Apocalypse Endeavor

Books by Cap Parlier:

Anod series
The Phoenix Seduction (1995)
Anod's Seduction (2004) [reprint of The Phoenix Seduction]
Anod's Redemption (2004)

Sacrifice (2000)
The Clarity of Hindsight (2016)
Apocalypse Endeavor (2019)

To So Few series
To So Few – In the Beginning (2014)
To So Few – The Prelude (2014)
To So Few – Explosion (2015)
To So Few – The Trial (2016)
To So Few – The Verdict (2017)
To So Few – Frustration (2018)
To So Few – Deflection (2019)

---

and with **Kevin E. Ready:**
TWA 800 - Accident or Incident? (1998)

These and other great books available from Saint Gaudens Press
Post Office Box 405
Solvang, CA 93463-0405
URL: http://www.SaintGaudensPress.com
Visit Cap Parlier's Web Site at: http://www.parlier.com

Apocalypse Endeavor

by
Cap Parlier

SAINT GAUDENS PRESS
Phoenix, Arizona & Santa Barbara, California

Saint Gaudens Press
Post Office Box 405
Solvang, CA 93464-0405

Http://www.SaintGaudensPress.com

Print edition ISBN: 978-0-943039-51-0

Library of Congress Catalog Number - 2019904471

Printed in the United States of America

Dedication

—

To all survivors
past, present and future.

—

Acknowledgments

—

Authors have myriad sources for the inspiration(s) that moblize their commitment to the stories they write. My inspiration was one truly disturbing nightmare, one among many dreams and nightmares, some 25 years ago that seeemed far more vivid and colorful that the run-of-the-mill dream. The first five chapters came quickly. The following chapters consumed the intervening years. I am grateful my nightmare was not a premonition, as it was for Carl Parks.

First and foremost, I must convey my immense gratitude to John Richard and Jeanne Parlier, for his critical and constructive review of the manuscript. Their engagement with the story made it better in multitudinous ways. Thank you both so much for giving so generously of your time.

I would be remiss if I did not convey my sincerest appreciation for the courage and attention to detail of the staff at Saint Gaudens Press, for their continuing encouragement and support. They are truly a blessing.

Authors of fictional stories do not often recognize the tools they use to research the details they need; yet, in this instance, I would be derelict if I did not acknowledge the extraordinary investment in and exemplary benefit of Google Maps and especially Google Earth. Particularly noteworthy are the Street View and Route line functions of Google Earth. While every road in every locale has not been covered, this story was the beneficiary of Google's investment. Hopefully, the detail made this a better story than it would have been otherwise. Thank you, Google.

Most importantly, I must publicly thank my wife Jeanne for tolerating my dedication to this story and taking such good care of me. She is a saint.

—

1

The slight, warm breeze in the shade of the back porch offered a very soothing moment after a long day finishing up the annual wheat harvest. The sweet, earthy smell of the rich soil around us with a hint of wheat dust validated the country setting. Birds of various species chirped, tweeted, whistled and sang like ocean waves caressing the sand. The cold effervescence of the beer added to the subtle pleasure. The last vestiges of golden sunshine illuminated the far tree line of cedars, pines and a few sturdy oak trees. A few fair-weather cumulus clouds dotted the darkening blue sky. The flash at the apex of an approaching aircraft condensation trail caught my attention. Yes, this is the life.

That's odd.

The bright glint in the clear dusk sky apparently coming from the fuselage of a large airplane attracted my attention. The four distinct white condensation trails that blended into one arrow-straight cloud silently approached. Seeing a large airplane headed west in the dusk twilight was not what struck me as odd; it was the silvery color, reflecting the setting sun at altitude. Most, no, probably all commercial airliners had painted surfaces in all colors – displaying their company logos. None of the American airlines used the polished aluminum finish, limited paint livery.

The aircraft traveled from the eastern horizon across the plains, passing north of our Wichita home. The front porch of the family home in the growing community of Andover, Kansas, faced east, so the view was unobstructed and broad. This airliner, if it was a commercial aircraft, was different. Why?

"What the hell!"

Four, relatively small, bright streaks shot from the rear of the aircraft, like massive, high-speed darts with long, white tails, back toward what had to be Kansas City.

I stood up and pointed to the phenomenon, wanting to look around, to see if anyone else saw what I saw, but I was not willing to take my eyes off this unique event. Then, after what had to be several long seconds, another object, large enough to be seen from miles away dropped from the aircraft, a rocket motor ignited, but it moved more slowly away from the launching aircraft along the same trajectory as the four fast objects. The target of the objects just had to be Kansas City. The smoke trail descended gradually, and then disappeared beyond the eastern horizon. Several more seconds, perhaps five to ten seconds, passed before confirmation of my supposition came.

The sun-like flash indirectly illuminated the eastern sky for several seconds. The actual source was not visible. As the light of the flash dissipated, a boiling cloud rose from the eastern horizon, roughly in the direction where the five objects had disappeared. As the cloud rose in the eastern sky, a round column extended below the boiling and rising main cloud. Roughly a minute later, a series of ripples under my feet, like vibrations, caught my attention, and then a major jolt shook everything from the house, the trees, the barn and even made dust rise from the driveway. As I had experienced many times in my California childhood, the ground shaking felt like a strong earthquake—quite uncommon for the Great Plains. As the shock wave passed, a series of larger ripples undulated the ground and porch structure beneath me like small waves rocking a sailboat or a massive bowl of Jell-O. The mushroom-shaped cloud was now well above the altitude of the aircraft that had launched the devices. I quickly looked along the contrail line. The aircraft was still traveling in an arrow straight line in the direction of Denver, as if nothing had just happened. As I watched the unfolding scene with abject fascination, three minutes passed before I heard a soft but odd, muffled series of pops. Then, a clearly audible boom reached me.

I watched, mouth now agape, frozen at the moment, not knowing whether to run, call for help, or be overwhelmed by what had to be some dreadful mistake. The source airplane continued on its straight-line path, as if absolutely nothing untoward had happened.

What have I just borne witness to? Was this some monstrous, unprovoked attack on the United States of America? ...Even worse, not some remote naval base in the Pacific Ocean, but in the very heartland of America.

I've never seen rear firing weapons like that. The last one was obviously a thermonuclear device, or at least a fusion weapon. But, what were the four, high-speed objects that preceded the larger one?

Whatever this was, it meant war! Somehow an international entity or nation-state had figured out how to penetrate the defenses of the United States . . . or perhaps worse a civil war or coup d'état. Some group had attacked the United States of America in most likely multiple locations. How many other cities had been attacked? An electric shock jolted me upright.

* * *

Carl found himself sitting naked in a bed. He felt the cool dampness of the sheet beneath him. Total darkness denied him orientation. Carl struggled with recognition. Had he just come out of a dream? Or, was he just in a different part of a dream? His chest still heaved above the focus of pounding within, as his body struggled with its recovery from some horrendous exertion. Confusion overwhelmed him.

Like in the movies, Carl Parks pinched himself on his damp left forearm. He felt a minor pain. He was awake. There were no lights, not even the green glow of the digital clock-radio-alarm that had been functional when they turned the lights out last night. Carl felt the sheet again. It was quite wet. His skin was clammy, damp and cooling rapidly. *Cold sweats*, he told himself. *Was this some strange aggravation from the vivid images and sensations of his dream, still hotly etched into his consciousness? What the hell was happening?*

Carl reached into the darkness to where he thought his wife should be. He was rewarded with the soft, smooth, warmth of her skin.

"What's wrong, honey?" she asked from her groggy state of awakening.

"Nothing, I guess. Just a bad dream . . . a nightmare."

"You don't have nightmares."

"I know, but this one was so . . . so . . . real . . . really bad . . . and vivid."

Carl felt her hand touch his arm. She stirred.

"The sheets are soaking wet, Carl. What on earth?"

"I know. Like I said, the nightmare was really bad. It must have scared the hell out of me."

"I guess so! Why is it so dark?"

"The power must have gone off." Carl's thoughts returned to his dream. "Did you feel an earthquake?"

"No. Why?"

"Did you happen to notice a flash outside?"

"No. Why? What's going on, Carl?"

"Just asking. It was in my dream . . . just wanted to make sure it's not real.

"Carl, really?"

Carl wondered, *is the power outage just us, or was it widespread?* He swung his feet to the floor. Carpet. They were not at home. Carl stood and stretched his six foot three inch, 200-pound frame, and then used his outstretched arms to feel for a wall, which came quickly. He then felt the pleated material of what had to be a window curtain. Yes. Carl felt the coldness of the glass.

Carl Parks pulled the curtain back. Starlight and the illumination of a waning quarter moon in the clear mountain air gave him sufficient view of the conifer forest and the snow-covered, jagged ridgeline in the distance beyond the trees. Yes, that was it. Now, he had his orientation. They were in Breckenridge, Colorado. This was the first night of the family's annual, week-long, pre-Christmas, ski holiday. Carl began to feel better although a strong shiver brought his awareness of the falling temperature. He found his heavy, terry cloth, robe in the darkness and his well-worn slippers. The power outage, if that was what it was, would not last long, but precautions were better than reactions.

Carl felt his way to the bedroom door. He knew where it was. This was the three-bedroom condominium they rented every year, and this was their fourth year using the same place. Carl shuffled, feeling his way down the short hallway, into the living room and across to the sliding glass doors that opened onto the balcony overlooking the parking lot and a portion of the city below. He pulled back the heavy curtain . . . darkness, well, except for the ambient light from the moon.

There were no lights to be seen anywhere, not even headlights of emergency vehicles that should be working on the power outage. *This is not a good sign.*

Carl worked his way back to the bedroom and the master bathroom, found the drain stopper lever, closed it, and turned on the cold and hot water. There was not much pressure, but water was coming out. This had to be whatever residual pressure might be left in the city water system, but was more likely line water draining from higher elevations. He thought about his act taking water away from others above them, but he had a family to protect. Carl then made his way to the other bathroom and repeated the process.

With water collection underway, he found the kitchen and the small toolbox he always brought with him. In the toolbox was a strong, industrial flashlight.

With the beam of light, he moved more quickly to check on his water collection. The master tub was nearly full. He waited until the water level reached the overflow, and then turned the water off.

"What are you doing?" asked his now awake wife, Janet, who was still snuggled down under the thick, down comforter.

"Just a minute. I'll be right back."

Carl went to the other bathroom tub and waited for the water level to reach the overflow level. The water flow was noticeably slower. There would soon not be any water in the lines above them. They had as much water as they were going to get.

Carl returned to Janet. Her sky-blue eyes peering up at him spoke the question.

"I'm just playing it safe, just in case this power outage lasts longer than expected."

"Is it everyone?"

"Yes," he answered, not wanting to convey his apprehension regarding the extent of the outage.

"So, you filled the bathtubs?"

"Yes, just to be safe."

"Do you need any help?"

"No. I can handle this. I'll build a fire. It is going to get cold in here."

"Oh, electric heat."

"Yes . . . precisely. Try to go back to sleep. I will take care of things."

Janet nodded her head, but did not close her eyes. Carl left her.

The fire was easy to start. There was sufficient kindling and split, hardwood logs to last several hours, and there was nearly a cord of wood on the balcony. Once the fire was going, Carl switched off the flashlight. The batteries would not last long.

Carl decided to use the quiet time of the early morning hours to gather a little more information. He dressed in his full cold weather gear.

"Where are you going?" Janet asked from the warmth of the bed.

"I need to obtain a better feel for what is going on out there."

"Be careful."

"Yes indeedie."

Carl checked the fire and thought about retrieving the M1911 45-caliber semi-automatic pistol from the backpack he always quietly carried with him on road trips, but decided against it. He confirmed he had the front door key to get back in, and then he ensured the door was locked behind him.

The cold air crackled his nostrils as he heard the crunch of old snow beneath his boots. He walked out to the street to give himself a better view of the valley. There were no lights anywhere, even in the distance that had to be ten miles. This was more than a local electrical power failure. Carl could not see the little regional hospital that provided emergency medical services for the county, but it would surely have temporary emergency power and lights. Nothing! One transformer or relay station would not take out the whole valley. While he did not know the details of the power distributions system in the Summit County, Breckenridge area, he did know the electric grid generally provided multiple paths to ensure service, so this had to be something big or important.

Carl scanned all of the buildings. Usually, you could see plumes of smoke or steam. But, there were none of those clues to be seen. He looked back to the condominium where his family was still in bed. One of the four chimneys serving the sixteen condos in their building had a tail of smoke rising into the night sky and disappearing. It was the only sign of life beyond himself he could see, hear and smell, or otherwise sense.

Carl thought about walking down the hill and into the town. The Breckenridge city police station and the Summit County Sheriff's Office were both at the north end of town. Instead, he decided to drive down, that way he could do a little more reconnaissance without using too much fuel. *Thank goodness I filled the tank upon our arrival yesterday evening.* He walked toward their gray, 1993 Jeep Grand Cherokee and checked to make sure the fuel cap cover was still locked and not tampered with. Carl retrieved the keys from his jacket pocket. He pushed the remote fob, door, unlock button, but he did not hear the usual clunk of pins unlocking. He tried the door just to check. It was still locked. He inserted the key and unlocked the door manually. When he opened the door, the courtesy light did not come on—not even a flicker or a dying ember glow. Carl tried the ignition . . . nothing, not a click or flicker there either. It was as if someone had taken the battery out of the car. He did not know how that would be possible, but thought he would check anyway. He pulled the interior, manual, hood release. Again, the normal courtesy light did not come on. The battery was still there with no signs of corrosion, arcing or damage. In fact, everything under the hood appeared perfectly normal except there was not one electron of electrical power.

This is really not good. "That's weird," he said aloud, confused by the odd occurrence.

Again, Carl thought about walking down the hill but recognized he needed to return to his family. His first priority had to be to maintain the fire, and keep his family warm and safe. He could go down to the police department later when everyone was awake, up and dressed.

The fire was still going but in need of another log. Carl carefully brought the fire back up to moderate intensity before he took off his thick jacket and insulated pants. His thoughts began grinding through the information he had.

All signs so far told him everything electrical had failed, either temporarily or permanently. Based on the Jeep's electrical state, he had to consider the possibility of permanence. *What could possibly cause such a widespread electrical failure?*

He could understand a municipal power failure; after all, those things happened due to thunderstorms, ice storms, and vehicle collisions with poles mounting transformers, among so many other possibilities. Those electrical power outages lasted minutes or hours, and sometimes days. *But, why would an independent automobile electrical system totally fail? For that matter, why did my flashlight work?* It was electrical. Carl tried his cell phone. Nothing. He tried the battery powered, small AM-FM radio. Nothing . . . not even static noise. So far, the only thing electrical that he could find working was the flashlight. Why?

Carl looked around the kitchen and the living room. He tried everything he could find that was electrical. Even the battery powered wall clock above the breakfast counter had stopped at 12:37 . . . must be AM, since the clock was working when they went to bed at 10:30 PM, or 22:30. Then, like an epiphany, the realization came to him.

His toolbox was steel – a complete metallic enclosure. The flashlight had been securely stored inside the latched, sealed toolbox. His nightmare flashed back at him—Electro-Magnetic Pulse or EMP, as the military like to refer to it.

No! That could not be. One of the many consequences of nuclear detonations was an enormous surge of electromagnetic energy that literally fried anything electrical.

My God, Carl said to himself. *Could his nightmare be true? Or, at a minimum, could it be a premonition?* Something happened at 00:37, just after midnight; that was close enough to the moment of his awakening in his cold, sweat soaked bed. If it was EMP, this power outage would be permanent, or essentially permanent as far as their winter survival was concerned.

The nauseating, sinking feeling of helplessness washed over Carl Parks sitting in a straight back, wooden chair several yards from the fire. His family – his wife, his daughter eight months pregnant with their first grandchild, their three sons and a friend of their middle son – was in a valley, high in the Rocky Mountains at the beginning of winter. He remembered the Donner Party disaster in 19th Century American history, the Argentinean soccer team stranded in the high Andes Mountains after a plane crash, and all of the other stories of people being where they should not be in the snow and ice of winter in the high mountains. What had been confusion, then curiosity, then anxiety for Carl Parks, had now become life-threatening to him and his family.

Carl sensed there would be no rescue. He also knew if they had to walk out of the mountains, their best chances until springtime would be now. However, even if he was by himself, the likelihood of making it through Loveland Pass to Denver, or even through Hoosier Pass toward Cañon City, Albuquerque and the south before the next snowfall would be very risky at best and more likely suicidal. There would be no way, period, with a pregnant woman within a month of delivery. They would have to figure out how to survive in the winter of the Rocky Mountains in an environment that had been artificially created by bountiful electricity . . . electricity that would not likely be restored for a long time. They did not have the option to leave until the baby was born, and even then they would need several months before the child was sufficiently stabilized, if she or he survived that long, before such a journey could be attempted.

Damn, if my nightmare premonition was somehow real, then there was probably not much of Denver remaining to be worthwhile for the effort. The Interstate-70 highway was certainly a better roadway than Colorado Route-9;

however, Southern Colorado and New Mexico were less likely to be involved in whatever happened last night.

First and foremost, he had to protect his family from the winter and keep them safe from the more base elements of mankind they were sure to encounter. Second, he would have to find a way to provide for them during the long months ahead with their surroundings virtually devoid of game. Third, they would have to prepare for the impending birth of their first grandchild in less than adequate conditions at best one month away, or less. There was no way to predict the weather. They were now relegated to observation of the skies as their ancestors had done. And fourth, they needed to prepare for the arduous journey out of the mountains next spring. Here was the skeleton of a plan. He would need the rest of the family to help flesh out the plan. These were not going to be easy months ahead.

Carl also recognized what else would be coming. While the threat of deep winter cold survival was palpable, the greatest threat would be man.

Law and order would soon break down. The situation would soon degenerate into survival of the fittest— Darwinian theory transformed into living practice. He had borne witness to the brutality of man from his service in the United States Marine Corps, and as a student of history and world events. He did not relish the thought of extending his education regarding the inhumanity of man. But, this was a condition not of his choice, and he would make the best of a very bad situation. He would have to educate, train and lead his family and whatever like-minded strangers they could gather up in the next few days and weeks. The hard part of connecting with people they did not know was what would be literally a life-or-death assessment, and decision on their trustworthiness and loyalty, when others would be confronted with the same or similar decisions. They had to find the common intersections of different familial dynamics to form some kind of collective for their mutual defense and survival.

If this was the worst-case scenario playing out around us, there would be no cavalry—no one to rescue us. They would be on their own, in many more ways than one. They would have to plan for no expert support—no doctors, no nurses, no police, no firefighters, no one. They would have to quickly improvise all sorts of routine tasks they had taken for granted for so long—finding food, cooking, cleaning, treating wounds, injuries and illnesses, all of life's little challenges had become potentially life-threatening in an instant.

—

2

"It's cold in there," declared Alex, their youngest and tallest son, and the first to join Carl in the living room. Alex stood just a few inches shorter than his father, had the same light brown, straight hair like his father, and fortunately for him possessed his mother good looks rather than his father's average appearance.

Carl Parks had been alone with his thoughts for several hours. He was not yet prepared for the questions that would soon come to him, but he was thankful for the company. "Yes, it is son."

"Is that why you have the fire . . . the heat not working?"

"Yes."

Alex found a companion chair and sat next to his father, staring into the flickering flames of the fire. The occasional crackle of the fire added the only sound to the silence.

After several minutes, Alex went to the kitchen, pulled out the Cheerios cereal box, poured a bowl and opened the refrigerator door.

"The power's out."

"Yeah."

"How long do you think the power will be out?" he asked.

Carl considered the moment. He had always preached to his children that they should face reality and deal with the issues as they were, not as they might want them to be. "A very long time," he answered with solemnity and calm, "I suspect."

"Really?"

Carl only nodded his head, as he continued to stare at the fire.

"Then, I guess we should finish the milk soon since it won't last."

"Yes, but save some for the others. We need to share what we have."

"By the way, Dad, why is the tub in our bathroom full of water?"

"Precaution, son."

"For what?"

"I just wanted to be as prepared as we just . . . just in case."

"Is something going on here?"

Carl turned to see the concerned face of his youngest son waiting for his answer. "I would rather wait until everyone is up."

"A family meeting?"

"Yes, I am afraid so."

"OK," came his response, as he poured some milk into his cereal bowl and replaced the gallon, plastic container in the dark refrigerator.

They returned to silence. When Alex finished, he went to the sink to rinse out his bowl.

"No water either?"

"Nope. I'm afraid not. No pumps. I drained the lines in the building to fill the tubs."

Alex put his bowl on the counter next to the sink, found the paperback book he was reading, lay down on the floor with this head toward the fireplace, and started to read. It was not the best light, but it was all they had at the moment.

As Carl pulled back the curtain to restock the small woodpile inside, the clear twilight mountain sky was being illuminated by the approaching dawn. It would be a beautiful weather day in the high Rockies, but Carl instinctively knew that would be about all that would be good. After carrying in a small armful of split logs, Carl closed the sliding door, locked it and pulled the drapes closed again. As he turned around, he saw the same concerned expression looking up at him from the floor.

"It is nearly dawn. Let's wake everyone up. We have a lot to discuss. Tell them not to flush the toilet."

"That could be gross, and I flushed when I got up."

"Yes, perhaps, but tell them just the same. I doubt the tank refilled."

Without questioning the request, Alex made his way to the kid's bedrooms. Carl went to the master bedroom.

He could barely see in the darkened room with the multiple reflections of the firelight. Carl carefully moved across the floor remembering basically where everything was . . . a skill he knew he would be using more of from now on. He gently shook his wife's hip.

"What is it?" she asked from her sleepy stupor.

"You need to get up."

"I'm tired, Carl. Just let me sleep."

"I am getting everyone up. It is dawn, and there is much we need to discuss."

Janet did not protest further, but her movements were not enthusiastic either. Carl returned to the living room.

Alex was the first to return. Lisa, their oldest child, actually a fully grown young woman who had decided it was time for her to have a child of her own and was eight months along, was the next and usual quick riser. She was slightly taller than her mother, at five feet seven inches, with longer and thicker, not as blond hair as her mother, and her young body handled pregnancy exceptionally well. Oldest son and shortest of the three Parks sons, Mike, followed by middle son, Nick, and his school friend, Dave Baker, joined the group. Dave's curly, dusty red hair readily distinguished him from the others of the group. Janet was the last to arrive with her striking good looks, making make-up unnecessary, and her shoulder-length fine, blond hair still showing the kinks of bed-head. She was wrapped up tightly in her heavy, terry-cloth robe and found a place on the large sofa against the far wall opposite the fireplace. There were no complaints, as Carl would have expected to hear given the early hour. Carl stood to the left of the fireplace and looked at each of them to find various expressions from blank to Alex's apprehension. All eyes were open and on him.

"I do not think there is an easy way to start this conversation, so forgive me for my bluntness." No one reacted. "For numerous reasons, I believe we are in a very dangerous situation." Expressions changed. For those who might not be fully awake or paying attention, there were no longer any doubts about their alertness. "I think some major event has occurred, and we have no electrical power, and I don't think we will find any electricity for a long time."

"Why?" asked Lisa.

"I am not entirely sure. I have my suspicions, but I do know that virtually nothing electrical works in this village."

"My watch is blank," said Mike.

"A digital watch . . . electrical."

"Mine works," added Lisa.

Carl looked at his daughter's left wrist then listened to it. "Mechanical . . . not affected."

"So, everything electrical?" Nick asked.

"Yes, everything, well, except for my flashlight, but that is only because it was completely protected by my metal toolbox."

"What does that mean?" asked Lisa.

"Before I answer Lisa's appropriate question, let me ask each of you, did you notice a flash outside just after midnight?"

Several answered with a smile, while the rest shook their heads in the negative.

"OK. To Lisa's question and I'm afraid I must continue to be blunt, it means we will be in a desperate struggle to survive a winter, snowbound in the high mountains of the Colorado Rockies."

"I don't understand," Lisa said. "Power will come back on. It always does."

"Not this time."

"Why? What is different?"

"First, the electrical power outage is widespread. This is not just a building or section of the village. It is the entire valley as best I can tell, and I suspect it may be much bigger than just Summit County, Colorado. Second, everything electrical has been affected, not just the wall power. Nothing electrical seems to work . . . not the cars, not the clocks, not the radios, not anything, unless it was fully shielded by conductive material."

"That sounds serious," Janet offered.

"Yes, I believe it is. Everything up here depends upon electricity – telephones, heating, appliances, water, lighting, transportation, everything."

"What about emergency generators?" Lisa asked.

"I am sure there are emergency generators in this valley for the medical clinic emergency room, for example. They would have kicked in long ago, but I can see no signs of electrical power, even from emergency generators. If my guess is correct, this event fried the electrical control circuits for those emergency generators as well."

"You have mentioned this event several times, now, Dad," Nick stated. "What exactly do you think happened?"

"I think there is only one thing that can explain all these simultaneous or near simultaneous failures. The military calls it, EMP—Electro-Magnetic Pulse. All nuclear weapons produce the phenomenon, but today there are specifically designed, modest yield weapons that produce an enormous surge of energy that will fry any unprotected electrical circuit and render it worthless and un-repairable. That's why I asked you about the flash. An EMP device would have been like an instant sun in the night sky that lasted for a few seconds and disappeared."

"Now isn't that great," Nick added, as the family's most ardent pacifist.

"What about our military?" asked Dave, joining the conversation for the first time.

"I know some of the military's systems and equipment are protected, but that does not matter to us up here. While our military probably defended the country, they have enough to worry about without mounting a risky rescue mission into these mountains during winter. I'm afraid we are on our own."

"So, you think your dream—your nightmare—was a premonition?" Janet asked.

"From everything I have seen . . . yes."

"What dream?"

"Your father had a nightmare last night that really . . . well . . . affected him."

"You rarely dream, Dad," Lisa said.

"Yes, but this one was bad and seemed so real."

"I guess so, if it's caused all this," said Alex, producing a series of strained chuckles.

"So what do we do?" asked Janet.

"What about my baby?"

"Oh yeah," Mike said with his realization.

Carl stood, walked to the window, saw the sun was up on a bright, clear day, and then replaced the curtain. He placed another log on the fire and turned to his family. "Our only chance to make it out of these mountains is right now."

"Then, let's go," Lisa said.

"It would take at a minimum of a week or more without any problems. It would be a tough walk even in the summer, since we must climb to the passes on either route out. Further, with just one snow storm while we were on the road, we would likely be stranded in the open with no shelter and unable to move."

"Walk?"

"No cars, buses, trains, airplanes—yes, walk."

"I can't do that," Lisa recognized.

"Precisely."

"What about some of us going for help?" Mike asked.

"Three thoughts. One, if I am correct, everyone everywhere will have more than enough to deal with on their own. Everyone will be in a survival situation of one degree or another. Second, it is winter. Even those outside who might be able to rescue us will not be able to move until at least springtime. And third, we need to stick together for protection."

"Protection from what?" asked Lisa.

"Do you want the truth?" Carl looked at each set of attentive eyes. Alex and Nick nodded their heads. No one refused. "Simple survival—keeping warm, finding food—will be hard, but our greatest threat will be man." Carl paused for a response or questions, but none came. "In this situation, law and order will break down . . . and probably quite rapidly. We can expect rogue marauders or even other families like us to be foraging for what they need, and some will be willing to kill to get what they want."

"The police have guns."

"Yes, they do, but they are in the same survival situation we are. I'm sure some have families of their own to protect, and they can't be everywhere at once."

"To repeat my earlier question, what do we do?"

"First, no one does anything alone. We go in pairs for everything."

"Even going to the bathroom," Lisa protested. Everyone laughed.

"Yes, even going to the bathroom."

"Oh, gross," Nick said.

"Is that really necessary?" Janet asked.

"There will be too many opportunities for something to go wrong. Each of us may need help, and if nothing else, the other person will need to be a lookout for trouble. We must treat this as a quasi-combat environment for our survival. A mistake could be swift and final." There was no laughter, only serious expressions. "We will need to set up a watch system so that two of us are awake and alert all of the time. We must establish a protection system, a defense system, to deal with threats in a proper, measured, and final manner. From here on until order is established, this will not be a game. It will be brutal, ugly, disgusting, and most of all, required." Carl paused again for reactions, responses or questions. Stares of disbelief faced him. "The rules of human behavior that you have known all your lives must be suspended. We have been pushed into a different world."

"It cannot be as bad as that," proclaimed Lisa.

"I am afraid you will have to trust me, because you may not get a second chance. While the situation may remain civil for a few days, it will rapidly deteriorate, as more people become hungry and desperate. We must trust no one until they have truly earned our trust."

"Carl, you are scaring me and the children," Janet said.

"Perhaps I am, but these will be scary times, and we must be prepared."

"OK, Carl, you made your point," she acknowledged. "You need to tell us what you want us to do now."

From the expressions that faced him, Carl felt he had gone too far with his candor. It was time to focus on other things. "Let's make sure all the curtains are closed and remain closed, and any windows that do not have dark coverings are securely covered. We do not want others to know we are here. They will come eventually, but that is a different problem. Next, we need to move our stuff into this room. This will be the only room we use, and we will close off and seal the other rooms as best we can. It would be better to use the master bedroom since it faces away from the other dwellings, but this is the only room with a fireplace. This fire will be our only warmth. To that end, we need to bring the wood we have inside, stack it in the corner," Carl said, pointing to the corner next to the fireplace, "and, we need to quickly gather up the wood from other apartments with no signs of occupancy. I know this is not going to be a pleasant topic, but we will also have to step back a century or more and start using a chamber pot for our bodily waste."

"What is a chamber pot?" Alex asked.

"We need to find the largest pot we have with a lid. We will have to urinate and defecate in that pot. We'll have to take turns carrying it outside to empty it. We will not be able to dig a hole with the frozen ground, so I'll try to find an appropriate disposal point to empty it."

"Gross!" exclaimed Alex.

"Yes, well, this is what happens when we lose all electricity in the high mountains . . . in winter. We've been pushed back to the Middle Ages."

"What about food?" asked Mike.

Carl stared into the waiting, inquisitive eyes of each person. They looked at him, as if he had the answer. "There is no easy way to put this." Not even a blink came to him. "We are going to have to forage . . . find it wherever we can."

"You mean steal," Lisa stated.

"If you want to put it that way, yes, steal. And, we may have to kill as well."

"Animals?" Janet inquired.

"And others perhaps."

"Oh, Carl, you can't be serious," responded Janet.

"Yes, I am afraid I am quite serious . . . deadly serious."

They continued to stare at him. Now, signs of disbelief mixed in. Clearly, they did not accept his assessment.

"We have perhaps two, three, four days or more of food with us. I recommend we wait for a day or two to see what happens. We can plan our next few moves, and other than defense, should the need arise, I do not think we need to do anything just yet. But, I need to prepare us all for what lies ahead."

"So, no skiing today," quipped Nick.

"You are welcome, but you will have to climb. There will be no more lifts."

"I was just kidding, Dad."

Carl nodded his head in recognition. He wanted to say more but knew this was probably more than they were able to absorb at the moment. There would be plenty more time to commiserate and discuss.

Carl turned, pulled back the drape slightly, opened the sliding glass door, stepped out onto the small balcony, and closed the door behind him. It was a gorgeous, bright, calm winter day in the high Rocky Mountains. The fresh air invigorated everything. The temperature was still below freezing but not by much. Carl carefully scanned the entire vista starting from the near field to the far ridgeline. The only movement he could detect was the few additional tails of smoke from chimneys across the valley. But even with that, it was far less than he expected. Maybe there were fewer people in the village than he thought, which would make the available food last longer. The parking lots he could see were about half to perhaps two thirds full, so there had to be a significant stranded population . . . that would soon become a threat and competition for survival. Carl said a little prayer to give him and his family the strength to do what would become necessary in short order. He waited until he began to feel the cold before he returned to the group.

—

3

The sliding door opened behind him, but Carl Parks did not turn.

"How long are you going to be out here, Dad?" came Lisa's voice.

"I need to think things through. I need to anticipate what is going to happen next . . . tomorrow, next week, the months ahead . . . and what we will need to do."

"But, it's cold."

"Yes, Lisa, it is cold." Carl wanted to add, his comfort was the least of his worries, but he knew his anxiety would not help his daughter.

"What are you looking for?"

"Movement. I want to see what other people . . . what they are going to do?"

Lisa Parks moved next to her father, grabbed the railing with her gloved hands, and stared across the town. "Is it really that bad?"

Without taking his eyes off his task, he answered, "I would like to think this is just a simple power outage, but the evidence suggests something far more serious."

"And, you really dreamed about this last night?"

In all this potential threat, Carl smiled and turned to his daughter. "Well, at least what may have caused this type of power outage. So far, the result that might have caused this in my nightmare and what we find now are the similar . . . and, I must say, the damage appears to be far worse than what I remember from my service days."

"Has this happened before?"

Carl laughed. "Not in my entire life. Before I was born, I think it was around 1958, if memory serves, there was a nuclear test in the Pacific that knocked out a lot of electrical equipment from Hawaii to New Zealand, and that was when electrical circuits were analog rather than digital, as they are today. I rarely have dreams that leave any awareness. Nightmares are even rarer for me. And, I can remember nothing that has made the connection to reality. This is really bizarre for me. I am still struggling with what happened last night and what we face now."

"I still have trouble believing this is not just an ordinary power outage, and in a few hours or days, the power will come back on."

"I know, Lisa. I sure hope you are correct, but I don't think so."

"Why?"

"If it was a simple power outage, the cars would operate until they ran out of fuel. Our car is stone cold dead. I checked the battery. It was connected.

The interior lights offered not even a flicker. So, yes, I believe whatever happened is much more than a simple power outage.

"I'm getting cold. I'm going inside."

Carl touched her shoulder, as his daughter turned to leave the balcony. He took another quick look across the town, but saw nothing significant or even of interest. Carl Parks followed his pregnant daughter into the apartment. Everyone was still sitting around the fireplace.

"This seems silly," Nick offered.

Carl stared at his middle son. The thought that the teenager could be correct came to him. But, his instincts told him differently. "You may be right, which is why we should take a wait-and-see position."

"What are we waiting for?" Nick pressed.

"I would like to think we are waiting for the power to come back on, so we can all laugh about my overreaction and go skiing. However, at the moment, I think we are waiting for events to play out."

"How long will that take?"

"Could be a few hours or a few days . . . hard to say. If I am correct, the process will not take long to start."

"What did you see outside?" asked Alex.

"There is really nothing outside, yet . . . well . . . other than a beautiful Rocky Mountain day. It won't take long for things to breakdown."

"So, you want us to just sit here," Janet objected.

"There will be confusion, frustration and what I am the most afraid of, emotional responses to this situation. I want to make sure we are not involved in those events. So, here is what we will do while we wait. First, we will set up a watch schedule to keep an eye on events around us. This afternoon, we will need to rearrange things inside and outside for our protection, and we will set up defense procedures." Six sets of eyes waited emotionless and patiently for Carl to continue. "There are seven of us, but Lisa's pregnancy is an immediate concern, so I think she should be exempted from watch duties." No one objected. "Let's start with Mike and Nick as team one, Mom and Alex as team two, and Dave and I will be team three. We'll start with two-hour cycles. Each team must stay together, stay awake, and I think keep a log of what we see. For the rest of today and tonight, we will do nothing but watch, just in case I am wrong about this power outage. Agreed?"

Everyone nodded their heads. Mike rose to retrieve the log poker, consolidated the burning logs and put a new log on the fire.

"Wasn't there a news broadcast on the radio yesterday about an approaching storm?" asked Nick.

During the long, ten-hour drive from Wichita, Kansas, several radio stations reported the movement of a powerful storm system passing through the majority of the West Coast of the United States. If the reports were correct, the storm had been forecast to reach Colorado tomorrow, and they said it was likely to gain strength with unusual moisture from the Gulf of Mexico. Just another complication as far as Carl was concerned.

"Sure," answered Dave. "I heard it."

"There is nothing we can do about the weather," Carl responded. "We will deal with it when it comes. And, if my nightmare is correct, a storm like that will probably help sort things out quickly."

"What do you mean?" Janet asked.

"We are prepared. We can stay as we are without any adjustments for at least several days, if not a few weeks. Others will not be so prepared, and the weather will accelerate the natural selection process that has probably already begun."

"Isn't that a bit cruel . . . a bit harsh?"

"In normal times, yes, but these are not and will not be normal times. People are going to die – some quietly in the cold, some violently. It is just that simple. As I said earlier, this is about survival."

A couple of grimaced expressions punctuated Carl's comment. He also resolved to tone down the bluntness of his thoughts, at least for the time being. Carl pulled Janet's watch from his pocket.

"It is ten minutes 'til nine. We start the watches now." Carl handed the watch to Mike. "At eleven, pass the watch to team two, and so on, every two hours."

"Where do we stand watch?" Mike asked.

"I think the best place is the balcony," answered Carl motioning toward the curtains covering the sliding glass door.

"It's cold out there."

"Yes indeed, so dress warmly."

"Why do we need to be out in the cold, freezing our butts off?"

"Because we need to be able to see as much as you can, but more importantly, we need to be able to hear, or smell if some odor comes along. We need to use all our senses, and we can't do that inside."

"But, it's cold."

"This is not going to be a debate," Carl said, probably a little more sharply than he should have. "You will have to trust me. I will stand my watches outside as well. If we need to shorten the time to an hour or even 30 minutes, we can do that so we avoid any cold injuries. OK?"

Mike nodded his head and motioned for Nick to follow him. They put their full ski suits on along with their knit caps and heavy gloves. Neither of them looked back, as they stepped out on the porch and closed the door behind them.

"What do we do?" Janet asked.

"Well, I would suggest we try to nap, or read, maybe play a game or something. I don't think there is much we need to do today, unless something starts to happen. I'll check on the boys here in a little bit to make sure things are working right."

"That's it?"

"I think the best thing for us to do is stand back and see what develops. I would like to go out, to go into town, to see what is happening, but I am more worried about being caught up in something bad or precipitating something by my presence alone. We just have to wait and watch for now."

Janet nodded her tacit agreement, and then rose, going to the kitchen. She fidgeted with kitchen utensils, dirty dishes in the sink, and other objects on the counter. Carl watched his wife. There was something serious on her mind. Carl considered his probe but rejected the thought. He knew she would voice her concerns when she was ready. She turned to the refrigerator, opened the door, and then closed it.

"What should we do about the frozen stuff?" She turned back to Carl. "What about all the food we have here?" she asked, motioning to the refrigerator.

Carl joined her at the refrigerator. He opened the top freezer and lower main compartment doors. The box was nearly full. He considered the possibilities.

"Well . . . we need to do something, don't we?" Carl responded. Janet just glared at her husband. "Let me think about what we should do. For now, let's minimize the opening of the refrigerator." Carl turned.

"Don't take too long figuring this out," Janet grumbled.

Carl thought about using the freezing air outside, but that might be harder to control. He walked to the bedrooms in the back. They were already cold. He checked the water he filled in the bathtubs. Neither showed any ice formation, but the water was definitely cold. Carl carefully studied the configuration of the rooms, the construction, and thickness of the walls. First, he closed off all the air vents to prevent any warm air escaping from the living room via the vents. The apartments above and below theirs would have some effect but not a dominant one. He also took inventory of mattresses, bedding, specifically blankets and other material that could be used as insulation. Carl pulled two, extra, heavy blankets from the top of the linen closet. One was a king-size blanket for the master bed. It could easily be doubled to cover the hallway. Carl returned to the living room.

"OK. Here's what we need to do. We can insulate the back two bedrooms from the rest of the apartment. We will use the room on the right as our cold storage . . . that will give us the most protection. So, I need the back two bedrooms cleared of anything you don't want to freeze. I would also recommend we move the mattresses, clothes and anything else out of those rooms. We should probably freeze whatever can tolerate freezing to help us stretch our supplies."

No one moved until Carl gestured—well? Lisa rose first.

"Carl," Janet interjected, "I've made some light sandwiches. Can the kids eat first?"

"Sure. In fact, let me take a couple out to Mike and Nick."

The other kids sat at the breakfast bar to eat in silence. Carl took a paper towel to wrap a sandwich for the two boys on watch. He pulled aside the curtain, opened, and then closed the sliding glass door behind him. Carl handed each of the boys a sandwich.

"Seen anything?" Carl asked.

The two boys looked at each other.

"No," answered Nick. "Not really."

"Then, you've seen something."

"Just one or two people walking into town. Nothing important."

"We need to watch for anything that might be illegal or inappropriate like breaking into cars or other apartments, any fights or violence, anything like that."

"So far, it's just been boring," added Mike.

"Yes, well, I'm afraid that is not going to last. If you see anything strange or curious, call me."

"It's cold out here," Mike said.

"I know. We will have to see how things go. Try not to move too much or make noise."

"How do we keep warm?" asked Nick.

"Some amount of cold is probably good to keep you awake and alert. If you start to feel tingling, or lose feeling in your toes or fingers, we will need to get you inside. But, movement, or noise, or anything else that might draw attention to you, or us, will not be good. We do not want anyone else to know we are here." Both boys looked at each other, and then back to their father. There was at least some combination of confusion, disagreement, disbelief and resentment. "Look. I know this is not exactly what y'all wanted to be doing right now. I am convinced things are going to get ugly before they stabilize. We cannot afford to get caught up or behind in these events."

"OK, Dad," Nick answered. "You made your point. We will do our best."

Carl nodded, slowly went to the rail and took a good look around. "Clouds are coming in and thickening. The storm system Nick mentioned earlier may be closer than expected."

"We'll keep an eye on it."

"Please do. The weather may force some folks to take dangerous action."

"We'll do our part."

Carl patted each boy on the back and returned to the interior. The others looked at him for some explanation. They all appeared to be looking to him for so many answers to unasked questions. Part of the problem would be keeping their minds busy with something constructive during all the periods of inaction, and yet ensure their readiness to deal with whatever might come their way.

"How are the boys?" asked Janet.

"Cold. Bored. Frustrated."

"They aren't the only ones," Lisa quipped.

"Everybody has had something to eat. Let's get the back bedrooms cleared out. Alex, you and Dave should move the mattresses out here. We'll have to rearrange things so we have a place to sleep as well as do other things."

The boys moved to start their work. Lisa followed them. Janet stared at her husband.

"This isn't going to work, Carl."

"We have no choices here. Society is going to deteriorate around us. We must be ready. We are entering an environment that will not be forgiving of errors, mistakes or oversights."

"Maybe so, Carl, but you are going to have to figure out something. We're all going to go crazy confined to this apartment with nothing to do."

Carl knew she was correct. "I know."

They worked the rest of the day rearranging the apartment. The living room furniture was pushed back to the walls. The mattress occupied the space between the chairs and the fireplace. Clothes and other items were stacked in separate piles around the living room.

As the rearrangement process proceeded, the watch team was changed. Janet and Alex began their watch period while Nick and Mike warmed themselves in front of the fire.

By the end of the day, the back rooms were cleared. Carl nailed the heavy blankets over the hallway. The first blanket, the lighter one, was nailed into place just after the hall bathroom door with a flap opening un-nailed on the right side. The second curtain was installed at the end of the hallway about one and a half yards behind the first one with the opening on the left side. Once everything was settled, Carl opened the window of the right bedroom about two inches. Carl wanted the temperature to drop before they moved the food. They removed the curtains from the windows of the two back bedrooms to rig up another baffle for the sliding glass door to reduce the cold air intrusion and primarily to minimize the light from the fire escaping to the exterior when the door was opened especially at night.

By the time Carl finished his second watch period, everyone except the watch team was asleep. The frozen foods were safely frozen in the right bedroom. The refrigerator food seemed to be all right in the left bedroom. The fire was modest and stable. So far, there was not much activity outside. More significantly, light snow had begun to fall.

—

4

By dawn, or at least what Janet's small wristwatch indicated should be dawn, more than a foot of new snow had fallen. Even in the dark, everything was white, and the snow kept coming and worse it was coming horizontally on the wind. The really serious aspect of the storm was the wind, joining the snowfall and becoming a classic blizzard. Carl could not see the evidence, but he imagined there were substantial snowdrifts measured in many feet. Any movement in a storm like this would be nearly impossible.

Each watch team had kept the snow away from the large, balcony window and sliding glass door. They had shortened the watch periods first to an hour, and then to 30 minutes when the wind picked up.

Carl pulled the curtain back slightly, moved behind and pulled the sliding door open just enough to slip out, closing the door behind him. His wife and youngest son, Team Two, moved back and forth in a futile effort to generate some warmth. The crystalline beads of snow and ice caked on their clothing.

"How is it going?"

"Not well, Carl," snapped Janet. "We have been out here in this bloody blizzard, watching for God knows what."

Parks scanned the area within view of the balcony. There was only wind and snow -- not a single sign of any creatures of any kind moving in the storm. He could barely see the trees behind the building. "Let's come inside."

There was no hesitation. Carl opened the door. The two watch-standers passed him without words. By the time Carl entered and closed the door, there were already protests from the others, as frozen water flaked off the two cold ones. Janet and Alex tried to take off their outer clothing as carefully as they could and move close to the fire.

"This is crazy, Carl. We can't keep going like this. We need to get out of here." Carl took off his parka and poured a small drink of water. "Did you hear me?"

"Yes, Janet, I heard you."

"Well?"

Parks turned to face his angry wife. All the faces looked at him. "You have only been outside for twenty minutes . . . ."

"I don't mean right this moment," she responded sharply.

"As I was saying, you know how difficult it is out there. There is no transportation. It would take us several weeks to make it out of the mountains in summer with no weather. There is no way anyone will survive an attempt to make it out of these mountains in the dead of winter."

"We just can't keep going like this."

"There is no other choice, Janet. We have only been up here for a couple of days. We have a long way to go. We must hold together, survive the winter, and then make our way out of the mountains and hopefully home."

"It's December, Carl," she protested.

"I know that. And, we won't be able to move safely until spring . . . probably May or June . . . April, if we're lucky."

Janet turned back to the fire. The others stared at Carl as though they were statues in a modernist sculpture exhibit.

"I don't think we can do this," Janet said softly into the fire.

"We have to."

Mrs. Parks turned around again. "But, why outside?"

"In any security situation like this, we need time. If we wait until an intruder is in the building or in this apartment, it may well be too late and probably result in unacceptable injury . . . and certainly will not help us survive."

"Intruder?" asked Lisa.

Carl shook his head and paced a few steps back and forth. "This may not be pleasant, but these harsh times warrant brutal honesty." He paused to search each set of eyes waiting for his pronouncement. "Once this storm is past, within a few hours or days, no more, we shall be faced with life-threatening marauders who feel their means of survival is to prey upon others, who are weaker. Whether we like it or not, it is a natural course of things in situations like this."

"You are saying we shall become animals," said Janet.

"If you wish to state it like that, yes. This is purely a survival of the fittest situation . . . in the classic Darwinian sense."

"Really?" their middle son challenged.

"Yes, Nick. I'm afraid we shall soon see what happens among humans when the rule of law is dismissed, and survival becomes the only motive."

"What do we need to do?" asked Mike.

"We do not have the luxury of defense in depth, but we must find a means to gain time . . . time for us to react to any threat. There will be those who will see our preparations as an attractive acquisition. Our survival will depend upon preventing any intrusion or compromise of our," he sweeps his arms around the room, "our environment, our haven."

"Do you really think it is going to get that bad?" Lisa asked.

"Unfortunately, yes. I have seen some of the worst of humanity. I'm afraid we will soon see how brutal humans can become, and we must be prepared to deal swiftly, violently and permanently with those who would harm us."

"You mean kill people?"

"Yes."

"You can't be serious," said Janet.

Carl looked each of them in the eye. "I am deadly serious." Shock painted the faces of his entire family. "Even if the power was restored this instant, we are likely to experience bad behavior before things could return to normal. We no longer enjoy the luxury of any semblance of normalcy until law and order . . . and electrical power are restored."

A knock at the door instantly turned all heads toward the door, and then back to Carl. He placed his right index finger to his lips, and then motioned for them to quietly leave the living room. Lisa held her hands out and shrugged, as if to say why do we have to leave the room. Carl waved his hand to stop, added a stern expression and signaled to her to move quietly.

Carl waited for all of them to move behind the thermal curtain blanket to the hallway. He withdrew the M1911 45-caliber, semi-automatic pistol from his belt at the small of his back, pushed the slide back at the muzzle to ensure he had a round chambered, let it go home, and then pushed the safety off. He looked out the front door's observation port. A middle-aged man in ski clothing and a three-day growth of beard stood staring at the door. Carl held the pistol at his side with his finger inside the trigger guard. He unlocked the door, placed his foot a couple of inches short of the door to jam it if need be, and opened the door.

"Sorry to bother you," the man said. "Are you without power?"

"Yes."

"The telephone doesn't work."

"I know."

"Do you think it will come back on soon?"

"I don't know," Carl answered, not wanting to be discourteous, and yet offer only minimal responses.

"Do you have food?"

Carl placed his finger on the trigger and raised the pistol behind the door. "Not much."

"Well, my wife and I did not bring much up with us. We are going to have to do something."

Carl only nodded his head.

"Well, sorry to disturb you. Thank you," the man said, nodded his head and turned to leave.

Carl said, "Good luck," to the man's back.

He closed the door, returned the locks, and checked the observation port. The hall was empty. He relaxed his trigger finger and engaged the safety. "It's clear," he said to the blanket.

Janet was the first to return and see the pistol in Carl's hand. "Jesus, Carl. Is that really necessary?"

He answered, as he replaced the pistol in his belt. "The risks of not being prepared are too great."

"You're scaring the hell out of all of us."

"That is not my intent. I just want us all to survive this winter and make it out of these mountains next spring."

"But, Carl, my God . . ."

Parks held up his right hand to stop. Enough. Carl looked to the only non-family member of the group and his teammate, Dave Baker. Carl considered whether he should take Dave with him. He turned to the door.

"Where are you going?" asked Janet.

"To check outside. Lock the door after me. If anyone knocks, stay quiet and do not answer the door. Don't even look in the port. I will knock twice, once, and then three times. Only then, confirm it is me before you open the door."

"Carl, really . . . "

"I am only going to say this once," he snapped, "you may think I've gone off the deep end. I can only say that y'all will soon see why I've gone crazy. Now, no more. Just do what I tell you to do. We will all be safer that way." He did not wait for a response.

He waited at the door to hear the locks re-engage. Several deep breaths helped his lungs adjust to the cold. He moved carefully down the short hallway and split flight of stairs to the small entryway atrium, and stopped three feet short of the door. A light flurry added slightly to the already thick blanket of fresh snow that covered everything. There were no tracks. Carl carefully scanned the few windows he could see surrounding the parking lot. All the curtains were closed. There was no movement other than the small snowflakes floating in the diminishing wind. He moved a little closer to the door to gain a view of more windows. The result was the same. When Carl reached the door, he meticulously searched every possible observation point—still no signs of life.

Nearly three feet of snow blocked the door. Carl considered pushing out the door to continue his reconnaissance, but he chose not to leave any evidence of his presence. There were no signs of activity inside the building. That means his earlier visitor occupied one of the twelve apartments in the building; so, there was at least one other group in the building. *I've got to determine who else is in this building.* The parking lot was perhaps two thirds full, and the lumps of mounded snow indicated none of the cars had been able to move. He thought for a moment of conducting a census, but decided to let things float for a bit. He searched the darkened area down the last half-flight of stairs for the two lowest apartments. The hallway was clear, and the window at the far end appeared to be clear as well. Carl continued to move cautiously to the window—again, no signs of life. The snow was less deep. The sill of the window sat just above the top of the snow and could easily serve as an exit point, although a step to the chest high sill would be helpful.

Carl Parks methodically checked each of the two floors below their apartment. The building was not the most defensible location, but it would have to suffice as a place to live and survive. He used the highest hallway windows on both sides of the building to gain a better view. A small view of the town below yielded no additional information. The two upper windows would probably be the best observation posts, but it was too risky as long as the intentions of the other occupants of the building were unknown.

The prescribed knocks unlocked and opened the door. They waited for Carl to remove his gloves, knit hat, and unzip and remove his coat.

"What did you see, Dad?" asked Lisa.

"Snow. Lot's of snow."

"Did you go outside?" Alex asked.

"No. Too much snow. I didn't want to leave any tracks."

"So, what are we going to do?" Janet asked, adding her question.

Carl searched every set of eyes watching him. He sat on the single chair and rubbed his hands together, as he exhaled forcefully into them. "Since my precautions are a bit upsetting, perhaps I should not be too expansive or expressive. So, first, we will sit tight . . . basically to stay out of the way when the craziness begins. Second, we need a couple of pairs of snowshoes to be able to move safely in all that snow. And, we need more weapons."

"What do we need snowshoes for?" Nick asked.

"To be able to walk through fresh snow without sinking in," responded Carl.

Carl found a piece of paper and a pencil. He sketched a teardrop-shaped frame with a lattice spanning the inside and a strap to tie it to a boot. They talked about material that would be flexible, and yet strong enough to support Carl's 200 pounds and the abuse of movement. The boys took up the task of finding suitable materials.

They tried several different items without success -- too stiff, too inflexible, too absorbent, too weak.

"Maybe we should go into town to see if we can find some stuff," Nick said.

"Yeah, I think I saw some in one of the ski shops," added Alex.

Carl stopped his experimentation. "You are probably right, and having a couple of sets of proper snowshoes would be ideal. However, just getting there through all this fresh snow without something on your feet will be a horrendous effort. But, I am more worried about the lawlessness that is soon to erupt and the probability that by the time we got into town they would have already been looted."

"You really have a pessimistic attitude," Janet sneered.

Carl ignored the comment, as he returned to his materials experimentation. "Isn't it worth a try?" pressed Janet.

Carl turned to face his wife. "No, it isn't. None of you have seen war. None of you have seen what happens to human beings in war, or when the rule of law breaks down. The power is not coming back on. The few sheriffs in this mountain town are going to be taking care of their families. We will soon face a true survival of the fittest situation. We must preserve what resources we have. We must be smart, cunning and coldly ruthless to make it through the winter, and the threats we will soon face. To be brutally graphic, we must stay out of the way, not attract attention, and let the hooligans kill each other off. None of you may believe me and that is your choice. But, my concern now is survival and protecting my family through perhaps six months in a very hostile and unforgiving, high mountain, winter environment. Now, unless anyone among you are prepared to lead us out of this situation, I will ask you to listen to what I say and do what I ask you to do." He searched their eyes. "This is not a game. This is not pretend. We will get no second chances for mistakes." He waited for any response.

Carl went to the dining room table, strewn with various materials pulled off the kitchen counter, battens from the bedroom curtains, strips of carpet and a wicker chair, molding from the baseboard, the copper piping under the kitchen sink, and even plastic from food containers. Each piece possessed unique properties. He played with bends and breaking a few. The material that seemed to have the most promise was the baseboard molding, but he could not bend it enough to shape a large, flat shoe. Carl thought about soaking the molding in one of the bathtubs, but could not risk contaminating their water. He found two plastic bread loaf containers, cut off the ends, wedged one slightly inside the other, and then used duct tape to give the combination at least a temporary seal. He took the crudely elongated tray into the hall bathroom, since it had a window allowing in the ambient light of the now thinning overcast sky. Carl ladled out sufficient water to half fill the tray, put the middle of the molding strip into the water, and added a decorative stone from the living room to keep the wood under water.

Words did not pass among the family. Janet and Lisa read paperback books. Mike stared out the window. Nick, Alex and Dave worked on some of the materials. Carl watched them and returned to his molding experiment.

Carl placed his left foot on the stone and gently pulled up on each end of the six-foot strip. He was making good progress until he pulled a little too much, and the sample broke, not with a snap but a muffled, 'wet' thud -- actually an encouraging result. He retrieved another strip and started again.

The snow stopped and the wind diminished. A solid, low overcast moved swiftly across the mountain peaks. Carl checked out of the balcony window—no tracks. He went to each bedroom window to get different angles. From the master bedroom window, he saw the first signs.

Carl could not see any direct movement, but the unmistakable tracks of perhaps two or three large males crisscrossed the parking lot. The snow had been swept aside on the driver's door on virtually every car, including the Parks' gray Grand Cherokee Jeep. Several car windows had been broken. The tracks did not go to any of the buildings . . . yet, but they would soon enough. Carl watched from the shadows for several minutes without seeing any additional indications.

The molding strip experiment received several more pulls before Carl returned to the living room.

"There is activity outside," Carl announced. "We need to re-post our watches to get as much warning as we can."

"Who is up?" Alex asked.

"Since you and Mom stood the last watch, I think Dave and I are up. I also think the primary threat is probably going to come from the parking lot, so let's drop the balcony watch and stand in the master bedroom only. Please make sure you do not open the curtains or get too close to the window. We need to do our best to keep our presence here indeterminate for any observer outside."

—

5

They watched. They listened.

As the weather cleared, people began to move. Tracks of various sizes laced the snow.

Car windows were broken in what appeared to be a random basis. Personal items presumably from the vandalized vehicles littered the ground between the machines.

Some tried to leave the condominium complex. Carl Parks knew they were doomed, but he kept his assessment to himself. There was a sense of desperation in the people he could see. The reality of their predicament sank into the lives stranded in the high mountains during wintertime. Then Carl spotted what he had hoped would be the most distant. A partially buried body of what appeared to be a man caught Carl's attention laying beyond the central parking lot in the U-shape of their condominium complex and across 4 O'Clock Run Road, now laced with lines of footfalls. It was the pinkish tint in the snow around what appeared to be the upper torso that focused his thoughts. The trampled snow around the body suggested several assailants with virtually no struggle, as well as a swift and violent end.

Carl watched calmly and quietly. As the gravity of the situation in the high mountains in the middle of winter dragged his thoughts into the gutter of humanity, Carl used his experience as a surgical instrument to cut through the ugly mess. His mind kept returning to Maslow's Hierarchy of Needs. He remembered that distant education and training on human psychology. What had begun just a few days ago as a family holiday to enjoy time together and celebrate Christmas in the picturesque Rocky Mountain community now became something quite different. They would be quickly descending to the base of Maslow's hierarchy of needs. Safety and security occupied his thoughts, and he knew those thoughts would soon drive his actions. He had a family and a soon-to-be-born grandchild to keep safe. Carl also recognized the most fundamental and rudimentary of those needs would probably demand he take risks beyond his imagination. This was survival—plain and simple. The family remained warm and dry . . . for now. They had food that could be stretched for a couple of weeks, but Carl estimated they had perhaps four months to survive before they could begin the arduous journey out of the mountains to whatever lay beyond, if there was no rescue effort before spring.

"What's bothering you?" Janet asked from behind him.

Carl glanced at his wife and turned his gaze out the window. "Do you want the truth or the politically correct answer?"

"How bad is the truth?"

"Pretty bad, I'm afraid."

"What is worse than killing other human beings?" Janet asked.

Carl turned to look directly into Janet's eyes. "I really do not think my assessment will prepare you, or help you feel better about our situation."

"Are you being dramatic to scare me?"

"I'm afraid not, Sweets. I am deadly serious."

"Now you're scaring me."

"Janet, over the coming days, weeks and months, we are going to . . . we are going to witness the worst and most savage base aspects of human nature. My first priority will be protecting you and our family from harm. My second priority will be finding sufficient foods in a very hostile environment. In fact, before things get much worse, I need to make a run on the grocery store . . . or maybe even one of the gas station convenience stores, to gather up whatever we can find. It will not take long before the infrastructure will be stripped clean, which will make foraging all the more difficult."

Janet stared to the distant horizon at nothing in particular. After what seemed like a minute or two, she muttered, "No one is coming to help us."

"If my assessment is correct, there is no one to rescue us. Everyone else is most likely facing exactly the same situation we are. Denver probably got hit directly. Those who survive are fending for themselves."

"Hit?"

"The signs I see and my nightmare, which I think was some kind of premonition, tell me this country was attacked on a large scale by a very sophisticated and capable adversary."

"The whole country?"

Carl considered how he should answer. What he wanted to say would undoubtedly be very depressing. At the end of the day, the brutal truth would have to suffice. "I have no way to know until I get more information, but even if it is just Denver, this is more than enough for us."

"Dear God above! Denver is the middle of the nation. Who would do such a thing to this beautiful country?"

"I could guess, but the answer is irrelevant. It does not alter our situation," Carl answered. "We need to survive this winter, and if we do, there will be time enough to address that question."

Janet and Carl sat quietly. Carl instinctively kept his eyes scanning left to right, near to far. Ten minutes passed without the slightest sign of movement.

Carl turned his head to look at Janet. "I think it's time for me to reconnoiter the town, to see what I can turn up."

Janet looked into her husband's eyes. "Should you take the boys with you?"

"No. If I am alone, I will be less threatening to any bad actors out there. Plus, it would probably be best for them to be here with you and Lisa." Carl checked his mechanical wristwatch. "It's nearly 10:30. I'd better get going."

Carl quickly scanned the area to make sure, as best he could, that no one was watching them or would notice their movement, and then he stood. He waited for Janet to stand before he pulled the sliding door and the makeshift blackout curtain back for her to precede him into the warmth of the interior.

Carl checked to make sure everyone was present. "I'm going to take a trip into town to see what I can find. Mike and Nick, I'd like y'all to extend your watch period to cover the remainder of the Team Three watch."

"Shouldn't at least one of us go with you?" asked Alex.

"Thank you for your concern, but no. I think it's best I do this alone. It may take me the rest of the day, since the snow has not been cleared. I intend to make it back here before dusk. Please do not open the door for anyone. Just remain silent and motionless, if anyone knocks. Also, Dave, please help Mike and Nick tie a white sheet to cover the balcony railing and camouflage our watch station. Make sure you tie it down as tightly as possible. Any movement will attract unwanted attention."

"Dad, you keep telling us all these things," Lisa interjected. "What do you think is going to happen or might happen?"

"Nothing good," answered Carl. "You will see direct evidence soon enough. For now, you will just have to trust me." Carl looked to each face. "Any other questions?" He scanned his family and guest, again. "OK. Let's hop to it."

Carl did not wait for consent. He grabbed his backpack, leaning against the wall, and went to the bathroom. Carl removed his venerable 45-caliber pistol, pulled the slide back a quarter of an inch to check for a round in the chamber, re-engaged the safety, and placed it in his right jacket pocket. He put the only spare clip and the only box of ammunition he had in his left jacket pocket. Carl checked himself in the mirror to ensure none of his additions were visible or detectable. Satisfied, he zipped up and donned his backpack, adjusting the shoulder straps across the bulk of his winter coat. Carl rejoined the family gathered in the living room near the warmth of the modest fire.

"When I return, I will knock softly, low on the door . . . once, three times, and lastly, two times." Carl went to the coffee table in front of the couch. With everyone watching him, he knocked softly on the table—1, 3, 2. "Please remember the sequence. I do not want to speak outside this apartment." He pointed to each of them and received an affirmative head nod. "Very well, then, wish me luck."

"Good luck, Dad," Lisa said—the only one to speak.

Carl nodded his head. He went to the front door, checked the peephole— landing clear—and picked up the set of makeshift snowshoes they constructed. He inhaled a deep breath and opened the door. Closing the door behind him, Carl quickly and quietly descended the stairs to the building lobby. The snowshoes strapped to his boots easily enough. He opened the door slowly, scanned the outside, stepped out and quietly closed the door behind him.

The combination of an underlying hedge and the snowdrift line kept a narrow path next to the building comparatively clear. Carl shuffled sideways to blur his tracks and did the same along the narrow path to the end of the building. He scanned the area around for any witnesses, and then he looked to the windows above as best he could. All the windows appeared to be covered in some form. Carl found a break in the hedge, climbed the drift and began his trek into town. He had decided to take the Four O'Clock Run ski trail behind the condominium complex to the end at North Park Avenue. Only fresh snow covered the ground. Carl continued to shuffle his feet to leave long indistinct tracks rather than specific footfalls that might convey his size to any tracker. He considered trying to brush off his tracks, but he decided the effort would have little value versus the work to accomplish the task. As expected, the street had not been cleared of fresh snow and clearly showed more foot traffic, nearly all since the snowfall ended. Carl scanned the streets and buildings—no movement. He stepped out of the woods and moved smoothly north, turning east on Ski Hill Road to cross over the nearly frozen Blue River, which was really not much of a river, rather more like a creek. Regardless of the name, water was still flowing, the ripples clearly visible through the few remaining holes in the covering ice and snow. The signs of human activity were more apparent—more tracks, discarded bags and boxes.

As he reached Main Street, Carl scanned the streets, left, right and ahead. Several men were searching the stores and not moving with any urgency or particular concern for his presence. His first objective was Climax Jerky, inside the Lincoln West Mall on the southwest corner. He remembered visiting the specialty shop during the ski holiday last winter. Two men cradling shotguns stood guard on the entrance, which had been shoveled clear since the last snowfall. They did not look particularly menacing, just cautiously protective.

Carl scanned the streets one more time, and then made eye contact with one of the guards. He approached and held his hands in front of him, chest height and palms out. "Are the stores open?" Carl asked.

"Some," the man answered succinctly. "Cash only."

"Sure. That's OK. May I enter?"

"Yes."

Carl entered the darkened interior, lit only by various candles distributed around the corridor. Most of the stores were still closed—clothing, knick-knacks, and such. Carl saw a steady light from the Climax Jerky store. Only one person remained in the store. A 19th Century kerosene lamp illuminated the store fairly well. "Are you open for business?" Carl asked.

"In a manner of speaking, yes. I still have product, but it is cash only. Telephones and computers are not working."

"I know," Carl responded. "The power is not likely to come back on anytime soon. I would like to buy as much of your products as I can stuff in my backpack."

"If you have the cash to pay for it, I think I can handle that. What would you like?"

"I was here last winter, and there was nothing I did not like. So, a little bit of everything I would say."

"We are almost out of beef. I'll give you what's left of the beef. We still have all the others."

"Our kids like beef and turkey. I like all of it . . . well, you can hold the gluten free stuff."

"Do you want me to wrap it?"

Carl removed his backpack and unzipped it. "Fill 'er up." Carl smiled. "I want to get as much as I can into my backpack, and I do not want to waste space with paper or wrapping."

The store clerk, perhaps the owner, donned server gloves and gathered up all of the jerky strips in the display case tray marked "beef." "Are you sure you can pay for all this?" the man asked.

Carl reached into the left front pocket of his Levis, and withdrew a folded and bound stack of $100 bills. "Yes, I do."

Satisfied he would get paid, the clerk placed the handful of beef jerky into Carl's backpack. The clerk jotted down the amount with a pencil and paper. The next handful was roughly half of his venison jerky. He followed with similar amounts of elk, buffalo, salmon, turkey and even wild boar jerky. Carl signaled for him to continue, since his backpack was not quite full. The clerk tallied his worksheet. "That's $127, so far."

Carl peeled off two $100 bills and placed them on the counter next to the man's notepad. Again, satisfied, the clerk grabbed a slightly smaller amount of each type of jerky with further additions to his accounting sheet. The clerk did not stop after adding the wild boar jerky and picked up five more strips of each jerky. He paused to look at Carl, gesturing as if to say looks like its full.

Carl nodded his head and said, "How much do I owe you?"

The man completed his tally and responded, "$196."

Carl pushed the two $100 bills toward the clerk. "No need for change." Carl zipped up his backpack, placed it fully on his back and adjusted the straps for smooth carry. "I'm going to go empty this. Can I buy more?"

"As long as you have cash and I have product, you can buy as much as you wish."

"Thank you. I'll be back in an hour or so."

"What are you stocking up for?" the man asked.

"Just being cautious. It will get eaten. I will not be reselling any of it. I have a family."

The man nodded his head and apparently accepted Carl's explanation.

Carl turned toward the door and glanced over his shoulder to say, "Be safe, my friend."

Outside, Carl thanked the two guards and quickly scanned his surroundings. There were more men and boys on the streets, and no females that he could tell. He moved out smartly west on Ski Hill Road. Carl remained vigilant without being obvious and returned to the condominium in his earlier tracks. Fortunately, no one interfered with his transit. Before entering their building, he scanned the area one more time, and then quickly opened the door, stepped inside and closed the door behind him. Carl removed his snowshoes and carried them to the condominium. He knocked softly, low on the door—once, three times and twice. He waited and was just about ready to knock the sequence again when the door opened.

"How did it go?" asked Alex.

"Good, Son. Thanks. Please ask Mike and Nick to join us. Sweetheart," Carl said, looking to Janet, "would you find a container for a lot of jerky?"

"Really?"

"Yes, really." Carl took off his backpack, unzipped it, and removed a single strip.

"Do you really think we need that much jerky?"

"Yes, and I'm going back for more, now, before it's gone."

Janet did not question her husband, again. Carl unloaded his backpack. Janet found a large pot and stacked the jerky strips vertically into the pot. Alex returned with Mike and Nick, closing the balcony door and restoring the blackout curtain.

"I need to say this, very quickly," Carl began, "the jerky store in town still has product. I don't know how much longer it will last. I'm going back into town. The jerky is not for snacking. It is for survival. I do not want anyone helping themselves. We will ration what we can collect. Does everyone understand?" Carl looked to each person for a verbal or gestured affirmation. "OK. This time my return knock sequence will be two, one, three." He demonstrated softly. "Very well, then. I'm going to the jerky shop and straight back here. It should take me 90 minutes or so."

"OK, Dad. We got it," Lisa said with some irritation, as she held her belly as if she was holding it up.

Carl did not pause for argument. He donned the empty backpack and left.

The journey was uneventful, although there were even more males moving around. Carl kept his head down, avoided making eye contact or responding to calls, and also kept his hands in his jacket pockets, as if he was keeping his hands warm, although his right hand was gripping the pistol with his thumb on the safety, just in case he needed to react quickly. The guards at the Lincoln West Mall were more animated, agitated and their shotguns were held at the ready. Something had happened during the short time he was gone. They recognized him and nodded him past. Their apparent nervousness made Carl more cautious as he entered the mall building and made his way to the jerky store. The same man was there and alone, although he now had a large 44 Magnum on the counter in front of him.

"You're back," he announced.

"What the heck happened while I was gone?" Carl asked.

"A group of boys thought they could take what they wanted."

"Did anyone get hurt?"

"They came close, but no. They wisely left without incident and were invited not to return."

"Sorry you had to deal with that."

The man waved his hand dismissively. "The longer this blackout lasts, the worse it will get."

"Yes, it will." Carl pulled off his backpack and unzipped it. "I would like another load," he said. Carl placed another $200 on the counter beside the pistol.

"Unfortunately, the price has gone up."

"Why?"

"Demand."

"Are you kidding me?"

The man placed his hand on the pistol grip and simply answered, "Nope."

"Easy," Carl said calmly, as his right thumb was removed from the safety on the pistol in his hand. "I mean no harm and want no trouble. I just wish to buy some of your products. What is the current price?"

"Double," he said flatly.

"That sounds like price gouging."

"Call it what you will. Do you want the jerky or not?"

Carl felt a reinforced sense of unease. The change in the demeanor of the clerk/owner heightened his sense of foreboding. Carl looked quickly and carefully around the small store for even the slightest sign of compromise or abnormality to the new normal. He detected none. "Yes, please," he eventually responded. He released his grip on the pistol and laid down two more $100 bills.

The clerk released his grip on the powerful pistol. He repeated the earlier process. Once the backpack was full, he tallied the cost. "That will be $407."

Carl stared at the man and reached into his left pocket. He added a $10 bill to the stack.

"Nice doing business with you," the man said.

Carl only nodded his head, not feeling particularly good about the transaction. I'll not be back here, again. Carl gathered his backpack and headed out. The two entry guards were still quite nervous about something. Carl felt no urge for conversation or inquiry. As he had done earlier, he moved quickly through the streets to the trailhead at the edge of the woods. Halfway up the ski trail, three boys in their late teen years stepped out from behind bushes blocking his passage.

"We'll take your backpack and whatever you have in your pockets," the middle one announced.

Carl stood very still. He quickly scanned the three boys, as he felt to make sure the safety on his pistol was OFF—it was. He could see one hunting knife, a baseball bat and what looked like an ax handle. "You boys are making a grave mistake."

"How so?" the middle one responded.

"I do not want to hurt you, but this will not end well for any of you, if you do not leave now."

They were clearly not impressed and not likely to act favorably.

"I said, hand . . . ," he did not finish his sentence, as Carl withdrew his pistol and fired three quick shots into the center chest of each boy. Two of the boys were dead immediately. The boy on Carl's left was still alive, but would not be so for very long. The boy tried to say something, but only blood and gurgling could be seen or heard.

Carl searched the area around the incident. He found a spot with a large fallen tree that met his requirements. The tree had fallen a year or so earlier, so it was still solid. A slight depression just beyond the ski trail made a good spot for his purpose. Carl removed the first dead boy's jacket and pants. He then cut the shirt off his torso, tore it into strips, and used two of the strips to plug the holes in the front and back of his chest to minimize the escape of blood, seeping now rather than pumping out. Carl lifted the boy's limp body over his shoulder and carried him to his final resting place. He laid the boy in the snow, and straightened the legs and crossed the arms over the lower torso. Carl repeated the process. By the time he completed the movement of the second boy and returned to the third, he was dead as well. With all three bodies plugged and stripped, and laid out next to each other, Carl covered them with snow from a nearby drift. He then broke off a pine branch to cover his tracks as best he could. He also dug up the blood spots in the trail snow, throwing the remnants into the woods, spreading them out. Carl filled in the holes with snow and tamped them down to obliterate any residual evidence of what had just happened. He checked the area to first make sure he had masked the event and second to remember where the three bodies were located, since they might have to be relocated for one reason or another.

The condominium complex was thankfully quiet. Carl repeated his entry process and knocked on their apartment door—1, 3, 2.

Alex opened the door. "Another load . . . ay Pops."

"Yep."

Janet had already moved to the kitchen counter with another large pot ready. Carl handed the backpack to his wife. She began unloading and storing the returned jerky. Carl checked to make sure the pistol safety was engaged, and then began unzipping his jacket.

Janet leaned toward him and whispered, "You have what looks like blood on your jacket."

Once he had removed his jacket, Carl checked what she saw. Sure enough, there was more blood than he imagined. Without words, he dampened a couple of paper towels and wiped off his jacket.

"What happened?" Janet whispered.

"I'll tell you later," Carl answered in a whisper as well.

"Are you OK?" she asked in a more normal voice.

"I'm fine."

"Do you want to talk to the kids?"

"Not necessary. How about Dave and I switch with you and Alex. I'd like to watch the exterior until dusk."

"OK by me. Do you want to ask Alex?"

"Do I need to?"

"It would be good form, Carl. They may not legally be adults, yet, but our circumstances are going to thrust them to adulthood very quickly."

"Good point," Carl said. He turned to the living room to find the faces he wanted. "Dave, Alex . . . a word, if you please."

Both boys joined Carl and Janet in the kitchen. Lisa joined them out of curiosity.

"Dave, I'd like you and me to relieve Mike and Nick early, and trade the duty with Janet and Alex, so I can watch the outside before sunset."

"Sure," responded Dave.

"Fine by me," Alex added.

"What's going on, Dad?" asked Lisa. "What are you concerned about?"

Carl considered whether to confide in the children what had happened on the ski trail. In the end, he decided to keep it simple. "Things changed substantially from my first trip into town and my second trip. I am concerned things may be deteriorating faster than I expected."

"Is there anything we can or should do?" Lisa pressed.

"Not that I can think of, but thank you for asking. Your first and only priority is to take care of your baby. We will handle the rest."

"OK. Just thought I'd ask."

Carl nodded his head and gestured toward the balcony door. He retrieved, put on and zipped up his jacket. This time, he grabbed his heavy winter gauntlets. Dave dressed himself up for the cold. Carl went to Janet and kissed her. "I love you," he said softly.

"I love you, too. Just be careful."

"I will."

First Dave and then Carl stepped beyond the blackout curtain. Carl made sure the curtain was in place. They had less than an hour until dusk. He knocked once on the glass. Both Mike and Nick turned to see Carl, who gestured for both of them to come in. Carl scanned the outside—nothing noteworthy. He opened the door. Both boys stepped inside.

"Dave and I are going to relieve you early and take Mom and Alex's shift. Have you noticed anything?"

Nick answered, "Only a few groups of boys and men moving around. They appeared to be searching cars and apartments."

"OK. It is only a matter of time before they come to us." Carl thought for a moment and looked to Mike. "Would you find a piece of paper, a pen or pencil, and something to write on for me?" Mike nodded his head. "Thank you. We'll take over from here."

Carl and Dave checked the exterior surroundings to minimize the opportunity for any potential observers, and then stepped out onto the balcony. They quickly settled onto the stools. Carl then checked the bed sheet camouflage installation. *Well done!* A few individuals or couples were spotted walking toward town down the far street—4 O'Clock Run Road.

Mike knocked at the door. Carl quickly scanned the area and turned to nod his head. The door opened slightly, and Mike handed his father a blank sheet of paper, a pen, and a rather large coffee-table book. Carl mouthed but did not speak—thank you. Mike nodded his head once and closed the door.

Carl immediately began to fill the page with a sketch of the scene that lay out before them, with every door and window represented, as well as enough of the buildings to orient the sketch.

Carl leaned toward Dave and whispered, "We need to mark down any sign of life—a light, a displaced curtain, anything. We need to identify which apartments are occupied and eventually who might be allies."

Dave's left thumb up confirmed his understanding.

They began to mark the sketch. Most folks were not particularly careful. Curtains moved. Faces appeared in windows. As twilight progressed, dim candlelight could be seen in a half dozen windows with open curtains.

Darkness enveloped the valley. The clear mountain air made the blossoming starlight all the more vivid than he remembered. The waxing half moon just began to peak over the eastern horizon on the far side of the valley. The single soft knock on the glass behind them probably meant their shift was over. Dave and Carl stood and pulled the sliding glass door open just enough to slip inside.

Carl kissed Janet quickly but dispassionately. He held the book and paper, and explained the purpose. Janet and Alex nodded their heads. Janet took the book and opened the door. Carl waited until the door closed before pulling back the blackout curtain far enough for them to enter.

Mike and Nick were playing a game of chess by the modest fire. Lisa was lying on her mattress, reading a book by candlelight.

"Mom made a tuna sandwich for each of you," Lisa said matter-of-factly without taking her eyes off her book.

"Thanks," Carl and Dave answered in unison. They consumed their sandwiches with a glass of water in silence.

Carl looked around the room. Everything was peaceful and calm. The fatigue of his adrenaline-descent brought the urge to sleep. Carl went to the mattress he shared with Janet, laid down, pulled the blanket over him, and was soon in deep sleep.

—

6

Returning to consciousness took an uncharacteristically longer time than usual. Carl could smell the delightfully earthy aroma of the modest fire. He searched for some indication of time. Lisa sat on the fireplace hearth to the right of the fire reading what looked like another book different from the one she was reading last night. Dave, Mike and Nick were sleeping. That meant Janet and Alex were on duty. Carl gave up and checked his wristwatch in the dim light of the fire—08:45. It has to be in the morning since he and Dave had finished their shift at 20:00 last night. The time also meant he had missed the Team Three shift and Dave had stood watch alone. *That was not good.* Carl sat up for a few seconds, and then stood. He joined Lisa on her left side, away from the fire.

"What happened?" Carl asked her.

Lisa finished the paragraph she was on, put the bookmark in the book and closed it. "Apparently, you were sleeping so hard and deep, Dave asked Mom whether he should wake you up or stand watch alone. Before Mom could answer, Alex volunteered to stand back-to-back watches with Dave. That's why they both crashed."

"Where's Mom?"

"She's in the bathroom . . . cleaning up, I think."

Carl moved past the hallway blankets. The temperature was decidedly colder beyond the blankets. He knocked twice on the door, heard no response and opened the door. Janet was standing, surprisingly naked, and apparently finishing her sponge bath. Two large candles illuminated her body adequately. She glanced up to see Carl and returned to her task. "This is freakin' cold . . . but necessary," she pronounced without looking up again. "We've got to figure out a better way. Our water supply," she said, nodding her head toward the tub, "is nearly frozen. It won't do us much good like that."

She is such a gorgeous woman. "True."

Janet finished and rinsed the washcloth in the remaining water she had in the sink. She began to dress. "Did you come in here just to see me naked?" she chuckled.

Carl smiled broadly. "Not a bad idea, my dear . . . but alas, I wanted to hear what happened last night."

"You were dead to the world. My turn . . . what happened in town yesterday afternoon. I've never seen you crash like that. Something really got to you."

Carl stared into her concerned eyes as she completed dressing. "I'm not sure how my answer will help our situation."

"Stop! I don't want to hear any more of that patronizing bullshit. What happened?"

OK, you asked for it; you got it. "I was ambushed by three teenage boys on the way back from my second run into town . . . on the trail just short of home."

Janet's expression instantly transformed from curious to fear. "Were those the three shots I heard yesterday afternoon?"

"Yes."

Janet inhaled sharply. Tears welled up in her eyes. Her hands covered her mouth and nose, as if in some form of prayer. Shock trammeled her whispered voice. "Three? You killed all three?"

"Yes."

The tears now descended her cheeks. "Oh, Carl, did you really have to kill those boys?"

"I gave them the opportunity to leave and not bother me. They did not move. They made their choice. I ended it quickly. This is the ugliness that is coming, and it's going to get worse before we come out the other side."

"What did you do with the bodies?"

"To be blunt, I stored them. They will remain frozen until spring."

"Why?"

Carl again searched his wife's expression. "Again, to be blunt . . . for evidence or necessity?"

"Necessity?"

"Janet, do you really want to hear how bad it is going to get?"

"Yes."

"Very well," Carl answered, "our food supply will not last until springtime. The looting in town has already begun, and it will accelerate rapidly. In our situation, we should be driven by the ancient wisdom—waste not, want not."

"Are you suggesting we will eat those boys?"

"It may come to that. Such necessity is not without historical precedent. I'm not eager to take that step, but I am primarily driven by our survival. People will try to find food however they can. Normal behavior no longer applies. This is going to get ugly. OK, so now you know . . . what happened last night?"

"Dave tried twice to wake you, without response. He was going to stand the Team Three watch alone. Alex volunteered to stand watch with Dave."

"Well, I must laud their teamwork, but if this happens again for any of us, I must be awakened. Throw cold water on me . . . that usually works."

"We did the best we could and I supported the decision to let you sleep."

"Thank you . . . I'm just sayin'."

"Anything else?" asked Janet.

"No, I guess not. We need to get back out there."

"Yes, we do."

Carl opened the door, blew out the two candles and followed Janet out of the bathroom. She stopped before the curtain, leaned toward Carl and whispered in his ear, "Let's not talk about cannibalism with the kids, just yet."

"That was my plan," he whispered in reply, ". . . until you pressed me."

Janet nodded and pulled back the blanket. They stepped into the welcome warmth of the living room.

"What were you two doing back there," Lisa said, "creating your own heat?" She giggled.

"Nice thought," Janet responded, "but, no, just talking."

Carl went to the kitchen. "Has everyone had their strip of jerky this morning?"

"Everyone except you," answered Lisa.

"OK." Carl retrieved one of the pots of jerky and pulled out what he thought was venison. His first bite confirmed his assessment. He felt the strong urge to try buffalo and elk, but he resisted, knowing they had to stick to the plan.

Once he had consumed his morning allotment of jerky, Carl went to the edge of the blackout curtain and peeked out on the balcony. Mike and Nick sat near motionless on their stools, behind the covered railing. Carl watched them annotate the record sheet a couple of times without looking past them to see what they were noting. He checked his wristwatch; they had a little over three more hours to go on their watch period. Alex and Dave were still asleep. Carl glanced over at Lisa, who was quite absorbed in her book. *What is she going to do when she has read all the books we have?* Carl added a log on the fire to keep it going at a modest level. *I'm going to have to shovel out the accumulated ash in a few days.* Carl went to his mattress, laid down, caught Janet's attention and patted the mattress next to him. Janet got the hint. She laid down next to her husband and snuggled up to him.

They dozed off. The next thing that brought Carl to awareness was Dave wiggling his big toe.

"It is our watch time," Dave said softly.

"OK." As Carl began to extricate himself from Janet's embrace, she woke up. "It's OK. Just watch time." Janet smiled and kissed her husband. Carl went to the blackout curtain and peeked out. A bright, sunny, picturesque, mountain day greeted him—not a cloud in the visible sky. Everything appeared to be calm. Carl knocked once on the glass door. Both Mike and Nick looked back, gave a thumb's up and came inside.

"How're things outside?" asked Carl.

"Fairly quiet, actually," Nick responded.

"More folks wandering around," added Mike, "probably trying to figure out what to do next."

"It will be that way until it becomes dreadfully obvious. Let's have a family meeting before the next watch."

When Carl followed the boys inside from the blackout curtain, everyone had taken a seat on the couch or various chairs. Carl poked the fire a little to freshen it up, and then turned to face the group. "First, I must apologize to everyone for missing my watch shift last night. It was a rough afternoon. Second, there will be difficult times like yesterday that each of us must deal with, but it is imperative that we remain vigilant to avoid disaster as best we can. If I fail to wake up for a shift . . . some cold water to the face should do the trick. Our protection will depend upon our discipline. We must each carry our weight equally, or all of us will suffer. Lisa's baby is due in a month or less. While she must bear the preponderance of support for the child, as she will be the sole milk producer among us, we will have to assist her with infant care, as necessary . . . which reminds me, we really should conduct another rehearsal or two before you go into labor for real," he added to Lisa directly. Lisa nodded her head. "Lastly, before things get too much crazier in town, I need to reconnoiter the grocery stores and the police stations."

"Shouldn't at least one of the boys go with you?" interjected Janet.

"Normally," Carl answered, "I would say we should never do anything outside this apartment alone. We should always be at least in pairs, like we are doing with our security watch. However, whomever ventures outside really should be armed, and right now we have only one pistol."

"Where are we going to find more guns?" Nick asked.

"I am fairly certain that the process will come in time as the population begins to thin." The expressions suggested they understood what Carl's statement meant. He decided elaboration was not necessary at this juncture. "Very well, then. If there is no objection, I would like to return to the normal sequence, which means Alex and Mom will take the current watch." Carl looked for an affirmative gesture from Janet and Alex. Both nodded their agreement. "I will try to return in time for the Team Three watch duty. Please do not forget to mark the sketch with signs of life. We will need that information in the next day or so." Carl paused to check everyone's eyes. Several nodded agreement. "Has anyone seen any aggressive activity?"

"Only that dead guy we saw by the parking lot entrance," answered Nick, "and, he's still there."

"Yeah," Carl responded. "He will probably stay there for a while. We are likely to see hunting parties searching for food and domination. We must detect the signs as soon as possible. Just pay attention to what you can see and hear. OK then, let's get to it."

Alex and Janet stood, donned their jackets and gloves, and headed to the balcony. Alex retrieved the activity sheet from Mike. Carl remembered he needed to fill the pistol's magazine, which he did quickly and smoothly. Before Team Two moved past the blackout curtain, Carl said, "My return sequence will be three, two, one, this time." He knocked the sequence on the table softly. Carl zipped up his jacket and grabbed his gloves, although he would not wear them in order to handle the pistol as swiftly and precisely as possible.

Team Two disappeared beyond the blackout curtain. Carl headed out as he had done yesterday, except he left the snowshoes in the apartment since there was sufficient packed snow to use his snow boots only. He felt no need to check on his stash of bodies. Carl considered staying on North Park Avenue and avoiding the risks of Main Street, but he convinced himself he needed to check the small Local Market on Main Street at Wellington Road. There were more people about. Carl kept a suspicious eye on everyone he could see. He walked down the middle of the street to give himself a little margin if anyone tried to approach him.

As he reached the Local Market, the broken windows, open doors and littered parking lot convinced him entry would most likely be a wasted effort with unreasonable risk. Carl continued north on Main Street. There was no footbridge across Blue River, so Carl turned west on North French Street until he was across Blue River, and then used the rear service road. City Market exhibited the same signs of looting as Local Market. Again, Carl felt little motivation to check the interior.

Carl continued his reconnaissance, crossing North Park Avenue. He found the sign for the Summit County Sheriff's Office. At least the windows were not broken, but the doors were locked. A handwritten cursive sign had been taped to the inside of the door.

We have our families
to protect.
You are on your own.

"That is not an encouraging sign," Carl spoke aloud to no one. He looked around in search of other signs of activity. Other than tracks in the snow, he saw no other signs in that area. Carl pressed on north up Airport Road to Valley Brook Street and the Breckenridge Police Station.

The doors and windows displayed signs of attempted break-ins—several hard, blunt impacts and a few bullet impacts. The sign on the inside of the transparent door was far more succinct than the one at the sheriff's office.

NO POLICE

Carl saw movement reflected in the window. Without moving his head, his focus immediately shifted from the empty, dark interior to the source of that movement. His thumb instinctively found the pistol safety. A group of four young men appeared behind a short fence along Airport Road, perhaps 70 yards away. They were watching him and had not been anywhere in sight when Carl arrived. The men could just be wondering what the single man was doing or going to do, or they might be calculating what they were going to do next.

Carl did not want to wait around for clarity. *I can't stand here forever.* When Carl turned away from the station doors, he looked directly at the group to make sure they recognized his awareness. All four faces watched him. He began walking back the same way he had come. As he turned south on Airport Road, Carl glanced to his right, as if he was checking for traffic. The group of men had not moved and continued to watch him. He did his best to act as though he did not care. As he walked, the urge to look behind him to check on the group grew with each step. On the plus side, he only heard the crunch of his footfalls in the partially packed snow on the roadway. Carl listened intently for a sound to naturally cause him to look behind him. When he reached North Park Avenue, he looked both directions, and then behind him, as if he was checking for traffic. The group had moved with him down Airport Road, but remained a respectable 100 yards behind him.

Once across North Park Avenue, Carl walked at a modest pace to maintain his footing and moved to one of the broken windows with the largest piece of remaining glass at the City Market building. He pretended to be examining the interior, but he was actually using the glass as a crude mirror to check on his trackers. They had crossed the street and stopped at the edge of the road. Carl was fairly certain, now, that they were following him, probably to track him back to his residence and additional booty. He quickly considered his options and the best way to execute those options. He did not want to confront this group. These men were more than teenagers and probably had more experience than the boys he dispatched yesterday. Carl knew he could not just continue down Park Avenue, unless he intended to ambush them on the 4 O'Clock Run trail, as the boys had confronted him. *No. I do not need that risk. I've got to ditch these guys somehow.*

Carl checked the reflection, again. They had not moved. Carl peered inside the store. He detected at least two men moving around the interior of the ransacked store. Carl decided his best option was to risk passing through the store, make it out the back service entrance, move along the bike path adjacent to the river, and then pick up French Street, to Main Street, and use Watson Avenue to return to Park Avenue and the trailhead. That route would give him several discreet surveillance points to check for followers. *That's a plan. Execute.*

Checking the reflection one more time, Carl confirmed all four men remained stationary. Without glancing toward them, Carl turned away from them and entered the store. He gave his eyes a few seconds to adjust to the darkened interior. He could not see, but he heard at least two people rummaging through debris in the store. Carl withdrew his pistol from his right jacket pocket and flipped the safety off. In this situation, he would likely have very little reaction time margin. His left hand grasped the spare magazine and felt the small container of ammunition. Carefully selecting his steps, he moved quietly and swiftly through the store. He encountered two more men in the rear service room. They froze, wary of the intruder. Carl kept his pistol close to his side, not wanting to alarm the two looters, and held up his left hand, palm out. He did not wait for any sign and made for the open rear door. Carl glanced over his left shoulder to make sure the two looters were not making a move on him, and then quickly checked left and right. *Clear!* The packed snow behind the store and on the path made his fast-paced walk comparatively effortless. At French Street, Carl glanced over his left shoulder—no one visible. At the first shop south on Main Street, Carl stepped into the entry alcove and watched. *Nothing. Good.* He continued south on Main Street. Fewer people were out and about. At Watson Avenue, Carl scanned completely around him. He was not willing to declare success, just yet, but there were no signs the group of men was still following him and no one else seemed to be interested in him. Carl evaluated his situation several more times before making it safely back to the apartment building without incident.

"How'd it go?" asked Nick, as he opened the door.

Carl placed his right index finger to his lips, seeking silence. He checked the stairwell one last time to ensure no one was attempting to follow him, and then entered. Nick closed and locked the door.

"Sorry, Dad."

"The more information we give others outside our family and this apartment, the more vulnerable we become."

"I got it, Dad . . . again, sorry. So, now, the door is closed. How did it go?"

Carl checked his wristwatch. "It's almost time for Mom and Alex to be done with the shift. Let's get them in so I can do this once for everyone."

Mike went to the curtain and called Team Two inside.

"Is everything OK out there?" asked Carl.

"Yeah," Janet answered, "pretty quiet for our watch."

"Before Dave and I start our watch, I want to update everyone on my latest recce into town."

"Recce?" asked Dave.

"A contracted or slang version of reconnaissance." Dave nodded his head. Carl continued, "The grocery stores have all been looted already. Both the sheriff's office and police station are closed, and we are not likely to find any assistance from law enforcement, which means we will probably continue our descent into anarchy and chaos. We must be prepared for the worst. Gangs are starting to develop. A group of four men followed me for a while. I suspect they wanted to track me back here to see what they could find. Unfortunately, we are going to do the same thing for our own protection. Where is the activity sheet?" Alex handed the sketch to his father. Carl examined the sheet. Multiple marks covered about half of the windows and all of the doors observable from their balcony. "We need to keep tracking activity. We are also going to start searching the no-activity apartments to see what we can find of use to us."

"Break in?" Mike asked.

"Steal?" added Janet.

"Yes, that is exactly what I am saying . . . and we will undoubtedly have to defend what we have and what we can accumulate."

"That's against the law," Nick commented.

"Son, in these circumstances, there is no law . . . only survival of the fittest. I want . . . I must . . . keep this family as fit as I possibly can. We do not have enough to make it to spring and make the arduous journey out of these mountains. We must remain strong and fit to accomplish both. Others have already started the process."

"That does not make it right," Janet pronounced with the emotion of disdain.

"No. There is no more right and wrong. There is only survival."

"That is pretty grim, Carl," Janet protested.

"Yes, Janet, it is. We are stranded in the Rocky Mountains in the middle of winter. Law and order have evaporated in a matter of days. Our choices have narrowed to just two . . . survive . . . or not. Hopefully, we will make it to springtime with sufficient strength to make the difficult journey out of these mountains."

"You're scaring me, Dad," Lisa said, grasping her distended abdomen, as if she was trying to hold it together.

"For that, I am sorry, Lisa, but I am not trying to scare you or anyone. I am only attempting to be honest and direct . . . to prepare us for what is ahead. I desperately want to be wrong . . . completely wrong; however, I see no signs that I am wrong. Every single indicator I can detect tells me we are going to see the worst elements of humanity. I must prepare us all to do the necessary things without blinking or hesitating to survive. Among these very dark realities, I will urge us to be as observant as we possibly can. Implicitly trusting others who are likely desperate and reactive could be deadly. As we are gathering up the materials we need for survival, we need to look for others to safely join us. There will be no second chances." Carl looked down at the not-so-clean carpet. "The hardest part of all this . . . we must eliminate anyone and anything at the first hint of threat. If a confrontation can be avoided, do everything you can to move around it, but if avoidance is not possible or even likely, then those who threaten us must be permanently eliminated."

"Kill?" Nick asked directly, succinctly and solemnly.

"Yes, I am afraid so. There is plenty to think about. After my experience in town yesterday and today, the need to teach each of you the necessary skills has arrived sooner than I had hoped." Carl checked his wristwatch. "Now, night will be here shortly. Dave and I need to get back out on the balcony. We will continue this tomorrow, as long as we can find a stable time."

Dave stood and prepared himself for the cold of their watch period. Carl did the same. He stopped when Janet came to him and whispered in his ear.

"I love you, Carl," she said softly. "I know you are doing what you think is best, but I sure do hope you are wrong. I'm with Lisa. Your words are scaring me and probably all the children."

"I hope so, too . . . truly."

Janet kissed her husband on the cheek and went to the kitchen.

Dave stood at the blackout curtain with the activity sketch, book and pencil in his hand. Carl felt the pistol in his jacket pocket to ensure the safety was still engaged. He put on his ski gloves to give him as much warmth as possible. Carl glanced over his shoulder before he followed Dave beyond the blackout curtain.

Carl scanned the scene. He saw no movement or indications they were being observed. Satisfied they were clear, Carl nodded his head. They quickly stepped out onto the balcony, closed the sliding door, and settled onto their stools. Carl took the activity sketch from Dave. Clear trends were beginning to evolve. Perhaps a third, approaching half, of the apartments, condominiums, and other inhabitable dwellings showed no sign of human activity. Fortunately, thus far, there were fewer signs of looting in the residential areas than he had seen in the commercial areas of Breckenridge. They would focus on the no-activity units. But first, he had to prepare everyone for the defense and search techniques. Carl knew they needed to get out there before the developing gangs became desperate or emboldened enough to venture into the riskier residential areas.

Dave leaned toward Carl and whispered, "I know how to shoot, Mister Parks."

"Do you now?"

"My Dad taught me years ago."

"That is a good step. I wish I had done that with our boys, but I suppose I hoped it was a skill they would not need in their lives."

"I think my Da . . . ," Dave stopped his sentence when Carl raised his left hand.

A group of three men appeared, coming up the road from town. The sun was below the western ridgeline, yet they were not quite to dusk. The men stopped at the entrance to the parking lot and appeared to be conferring on what to do next. One of them pointed to the dead man near the entrance. They displayed no signs of noticing Dave and Carl watching them. The men decided to move on and soon disappeared beyond the apartment building to the west, upslope.

This time, Carl leaned to Dave. "We may have to put your skills to use soon." Dave nodded his head.

As the sky eventually darkened, light began to appear in some windows. Carl dutifully added tick-marks at the appropriate spots on the activity sketch. The early evening watch remained comparatively quiet. No other movement was detected before the single soft knock marked the end of their watch period. Team One, Mike and Nick, relieved Team Three.

Carl spent the remainder of his waking hours thinking about the procedures for implementing the search process. While he was thinking, Carl worked on adjusting the hung blankets that served as a thermal barrier and blackout curtain for the back bedrooms. It took him a little over an hour to accomplish. The warmth of the fire and living room would slowly warm the bathroom and melt the nearly frozen water supply. Carl took the opportunity to clean his body as Janet had done.

—

7

"Look's like we've got weather coming in," Carl whispered to Dave.

"Snow?"

"Given those clouds and the air temperature, I would say, likely a lot of snow." Carl scanned as much of the sky as he could see from their observation post. "The wind is picking up. Wind and snow make for a blizzard."

"It also might slow the bad guys down," Dave added softly.

"Indeed."

Carl checked his wristwatch. They had another 45 minutes of their watch period. Neither of them had spotted any movement, outside or in any of the dwellings within their sight in the last two hours—a positive sign to David's observation.

Snow began to fall. Carl had no idea how heavy or long this storm would last. He felt it would at least be the rest of the day and a welcome respite from the worries of intrusion. He decided they would suspend the balcony over-watch duty for the duration of the storm and use the time together to train the family in the defensive skills they would need to survive.

By the time Mike's soft knock on the glass door behind them came, the snowfall had become quite heavy, obscuring visibility to just a hundred yards or so. Carl glanced over his shoulder, shook his head and gave the universal 'cut' gesture below his chin. He looked to Dave, nodded his head toward the door, and began dusting off the accumulated snow on his clothing. Dave did the same, and then entered the apartment. Beyond the heavy curtain, the interior warmth felt very reassuring. Both Dave and Carl removed their outer, insulated clothing and stood in front of the modest fire to warm themselves.

"Pretty heavy snow out there," Carl pronounced. "No point in standing watch in those conditions. We haven't seen any movement in hours." Mike and Nick removed their winter gear as well. "I thought we could use this collective downtime for some useful training and preparation." Carl checked his watch and began to grin for the first time. "By the way, Merry Christmas to everyone. I know we did not plan on being up here this long, but it is what it is. We can be grateful being alive, warm and safe," he said, and then mumbled, ". . . at least for now."

The family shared words of praise, celebration and gratitude.

"I wonder how my family is?" Dave said.

"We all do," added Janet.

"I truly wish there was a way to answer that question for you, Dave. My guess, for what it's worth . . . they are probably in a similar situation, without electricity in wintertime, but they are probably better off since we are isolated and stranded up here. So, hopefully, you can draw some comfort from that assessment."

"Although I am not eager to know the answer," Janet said, changing the subject, "what did you want to talk about today?"

"At our present rate of usage, we have perhaps a month of wood accumulated. We need at least two additional months of wood and perhaps more. We have conserved the water we have, so we are in pretty good shape there, plus as long as we have fire, we can melt more, if need be. It is the food supply I am the most concerned about now. We have a few weeks of food remaining. The baby is coming soon and that will change our consumption process. Once this storm passes, we are going to have to send out hunting parties in search of food." Janet caught Carl's attention and shook her head almost imperceptibly. *No, I'm not going to talk about that.* "I was hoping in vain that we could acquire other weapons. There is still hope during our searches, but we cannot wait or depend on that. We have other weapons in here, so the pistol can and should go with the hunting parties. Although I do not think the women should be included in the hunting parties," he stopped to look at Janet and Lisa, "I think both of you should know how to use the pistol safely, should the need ever arise." Janet nodded her head in agreement. "So, let's begin with the pistol."

Carl went to his heavy winter jacket and withdrew the pistol along with two magazines. He extracted the clip and ejected the chambered round, catching it before it hit the floor. For extra measure, he visually checked to ensure the chamber was clear and inserted his little finger into the empty chamber as he had been taught all those years ago. Carl dropped the slide catch to let the slide go home and un-cocked the hammer.

"First, we'll pass on the proper care and maintenance for the time being. I will handle that task for now. The pistol is safe. I would like each of you to hold it, just to feel its shape and weight in your hand." Carl held up the pistol and pointed to the major external features—trigger, slide, slide lock, hammer, thumb and grip safeties, and the magazine slot and release. The purpose and function of each of the primary components were shown to the family. He handed the pistol to Janet first. They passed it from one to the next and eventually back to Carl. "The M1911 is a heavy and powerful pistol . . . probably not the preferred weapon for a novice shooter, but we have no other choice at present. The initial action always when taking custody of a firearm is to make sure it is clear and safe. That is what I did first thing. I'll repeat the process for demonstration purposes, and then I would like each of you to duplicate the process." Carl used the empty pistol, as if it was loaded, to show the family the process again. Each of the family, in turn, performed the clearing procedure. When the pistol was returned to Carl, he said, "Again," and handed to Janet. They each performed the clearing process without a hiccup. "Next, when the pistol is loaded as it will be most of the time, the safety should be ON." Carl pointed to the safety lever on the left side of the pistol and activated the safety for each person to see. "Try it," he commanded. Each of them, without being told, accomplished the clearing procedures, and then worked the safety several times with their right thumb as they held the pistol. "OK. Good. Now, before we load the thing, I would like you to feel the trigger pull. When you pull the slide back to chamber a round, the hammer is cocked, like this," he said demonstrating the process, pointing to the hammer in the cocked position. *I'm not going to confuse them with the half-cocked position, since that will be irrelevant for their operations.* "You can also cock the hammer manually, like this." Carl demonstrated. "Further, you can un-cock the hammer as I've done, but I'd recommend you not worry about that until you have more experience with the weapon. As we pass the pistol around, I'd like each of you to feel the force of the trigger pull. Always remember, squeeze, don't jerk, the trigger, which will help you control the trajectory and hit your target." In turn, they followed suit. Carl watched each of them intently to make sure they were doing the process correctly. He saw the barrel waggle on a few of the trigger pulls, so he took the time to coach them as necessary to control their trigger pull.

When the pistol returned to him, Carl cleared it for consistency, un-cocked the hammer, and held the pistol up in his right hand. "From this point," he said, "we are going to be dealing with live rounds and a loaded pistol, so it is imperative that you be careful and deliberate with a loaded weapon. Second, we do not have a large supply of ammunition for our only firearm, thus we will be unable to practice with live fire." Carl placed the pistol on the coffee table in front of him and retrieved the lone round from his pocket that he had ejected earlier. He held up the cartridge between his thumb and index finger. "This is the type of round used in this pistol." He pointed to each component. "This is the bullet—the projectile. The bullets are always pointed toward the muzzle of the barrel. This is the casing that holds the propellant, the powder, that when ignited by the primer expands very rapidly and sends the bullet down range. This pistol holds . . ."

"Really, Dad," interrupted Lisa, "do we really need to know all this man-shit?"

"Yes, Lisa. I think you and Mom need to know how to use this weapon. We cannot predict what is going to happen, and there might come a time when a bullet like this will decide whether you live another day."

"Carl!" protested Janet.

"We have been thrust into a brutal situation, not by our choice or making. I will have failed as a father and a husband, and as a citizen, frankly, if I did not do my utmost to prepare you for any eventuality."

"OK," Janet responded in a softer tone, "just bring the bluntness down a notch or two. To take Lisa's point, if you are here, you are going to handle the pistol. If you, or one of the boys, have the pistol on one of your patrols, what good will this lesson be to us remaining here?"

Carl nodded his head in acknowledgment. "Point taken. I just thought everyone should be prepared to defend the family and our safety." This time, Lisa held up her right hand, as if she was still in school. "Yes Lisa."

"It's OK, Dad. I understand. I shall try to learn as best I can."

"Thank you. Our magazines," Carl continued his lesson, holding up the loaded magazine, "holds seven rounds. When we can, we'll load an additional round in the chamber."

"How do we do that?" asked Alex.

"The easiest way, which shall suffice for now, is to jack a round, and then pop the magazine and load a seventh round back into the magazine." Carl demonstrated the process twice. "Now, never forget, if you are in a fight, change the magazine and use the seven you've got. Make damn sure the pistol is not pointed at anyone you do not intend to kill, just in case—accidents happen. For this exercise, I want you to stand beside me, when it is your turn. Now, what I would like each of you to do in turn is insert the magazine, load a round, and then engage the safety." Carl demonstrated in slow motion first, emphasizing each action. He cleared the weapon, and then performed the procedure at normal speed. He cleared the weapon, again, and reloaded the magazine. Carl nodded his head for Janet to go first. He handed the pistol and magazine to her. She looked at him. Carl nodded his head for her to proceed. Janet performed the loading process flawlessly. Carl agreed. She cleared the weapon. Carl caught the round in flight. Taking the pistol and magazine from his wife, he reloaded the magazine, and then gestured for Lisa to take her turn. She stood slowly and awkwardly, and then waddled to her father. Like her mother, Carl was impressed with how well she performed the procedure. The boys followed and accomplished the task precisely as shown.

"The last step in this session is the purpose of this tool. Never use this pistol to threaten anyone. You should not pull it out of wherever you carry it unless you intend to kill. That is the only purpose for this weapon. This is going to feel awkward and it should. The weapon is clear. I will hand it to you, as if there was a round in the chamber and the magazine fully seated. The hammer will be in the cocked position and the safety will be on. I want you to extract it, point the pistol at my chest, disengage the safety and pull the trigger. You may have a sick feeling in your gut. That is normal. Killing someone is serious business. Does everyone understand, so far?" Each of them nodded their head in the affirmative. "Normally, I would very much object to anyone pointing a pistol at my chest, since I hope no one here wants or intends to kill me, but it is important that you feel and see exactly what you may have to do. This pistol has a bit of a kick to it. It is a powerful weapon. We do not have time or ammunition to practice your marksmanship. So, I want you to use an operational stance to aim the pistol and control the recoil. Hold the pistol straight in your hand. Lock your elbow and wrist slightly across your chest and cradle your right hand and the pistol in your left hand. I want you to pull back against your locked arm. Point your arm at the middle of your target's chest and squeeze the trigger." Carl demonstrated and emphasized each aspect of the stance and aiming process. "Try not to consciously pull the trigger. It will likely cause you to jerk, which is not good. Just squeeze. It should surprise you when the gun fires." Carl purposefully cleared the pistol again, simulated loading the magazine and chambering a round. He accentuated engaging the safety, and then put the weapon in the waistband of his Levis. "Drawing the pistol is not about speed. It is all about precision that will save your life. Do not worry about how fast you get it out. Once the barrel is pointed away from you and friendlies, disengage the safety, turn slightly to the right and point your arm at your target's chest. Here is the important part, if you feel threatened sufficiently to draw your weapon, I would recommend you do not hesitate. Do not try to frighten or dissuade the threat. Kill him."

"Damn!" exclaimed Mike, as he shook his head in disbelief.

"As I have told you many times, we are in a pure survival mode. Mistakes or hesitation can be fatal. Does everyone understand?" Carl looked carefully and purposely into the eyes of every family member for any sign of confusion.

"We're not even going to give them a chance?" asked Lisa.

"Their chance was not to confront you. You must think everyone out there is trying to kill you. They must prove they are not and can be trusted with your life. Trust your gut. If your gut tells you something is not right, or is threatening or aggressive, take action. Do not wait. Do not hesitate. Shoot to kill."

"You are telling us to kill people," protested Janet.

"Frankly, it is you or them. As you have heard me say for many years, better safe than sorry." Carl looked again at every set of eyes on him. "Sorry, in these circumstances, in a split second, it may well be death or worse."

"What is worse than death?" Alex asked.

"Rape, torture, or being kept alive and dismembered limb by limb without anesthesia until there is nothing left."

"Dear God above, Carl. That is outrageous . . . obscene," Janet said in disgust.

"Yes, well . . . truth be told, it would not be the first time for any of that when anarchy and survival prevail. Our objective is to survive no matter what comes our way. There are bad people who will resort to the easiest path for their survival, and they could care less about your humanity." Carl paused and looked around the room. No one spoke or reacted. "A word of caution to what you call my doom & gloom here . . . we need to look for the humanity in people we encounter. There are good people out there. We need to connect with them . . . to join with them for collective protection. The critical issue for all of us is there is a very thin line between good and bad in the type of situation we are in now. Because the margin for error is so narrow, I would much rather each of us err on the side of caution, of protection, of safety. Remember, a mistake by any one of us could endanger the whole family. So, it will come down to fractions of a second to make that decision. Think about what I've said. Imagine that confrontation. The time to think is now. You will not have that time when the confrontation comes."

"Enough!" Janet exclaimed. "What's next?"

"I appreciate your frustration, and probably the kids share your frustration, with my bluntness in this situation. It is just I see bad things ahead, and we do not have much time to prepare. I cannot be everywhere all of the time. I cannot do it all. Each of you must do your part in our defense." Carl paused. The boys nodded their heads. *At least I have that.* "Let's get the shooting practice done without bullets." Carl gestured to Janet to go first.

Each of them, in turn, accomplished several cycles of the shooting practice. Each of them needed coaching to one degree or another. Dave was the closest to acceptable. His handling of the heavy pistol demonstrated his familiarity with the various processes in utilizing a firearm. Carl was encouraged by the performance of the family on such a difficult mental task.

"OK. I think we have done as much as we can without using ammunition. I urge each of you to use this time before any confrontation to think through exactly what you must do." Carl went past the curtain to the sliding glass door. The snowfall remained heavy with very low visibility. He returned to the family. "The snowfall remains prohibitively heavy. Let's take a break. Perhaps, we can eat our evening meal."

"How about a half can of tuna each," suggested Janet.

"That would be nice," Carl responded.

"I'll have a glass of water with my meal," Mike added. Everyone laughed.

A door slammed. Carl jumped to put on his jacket, grabbed the pistol, loaded the magazine, chambered a round and engaged the safety. He put the spare magazines in his left pocket. Carl went to the door, looked out the peephole. *Nothing there.* He looked over his shoulder. Everyone was looking at him. He held up his left hand and held up three fingers, three fingers again, and then one finger, and then pointed to the door. The boys nodded. Carl then held his left index finger to his lips, signaling quiet.

Carl opened the door, stepped softly out onto the landing between the two top apartments, and then closed the door behind him. He heard the door bolt softly engage behind him. With carefully placed steps, he moved quietly to the stairwell. Several people were conversing, albeit in muffled tones, and making their way up the stairs. Carl determined the intruders were a man, a woman and what appeared to be an early teenage boy. He took quick glimpses to detect anyone else ascending the stairs. The man started up the last two flights of stairs. They were coming to his level. Carl backed up several paces, removed the pistol from his jacket and placed his hands behind his back. His right thumb rested on the pistol's safety.

The man turned on the last mid-landing. He looked up as he took the first step up the last flight. "Who the hell are you?" The three of them froze and their heads turned to Carl. The man appeared to be a half a foot shorter than Carl, with a trim but modest build, although it was hard to tell with the cold weather clothing. A knit, ski cap covered curly black hair and matching week growth of beard, but did not mask his stern expression. The woman was essentially the same height, comparably bundled up with a delicate, but determined face devoid of make-up. Her hair was not visible, tucked completely into her ski cap. The boy was nearly as tall as his parents with his father's hair without facial hair and a far more apprehensive expression in his eyes than either of his parents.

"I am here," Carl said calmly. "You are the intruder. Why are you here?"

"Why are you here?'

"My question first, if you please."

"No. We own that condo," he said with sternness. "We belong here. You do not own that apartment." The man nodded to the condo containing Carl's family. "You are the intruder. You should leave now before I call the police."

"First, there are no police. I've checked. They are taking care of their families, as I am taking care of mine. We were stranded here," Carl nodded to their apartment, "when the power went out a week ago."

"OK. OK. May I?" the man said, pointing to his jacket pocket.

Carl disengaged the pistol safety, and then nodded his head in the affirmative. "Slowly, please."

The man moved carefully and deliberately. He removed a collection of keys. Holding his left hand up, palm out, the man fingered his keys, found the one he sought, and held it up. Carl did not react in the slightest. The man motioned to the door across the landing from the Parks. Carl nodded his head once. The man moved slowly up the remainder of the stairs with both hands held at shoulder height. The woman and boy did not move. Carl backed up two steps to the wall behind him, to give the man room to get to his door. He inserted the key, turned the lock, opened the door a few inches, and then turned back to face Carl. "Hopefully, this little demonstration satisfies the friendly test," the man said.

Carl engaged the safety and shifted the pistol from his right hand to his left hand, but he remained ready to use it in an instant, if need be. He extended his right hand to the man. "I'm Carl Parks." The two men shook hands. *He is cold.* "We're in the apartment across from you. We've come up here every pre-Christmas week for the last half dozen years. We live in Andover, outside of Wichita, Kansas." Carl watched the woman and boy slowly and warily move up to join the man.

"My name's 'Pete,' Peter Higgins. This is my wife, Barb, and our son Larry." Carl shook hands with both Barb and Larry. "We live in Denver. We've owned this condo for more than a decade."

"What happened to you, if I may ask?" Carl asked. Pete only shook his head. "Electricity disappeared a week ago. Where have you been . . . to just arrive now?"

"Why don't we go inside," Pete suggested. Carl followed them into their apartment and shut the door behind him. He waited for the appropriate moment, shifted the pistol back to his right hand behind his back, and then quickly returned the pistol to his right jacket pocket. "It's cold in here. Let me get a fire going." The process did not take long. Pete motioned to the living room chairs. They all sat. "We were nearly to Silverthorne when it happened."

"What happened?"

"We were driving up that night. A bright flash high in the sky . . . like a sun, and then it faded. Sparks popped out everywhere. The car died instantly right on the interstate. Every vehicle out there—cars, trucks, everything—went black and stopped . . . all at the exact same instant. Everything electrical seems to have failed . . . everywhere."

That confirms it! My nightmare that night a week ago was some kind of premonition . . . more than a nightmare.

"Fortunately," Pete continued, "we have friends in Silverthorne. We stayed with them for a few days. It was closer to get here than try to return to Denver. We left yesterday morning. It took a day and a half to get here."

"You're lucky. It's brutal out there."

"Yeah. I thought we could make it before the next snowfall. Not quite. The last few miles were really rough. People seem to have gone crazy."

"We were already here. We did not see the flash, but I dreamt about it. With your experience, I think all of this is due to what the military calls Electro-Magnetic Pulse—a special form of a nuclear weapon."

Barb gasped. "Oh my God."

"Then," began Pete, "the electricity is not likely to come back on."

"Nope . . . not likely."

"So, we're stranded here for the winter?"

"Yes. I'm afraid so."

"Then, it's survival of the fittest time."

"That's my assessment. It has already begun in town."

"Perhaps we can pool our resources for better protection," Pete suggested.

"That would be positive. Collective is better than separate."

Barb yawned in the letdown from their minor confrontation after their extraordinary exertion.

"Carl, we have much to discuss and negotiate. However, if you will excuse us, it has been a very long couple of days. We need to have a quick bite to eat, and then get some rest. How about we knock on your door when we've recovered."

"Sure," Carl answered and stood. "Whenever you feel better. With that heavy snowfall outside, we're not going anywhere. By the way, Merry Christmas."

"Thank you, Carl. Merry Christmas to you and your family. We look forward to meeting the rest of the family."

"Again . . . whenever y'all are ready. Nice to meet y'all. Stay warm. See you soon." Carl departed. The door closed behind him. He went to their door, made sure his hand was in front of him and knocked softly—3-3-1. The door opened.

Alex closed the door, locked it, and then said softly, "What happened?"

Carl motioned for everyone to gather on the couch. He went to the curtain to check outside. The snowfall remained very heavy. Visibility was still quite low. Carl returned to the family. "Our neighbors arrived—the Higgins family—Pete, Barb and Larry. They were driving up near Silverthorne when the power went out. Pete saw a flash in the sky that pretty much confirms my premonition. We have suffered an EMP event and the power is not going to come back on anytime soon. But, that does not explain why the damage we see is so extensive, pervasive and absolute. They've been on the road since yesterday morning and they're very tired. We will probably talk to them collectively when they have recovered. They own the apartment across the landing, so they might have valuable intelligence as we begin our search parties." Carl checked the balcony door and the weather one more time. "There is a lot of accumulation out there, and it's still coming down. No need to stand watch. Let's make sure the doors and windows are locked before it gets any darker. The balcony is good. I'd suggest all of us get a good night's sleep. The balcony door is secure. Tomorrow is another day in paradise."

The boys each took a back room and the bathrooms. Janet handled the front door. To Carl's surprise, his wife actually jammed a straight back wooden chair under the doorknob for an extra measure of protection.

"We're secure," announced Mike.

"OK. Goodnight everyone. Color me gone." Carl lay down on their mattress.

Janet kissed all of the children goodnight, and then joined Carl on their mattress. She snuggled up to her husband and moved her lips near his ear. She whispered, "I may not always agree with your methods, but I'm very proud of what you are doing to protect us."

"Thank you," he whispered in response. "I love you, sweetheart," he added and turned his head to kiss Janet.

"I love you, my hunk of man." Janet kissed her husband.

Carl pulled the blanket and comforter over them. He would soon be fast asleep.

—

8

Carl awoke early, as was his nature. His wristwatch told him it was 05:17. Everyone else remained asleep with a few audibly snoring. The fire had burnt itself out of fuel, allowing a definite chill. Before he would jump to rejuvenating the fire, Carl looked beyond the curtain. The snow continued to fall. The dark made it difficult to determine how heavy the snow was still falling. Carl turned back and quickly restarted the fire. He kept it modest rather than waste wood for a quicker warm up. They were consuming their firewood at a slower than calculated rate, but there was never enough and only perhaps a month's worth. While he was back in the wood room, he also decided to check on their frozen food supply in the master bedroom. Of all their necessities to sustain life in the high Rockies during winter, food was the most worrisome and had to be the priority of their pending search parties.

Carl decided to let everyone sleep as long as they could. He considered reading to pass the time, but his mind just could not embrace that activity. Instead, he carefully and quietly moved one of the straight back, wooden chairs to the edge of the blackout curtain. He peeked out. There still was not much to see. He felt no urge to obtain a better view of the exterior. The wind continued to blow the snow, although the sounds of the wind were fortunately muted. At least three or four inches covered everything on the balcony. Visibility remained very low. Carl could not discern anything beyond the balcony railing other than a hint of blowing snow. His mind churned through the options for the next steps. He could not do it all. They would have to depend upon the boys to carry some of the load. Carl was not sure how to judge Peter and whether he would be a worthy teammate; however, necessity pushed him toward giving the Higgins family a chance. He needed to prepare his family, especially Janet and Lisa, since they would most likely be the family members remaining in the apartment the most.

Carl heard a muffled shuffling sound behind him. He chose to keep his eyes outside. A hand lightly touched his left shoulder. Carl looked over his left shoulder to see his daughter's calm face in the firelight. "Are you OK?" Carl whispered.

"I suppose . . . I'm just tired of feeling like a swollen pig," she replied softly, as she leaned her head against his shoulder.

"Not for much longer," he replied with a light chuckle. "Soon . . . you will feel like a cow rather than a pig."

"Dad!" They both laughed softly.

"Was there something you needed?"

"No." She quietly shuffled to lean against the chair next to him. "I just woke up and saw you here. Is it still snowing?"

"Yep. No sign of let up, yet. It's still dark out, so it's hard to tell." Carl strained to see his wristwatch. "It's just after seven. The sun should be up soon, and hopefully, I can get a read on this storm."

"I've been in the apartment for over a week. I need to get some fresh air."

"You can step out into the snow drifts on the balcony."

"It's not that important." They both laughed softly, again.

"I know what you mean. Once the storm ends and we get things cleared, we'll try to get everyone out the backside into the forest."

"That would feel good, Dad. Thanks." Lisa turned partially away, and then turned back to her father. "I'm hungry, Dad. Can I get something to eat?"

"I know. So am I. But, I think we need to stick to the plan. We need to eat together, so that everyone sees and knows that everyone is being treated the same." Carl glimpsed outside. "It is starting to lighten. The others should be awake soon. Let's all eat our portions together."

"I just want to eat my portion now," Lisa whined softly, as she looked at her feet.

"Lisa, you are already getting extra ration for the baby. We are living on very thin margins, which are critical to our survival." Carl paused to let the words sink in. "As soon as we allow the first crack of doubt to germinate, the cancer spreads quickly, so let's stick to the plan."

"OK, maybe we could wake them up?" Lisa, once again, held her father's eyes.

"How would you feel if you were in their position?"

Lisa actually considered her father's challenge. "Good point, Dad. I'll go read and try to get my mind off of my growling stomach."

"I expect everyone to be awake soon. How about this, it's 20 to eight. The sun is up, although the clouds make it fairly dark. The sun won't break the eastern ridgeline for another couple of hours. If everyone is not up by eight, I'll wake them so we can all eat."

"OK. Deal. Thanks Dad." Lisa worked her way to the fireplace and retrieved her book.

Carl returned his attention to the exterior. The combination of daylight and lessening snowfall enabled Carl to see the street beyond the condominium complex. There were no tracks in the fresh snow—a temporarily positive sign. *That won't last much longer.* Carl went to the coffee table, picked up their activity sketch, and returned to his observation seat. Circles marked the locations of various units that showed no signs of activity or change. Carl added an asterisk at those units that exhibited little activity. They would focus on the circles first, and then take on the asterisks to gather up as much usable food as they could, as well as other items that might aid their survival.

Sounds of movement behind him suggested other family members were waking. Carl checked the time, again—07:56. *OK, close enough.* He turned away from the window. Everyone except Nick was at least sitting up, if not standing up. Carl encouraged them to tend to their bodily functions. The process took another 15 minutes, and by that time, Nick had awakened and joined the family. They each ate a large strip of jerky along with a glass of water. Lisa consumed four Triscuit crackers and the last of their cheese in addition to her jerky allotment. Carl was silently pleased that his family had endured the challenges of winter survival and especially food rationing with essentially no conflict. This was the beginning of their ninth day in the mountains without electricity.

Once everyone was done, Carl gathered the family around the fire. "As we discussed yesterday, we are going to start searching the other units in this complex, and then work our way out. We also need to resume our observation watches. We left off with Team Three, so Team One will resume that watch as soon as we conclude here. We'll stick to the four, eight, twelve transitions, so Mike, you and Nick will get a short watch." Carl held up the activity sketch. "I have circled the no-activity units and placed an asterisk next to those units that have very little detected activity. Dave and I will make the first foray. We'll start with the building on the left first, since it has the most circles. I'll teach each team the search technique we should use after we make this first attempt."

"Dad," Lisa protested with an accusatory tone, "you are talking about breaking into someone else's home and stealing!"

"Yes, sweetheart, that is precisely what I am suggesting."

"That's not right!" Lisa looked at her mother for support.

"No, no it is not . . . in normal times; but, these are not normal times, and those days will not likely return any time soon. This is all a matter of survival."

"I'm with you, Dad," Mike interjected.

Carl scanned his family. Everyone nodded their heads. Even Lisa eventually nodded her head, as well. "We must survive the winter . . . and the human desperation that is inevitably going to overwhelm any remaining civility. I am not suggesting we steal from other people who are stranded up here with us. Unfortunately, it may well come to that, though, if we run low on supplies before spring. Once the roads clear, we can make our way out of the mountains . . . and hopefully back home."

"We understand," said Alex.

Carl nodded his head. "Once the snowfall lets up, we will clear the balcony, so Team One can take their watch station." Carl looked to Mike, and then Nick. "We will need you to keep a vigilant over-watch in case anyone approaches a building while we are inside. If anyone even appears to be heading toward the building we are in, bang two pans together several times like cymbals; that will avoid wasting ammunition or making a human voice, which will attract unwanted attention from any roamers."

They cleared the porch-balcony of snow, set up their signal system, and waited for the snowfall to taper off to near zero. Carl laid out their search plan. Team Three would start at the ground floor apartment farthest away from the handful of occupied apartments. They set the order of the search, if they got that far, and agreed to evaluate their immediate circumstances as they completed the search of each apartment. They also agreed to minimize the disturbance to each property; they would not trash the place. They would use pillowcases as their carrying satchels. Their priorities for each search were:

1. Food, especially preserved foodstuffs like canned goods or jerky;
2. Weapons, especially firearms and ammunition;
3. Firewood or other fuel to sustain their warmth giving fire;
4. Medications, like antibiotics, painkillers, and any necessary prescription medications; and
5. Non-electric tools that could be utilized for construction tasks.

Once Carl was satisfied the latest snowstorm was ending, they suited up for the cold weather. Carl and Dave stepped out onto the landing. No signs of life or activity could be detected in the Higgins apartment. Carl waited for the sound of the door lock behind him, and then the pair made their way down to the ground floor. They would use the back door, along with the space between the building wall and the hedges to mask their path at least a little. Their tracks would leave a clear path in the snow from the closest corner of their building to the first target search building.

Their first objective was a ground floor apartment on the left after entering the building. With the door closed behind them, they froze to listen. Would there be any reaction to their entry? They detected no signs of life. Carl moved to the first target door. Again, he listened with his ear to the door. Nothing. He tried the doorknob. Locked. Carl did not know how to pick the lock, and a forcible breach was not going to be quiet.

Carl leaned to Dave's right ear. "This is going to make noise," Carl whispered. "We will need to move quickly. You take the bedrooms and bathrooms. I'll take the kitchen, utility room and closets."

Dave nodded his head in consent.

Carl stepped back and struck the door with his right foot just next to the doorknob and deadbolt. A loud crack of the door jam wood breaking marked the breach. Carl entered first, quickly scanned the dark apartment, and signaled for Dave to enter. The young man moved quickly to the bedrooms. Carl checked behind them and closed the door to make it a little less obvious.

There were no signs of occupancy. The apartment was minimally furnished, typical for a unit intended just for rental. Carl quickly searched each cupboard, drawer and small pantry shelf. There was nothing on their priority list except two cans of soup that he placed in his pillowcase. Carl swiftly checked the utility room—absolutely nothing. He made quick work of the living room and coat closet—again, nothing.

Carl finished his search tasks and moved quickly to help Dave. He started with the first bathroom. He passed on the towels and common cleaning products. Carl grabbed two rolls of toilet paper. You can never have too much. He met Dave in the short hallway. His pillowcase had only a few items in it.

"Not much," Dave whispered.

Carl nodded his head and led Dave out of the apartment. He quickly and carefully scanned the exterior to make sure no one was waiting to ambush them. Nothing. Carl put his right index finger to his lips, signaling for no sound, as they moved on with their search task. He picked up a few wood splinters outside the door, threw them into the apartment, and closed the door as best he could.

Their next target unit was two floors up. Carl gestured for them to move up two flights. They stepped carefully and smoothly up each half flight of stairs. At the first landing, Carl scanned both doors—no signs of disturbance. He signaled for them to continue. At the second landing, Carl scanned both doors, again. Neither door showed any sign of abuse. Their target apartment was on the left.

Carl kicked the door. The door jam broke like the first one, but he instantly noticed the door security chain had been engaged, which meant someone was inside. Carl immediately drew his pistol and entered the apartment. He cleared the living room and kitchen, and then signaled for Dave to enter and close the door. Carl cleared each room and closet. In the master bedroom, he found them. An elderly man and woman on the bed next to each other clearly deceased. There were no signs of blood or injury to either body. They had frozen to death, most likely several days ago, if not shortly after the crisis began.

Leaning to Dave, who was directly behind him, Carl whispered, "They're dead. Let's leave the bed alone and get our search done quickly, so we can get out of here." Dave nodded his head in agreement, and then went directly to the closet.

Carl left the bedroom and went to the kitchen. The whole apartment had become a very effective freezer. The small pantry was full of canned goods. He would not be able to carry them all, so he unloaded everything he thought they could or should take onto the breakfast bar-island that separated the kitchen from the living room. Carl was still working on the pantry when Dave appeared.

The young man whispered, "I got some toilet paper and bar soap, but that's it. Wow! Look at all that."

"We're going to need a few more pillows cases and some rope or spare sheets."

Dave nodded his head and left to retrieve the requested material.

Carl left the near worthless stuff like potato chips. He checked the perishable items like bread; no mold he could detect in the darkened apartment, so he put the two loaves on the counter as well. Once he finished clearing the pantry, he checked the refrigerator-freezer—nothing usable beyond four packages of frozen vegetables that were still frozen. The cabinets yielded nothing more.

Dave returned with three sets of different colored pillowcases and a few straight sheets that matched some of the pillowcases. Carl immediately began loading the pillowcases and checking the mounting weight as he went. Dave watched attentively and followed suit. When the counter was cleared, they had eight heavy pillowcases. Carl found a knife and cut each sheet into four wide strips lengthwise. Each strip was then rolled and tied to a loaded pillowcase at each end of the sheet-rope.

"This is going to be very awkward," he whispered to Dave. "Be careful with your steps and try to keep the bags from swinging or bouncing." Dave nodded his head and started to lift the first load. Carl grasped his arm to stop him. "We need to get these directly to our apartment." Again, Dave nodded his head. "Keep your eyes out as best you can to look for anyone that might see us. If you see anyone, let me know immediately." Carl did not wait and loaded his two pairs across his shoulders. They were heavy . . . heavier than expected. Dave did the same. "Are you OK with that load?"

"I think so," Dave answered, and then tried a number of steps. He was clearly struggling with the awkwardness of the weight.

Carl practiced his movement a few times and quickly figured out how to dampen the motion of the sacks. Once they both felt they were ready, Carl leaned into Dave's left ear. "Stay behind me. Try to keep an eye on what is behind us, as you mind your steps. We will go directly to our apartment, as quickly as possible. We will use our previous tracks in the snow. And Dave," he paused and drew back to see his eyes on his, "we may have to fight our way out. Be prepared." Dave nodded his head.

Carl moved to the door, checked the peephole glass, and when he was satisfied there was no one waiting for them outside, he drew his pistol and opened the door. Once outside, he gestured for Dave to close the door as best he could. They stepped carefully down the stairs without stopping at the next landing. *So far so good . . . no changes.* Carl checked the window on the exterior door. *Nothing changed outside—no new tracks in the snow.* He opened the door and nodded for them to move. Carl scanned the area continuously. Dave stayed a few steps behind him. They moved more easily through the deep snow despite the heavy shoulder loads they carried thanks in large part to the prior path they had made. When they reached the corner of their building, Carl motioned for Dave to proceed ahead. He remained at the building corner to assess the entire scene. Satisfied no one was following them, or even paying attention to them as far as he could tell, Carl followed Dave along the edge of the building inside the snow-covered hedge.

Dave waited for Carl inside the ground floor lobby. Carl gestured for them to move upstairs—*still no changes.* Carl rendered the agreed-to knock sequence. Their door opened immediately. Again, Carl gestured for Dave to enter first. Carl entered and Janet closed and locked the door behind them.

"Wow!" Janet exclaimed. "You must have found a treasure trove."

"Let's get this food taken care of first," he responded to Janet, "and then I'll report on what we found and what we learned."

Janet supervised the storing of their acquired foodstuffs, which added substantially to their inventory.

Carl looked to Alex and directed, "Take the frozen vegetables to the back bedroom." The master bedroom had become their cold storage, since it was the farthest from the interior warmth and the refrigerator-freezer was no longer working.

After Dave and Carl unloaded their take, Carl checked on everything. He went to the blackout curtain, peaked out to see both Mike and Nick continuing to search the scene before them. The overcast was thinning and brightening. The storm was clearing. Carl knocked softly on the glass. Both young men looked to the sound. Carl motioned for them to approach the door and stay low, as he cracked the door and lowered himself to his knees.

"Is everything OK out there?" asked Carl through the gap in the door. Both men nodded their heads in the affirmative. "Have you seen any activity before or after our search?" Both shook their heads in the negative. "OK. Come inside." Carl moved to the side and pulled the door open a little more. Mike and Nick crawled in. Carl closed and locked the door. He returned the curtain to its proper place. Dave had already removed his cold weather clothing. Carl did the same, and then gathered the group around the modest fire.

Carl recounted the story of their first search foray and what they found. Predictable questions were asked and answered. Nick volunteered that they watched both the ingress and egress transits, and had seen no signs of human activity in the target building or anywhere else within visual detectability of them. Carl reviewed the compound chart with the group and 'X'ed out the two apartments they searched in the adjacent building. On their chart, there were three target apartments in the adjacent building to the right of their building.

Carl proposed, "While others around us are still being cautious, I'll take Alex with me on the next building. We'll reassess our situation after that and go from there." Mike and Nick still had 30 minutes left on their two-hour watch cycle. He looked to Team One, "Would y'all mind extending your duty time, since Alex is in Team Two?"

"No problem, Dad," Nick replied.

Carl nodded his head. It was time to set this segment of their survival plan in motion. They began to suit up for the cold. A knock at the door stopped their task. Carl held his right index finger to his lips for silence. He finished donning his jacket and retrieved the pistol. Cocking the hammer and thumbing the safety off, Carl moved to the door. The peephole revealed only Pete Higgins on the landing.

Carl aimed the pistol at the door, placed his right foot to block the door, and cracked the door an inch, stopped by his foot. "Yes, Pete?"

"Can we talk, Carl?"

"About what?"

"About joining forces."

Carl's instinct wanted to say no thanks; yet, his logical side recognized the wisdom of expanding the team for their mutual survival. He flipped the safety back on and placed the pistol in the waistband of his thermal trousers. Behind the door, he motioned for one of the boys to come observe, just in case something went wrong. Carl opened the door and stepped out onto the cold landing, and then closed the door behind him. He heard nothing inside their apartment, which was a very good sign.

"Good morning," Carl said, as Pete stepped back two paces, opening space for Carl.

"Good morning to you. We had a long sleep . . . rough few days. We really needed it."

"Good," responded Carl, not wanting to take the initiative and allowing Pete to play his hand.

"I saw your search foray." Carl remained stone-faced, motionless and non-responsive. "I think I can help." Carl only slightly nodded his head, and if to say and? "We own this condo," Pete continued, gesturing to the door behind him, "and, we live up here half the time or more. I know most of the people who live in or own these condos. I know where to search and who the friendlies are."

OK, he's sounding like one of the good guys. "What do you propose?" asked Carl.

"Team up."

"How so?"

"Watching you and the other fellow with you suggested to me that you are former military." Again, Carl chose not to react in any manner. "Have you thought more about my proposal yesterday?"

"Yes. Did you serve?" asked Carl.

"Yes. Marines. I was a platoon sergeant with 2/7—2nd Battalion, 7th Marines."

"Semper Fi," Carl finally smiled and extended his hand to Pete. "I had a platoon with 3rd Recon, attached to 1/9 in the bad war, before I went to flight school."

They shook hands vigorously. "Damn, I was hoping you would say something like that. So, what do you say to my proposal?"

"I think we can make that work. Probably the first step is to introduce ourselves and our families to each other. Are Barb and Larry available? My family is up."

"They were getting something to eat when I saw you come out. Let me go check. I'll knock on your door when we're ready."

"OK. It's warm inside, so you won't need to dress for the cold."

"Good. We'll be right there."

Pete returned to their apartment. Carl did the same.

Everyone was looking at him when Carl entered and closed the door. "The Higgins family—Peter, Barb and Larry—are going to come over. He's a former Marine and will be a good addition to our merry little band of campers."

"Do you trust them?" Janet asked.

"It will take a while for the trust to build, but yes, I get a good feeling talking to him. We can use the extra watch-standers, and I suspect they have supplies. More importantly, Pete said they own their apartment, have been coming up here for years, and he knows most of the residents. He could be very useful in our search efforts for supplies."

"How old is their boy?" Alex asked.

"He said 14 years old."

The knock at the door announced their arrival. Everyone stood and faced the door. Carl checked the peephole. It was the Higgins family with no additions. Carl unlocked the door and opened it. "Please come in," he said.

Introductions were completed all around. Carl chose not to disclose their very limited arsenal—one pistol—or, to give them a tour of the apartment, and thus their supplies . . . at least for now. He explained their watch procedures, the blackout curtains and their routine for living, along with their rationing process. When Carl picked up their survey map, Janet nodded to Barb and moved to the kitchen area. Lisa joined them. Carl checked on Mike and Nick. They were still OK. The boys engaged Larry in their own discussion.

"We've been observing the buildings, windows and such," Carl began his explanation. "We've noted signs of human activity that give us an indication of which apartments are occupied." Pete nodded his head. "We checked these two this morning," Carl said, pointing to apartments 211 and 232. "The upper one has a dead couple . . . frozen to death it appeared."

"That's the Wazinskis . . . elderly couple."

"OK. There were no signs of trauma. It looked like they froze to death in their sleep."

"They lived there year 'round. It looked like y'all cleaned them out."

"Yes, we did. Apartment 211 had virtually nothing in it."

"Yeah, that's a rental owned by the Johnson family," Pete volunteered. "They generally stay in 412, when they come up from Boulder." Carl noticed that 412 had shown no signs of occupancy either and was on their list. Pete placed his right index finger on 532. "We're going to want to hit this one real soon." Carl gave him a gesture—and. "No stars on that one. It belongs to an old guy named Kramer--widower. He is quite the hunter . . . shares his meat with many of us. Anyway, he has quite the collection of weapons—pistols, shotguns, long guns and even a crossbow, and what looked like an English longbow."

After a moment of deep thought, Carl proposed, "Why don't you and I go together on this one? We can come to an agreement on procedures, and then both of us can teach the boys?"

"Good idea. How do you want to integrate us into your watch schedule?" Pete asked.

Carl glanced at his watch and took a quick peek outside. "Let's do that after this foray. We need to get this search behind us."

"Very well."

"It's past time to relieve Team One. Janet, would you take Alex and start your watch cycle. Perhaps, Barb and Larry can join you and learn the ropes. Just make sure you keep your conversation at very low volume, stay as hidden as you can, and please keep a good eye out to watch our backs while we're in the building."

Janet nodded her head and led the other three out onto the balcony.

Pete and Carl suited up, grabbed their shoulder bags and headed out. Pete followed Carl in good team fashion. They crossed corner to corner from Building 3 to Building 4, made their way along the wall inside a similar hedge. They had to tamp down several drifts that blocked their path and made marks, as if they had entered Building 4. They crossed again to the corner of Building 5, using the same procedure. Once inside Building 5, they moved smoothly, quietly and swiftly to apartment 532. Carl drew his pistol, checked to make sure they were not being followed or watched, and kicked in the door. He quickly cleared the apartment—not occupied. They found their target in the master bedroom closet—a large, seven foot high, gun cabinet. Both men searched for a hidden spare key and found none.

The lock on the door was substantial—a serious lock. They could see ammunition shelves, several pistols of various sizes and types, but an inner door covered half the locker. Carl struck the glass with his pistol. It did not break or even crack. "Polycarbonate," he said aloud. Carl was quite mindful of time. They could not ponder breeching the lock for very long. Other foragers might be coming out at any time. "Let's see if we can find a hammer, hatchet, ax, anything to knock the lock off.

Pete went to the kitchen and utility room, while Carl searched the bedrooms and bathrooms. Pete returned with a small toolbox that contained a hammer among other hand tools and a nice, clearly expensive hatchet.

"Good," Carl said. "Put those on the bed. We'll take them with us."

"He has some canned goods in the pantry."

"Why don't you bag everything that is edible and will last?"

Pete nodded his head and went to the kitchen.

Carl grabbed the hatchet and returned to the gun cabinet. He struck the transparency with the blade and barely marked it. Carl then turned the hatchet on the base of the door lock. It took him half a dozen, good, hard swipes at the lock before the outer portion gave way. Carl used the butt on the hatchet to punch the remainder of the lock into the case. The door popped open and revealed what amounted to the crown jewels. He did not touch anything and went to the kitchen. Carl whispered to Pete, "How are you doing?"

"I've got everything evenly divided between my two bags."

"Can you take more?"

"Sure. Why?"

"You were precisely correct. He's got a small arsenal back there. We need to try and move it all . . . if for no other reason than to deny those weapons to anyone else. And, there is a lot of ammunition."

"I can take more. We don't have that far to carry it," Pete said.

"Yeah . . . but the snow will make it harder. If you're finished in the kitchen, let's go back to the bedroom. I want you to see it all before we load it up."

Pete placed the bags over his shoulders to get a feel for their weight, and then followed Carl back to the master bedroom. The two men unloaded the gun cabinet into the bags. Pete carried six pistols and associated ammunition, which pretty well topped him out. He checked the .44 Magnum to make sure the cylinder was full and placed the big pistol in his back waistband . . . just in case, they might need it on the way back. Carl loaded his bags with the remainder of the ammunition, two shotguns and two long guns. They would inventory their haul back at their base. Carl also picked up the cleaning gear and supplies—gun oil, brushes, swatches, and tool kit. Carl grabbed another pillowcase and placed it over the barrels to mask the nature of their find. Satisfied they had everything, they both did one more check to make sure they had everything that could be useful, and then they lifted their heavy shoulder bags.

Carl checked the peephole on the broken door. Nothing could be seen. Carl drew his pistol. Pete did the same. Carl signaled for Pete to lead for their return to Building 3. Pete did not hesitate and moved smoothly, clearing the way down the stairway as he moved quietly. Carl continuously scanned behind them. After carefully checking the exterior, Pete opened the door and moved swiftly along the edge of the building. Carl stepped out and promptly scanned behind them. Still OK. They made it back to their building without incident and to the 332 unit. Carl provided the secret knock. They entered and went directly to the forward bedroom.

The two former military men unloaded their haul, laid out the weapons and ammunition on the lower bedsprings of the closest bunk beds. Pete carried the canned goods to the kitchen, leaving their storage to someone else, and then returned to the forward bedroom. Carl was standing a couple of paces back from the bed with their arsenal arranged for inventory.

Among the collection of weapons were:

-- M1A civil version of the military issue M14 rifle with 10x scope, and two full magazines plus four boxes of 7.62 x 51mm rounds (120 rounds)
-- M1903 Springfield .30-06 rifle with 16x scope and two boxes of stripper clipped, 7.62 x 63 mm ammunition (40 rounds)
-- Mossberg 500 12-gauge pump-action shotgun
-- Remington Model 1100 12-gauge semi-automatic shotgun with seven boxes of shells for both shotguns (100 no.4 shot rounds, 40 no.1 shot rounds, 20 no.00 shot rounds, and 12 flechette rounds),

-- M1911 .45 semi-automatic pistol with two full magazines and four boxes of .45. ACP ball rounds (214 rounds), and

-- M1873, single action, Army issue, Colt Peacemaker and one partial box of .45 Long Colt rounds (six rounds in the cylinder plus 12 rounds),

Carl looked at Pete and smiled. "You were certainly correct on that call. This is quite an arsenal."

Pete smiled. "Glad to be of service."

"We seem to now possess a weapon for every occasion."

"Yeah, so it seems."

"And, I'll be damned, he actually had a Peacemaker. I've never held one until now," Carl said, picking up the large revolver.

"Me either."

Carl handed the pistol butt first to Pete, who opened the cylinder, emptied the rounds onto a small table, closed the cylinder, and worked the action and trigger several times to get a feel for the pull pressure. He handed the pistol back to Carl, who did the same.

"Impressive," Carl pronounced. "The gun that won the West, they say."

"Yep."

"I feel a whole lot better knowing we have more than just my M1911."

Pete and Carl had returned with their haul. The two families integrated, with the Higgins spread amongst the Parks, allowing them to add watch teams.

Carl went to the blackout curtain and checked the exterior. It was local evening twilight in the high, winter, Rocky Mountains. They decided to use two large cans of Campbell's hearty beef stew. They warmed the contents on the fire, and then ladled up 10 equal bowls. The two families ate their first meal as one unit. Laughter actually punctuated a few quiet, calm discussion segments of their collective experiences before and after the blackout.

Once they finished their thin meal, it was nearly time for Team Four to begin their watch duty cycle. Pete and the boys, less Dave, moved mattresses and blankets from the Higgins' condo into their joint, tight living space. They rearranged the living room to make space for the additions. Carl and Dave stepped out onto the balcony to assume their watch duties. They all hoped for a quiet night.

—

9

The clear, cold weather of the following two days enabled the expanded Parks-Higgins group to complete the searches of the remaining unoccupied units of their apartment complex. Pete and Carl alternated taking and teaching each of the boys on the searches. They stuck to the plan and recovered a good cache of supplies—mostly canned and preserved food as well as ammunition that belonged to had no weapon they had recovered so far. They decided to remove and control all the ammunition and weapons they found, more to deny that material to others than for their use. They also found more dead bodies, three of which had died from blood loss from stab wounds. No gunshot wounds had been detected, as yet. They also met their first notional resistance when other occupants confronted several search teams. Fortunately, no action had been required other than a slightly more circuitous return route to add a little confusion to any observation. They were trying as hard as they could to avoid attracting unwanted attention to their little Building 3 enclave.

Once the group completed their searches of all five buildings, they agreed the responsible thing to do was move the dead bodies, although frozen at present, outside and away from the buildings. Pete and Carl agreed they needed little preparation beyond laying them side-by-side wherever they could find space—they thought it prudent to not mix the bones or clothing. Carl confessed his earlier kills and recommended they keep the two collections widely separate. He also confided in Pete his anticipation; they might need the fresh kill bodies later in their survival process, should it come to that. Pete displayed no surprise and agreed to Carl's recommendation.

The group finished the gruesome task a little after mid-day on the second day.

"Let's take advantage of the good weather, while it lasts," Carl said, with everyone except Team Three in the room.

"Sounds good," Pete answered. "What do you have in mind?"

"I'd suggest we make another, more purposeful search of the town. Early in the crisis, I took quick looks, but I was by myself and lightly armed. I suspect the town has been stripped bare by now, but we need to make sure. I see two possible plans. One, you and I plus two of the boys, all armed, could form a search party in strength, or two, one of us," Carl said, gesturing to Pete, "could take two boys into town, while the other takes up a position of overwatch from one of the bedrooms at the top of Building 1 or 2. You can see most of the streets, not all, and many of the far side stores." Carl's thumbs and index fingers formed a rectangle 'window' he moved around like a movie director to signify the perch field of view.

"Have you handled either of the sniper rifles?" asked Pete.

"Not the 1903, yet, but I have used the M14 . . . without the scope—the military version of the M1A."

"Do you think you have a feel for the ballistics?"

"That is the salient question, isn't it? To answer the question in the affirmative, I would have to zero, and then range each rifle, which in turn would broadcast the existence of long rifles, potentially disclosing our position, and using rather scarce ammunition . . . none of which we have the luxury of expending. The best we can do is adjust quickly from the first impact."

"What is the range?"

"My quick map study says about 800 meters to the north end of town, a little less to the south end, and roughly 500 meters to the center of town."

"Do-able shots."

"Under known conditions, yes. Both rifles certainly have the capability, but the best we could do is a crude estimate of the wind, and we have no range finder."

"I didn't see one in Kramer's place. Did you?"

"No, but I was not looking for one either."

"It might be worth a trip back to check. If anyone would have one, it would be Jack Kramer, especially with two long rifles like those we picked up."

"The revisit of Kramer's apartment is not quite so urgent, if we pick option one."

"I kind of like option two," Pete responded, referring to the search team with long-gun overwatch alternative, ". . . creates more uncertainty for anyone who might challenge us. At that range, the discharge report would arrive at the target a little more than a second after impact. Do you remember the ballistic drop for the 7.62 round at those ranges?"

"As I recall, something like 55 inches at 500 meters and 400 inches at 1000 meters, so perhaps 250 inches at 800 meters. I'd have to examine the scope knobs to see if I get a feel for the sight adjustments for those ranges."

"You're ahead of me. Do you want to take the overwatch?"

"We can try that, as long as you are comfortable going into town," Carl groaned, as he stood and stretched his muscles.

"I am," Pete paused. "Who knows, I might run into a few of the permanent residents I know."

"Good point."

"Do you want to run over to Kramer's place?" Pete stood, joining Carl.

"We have only another couple of hours of daylight. Even if I knew the exact range, without the actual ballistic tables, I'd still be guessing. I'll get as close as I can. Even if I miss, there will be no doubt a long gun is watching them, which should serve the purpose."

"Then, we'd better get to it."

Carl checked his wristwatch. "It is nearly time for Team Four to assume the duty. As the super, Alex, I'll ask you to take my watch with Dave. I'll take Nick for my back-up. Pete, I'd suggest you take Larry and Mike. I suspect 232, first, will have the best angles. Give me ten minutes to get up there and check out the view. If it's good, I'll have Nick give you a wave from the living room balcony. I'd suggest you use 4 O'Clock Run to town-center bridge. That should give me the longest contact overwatch for you."

"What do you mean . . . contact overwatch?" Pete asked.

"Things that can be seen directly. We'll see indications like shadows, puffs of snow and such, but a contact is sufficient for a bullet to be properly placed . . . with a little luck," answered Carl.

"Luck?"

"We don't have accurate ballistics tables for either rifle, so sight settings are at best a guess."

"That works." Pete raised his right hand, extended his index finger and gestured in a circle to signal startup in traditional aviator sign language.

Carl nodded to Nick. They suited up, and then went to the bedroom arsenal.

"Which one do you want me to use?" Nick asked.

"The Beretta will be easier to handle," Carl answered and handed the semi-automatic pistol with the safety engaged, to his middle son, butt first.

Nick grasped the pistol by the grip, pulled the slide back far enough to see that the chamber was empty, and then let it go home. He picked up one of the correctly loaded magazines, inserted it and locked it home, just as his father taught him. Nick racked a round and engaged the safety. He placed two loaded magazines in his jacket pocket.

Pete, Mike and Larry entered the room and silently armed themselves as well. Pete simply picked up a box of ammunition for the Model 29 he still held. Mike selected the other M1911 and Larry picked one of the .38 Specials.

Carl looked to Nick and nodded his head toward the door. "We'll signal you as soon as we are set." Carl pulled the bedroom curtain back at the edge to scan the view outside. Nothing.

The overwatch team made their way quickly to apartment 232. The door and interior remained as they had left it from their original search. Once he was satisfied the apartment was unoccupied, Carl went to the balcony window and peeked out. The tops of two heads and two sets of eyes were looking in his direction from the balcony of unit 332. He then went to the back master bedroom, moved the bed away from the window, and again peeked out the edge of the curtain to make sure there were no observers. Satisfied, Carl drew the curtain back completely, so as to minimize the chances of movement being detected.

The view of the valley and the town was spectacular. A few older pine trees poked up into his field of view of the town below him and across the frozen stream. Carl stood back, near the middle of the room, and raised the rifle and used the scope to scan the scene from left to right. It was as he remembered—a good overwatch position. He moved smoothly to Nick, who was standing at the door. Close enough to speak softly, he said, "The back cover choices are not good. Let's see what we can do to block the front door."

In the living room, Carl leaned the rifle against the wall next to the hallway. He lifted one of the sturdy wooden chairs from the dining table and propped it under the doorknob, pushing it as tightly as he could. "That should work." He checked to make sure the balcony sliding door was locked, and then gestured toward the back bedroom. Carl lifted the rifle on his way, and Nick followed.

Carl pointed at the medium size chest of drawers and motioned for them to lift it. Sliding the chest might make unwanted noise, and he knew they needed to minimize any sounds of their presence. They positioned the furniture a couple of feet back from the windowsill to allow passage across the length of the window, should the need arise. Carl checked the angles to ensure he had full coverage. He signaled Nick to come closer. "Go signal the apartment," he whispered. "Make sure you see signs of receipt." Nick nodded his head and went to the living room. Carl went to the far right of the window to get the best angle he could, to see the search team move down 4 O'Clock Run toward town. Their movement would be uncovered from the back door of Building 3 to the south point on the trail where they could be observed through the trees. The uncovered period seemed like a brief, acceptable exposure with minimum risk.

Nick returned. "They got the signal," he said softly. "I waited until I could see them head down 4 O'Clock Run. You should see them shortly." They both moved to the far edge of the window. Once they saw the search team among the trees moving down the trail, Carl stepped back, so that the muzzle would not be exposed to the window, and raised the weapon to use the scope. At such close range, it was awkward, but the scope enabled him to see deeper into the trees, if there was anyone lurking in ambush. He noticed nothing untoward or even remotely threatening. Once they made it to the street—North Park Avenue—Carl lowered the rifle and told Nick, "Keep an eye on them, especially looking ahead of their route of travel. I need to make sure the rifle is ready." Nick nodded his acknowledgment.

Carl sat on the edge of the bed and placed the rifle across his lap. Before he touched or moved anything, he examined the scope. The elevation and windage adjustment knobs appeared to be graduated in mils (milliradians of angle, or 0.056 degrees). Carl zeroed the windage knob. The elevation knob was left at 12.0 mils. Carl considered leaving the scope at that setting, but changed his mind with the thinking that it would be better for a shot to be low than high. He zeroed the elevation knob. *I'll have to try to do the range calculations later. I really should have done those calculations before taking on this task.*

"They've reached the bridge," Nick announced softly.

For better or worse, it is truth-or-consequences time. "Thanks," Carl responded. "Scan the whole scene. Let me know if you see anything unusual. Frankly, let me know if you see anyone other than our folks." Nick nodded his head. Carl placed his left elbow on the chest of drawers, resting the rifle forestock in his left hand. He looked over his shoulder at Nick. "Make sure you tap my shoulder if you hear the slightest sound from the living room." Nick again nodded his head. Carl looked through the sight and picked up the search team. "Nice," Carl whispered to himself, when he saw Pete had quickly shown the boys a modest tactical spread as they moved through various footpaths of packed snow. Carl scanned the street ahead of them—every window, door and corner. When he could he checked the tracks in the snow to get an idea of how many people have gone before them and where they had gone.

The wood and glass door on the small gallery of shops, where he had bought the jerky, was shattered, broken and essentially destroyed with lots of tracks into and out of the building. "Avoid that one," Carl whispered to himself. Pete surveyed the gallery, scanned south down Main Street, and then turned left heading north. Carl smiled. They disappeared behind a building. "Cross to the east side," Carl whispered, again, and soon picked them up on the far side of Main Street. Carl smiled. *He's giving me the best angles he can.* Scanning ahead, it was still clear. Carl scanned the market—their first target. Lots of tracks, broken windows and doors, the snow was so packed traffic direction could not be detected . . . but, no current activity. Carl methodically scanned the surrounding stores and adjacent streets as much as he could.

Carl watched as Pete evaluated the ransacked grocery store he had checked several days earlier. Pete stationed Mike at the entry and went into the store with Larry. Carl scanned the streets—still no activity. As he continued his overwatch scans, Carl returned to the storefront on a regular basis. Mike remained at the damaged door and appeared to be attentive to his watch task. Pete and Larry searched for probably ten minutes, appeared at the door to say something to Mike, and disappeared into the store again. Carl continued his overwatch. After the latest check on the storefront, he checked the Main Street north approach and saw them—four armed men heading toward the destroyed grocery store. If they had functional radios, Carl would have alerted the search team; unfortunately, he had no means to signal. He placed his sight reticle on the lead man. They looked like a gang rather than a tactical team—a positive sign. The men cleared the corner of the store just to the north across Wellington Road. Mike saw and called to the interior. Pete appeared next to Mike before the men had closed the distance.

"Open the window," Carl commanded to Nick. His middle son opened the window quickly and fully, and then moved behind his father. Carl flipped off the rifle's safety and placed his right index finger on the trigger. The sight crosshairs remained on the chest of the lead man. They were obviously talking. The gang made no threatening acts, but they were uncomfortably close. Pete and the boys did not brandish their weapons. As the conversation continued and no one moved, Carl became more concerned. He took up the slack in the rifle's trigger while his reticle remained on the lead man's center of mass. Carl held his state while he watched intently as he kept his breathing smooth and rhythmic. They were clearly discussing something. The conversation appeared to be calm and not animated. After several minutes, Pete and the boys walked away. The gang made no move to interfere, and soon turned and walked back the way they had come. Carl released his pressure on the trigger and engaged the safety. Without taking his attention from Pete, Carl said, "You can close the window."

Nick did as requested. When he returned to his observation position, he whispered, "Is everything OK?"

"It is now . . . just a confrontation that could have gone sideways. They appear to be headed back."

The search team made their way back the way they had deployed. Carl continued his process of watching their movement until they passed behind the corner of Building 2.

"OK. Let's break it down," Carl said and stood up. He rechecked the rifle's safety was engaged.

"Do you want to close the curtains?"

"Yes. We can leave the chest and bed where we've moved them. Let's get back home and debrief this thing."

They returned to apartment 332. When Nick and Carl entered, the group had gathered around the fireplace. Carl returned the rifle to the bedroom arsenal.

Nick did the same. To Carl's surprise, although he had not been taught to do so, Nick ejected the magazine from the pistol grip and drew back the slide ejecting the chambered round. He checked to make sure the chamber was empty, left the slide locked back and returned his items back to the bedroom arsenal as well. They returned to the living room. Carl went to the balcony blackout curtain, peeked out, tapped lightly on the glass and received a thumbs-up from both boys. Carl gestured for them to come inside.

Carl began, "What happened?"

"As you probably saw, we made it to the Wellington Road Store, or what is left of it." Pete paused, nodding to Mike, who concurred. "I asked Mike to keep watch at the door, while Larry and I methodically checked the store. We could find nothing of value. Everything edible, including pet food, is gone. Even clothing and gloves are gone."

"What happened with that group of men?"

"Mike alerted us as soon as he saw them. They are apparently a vigilante group, making an attempt to establish some sort of order. They know, as we all do, that people are hoarding what supplies there are up here."

"I watched," Carl interjected. "The reticle was on the lead man's chest and the trigger slack was taken up."

"Thank you for your overwatch, but I'm glad you did not shoot."

"Yeah. Tough to judge without radios."

Pete nodded his head in agreement. "I suspect the other stores are going to be in the same state. One place they might not have looted, yet, is the cold storage building. It is a rather non-descript, windowless block building with no signage, since it was built and operated for locals. That's where Jack Kramer and others stored their hunt meat. Whatever is there should still be frozen, even with no power."

"Better that we control whatever meat survived than leave it available for others to take," Carl suggested.

"Agreed. Do you want to make a search this afternoon?"

"It would be nice, but the sun is already behind the west ridgeline," Carl observed. "We probably don't have time. It also became obvious during the last mission that I had better do my homework if those long rifles and sights are going to be of any effective use. I need to do the calculations to get as close as I can and I really need a range chart, before we try that again. Where is the cold storage building?"

"French and Jefferson . . . southeast corner." Carl nodded his acknowledgment of Pete's statement. Pete continued, "I can help with the chart. I've got a detailed street map for Breckenridge. I even have a compass,

I think, if I can find it. How about I work on the range chart, while you do the ballistics calculations. What range rings do you want?"

"Well," Carl paused to think for a moment. "As I recall, the trajectory is pretty flat, out to 2 or 300 meters. Why don't we start at 300 and go out every 100 meters to say 1000 meters? We probably should know the range to the City Market and the Police Station, as well."

"OK. I can do that. Do you want the rings in meters or yards?"

"Meters . . . the math is easier. Let's plan to make the run to the cold storage when the light is good enough for overwatch . . . before the sun clears the east ridgeline. A different part of the problem . . . what do we do if the building is undisturbed?"

Pete considered the question. "If the meat is still there and still frozen, it will only be a matter of time before other locals raid the meat lockers. We need to move as much meat as we can up here. Carrying it will be quite difficult—a side of elk, for example."

"As soon as people see us moving meat, they will descend on the place. I am concerned we have passed the threshold of desperation and the unprepared among us will act out violently. And now, we have this vigilante group, and perhaps others like them, to contend with in that transport phase."

"Agreed."

"For tomorrow's search, let's have each team member take a backpack filled with paper or pine boughs, so they appear full to any observers. If the meat is there and good, then replace the filler with meat. I imagine some meat is already wrapped in butcher paper."

"Sure. We can bring back as much as we can and at least inventory what's left."

"If the meat's there, we'll need to make as many trips in as short of time as we can."

"Agreed. Who's got the watch?" asked Pete.

Carl checked his wristwatch. "Looks like Team One."

Pete looked at Larry. "Are you OK with that, Son?"

"Sure, Dad."

"Very well," Pete acknowledged. "Let's get to it."

Larry and Barb donned their cold weather gear and headed out to the balcony. Pete went to their condo across the hall to retrieve the materials he sought.

Carl placed a large candle on the dining table, lit the wick, and searched the utensil drawer, looking for a straight edge. He jotted down on a tablet of paper what he remembered from his marksmanship training and annual requalification exercises. Carl sketched out a crude ballistics curve for the standard NATO round, as he remembered it, and with the angular mathematics, produced a table of sight elevation settings for the rifles every 100 meters from 300 to 1000 meters, which covered most the town. He completed his calculations for both mils and Minutes of Angle (MOA). Windage would be a little more problematic, but Carl did the best he could for estimated wind speeds from 10 to 30 knots at 90 degrees, and then a fraction for each 15 degrees from headwind to tailwind.

Carl went to the bedroom arsenal that was now very dark. He retrieved a candle, went back to the bedroom and returned with the rifle. He rechecked the elevation and windage knobs. They were still set at zero, where he had left them. Carl adjusted both knobs to feel the clicks of movement. He knew his calculations could not possibly be accurate, but the object was to get close enough to see the impact of his first shot in the scope, and then place the sight's impact point on his target. If he was close enough, the technique should work. *I'd better check the Springfield, while I'm at this sight calculation task.* Carl returned the M1A to the bedroom and picked up the M1903 Springfield. In the living room, Carl examined the adjustment knobs for the first time. The markings were not in tenths; they were in quarter marks. *Damn! This is an MOA sight rather than a mil sight.* Carl went back to the bedroom arsenal with the candle to establish the specific ammunition they had. To the best of his knowledge, they had standard military rounds – 150-grain bullets in the 7.62 x 63 millimeter cartridges. His calculations had all been in milliradians for a heavier projectile with a lower propellant charge. *I might have to use a slightly less elevation setting, but I still need MOA settings.*

Carl looked from his work to see the attentive, silent faces of his audience. He had been so consumed by the ballistics calculation task that he had been unaware of the interest the others had. He smiled, and then looked at Pete's annotated map. "Rings are in hundreds of meters?" asked Carl.

"Correct."

Carl studied the map. *I should be able to pick off specific ranges to at least 10 meters.* "This should work perfectly." Carl laughed, although no one else got the joke. He could not miss the puzzled expressions. "This is far more accurate," he said and gestured to the map, "than my crude ballistic calculations." Carl pointed to his new sight setting table. "I did the best I could from my feeble memory. At least I've seen the M14 ballistic chart. I've never seen one for a 1903 Springfield." Carl lifted the rifle off the table and held it for the boys to see the sight as clearly as possible in the minimal lighting of the apartment living room. "Both rifles are similar from a scope perspective. The elevation adjustment dial is on top and the windage knob on the side. The M1A has a 10-power mil scope, while the Springfield," he said, raising it slightly to signify the weapon he held in his left hand, "has a 16-power, MOA scope. MOA means Minute of Angle . . . just a different form of angular measurement. While the M1A is a gas-operated, semi-automatic rifle, the Springfield is a bolt-action weapon." Carl worked the action a couple of times. "I've made a range table with crude settings that will hopefully get us close, meaning to see the impact of a first shot, and then put that impact point on the sight reticle on your intended target and trigger another round downrange to hopefully hit your target. So, the process would be noting the range on the map," he added and fingered an example of the Wellington Road Market, "and then, going to the table to pick off the sight setting in mils for the M1A and MOA for the Springfield." Carl fingered each step, and then twisted the elevation knob for the range to the market. The audible clicks of the elevation knob sounded the adjustment. "Windage gets a little more complicated and subtle, so we'll hold for that."

"That's way beyond us, Dad," Mike said. "I think we'll leave the long guns to you and Mister Higgins."

"OK . . . probably so," responded Carl. He looked at Pete. "Do you see anything that doesn't look correct?"

"Nope. I could not have gotten this close."

"Do you think you can use this?" Carl asked, waving his right hand over the map and ballistics table.

"I think so, if need be. Until then, I think you should handle the sniper stuff."

"OK." Carl looked at his wristwatch. "Looks like it's past evening meal time."

"We were waiting on you to finish, Dad," Lisa chimed in.

"It's nearly the end of Barb and Larry's watch cycle. Let's get them in, so we can all eat together, then it will be Team Two's watch."

They did just that. Mike went to call in Team One. Janet began the process of dividing two medium-size cans of tuna into 11 equal portions with two portions going to Lisa, for her and the baby. They also had three Ritz crackers each with a glass of water. It was certainly not a gourmet meal, but it would sustain them. They ate in silence.

Once everyone had consumed their rations, Carl asked Barb, "How was it out there?"

"Flippin' cold, I must tell you. Two hours is a long time when you are not moving."

"No question," Carl said. "Did y'all see anyone moving around?"

"No humans," she responded.

"We did see a wolf or a coyote across the street," added Larry.

"Probably looking for something to eat himself," Carl observed. "Only one?" Larry nodded his head. "We probably need to lay a few traps to see what we can capture."

"Too late tonight," Pete contributed. "Larry and I can handle that tomorrow."

"Perhaps after we make the run to the cold storage building. It is only a matter of time before someone figures that one out."

"Yeah, you're right, if they haven't already. We should probably do that mission in morning twilight, before local sunrise."

"There ya go . . . sounds like a plan. Now, I'm going to try to get some rest before my watch." Carl stood to return the rifle to the arsenal room. By the time he reentered the living room, Pete and Nick had completed their dressing for the cold and were in the process of manning their watch station. Carl laid down on the mattress. Janet joined him before he pulled a heavy blanket over them. She snuggled up to her husband with her head on his left shoulder, his left arm around her, and her left arm across his chest. The warmth felt good and beckoned the inviting shroud of deep sleep.

"I'm worried about you," Janet whispered in his ear.

Carl could feel her warm, soft breath. Without opening his eyes, he responded as softly as he could. "Why so?"

"You are taking on so much."

"If I don't, who will? In this situation, we don't get second chances. Who has the skills?"

"Pete."

"And, he is picking up the slack."

"The boys can do more," she said. Carl kept his eyes closed and nodded his head slowly. "You have always told me, told us, to put our oxygen mask on first, to take care of our health first . . . without it, we cannot help others. I'm seriously concerned you are not taking care of yourself."

Carl whispered, "You have a point. I'll spread things out. Now, I need to sleep . . . to that end."

"I love you, Carl."

Carl opened his eyes and turned his head to look into Janet's eyes. He kissed her lovingly. "I love you, sweetheart, and thank you for caring. I just want to get us through this winter and out of these mountains."

Janet smiled and winked at him. They both drifted off to sleep . . . deep, seductive, peaceful, enveloping sleep.

—

10

The touch on his right foot shot Carl bolt upright. It took him a few seconds to become fully aware of his surroundings in the dim light of the waning fire. Mike was standing back, just out of range. Janet and the children had learned long ago that awakening Carl out of sleep often resulted in a jolting, prepared-to-fight response. Janet was missing from their crude bed. Mike was the only other person awake in the room.

"It's time for your watch, Dad," Mike announced softly. Carl nodded his head and checked his wristwatch. It was midnight. Mike found Dave and awakened him, and then returned to his father. "Nothing outside since Team One."

"OK. Thanks."

Dave and Carl suited up for the cold. Carl checked to make sure he had his M1911 in his jacket pocket.

"Ready?" Carl asked Dave.

"No, Mister Parks," he responded and smiled, "but we gotta do it, so let's get on with it."

"Good man." Carl led Dave to the balcony. He peaked out. Janet happened to be looking at the door in anticipation. Carl did not have to knock or signal. Janet crouched down and moved to the door that Carl opened for her to enter. He closed the door and turned to his wife.

Janet kissed her husband. Carl felt the deep cold from her lips and face.

"Mike reported no activity," Carl whispered.

"Nothing . . . not even an animal."

"OK. Mike put on a log. The fire should warm you quickly. Try to get some sleep."

"No problem there," she answered, kissed him again, and went to the fireplace.

Carl and Dave went outside onto the balcony, and settled onto the stools they used to keep them off the snow. They both silently surveyed the full extent of the field of view. The clear, cold night sky and the three-quarter waxing moon made the high Rockies winterscape appear serene and beautiful—majestic is the word that often came to mind. Even with the moon above the restricted horizon of the mountain valley, the sky was full of stars. It had been far too long since Carl had been able to admire the vast array of stars in the visible universe. *I'm sure we'll get the opportunity to see and perhaps enjoy the panoply of stars before this ordeal is over.* Carl saw nothing moving, nothing of interest, not even a sliver of light from some distant fire. As many times as the family had visited these mountains in wintertime, he had not fully appreciated the glorious beauty that showed through in the moonlight without any artificial lights to contaminate the scene.

Nothing moved or changed in the entire viewable scene during their complete, two-hour, watch period. No one had yet complained about seeing nothing, hearing nothing or even smelling nothing. Carl knew the cold would eventually bring the complaints and he was ready. Carl signaled for Dave to go wake up Team One to relieve them. The process took several minutes. Carl scanned the entire scene while he waited for the tap on the glass door. It was very boring . . . and that was a very good thing. Carl instinctively knew they would not make it through the winter with boring, and they had to be prepared to alert the families when a threat appeared, as it inevitably would.

The tap on the glass door signaled the watch change. Carl crouched low, in case anyone was watching, though he was fairly certain no one was watching. *Better safe than sorry.* Barb opened the door just enough for Carl to enter, as had become their common practice of courtesy toward the off-going watch-standers. Barb closed the door behind him and restored the blackout curtain.

"Did you see anything?" whispered Carl.

"Nope, not a thing."

"Nothing since your last watch—dead silence."

"Good. I hope it stays that way. We do not need excitement," Barb said confidently.

Carl chuckled softly. "Indeed."

Larry and Barb disappeared behind the curtain. Carl heard the distinct sound of the door opening, and then closing. Dave was already at the fireplace warming up. Carl joined him.

"I guess it is good that we don't see anyone," Dave spoke softly.

"You got that right," Carl answered in a near whisper, so as not to wake anyone sleeping. "Anyone moving out there in the middle of the night would not likely have good intentions."

"Do you think we will ever see anyone?"

"Yes. As the days go on, some people will become progressively more aggressive as they seek to survive. It is inevitable and only a matter of time."

"That is not a nice thought."

"No, it's not. We will soon see the uglier side of humanity. Best be prepared . . . better for us to deal with it and survive."

"Are we ready?" Dave asked solemnly.

I cannot answer that question directly or forthrightly, as reality deserves. "As ready as we can be."

Dave considered the answer and let his curiosity dwindle for the time being.

"We better get some more sleep while we can," Carl said finally, now that he was warm and knew Dave had to be as well.

Dave did not reply and went to an open mattress. Carl waited until his teammate was recumbent and headed toward sleep, and then he joined Janet, who barely stirred when he laid down beside her. He kissed her exposed cheek without response, laid his head down, and was enveloped by sleep.

His wristwatch said it had been four hours, but to Carl, it felt like four minutes. Janet was gone; she had arisen for her watch cycle without disturbing his sleep. Carl looked at Pete.

"It's just after six. Time to get the show on the road."

Carl nodded his head in agreement. "We probably should get everyone fed before we take this on."

"Good point. I'll get everyone up and going."

Carl quickly tended his morning bodily functions. By the time he returned to the living room, Lisa had chosen their morning ration, two strips of jerky and water. They were not getting the calories they needed, but this would have to do for now. If they found anything in the cold storage building, it would surely help.

"How do you want to do this?" Pete asked.

Carl thought for a moment. "How many backpacks do we have?"

"I didn't bring mine," interjected Lisa.

They took an inventory. All five boys brought their backpacks. None of the adults had backpacks.

"So, we have five. We should maximize the capacity of the search team."

"Five of us in the search team?" asked Pete for confirmation.

"I think that makes sense. We may only get one or two passes at the meat locker, before it becomes a fight. Yes, we need to make the most of what we can carry."

"What about the pillowcases we used for the apartment searches?" Dave suggested.

Carl thought about the option. "My concern would be tying up one hand and arm . . . or, in our case, the strain on our neck and shoulders. Carrying that potential weight over that distance with our shoulder bags may be too much and cause injury."

"But," Mike said, "if we only get one shot, we need as much as we can carry."

"Yes, that's true. However, impairing or injuring one or all of us is not acceptable."

"How about this . . . we can use the dual pillowcase carriers as packing for the trip out," Pete added. "We load the backpacks first, and then we can try to see how much we think we can carry with the pillowcases with the proviso we are careful not to overload them."

Again, Carl considered the suggestion. "OK. That should work. Just remember, you've got to carry the load for half a mile or so, and you may need to fight under whatever load you decide to carry." He paused. No one spoke. "The more we can recover in the one or two runs we can achieve, the better for all of us."

"OK, then," said Pete. "We have a plan. Now, who goes?"

"I need one person with me," Carl said. "I suggest Alex this time. Lisa can maintain interior watch, as she has done"

"I can help," Barb added. "I can go. I can carry a good load."

"That's up to you and Pete," responded Carl.

"I can help, too," Janet said.

Carl smiled. "I'd like you to stay here and maintain the exterior watch with one of the boys. If Barb and Pete agree that Barb will go on the search team, I recommend Larry stay with you. That would leave Nick, Mike and Dave to go."

"I'm good with Barb going. She's a trooper," Pete said.

"I'd like to go," Larry protested.

Pete smiled with pride. "I know you would, Son, but with Mom and I out there, it is probably best you stay safe. You will get your turn . . . of that I'm sure."

"Oh, OK," Larry conceded.

"Time is clicking on," Carl said. "Let's go."

They all suited up and armed themselves appropriately. Alex gave the Beretta to Mrs. Higgins and loaded the Mossberg with no.4 shot rounds. He put a box of shot rounds in his jacket pocket.

Once again, Carl and Alex deployed to apartment 232, confirmed that it was as they had left it, and signaled for the search team to proceed. They moved the chest of drawers to the left to give him the appropriate angular coverage through the portion of the window that would open, if he needed to take a shot. Carl used the same procedure to clear the route for Pete and the search team all the way to the cold storage building. As the team neared their objective, Carl carefully scanned the building several times. Satisfied the team was safe, Carl checked the range circles on the map and set his rifle sight in accordance with his calculated table. He scanned the pine trees surrounding them as well as the trees in the vicinity to the cold storage building and detected no wind, so he left the windage knob at zero. Carl quickly relocated the team and rechecked the building. Everything was calm and peaceful; no signs of other activity.

Carl could not see the entrance that was apparently along French Street. Pete and the team checked the complete building exterior. Satisfied the building was undisturbed, Pete appeared at the northeast corner of the building and held up his right arm with his thumb up. *All's well, so far.*

"Good," Carl whispered without taking his eye off the sight.

"Is everything OK out there?" asked Alex softly from the left side of the window.

"Yeah, so far so good. Now, if we can just get lucky and keep it that way."

While the team presumably disappeared, entered and searched the building, Carl continually examined as much as he could see of each of the cross streets and approaches. They were inside the plain, windowless, block building for perhaps 30 minutes, by Carl's estimate.

"There they are," Carl announced quietly. They appeared as they had going in. The backpacks hung perhaps a little lower under the added weight, but not obviously so. The pillowcase, shoulder bags were definitely loaded, but not overly so. They moved swiftly and surely. Carl counted all five of them. He carefully watched the streets behind them, as the team moved through the south end of Breckenridge. No one followed them. Several times he returned his sight to the building, to see if anyone noticed what they had done and gone in themselves. Again, nothing so far . . . thankfully.

The return journey took a little longer to complete than the outbound movement. When the team disappeared momentarily behind the trees at the terminus of 4 O'Clock Run, Carl looked up and to Alex. He motioned for his youngest son to come closer. "Go back to the apartment. Tell Mister Higgins: I'm continuing to watch the building. So far so good. If he agrees, another run should work. We'll signal vertical for clear, and horizontal for danger, before they cross the stream."

"Vertical?"

"I'll explain when you get back. He'll know what I mean."

"OK, Dad. I'll be right back." Alex left.

Carl located the building again. No new tracks in the snow. "Good," he whispered aloud to himself. Carl searched each of the roads leading to the cold storage building. He could detect no movement or even the slightest change—a displaced curtain, an open door, nothing.

Carl heard the door squeak. He quickly lowered the rifle to the top of the chest of drawers, and withdrew his pistol and disengaged the safety, as he kneeled on one knee and aimed down the hallway. Alex appeared without signaling or checking to make sure the apartment was as he left it. Carl re-engaged the pistol's safety and stood.

Meeting at the door, Carl leaned toward his youngest son. "Never assume a place is clear. You must be cautious, always, Alex."

"Sorry, Dad."

"Sorry doesn't cut it, Alex. Just be careful from now on. You should have at least signaled me. I could have easily shot you."

"It won't happen, again."

"Good. Lesson learned. How was Pete?"

"They got a huge haul . . . lots of meat of all kinds. They were finishing unloading in the back bedroom. They should be coming out soon. He understood your instructions."

"Good. You keep an eye out for them. I've got to keep watch on the building."

"Okey, dokey."

Carl picked up the rifle. He reestablished his overwatch from the target building outward. Carl cleared to the left and right of French Street several blocks, to the top of Jefferson Avenue, and then he saw movement at the bottom of Jefferson Avenue. It was fleeting, but something moved. He rechecked the team. They were still OK. They were crossing the Blue River at Adams Avenue.

"They're at the bridge," Alex announced.

Damn! I can't see anything, but I definitely saw movement. Should I call it off?

"Dad, they're waiting."

"Wave to them vertically," Carl commanded. Alex performed his role flawlessly. Carl looked back in the scope. "They got the signal." *I hope this is not a mistake.* Carl watched the search team cross the Adams Avenue Bridge over the Blue River. Barb had integrated well into the team's movement. If he did not know how she was dressed, Carl would not have been able to identify her as a woman. They were approaching Main Street. Carl carefully searched down Main Street between Adams and Jefferson Avenues. He quickly checked the range map—*550 meters*—and picked off the sight elevation setting—*2.5 mils.* The wind remained calm. The search team was nearly across Main Street, when Carl saw an armed man appear from the shop on the northeast corner of Main and Jefferson. He calmly and casually looked south down Main Street, and then north, up Main Street. The man noticed Mike, the last of Pete's team, moving across Main Street. The man turned and appeared to call to his comrades in the store.

"Open the window," Carl commanded. Alex did so swiftly and as quietly as possible. "Better stand behind me," Carl said, as he watched the man at the storefront.

Four other men joined the first man at the entrance. They appeared to be conferring . . . perhaps on their perceived situation. Carl could not tell whether the men believed the sighting was a threat or opportunity. Three of the men went back inside the store, while the remaining two continued to discuss something. The urge to check on the team grew; however, the potential threat deserved more attention. Carl did manage a few quick glances up Jefferson Avenue. On his third quick look, he saw Pete cross Jefferson Avenue on French Street, and then disappear behind the cold storage building. The sight returned promptly to the men at the store on Main Street. The two men were still talking and did not appear to be particularly agitated, or making moves to track or interdict Pete's search team. On his next quick look, Carl watched Mike cross Jefferson Avenue. The team was completely across without further detection. Carl also had not detected any awareness of the men in the Main Street store regarding the search team, so he was content to just watch.

On the second run to the cold storage building, Pete and the search team took just under 20 minutes to load up with another haul of meat. In yet another quick look, Carl caught Dave and Mike crossing Jefferson Avenue to the north. They had to be the tail end of the team. They appeared to be fully loaded, as they had been on the first run return. The two men at the store were now just watching without talking. They are going to see the team when they cross Main Street. *If something is going to happen that is probably the moment, or they might follow our folks back here.* Carl watched the team appear around the corner of a building and head west on Adams Avenue. The rogue men remained calm and casual. Pete's team was clearly transporting stuff that appeared heavy.

"This is not going to be pretty," Carl whispered to himself.

"What's going on, Dad?" asked Alex.

"I think the team is moving into a confrontation." Carl quickly glanced up to ensure the window was open and immediately went back to the sight.

"What are you going to do?"

"I may have to shoot them, Alex. Best stand behind me and cover your ears."

Alex was already behind him, and Carl assumed he was plugging his ears.

Carl quickly moved his sight reticle from Pete to the men at the store. *Three . . . two . . . one.* Pete became visible to the men. The two men noticed each other. Pete signaled for the team to freeze, which they did. Carl focused on the men at the store. So far, they just stared at Pete, frozen two steps into exposure.

"Can you see the team?" Carl asked Alex.

"Yes."

"I've got to concentrate on these men. Tell me what the team is doing."

"OK. They are not moving."

"OK."

The rifle sight reticle remained on the center of the closest man's chest. Carl disengaged the rifle's safety. His eyes darted to the elevation knob . . . still set correctly.

"Mister Higgins appears to be waving the team to move forward," Alex said.

The second man called to the interior of the store. Both visible men drew pistols. They appeared to be more aggressive and agitated than the vigilante group. This is too close.

"How many are in or through the intersection?"

"Three. Mister Higgins is standing at the corner, while the others cross."

Carl drew up the slack on the trigger. The first man took a step forward and stopped. He appeared to be deciding what to do.

"They are all across. Mister Higgins is facing to the south and walking backward."

He's not taking his eyes off the men. Pete had not brandished his pistol, which was a good, controlled sign. His motion was clearly signaling awareness and preparedness for action, if necessary. Both men started to move forward toward Pete. *That's it!* Carl squeezed the trigger. The rifle's loud report and heavy kick marked the first discharge. The bullet grazed the lead man's right calf and impacted the brick building behind him. The man went down. Carl noted the impact on the stadia of the sight reticle. He adjusted his sight picture to place that sight spot on the second man's chest and squeezed off a second round. The impact hit him squarely and knocked him back into the brick building. The man bounced off the wall and landed motionless on the sidewalk. The first man scrambled on his hands and knees back to the store they were looting. Carl placed the sight spot slightly ahead of the crawling man and squeezed off another round. The impact burst the man's head and ended his life. Carl moved his sight back to the storefront. He saw a head quickly look outside. Carl placed the reticle spot on that place. The third man stretched a little farther out the doorway in an effort to see his comrades. Carl squeezed off another shot. The impact hit him just below his neck and shoulders, knocking him back into the dark interior. *Three down; two to go.* Carl kept the sight on the store. He scanned for alternate exits. None were visible or detectable. The window offered no view of the two remaining men.

"Where are they?" Carl asked Alex without taking his sight off the store.

"Not quite to 4 O'Clock Run," came the response.

"Do you see anyone else around them, or that might be watching the team?"

"No. No one."

The store remained dark and devoid of any detectable movement. Out of curiosity, Carl swiftly and precisely checked the first two men. They had not moved even a little—no breathing that he could determine. They're dead. Carl returned the sight to the doorway. He thought he could see the sole of a boot, but he was not sure.

"They turned up 4 O'Clock Run."

"OK," answered Carl without diverting his attention.

"What are you going to do, Dad?"

"There are at least two more inside that store. I want to finish this."

Silence filled the room. "What do you want me to do?"

Carl thought about Alex's query, as he continued his watch on the store. "When the team reaches the building, I want you to go to the apartment. Help them unload the meat. Then, ask Pete to join me here."

"Are you sure you want me to leave you alone?"

"I've got to try to get those last two men, so they are not a threat to us." Carl removed his M1911 pistol and placed it on the chest just to the right of the rifle. "I should be OK, until Pete returns. If there is any problem, come back and tell me."

"OK, Dad. They're behind the corner of this building. I'm outta here."

"Be careful, Son."

Alex leaned over and kissed his father on the left cheek. Carl's only acknowledgment was to momentarily raise his right hand.

The muffled sounds of Alex's departure told Carl what he needed to know. No activity of any kind could be detected at the store. The last two men had to be inside. "Come on you bastards, let's be done with this," muttered Carl. I wonder if I should do a bait shot to the interior, to see if I can flush them out? Perhaps 10 or 15 minutes passed while Carl waited and watched. Then, it happened . . .

Two men burst out of the store running as best they could on the snow-packed, icy sidewalk. Carl sighted the trailing man, gave him a couple tenths of a mil lead, and squeezed off a shot. Behind. He added a couple more tenths lead and fired, again. The man was knocked violently off his feet. He shifted his sight to the lead man who was now slipping and sliding on the icy street with desperation to get away. The man stumbled and fell, but did not stop trying to get away. Carl felt no remorse. He put his impact spot on the man's nearly stationary flailing torso and fired. It was a solid hit. His target appeared motionless. Carl returned his sight to the previous man. He saw the blood stain in the snow and a clear trail of blood leading to a nearby juniper hedge. The entry to the hiding place was distinct. Carl scanned for any sign of movement, clothing, shoes, anything. He quickly scanned back to the last man—no detectable movement. He appeared to be dead . . . back to the hedge. There were no trails by compaction or by blood leading out of the hedge, so he had to be in there somewhere. Carl searched the base of the hedge, but there was too much of a snowdrift for him to see anything.

The sound of the apartment door opening instantly diverted his attention. He lowered the rifle to the chest of drawers, grasped the pistol grip, and released the safety, as he spun, knelt and extended his arms in a modified Weaver stance aimed down the hallway. He waited for anything to appear at the far end of the hallway.

"Carl, it's me," Pete called out without exposing himself.

"OK. Show me your hands," commanded Carl. Two hands extended out from the right corner at the far end of the hallway. Without lowering the pistol, Carl said, "OK, come ahead." Pete quickly glanced around the corner and withdrew. Carl lowered the pistol and engaged the safety. "It's OK, Pete. You're clear. Come ahead."

Peter Higgins cautiously, at first, stood in the hallway with both hands held shoulder height, palms out. Satisfied Carl was no longer in a defensive posture, Pete moved down the hall.

Carl put his pistol down on the chest, picked up the rifle and returned his sight to the hedge. No change. Carl extracted the rifle's magazine, topped off the ammunition load, and re-inserted the magazine. He returned his attention to the hedge—still no signs into or out of the hedge.

"That was exciting," Pete announced in a louder than desired voice.

"Yeah," Carl said softly without taking his eye off the hedge.

"I saw the two guys at the Smoke Shop. You must've seen them make a move. What happened behind us? I was more focused on getting Barb and the boys out of town and at least into some protection in the trees."

"They called to the others and started to move aggressively toward you. It was too much risk, so I dropped 'em."

"How many were there?"

"Five that I counted. I'm working on the last one. I wounded him and he managed to drag himself into that big hedge across Jefferson from the shop, while I was tending to his buddy. I want to get them all, so they are no threat to us."

"Do you think we should make another run?" Pete asked. "Nobody has been to the cold storage building, except us, so far, and there is more meat."

"If I can get that fifth guy . . . they were so intent upon looting that shop, I do not think they ever noticed y'all at the meat locker. I've seen no one else out and about. The rifle shots could have been heard all over the valley."

"A pair of binoculars would sure be helpful. I can see the hedge across the street from the shop, but I can't see anything else."

"The scope on the 1903 would work," Carl responded matter-of-factly. "The sun is going to be above the eastern ridgeline before you could make it back."

Pete ignored the first part. "I think you've got a good overwatch position. We've run twice with good yield. I'm inclined to strike while the iron is hot. We may not get another chance at this target."

"The risks have been manageable so far. However, the whole valley has heard the multiple reports of a long rifle; of that, I think there is little doubt. Anyone so inclined to interdict your search team is liable to shoot first, to minimize the effectiveness of an overwatch shooter."

"They have to find us first."

"True." Carl kept his attention on the hedge, while he considered Pete's proposal. "If you think you can manage the team, I am getting a better feel for this rifle with each shot, so I can support another run at the meat locker."

"OK, then, do you need anything before we launch, again?"

"I just need Alex here to watch my back."

"No problem. We'll launch out on the third run, as soon as I can get everyone ready."

"I'll be here and standing by."

Pete left. The hedge still remained unchanged. Carl carefully searched every leaf and branch he could see with the scope. A couple of times he thought he saw a small swatch of color—one blue, one red. He could not see any detail and saw no movement. The colors were not easy to reacquire, which made Carl doubt his original observation. A slight creak behind him caused Carl spin in one swift continuous movement, as he lowered the rifle, grasped the pistol, disengaged the safety and crouched in a firing position down the hallway. He heard only his adrenaline-charged breathing that he tried to control. Carl did not move a sliver, as he waited for whatever was out there. *Is that Alex?* The urge to call out subsided quickly, as he concentrated all of his senses on whatever was down the hallway. He considered moving to confront the intruder, if that is what it was, rather than wait defensively. Several minutes passed with no change—not one more sound. *Are they laying an ambush for him or Alex?* Then, he heard the door open.

"Dad, it's me," Alex called out. Two empty hands extended out from the wall corner. "It's Alex, Dad."

Carl lowered his pistol slightly but not fully. "Come ahead."

Alex darted his head around the corner for a quick glance. Satisfied the pistol was not aimed at him, Alex stepped into the middle of the hallway and walked quietly toward his father.

"Were you here several minutes ago?" Carl asked.

"No. I just arrived. Why?"

"I heard a creak, like a floorboard, several minutes ago."

"These are not wooden floors," Alex observed.

"No. They are not. I'm not sure what I heard, but it certainly got my attention."

"So, you and Mister Higgins agreed to another run."

"Yes. Pete thought they would be safe for at least one more."

"OK."

"Check on their position, while I get set up."

"Sure," Alex responded and went to the right edge of the window.

Carl reestablished his survey of the hedge. "I think they made it down to Park Avenue. Trees are in the way." Carl peered back into the sight and scanned the hedge.

"There they are," Alex said. "They just passed 4 O'Clock Run Road."

"OK. Do you see anyone else who might interfere or may be watching them?"

"No. I see no one else out there."

Movement. Carl adjusted his sight spot to a bloody man, stumbling out of the hedge and trying to gain his footing in the snow. He was clearly seriously wounded and probably figured whatever survival prospects he had left were worth the risk the shooter had gone to other tasks. "There he is," Carl whispered.

"Who?" asked Alex.

Carl did not answer, as he placed the sight reticle impact spot on the wounded man's torso and squeezed off another round. The shot missed just above his lower back. Carl made the appropriate adjustment to his sight picture and squeezed off another round. This one hit him squarely and instantly jerked him over onto his back. The man's chest was still heaving but soon ceased all motion.

"OK. That's done," Carl announced and looked up from the sight to Alex. "Where are they?"

"They were nearly to Adams Avenue when your first shot scattered them. I can't see them at all, now."

"Pete is probably looking to the window to see if it is safe. Give him a good vertical wave."

Alex did just that. As Carl anticipated, Pete rose from a small bush he had dived behind when the shots rang out. Carl watched the others stand up out of hiding and form up on the snow-packed street.

As he had done earlier, Carl used the scope to clear the route the search team was using toward the cold storage unit.

The team made it safely across the Blue River and Main Street. *No potential threats detected so far.* They turned south on French Street and disappeared behind the store buildings. Carl looked up and dialed in 5.9 mils in the scope elevation knob. He adjusted his sight watch to the intersection of French and Jefferson. Pete appeared in the intersection and crossed, followed by the others. Pete disappeared behind the cold storage building. Barb and Dave crossed, and also disappeared behind the building. Nick was nearly across and Mike just appeared in the intersection, when the two boys turned and ran north. "Oh oh," Carl whispered. Dave and Barb ran back across as well, and then Pete appeared with his pistol aimed back to the entrance of the cold storage unit. He fired a shot from the big revolver. Carl placed the sight reticle on the corner of the building. Pete disappeared off the left side of his scope. A large man in a camouflage, hunting suit appeared with a shotgun shouldered. Carl fired before he did, and the roughly one-second time of flight produced a torso impact. The shotgun fired into the air as the man went down, knocked off his feet by the momentum of the bullet impact. The man tried to scramble in an effort to at least attain a prone firing position. Carl squeezed off another round that kicked up debris just above the man's right shoulder. Carl quickly adjusted the impact spot and fired again. The impact hit the man in the shoulder, just below the neck, and stopped all movement. Not even twitches or chest heaving could be detected. Carl placed the reticle back on the corner of the building, expecting others to appear.

"Can you see them, yet?" Carl asked Alex without looking up from the sight.

"Not ye . . . wait . . . yes, they're coming down Adams Avenue toward the river."

"Good. Do they appear OK?"

Alex waited until he could see all members of the search team. "Mister Higgins appears to be favoring his left arm. He might be wounded. Everyone else appears to be alright."

"OK. Let's get 'em home. We've had enough excitement for one day." Just as Carl said it, another man appeared, going to his friend. He was wearing a different pattern, camouflage, hunting suit. Carl placed his impact spot on the center of the man's head, as he bent over his friend. The sharp report and rifle kick announced another bullet downrange. The shot hit squarely on the spot as intended and instantly ended the man's life. Carl kept the reticle on the corner of the building, just in case there were any more that might interfere with the search team. He did not take his scope off the building. "Where are they, now?" he asked quietly.

"They are across the Blue River."

"Is anyone following them?"

"No, not that I can see."

"Good. Keep a close eye on them. I've got to watch the building until they make it to 4 O'Clock Run."

"OK."

Carl quickly checked the backside of the cold storage building, as much as he could see, in case any accomplices tried to circle around. *Nothing.* There were no windows on the two sides he could see, so if anyone remained inside, they had no way to observe the search team's egress. The two bodies heaped in the middle of French Street remained motionless. No additional activity was detected.

"They all turned up 4 O'Clock Run," Alex announced.

"OK. Let's break it down. Close the window and draw the curtain closed."

Alex did precisely as he was instructed. Carl considered policing up the spent brass, but decided against it, since there was nothing they could do with it. They made their way out of the building and back to their apartment. By the time Alex and Carl joined the others, there was animated excitement among the group and the watch team had been drawn in.

Pete had taken off his jacket. He looked up to Carl and said, "Thanks."

"You're welcome. How many were there?"

"Only two that I could tell. I opened the door and must've surprised 'em. The big guy turned and fired, but he hit the wall. I took off running, firing a couple of shots to buy time."

"Alex noticed you favoring your left shoulder. Were you hit?"

"No. I slipped and hit my shoulder on the ice pretty hard. We're all OK."

"Whew! I was worried."

"So much for that third run. Did you get 'em?"

"Yes, both of them."

"That makes seven for the day, Dad," Alex noted. "Doesn't it?"

"I'm not interested in counting," Carl responded. "I am only interested in survival."

"We got a pretty good haul," interjected Barb, perhaps to divert the attention from the killing.

"Yes, you did," Janet added. "I've inventoried what you've recovered. There is a lot of venison, elk, beef, and a little bit of lamb, and even a couple packages of buffalo meat."

Carl felt some internal regret that he had to take so many lives, but each one of those men could have easily taken lives of our extended family, or threatened their safe haven. He was far more grateful that they found meat—protein to sustain them. Mostly, Carl felt relief at the team's accomplishment. "I think it is time we had a little celebration. Let's cook up some of the venison and heat up a couple of cans of green beans and new potatoes."

"Barb, Lisa and I can handle that part," Janet offered. Lisa rose and waddled off to the makeshift freezer and storage room.

"I think we have a couple bottles of wine in the lower cabinet," said Carl and placed them on the counter. "If there is no objection, I'm going out on the balcony to keep an eye on things until dinner is ready."

"No problem," Janet answered.

"I'll join you," added Pete.

The two former Marines sat silently outside in the cold, behind the camouflaged railing. Both men continuously scanned the complete field of view available at the balcony. The sun had already descended below the western ridgeline. Scattered, sunlit clouds offered some additional illumination to the local twilight. Neither man noticed any activity. Eventually, Lisa softly knocked on the glass door, signaling that dinner was ready.

For the first time in too long, their extended family enjoyed what for these times was a sumptuous meal, complemented by laughter and lightheartedness. The relief felt good. While there was not enough wine available for any of them, there was a sufficient amount to give each of them a taste and enhance the meal. Even their youngest, Larry, partook of one small glass. They took the time to enjoy the moment. They all knew and recognized there would be hard days ahead, but at least they could celebrate the success of the day's foray.

It had been a very good day, but the rigors of survival could not be cast aside. They returned to their routine of defense and protection.

—

11

Team Four completed their watch at midnight. The conditions were near perfect for the discussed and planned recovery patrol to secure the weapons of the seven men killed in the previous day's operations. The moon was a few days short of full illumination and the sky remained crystal clear without a single cloud in sight. Team Four took a few minutes to warm up at the fire before they headed out on their night mission. Team One was already on duty. Alex finished suiting up. They went to the arsenal room with a lit candle and selected their weapons for this mission. Alex chose the other 45 pistol. Dave selected the 9mm pistol. Carl loaded the Mossberg shotgun eight-round magazine, alternating no.4 shot and flechette rounds. Alex also loaded the Remington shotgun with four no.4 shot rounds. Carl held up a box of no.4 shot ammunition in the candlelight, so Alex could see he had the spare rounds, and then placed the box in his left jacket pocket, just in case. They also stuffed a set of pillowcase shoulder bags in a backpack for each of them. While Carl had seen mostly pistols during the day's engagement, he knew there was at least one shotgun out there.

The apartment was peaceful and quiet. The modest fire in the fireplace appeared to be adequate for an hour or so. Carl found the apartment key with its attached cord. He unlocked the door, let both boys out ahead of him, and then exited, turned and locked the door behind him. Carl placed the key cord around his neck and made sure the key was inside his parka before he zipped the jacket up fully.

They decided not to use the makeshift snowshoes, since the snow had been fairly well packed down. Without words, the small team made their way down 4 O'Clock Run to Park Avenue and across the Adams Avenue bridge. The gurgling sound of water was readily heard on the bridge, although the Blue River was now completely frozen over. They turned right on Main Street, heading south to the five bodies. By the time they reached the bodies, they were frozen solid and frozen to the sidewalk. Carl checked his handiwork as best he could, given the conditions. The moonlight gave them a surprisingly good sight.

Alex found a Glock Model G22 40-caliber, semi-automatic pistol with an extended grip magazine. He engaged the safety on the pistol and placed it in his backpack.

It took a little work, but Carl managed to find two fully loaded similar magazines in the right pocket of the dead man's jacket. He added those to Alex's backpack. He searched the body as best he could and only found a common pocketknife, which he extracted and added to the pistol find.

They repeated the search process on the body of the second man. He had been identically armed, also with two fully loaded magazines. The second dead man had been a little easier to search. Carl found a full box of ammunition for the Glocks in the man's left jacket pocket. The second man had no other weapons that Carl could find. The second man's weapon and ammunition were placed in Dave's backpack.

Carl waved his hand to gain the boys' attention. He signaled with his right hand—three, pointed to the corner shop, and held his index finger to his lips—the third body is in the shop; be quiet, just in case. The boys nodded their heads in acknowledgment. Carl shifted the shotgun to his right hand and fingered the safety to ensure it was off. He raised the shotgun and carefully advanced on the storefront entrance.

The store interior was ink-black dark. They had no way to illuminate the interior. A shooter could easily hide from view and have a clear, silhouetted target with the moonlit exterior. Carl eventually stood in the doorway, aiming the shotgun toward the interior. If anyone was going to be shot, it should be him. Satisfied to the extent possible, given the conditions, Carl held the heavy shotgun with his right hand and signaled for the boys to search the body. Alex and Dave moved quickly and silently to search the third body. Carl decided he would pass on examining the body. The boys found a semi-automatic pistol. Carl could not tell what type in the low light. They only found one spare clip and no other weapons. Carl nodded. Alex secured the pistol and magazine in Dave's backpack. Carl gave a thumb's up hand signal, and then pointed south on Main Street.

They heard nothing other than the crunch of packed-snow under their feet. They took several steps and stopped to listen. They saw no one and heard nothing, not even a breeze. The puffs of condensed exhalations punctuated their breathing. As they crossed Jefferson Avenue, Carl looked east to see the cold storage building that had been the target of their searches yesterday.

The fourth dead man was searched—another Glock 40 along with two spare extended clips. They also discovered a sheathed K-Bar combat knife that took a little work to free up from the frozen body. The weapons were loaded in Alex's backpack.

The fifth man was splayed out in the snow bank as he had died. Alex found one standard pistol magazine and surprisingly a long, 20-round extended magazine that he held up for Carl to see. They did not find the man's pistol. Carl saw the man's blood trail into the hedge in front of the small house converted to a curio shop. A substantial bloodstain in the snow between the hedge and the building marked the location the man chose in his effort to wait out the shooter. Given the amount of blood, which looked worse than it was, the man recognized that he was bleeding to death and had to make a break for any chance of survival. Carl found the man's pistol partially frozen in the snow near the bloodstain. He had to break down the confinement of the weapon and eventually broke it free. While the pistol still had small chunks of ice attached, Carl identified the pistol as a Sig Sauer 9mm semi-automatic pistol. He found nothing else of interest in the man's hiding place.

Carl made his way back to the street and held up the pistol by the trigger guard. Both boys nodded. Alex turned around to allow his father to place the pistol in his backpack. Once everything was settled, Carl signaled for them to proceed up Jefferson Avenue.

The last two bodies were exactly where they fell and died. To Carl's surprise, the first man chasing Pete and the team was larger than expected, perhaps 6' 5" and 260 lbs. or so. A Mossberg 500 Tactical shotgun with a pistol grip lay next to him. While Carl searched the first body, Alex and Dave searched the second body. Carl considered ejecting the spent round and chambering a live round in the shotgun, but did not want the sound of the slide action that could potentially be heard for hundreds of feet in the cold, windless, mountain air. He engaged the safety, pulled out his shoulder bags and placed it in one of the pillowcases. Carl felt a light tap on his shoulder. He looked behind him. Dave was holding what looked like a MAC-10 with a long muzzle suppressor and a 20-round magazine inserted. Carl mouthed a "wow!" without making a sound. Dave and Alex smiled and nodded. Carl examined the submachine gun. The selector appeared to be set on the semi position, and it did have an auto position. Carl engaged the safety and placed the weapon in the other pillowcase of his shoulder bag. Alex held up a backpack the second man had apparently been wearing, and then opened the flap, revealing a treasure trove of clips, boxes of ammunition and even another unidentified semi-automatic pistol. Carl saw no need to inventory the backpack in the dark, cold air, and simply loaded the backpack in the same bag as the MAC-10. He signaled with a circle around the man to ask whether they completed their search. Both boys nodded their heads. Carl returned to the first man. It took all three of them to move the body from its curled up, face down, near fetal position, so they could complete their search.

Carl felt a holstered pistol under his parka and left arm. They tried several different ways to reach the pistol, but the frozen state of the body thwarted each attempt. They did find three standard clips of what appeared to be 32-caliber, hollow-point rounds along with a tubular muzzle suppressor most likely for the pistol. Carl stood and the boys followed. He signaled for Alex to turn around, which his youngest son did. Carl opened Alex's backpack, reached in and withdrew the K-Bar. He handed the sheath to Alex and used the knife to cut through the dead man's parka. The holster was partially frozen to his body, probably from sweat long since frozen by the cold mountain air. Carl tried to unfasten the shoulder holster. He had to cut access slots in several places to eventually disconnect the holster with the pistol and remove it. Carl did not take time to examine the pistol, and he placed the firearm and knife in Alex's backpack and strapped it down. *No need to get them out of the middle of French Street. We'll leave them where they lay.*

Satisfied that they had recovered all the weapons associated with the seven dead men, Carl signaled for them to head back. He checked his wristwatch. They had been out for 75 minutes. Suddenly, Carl signaled stop. The boys nervously looked around, expecting to find some unspecified threat. After a few seconds thought, Carl signaled for them to go to the cold storage building. *There is no one out here but us. We have the shoulder bags. We might as well see if we can pick up some more meat.* Carl held up his right hand, and then gestured to eat, meaning for them to pick up additional meat. The boys nodded.

The cold storage building storefront on French Street had one, unusually wide door that remained open, and one appropriately sized window. The door and window were part of the business lobby with a counter opposite the door. Carl gestured for Alex to man the door and keep watch, so they were not surprised. His youngest son nodded his head in acknowledgment. There were two doors behind and to either side of the counter. Carl nodded to the right door.

Inside there were two banks of small lockers, about one-meter square, from floor to ceiling. It was difficult to see with no illumination other than the indirect moonlight from outside. Carl took several minutes to allow his eyes to adapt to the darkness. Of the lockers he could see, half of them had the doors open. He checked several of the open lockers and they were empty. Carl felt his way back into the darkness and selected one of the unopened lockers. He could not see what was inside, but cautiously felt the interior. It was about half full of butcher-paper-wrapped packages that were still frozen. Carl closed the door to that locker to indicate it had not been searched. He made his way back to the entrance, where Dave was waiting for him.

Carl leaned forward to whisper in Dave's left ear. "Check the lockers with closed doors. If the contents are frozen and you think you can carry them in your shoulder bags, load as much as you feel you can reasonably carry. If you empty a locker, leave the door open. When you are loaded, trade places with Alex, and tell him what to do. I'm going to check the other bank of lockers."

Dave nodded in acknowledgment. Carl gestured that he was going to the other door. Dave nodded, again, and started his task.

Carl went to the other door. As he reached the entrance, he stopped and whispered into Alex's right ear. "Dave is loading meat. When he has a full load, he will come out to trade places with you and will brief you on what to do. I'm going to check the other section." Alex nodded his head and held up his right thumb.

When he passed the open door, Carl thought he saw a distinctive shape in the deep darkness behind the door. He moved slowly and carefully to investigate, feeling with his hands for the wall, and then down, covering a foot either side of directly in front of him. His hand contacted a tube. Carl removed the glove from his right hand. The tube had a hole in the top end. He moved down the cold metal tube to a smaller diameter, metallic tube. It did not take long for Carl to ascertain that he had discovered a contemporary, military style, bolt-action, sniper rifle. Holy shit! He could not establish the caliber or whatever ammunition might be contained in the rifle; that would have to wait until they were back in their apartment. He placed the rifle in his right bag. Carl felt the floor, but could not find a bag, box or any container that might contain ammunition. *Odd; there is no additional ammunition. At least a rifle like this is not going to be available to anyone else.* Carl moved carefully to the barely visible left door.

The left section room was similar to the right section, except the locker doors were full size. None of them were open. Carl selected the first door on the right of the room. He could not see detail, but the locker contained several prepared sides of a medium size animal, probably deer or antelope. In the first locker, Carl could not detect any smaller portions or packages. He backed out of the first locker and closed the door. Carl crossed the room to check the first locker on the left with the same finding. Carl worked his way back, feeling his way into each locker, without being able to see anything beyond the first two lockers. He found small shelves in several lockers that held what felt like packaged meat. Carl placed all of the packages he could feel in his bags, trying to keep them balanced. Strangely, most of the butchered meat was not packaged, and he chose not to collect those pieces. When he reached the back of the large locker room, he turned to see a very faint outline of the entry door.

Carl carefully made his way out of the large locker room. Dave and Alex were both at the main entrance door. Carl leaned toward Alex's left ear. "Did you clear the small locker room, or is there more? I can carry a little more."

Alex shook his head and simply whispered, "Clear." Carl tried to check his wristwatch, but the luminous dial had not been charged.

The signal to return to their base started them on their way. They detected no other people out in the middle of the night, or animals of any kind—threat or not. The return journey was completed quickly. Nothing unusual or untoward caught their attention. Before they entered the base apartment, Carl whispered to the boys, "Let's not worry about unloading the bags, now. Let's drop them in the first bedroom. We'll inventory and store what we collected later. We need to get some sleep." The boys acknowledged Carl's directions. He used the key to unlock the apartment door as quietly as he could. They all quickly dropped their shoulder bags and backpacks. Alex and Dave laid down. Carl went to the balcony door and softly knocked on the glass. Both Pete and Nick looked. Pete came to the door. Carl cracked the door an inch and whispered, "We're back. Mission accomplished. All is safe." Pete held up his gloved right thumb.

Dave and Alex were both recumbent and motionless. Carl laid down next to Janet. He leaned over on his right elbow and kissed her gently on the left cheek. He whispered, "I love you."

Sleep claimed Carl in short order.

When he regained consciousness, Janet was gone and Mike was wiggling his left big toe. Mike softly announced, "It's your watch, Dad."

"Thanks, Son," Carl replied wearily.

Mike went to Dave and woke him as well. That meant it was 08:00—eight bells in nautical terms. Mike continued to wake everyone else for their morning meal. Carl called Pete in. They each had three pieces of jerky and the last slices of the last loaf of bread they had recovered, and of course water.

Pete was the first to talk. "How did it go last night?"

"Pretty good. No problems. We collected all the weapons. Some interesting items we did not take the time to assess or inventory. We also collected up the rest of the packed, butchered meat from the cold storage building. Quite a few sides of animals remaining."

"Yeah, we noticed that."

"We left the sides and unpackaged meat . . . just too hard to deal with."

"We probably have enough to make it to spring," Pete added.

"We need to accurately inventory what we have and lay it out for planned consumption. I sure hope you are correct.

"Can we plan to have another meat meal this evening?" Janet asked.

"Jerky is meat," Carl responded matter-of-factly.

"You know what I mean, Carl," she reacted a little more sharply than she intended.

"Yes. I think we can do that," he said without protest.

"I noticed some high cirrus approaching from the southwest when twilight came," Pete observed and paced a few steps back and forth before he continued. "We may have another snowstorm in the next day or so. I was thinking this morning, with a potential storm coming, we should probably check the food storage of a few of the larger restaurants in town, if you're up for it."

"Good point. Which ones do you have in mind?" Carl asked.

"I was thinking The Dredge and The Crown. They are both on the south end of town." Pete looked at Carl with seriousness in his eyes.

"We've eaten at The Crown," interjected Janet, "but, not The Dredge."

"Both pretty good restaurants," Barb added.

Before he answered, Carl wanted to know more from the watchstanders. "Did anyone see people roaming around during your watch cycles?"

"We could not even see you and the boys, either going or coming," answered Barb.

"OK, then let's go with your proposed mission," Carl said to Pete.

"Do we need more?" asked Janet. "We've recovered and stored a lot of meat back there. When the weather gets above freezing, what is left will spoil, and that will be a different problem."

"True, however, in our circumstances, better to have too much than not enough."

Janet raised her hand, and then spoke before any recognition, "But, you take so many risks with every foray out there."

"True, again . . . no argument," Carl said with a patient smile. "I think Pete and I look at this the same way. We are in a better position having stuff for our sustenance while controlling as many of the weapons as we can. It will be less threatening to us, until we can make the trek out of these mountains."

"I agree," Pete said.

Janet, Barb and several of the boys nodded their heads.

Carl checked his wristwatch—08:27. "The sun is going to be over the east ridgeline soon, so we'd better get going. As they had done yesterday, the group arranged for the continuation of the watches, while the search team was out. This time, Mike would provide back up for his father. They suited up and armed themselves, as they had yesterday.

The field of view from Carl's overwatch perch from apartment 232 placed The Dredge restaurant near the right limit of what he could see and cover. Further, several conifer trees partially obscured the angles he had on the two designated targets. The angles and obstructions would have to be dealt with, since there was not a better perch position available.

The team moved to stay out of town as long as possible and made their way directly to The Dredge. The converted and renovated gold dredge had been parked in a small pond with two, wooden plank, access causeways for access to the authentic restaurant—Old West ambiance and cuisine. The surrounding trees and buildings made continuous overwatch more difficult than he was accustomed to on the other town searches.

"Nice," whispered Carl.

"What?" asked Mike. When he did not get an answer, he added, "I can't see them."

Without taking his eye out of the scope, Carl whispered to his oldest son, "Mister Higgins has the team leap-frogging with at least one of the team visible to us, so we do not lose sight of at least one of them."

"Nice. Can I see what it looks like through the scope?"

Carl considered Mike's request. The team appeared to be heading to the south walkway to the restaurant, which would offer the best, unobstructed, field of view. "Sure."

Mike took his father's position, holding the rifle, and peering into the scope. Carl stood behind Mike and gently nudged him to help him pick up the team. "Wow!" Mike eventually exclaimed after acquiring one of the team members in the scope. He looked up and back down to the scope several times to appreciate the magnification. "Thanks, Dad," he said and turned the rifle back over to his father.

Pete waited in view of the overwatch perch until the whole team made it to the south path to the converted dredge. Carl saw no signs the team encountered or even suspected there might be resistance or a threat. When he was ready, Pete disappeared from view, moving to the entrance. He was probably clearing the building, to make sure no one was in the interior that could do them harm, or interfere with their mission. Pete appeared on the south boardwalk, clear of the building, since the north walkway was obscured by treetops, and signaled a thumb's up. The restaurant was now open, and the search team was busy searching the facility. He disappeared, again, to join the team. The process took roughly 15 minutes, until Pete reappeared. The rest of the team moved past him across the south boardwalk. They were not fully loaded, but they did have contents in their shoulder bags and probably their backpacks. Pete stood and signaled they were complete at The Dredge and headed to The Crown. He did not wait for a reply signal.

"They're headed to The Crown," Carl whispered without taking his eye out of the scope.

"Did they find anything?"

"It appears so."

Carl concentrated on his task of checking their path, as best he could, given the angles. Pete moved the team to the east side of Main Street to aid Carl's effort. The Crown was located on the west side of Main Street, so his overwatch task would become more complicated. At least he would be able to see the approaches to their target, although he would have no way to observe the storefront. *Why are the streets deserted,* Carl asked himself? *Surely people are getting hungry and perhaps even a little desperate. We can't be the only ones looking for food.* The paucity of any other human activity made him nervous. *What am I missing?* Pete stationed Dave on the east side of Main Street, opposite The Crown entrance, as their lookout and their signaler. Sure enough, Dave looked directly to the perch window and gestured that everything was OK, so far, and the team was going in.

On one of his cyclical checks of Dave, Carl caught the motion up Main Street, toward the north end of town. Carl worked his way in the direction of Dave's signal. A group of four men and two women were heading south on Main Street toward the search team. At least two of them were armed, as far as he could tell. Dave stepped back into the recessed store entrance where he was positioned; he was being appropriately cautious. Carl tried to watch Dave for signals and keep track of the approaching group. To Carl's relief, the approaching group stopped at Lincoln Avenue and entered the Town Square Mall; they were searching.

Dave noticed the group's stop and seemed to relax a little. Carl tried to watch Dave, watch the mall entrance for any possible confrontation, and continue his scan of the approaches. By the time he made it back to check on Dave, he was holding his forearms crossed, meaning, he presumed, the search of The Crown had not been successful. Pete appeared and started moving north on Main Street, probably to take a different route back. "No, not that way," Carl whispered to himself. He saw Dave bound up to the team leader and leaned in, probably whispering to Pete about what he had seen. Pete turned and reversed course. The mall group did not reappear by the time the search team made it to Adams Avenue and headed back across the Blue River. The search team crossed 4 O'Clock Run Road and were not quite to the 4 O'Clock Run trailhead when Carl finally noticed the mall group reappear. They were carrying a few things but nothing that appeared substantial or significant.

When the search team turned up 4 O'Clock Run, Carl whispered to Mike, "Let's break it down."

His oldest son closed the curtain. They left the furniture as they had moved it. They left the apartment as they had found it.

Carl and Mike arrived back at the apartment just after the search team. The debriefing was accomplished in short order. They had recovered nothing from The Crown. The restaurant had already been stripped clean, although the prior looters had not taken particular care of the furniture or equipment. To everyone's surprise, the team had collected, from The Dredge, several commercial size cans or containers of green beans, corn, peas, carrots and oddly, several large cans of Boston-style baked beans. There was no need to freeze the canned goods, so they stacked them at the edge of the kitchen area.

They agreed to pick up the standard watch cycle with Team Three – Janet and Mike. Lisa asked her father if she could go outside behind the apartment building to smell the trees and feel the cold. Carl agreed to accompany his daughter for her little excursion. She could not get a jacket closed, so they rigged a blanket wrap of her torso held in place by her jacket zipped down from the top. Carl helped her down the stairs, which took her far longer than expected to waddle down.

When she stepped outside into the partially packed snow, Lisa stopped and inhaled deeply. "The trees smell so good," she pronounced.

"Yes, they do."

Lisa walked through the thin tree line onto the one-lane wide ski trail that was called 4 O'Clock Run—the ski trail they took at the end of a day's skiing. The trail was one of the attractions they all appreciated about the apartment they rented annually for their pre-Christmas skiing holiday. *No skiing this year,* Carl mused. While Lisa held her distended belly, as if to keep it from falling down, she shuffled through the snow to enjoy the peaceful winter scene and stimulation of her senses. As was his nature, Carl noted very few, but there were some, tracks going farther up the trail beyond Building 3. By this time, it was a well-worn path from Building 3 to the trailhead. *We must change that sign.* Carl instinctively looked skyward. He moved outside the tree line to get a better view of the clouds, while he kept an eye on his only daughter, who displayed almost child-like enthusiasm for the snow, pine boughs, and segments of fallen trees poking up through the snow. *The clouds are thickening. We're probably going to get a storm tomorrow.* Carl returned to the trail.

"Have you had enough?" asked Carl, as quietly as he could and still reach her.

"No," Lisa responded promptly, "but, I know I can't stay out here." She turned and shuffled toward her father. "This may be my last venture outside. The baby is due soon. I can feel it."

"You're probably right, sweetheart. I'm good, if you want to enjoy it while you can."

"Thanks, Dad. Thank you for allowing me this and coming with me. I needed this," she said and swung her arms outstretched like the meadow scene from "*The Sound of Music.*"

"Sure. Take your time. Enjoy it."

"Yeah. I'm done. The cold is starting to get to me, so I'd better go inside."

Carl helped Lisa back into the apartment building. Climbing the stairs was quite the chore for Carl's pregnant daughter. She paused at each stairway landing to catch her breath. The inactivity of their confinement had not helped her cardiovascular conditioning at this altitude.

By the time they made it back to unit 332, Barb, Pete and the boys were napping. Lisa made her way through the recumbent bodies to the fireplace and the couch, as she disassembled her attire. Carl remembered the uninspected haul from their early morning foray, and his curiosity exceeded his urge to take a quick practice nap.

The arsenal room was quite dark, although light showed around the edges of the closed curtain. The room faced the forest behind the building. Carl peaked out the edge of the curtain to see if anyone might be out there. After checking in both directions without exposing himself, Carl drew the curtain back, opening about a foot gap and allowing in sufficient light to illuminate the interior of the arsenal room.

The boys had unloaded their shoulder bags onto the mattress-less, bedsprings for the twin set of bunk beds. Carl first moved the packaged frozen meat into their storage room, placing each package in its proper stack according to the labeling on the wrappers. When that task was done, Carl returned to the arsenal room and arranged the pistols they had recovered. The Mossberg Tactical shotgun appeared far more sinister next to the conventional stock weapon. Carl made sure the safety was engaged and laid it next to the other shotgun. He unloaded his shoulder bag. The Remington 700 Tactical rifle was a modern, serious, sniper rifle with an integrated muzzle suppressor and collapsible bipod. He knew he needed to check the caliber and cartridge for which the rifle was chambered, but that task could wait. The MAC-10 submachine gun was more like a machine pistol with a long over-sized, barrel mounted, muzzle suppressor. This was a very serious weapon and illegal in the United States. Carl ejected the grip magazine and ejected the chambered round—a 9mm parabellum like the Beretta used. He worked the action several times and felt the trigger pull. This particular weapon also had a collapsible, heavy gauge, bar stock. *This is not a hunting weapon; it was a killing weapon, and why on earth would someone have a weapon like this up here?* Carl pushed the ejected round into the magazine, placed the selector on SAFE and laid them on the bedsprings separately. *This thing can run through their available ammunition in very short order.* Carl turned his attention to the pistol in the shoulder holster they recovered from inside the big guy's jacket. It was indeed a 32-caliber semi-automatic pistol, a Walther PPK—James Bond's weapon of choice and a famous pistol model in use and popular since before World War II. Carl ejected the grip magazine. It looked like an eight-round clip. He worked the slide and ejected a chambered round. The pistol was already on SAFE. Carl unscrewed the muzzle suppressor, and then reinstalled it. He reassembled the shoulder holster; it was an X-strap harness across his back between his shoulders. The holster fit nicely under his arm. Three, loaded, spare clips were snapped into individual pouches on the harness under his right arm for easy access when quickly needed. Carl adjusted the harness for his body and tried drawing the pistol several times to get a feel for the suppressor extension. The process was awkward but manageable, to have the benefit of minimal sound. Once he was satisfied, Carl extracted the pistol, doffed the harness and laid the items with the other weapons.

Carl turned his attention to the backpack—the last item in his shoulder bags. It was heavy. As he suspected when Alex opened the backpack early this morning, it contained mostly ammunition for the weapons the two men had been armed with. He emptied the backpack first. Another loaded PPK had been in there. He could not find a suppressor for the second PPK, but the muzzle was threaded for one. Carl ejected the magazine, pulled the slide back to eject the chambered round, let the slide go home, and engaged the safety. He placed the pistol next to the other one. Carl sorted and arranged the boxes of newly collected ammunition.

That's what I needed to know—the same cartridge as the M1A rifle with a lighter projectile. He could use either round in either rifle.

Carl was admiring the haul when Pete joined him.

"Holy shit!" exclaimed Pete.

"Yeah. My thought precisely."

"These all came from this morning?" Pete asked, waving his hand over the collection.

"Yep. The Glocks and Sig Sauers from the first group, and these," he said, gesturing to the other, newly acquired weapons, "came from those two guys that chased y'all out of the cold storage building."

"Holy shit!" Pete exclaimed, again.

"Makes me wonder who those two guys were and why they had weapons like these in the High Rockies."

"These are not hunting weapons."

"Nope."

"Unless you are hunting humans."

"Agreed."

"Wow! At least we've got their weapons now."

"At least some of them. I wonder what else is out there."

"Have you checked out the Remington?"

Carl knew he meant the rifle rather than the shotgun. "Not yet. The ammunition is the same as the M1A with a lighter bullet—a standard NATO round. It doesn't take a rocket scientist to recognize that it is a very sophisticated weapon. The scope is a 16-power sight with a milliradian windage and elevation grid, military grade reticle, and mil adjustment knobs, so my calculations will get me close. The lighter round won't give us as much drop."

"Impressive."

"Indeed. You're welcome to check it out. I need to clean the M1A. We've put more than a few rounds downrange . . . need to keep it in fine form."

The two men went about their activities without words. Carl was still servicing the M1A rifle, as Pete dry-fired the Remington 700, and then the 1903 Springfield. Pete evaluated some of the other weapons they had collected until Carl finished cleaning the M1A. Carl held up the weapon and Pete continued his evaluation, while Carl turned his attention to the Remington.

With the bolt opened on the Remington, Carl hand-fed one of the rounds he had been using with the M1A; it inserted and withdrew smoothly. The rounds were interchangeable. *The bipod will certainly be helpful. I like the semi-automatic action of the M1A, but the bolt-action is smooth and positive, and the integral muzzle suppressor makes localization far more difficult, if not impossible.* Carl went back to the retrieved backpack, looking through every compartment and pocket for just one spare magazine for the Remington 700. Nothing. The backpack was empty. *Did we miss anything in their clothing? I can't believe they only had one five-round clip for a weapon like that.* Carl extended the bipod legs and locked them in place, and then rested the rifle next to the M1A and 1903.

"We have quite a developing arsenal," Pete finally said.

"You got that right. Better that we have these weapons; at least, they are out of circulation. We haven't faced a sniper, yet, but clearly, such weapons are out there and we need to anticipate facing another shooter." Carl smiled. He was certainly not a shooter, a professional with a long gun, but he had proven to be good enough.

"I hope we never have to deal with a sniper, but you are quite right."

"Me as well."

"Hey Carl," Pete said, as if he had not been listening. "Nick mentioned to me during our last search mission that the boys would like to do more to help . . . do their own searches to help out."

Carl laughed softly. "I think Janet may have put them up to it. She's concerned we are taking too much and burning our wick at both ends."

"It is a concern of all of us."

"You've been out with them more than I have. Do you think they are ready?"

Pete hesitated just a little. "They have not been through boot camp like us . . . well, like me," he laughed in recognition that Carl had been an officer.

"The Basic School for me . . . quite similar."

"Yeah, anyway, I think they can handle it."

"What do you think their mission should be?"

"I've been thinking, after watching them on several missions, now . . . I'm thinking we could give them a comfortable test." Carl nodded his head. "The Heartstone Restaurant is at the northeast corner of Ridge Street and Washington Avenue. You should have a clear view of the entrance."

Carl considered the proposal. He was fairly confident that Pete was correct in the worthiness of the target—at least the overwatch angles. The Parks family had eaten there a few times. It was a small restaurant, modest menu, and well-prepared meals. Carl suspected there would be deep stores, but it was worth the run and test of the boys. "Who do you think should go?"

"I thought I would join you at the overwatch perch with one of the other long guns, and we could take Larry as our backup. I'd suggest we send the other boys as a team. The ladies can manage home base."

"OK. That should work."

"When should we do it?"

"Now, there is the conundrum. Daylight is waning. The sun will disappear behind the west ridgeline in less than an hour, and we have signs of an approaching storm that will probably reach us tomorrow."

"Should we wait until the storm passes?"

Carl considered the salient question. "We've had a pretty busy day, so I'd not recommend going this afternoon, although it would be better weather-wise." He paused to think. Pete did not intrude. "What do you think about evaluating the weather in the morning. If it is acceptable and appears to be holding off for what the expected duration of the mission would be, then we go in the morning with your proposed plan. If we do not meet those constraints, then we wait. It would be better to go before the storm, so we do not have to deal with fresh snow and drifts."

"That sounds reasonable."

"I'd better get a quick combat nap. My watch starts in less than an hour."

Pete nodded his head. Carl took a quick look outside—no detectable observers. He closed the curtain returning the room to darkness. The two men made their way back to the modest light and warmth of the living room. Carl saluted Pete and laid down. Janet was on watch with Mike. Sleep claimed him quickly.

—

12

The weather was looking progressively more ominous. A solid overcast now blanketed the visible sky and it was darkening. The wind velocity was increasing from the south, which was yet another indication of an approaching low-pressure system. Pete had joined Team Four (Dave and Carl) on the balcony watch station and sat on a hard plastic storage box.

"What do you think?" asked Pete.

"Not looking good. We have a couple of hours . . . maybe four to six hours at the outside from the look of those clouds," Carl answered, as he looked to the sky.

"Do you think we should send the boys into town?"

Carl thought carefully for several minutes. "It will be easier before the fresh snow . . . and no telling how much snow we're going to get in this storm." Carl lapsed into thought, again. "The decreasing ambient light will make sighting a little more problematic . . . ." Carl scanned the ski trails above them and what little they could see of the town. Carl looked directly at Pete. "I think we have time. I'd say, let's go. Are the boy's ready?"

"Are you ready, Dave?"

"Yes sir," he answered without hesitation.

Pete looked back to Carl. "Looks like we're good to go."

"OK. Let's go inside, get a quick bite to eat, and get this show on the road."

The boys were indeed suited up. The three women had anticipated the morning mission. They ate their modest meal in silence.

Pete briefed the team on their procedures, as well as what they would be doing in their overwatch. The boys asked no questions and nodded their heads in agreement. The search and overwatch teams completed their preparations and armed up. Pete chose the 1903. Carl decided to try the Remington on this mission and carried the M1A rifle as well, just in case. The overwatch team deployed first with all three long guns, plus two full boxes of ammunition of each type. Larry signaled their readiness.

Mike led the team down 4 O'Clock Run and into town.

Carl and Pete both detected several groups apparently searching other businesses; fortunately, the other groups were at least a block away. As Pete had taught them, Alex remained at the entrance and signaled clear, when the search team entered the closed restaurant. The overwatch team had much more to keep an eye on. By mutual consent, Carl took the north side of Washington Avenue, and Pete watched the south side of town. Both of them alternated checking on the search team. Alex remained vigilant and calm.

"Oh, oh, we may have a problem," Pete said.

"What?"

"Two groups ran into each other at Adams and Ridge."

That's just a block south of the boys. Carl scanned south. The image in his scope confirmed Pete's observation. Both rifles were pointed at the group. "If this turns ugly, let me take the first shot or two. The suppressor will make localization difficult. I've only got five shots. At that point, you can take over. That should confuse the hell out of 'em . . . the report suggesting a very long range."

"No problem."

"Larry, open the window please," Carl requested.

Pete's son did as he was asked.

Carl checked the wind. The best he could determine was from the right at perhaps 15 knots. Carl dialed in his windage setting. "I've added 1.5 mils of right windage."

"How much is that in MOAs?"

Carl did the calculation in his head. "5.2 should get you close."

Pete added the windage setting to his sight.

Just then, a gunfight erupted between the two groups. Several bodies dropped quickly and the others darted to take cover. Carl swiftly checked on the search team. They clearly heard the gunfire and were showing concern. Two of the antagonists retreated north on Ridge Road, toward the search team. Carl drew a bead on the closest man. "I've got the lead guy. Take the second one."

"I'm on him."

The two men continued to fire their weapons at obscured targets. Impact puffs of brick were seen in their vicinity. They were clearly being shot at from positions not visible to Pete and Carl.

Mike must have assessed the approaching gunfire as an excessive threat. The team made a break to extricate themselves from the growing threat. Alex was the first to cross Ridge Road, running as best he could on the packed snow. The closest man must have heard or sensed movement behind him. The man quickly looked both ways and probably felt threatened. Dave ran across the street, and then Nick. The threat must have exceeded his threshold of tolerance. He turned and fired a pistol shot. Carl squeezed off a shot. The dull thud marked the shot downrange. Carl withdrew the bolt, ejecting the cartridge without taking his eye off his target, and chambered another round. The shot hit the man dead center in the chest and knocked him against the wall. He bounced down and lay motionless. The sharp report from the M1903 startled Carl. He took a deep breath, focused on his sight, and moved his sight reticle to the second man. He was on the ground, as well. The second man struggled to rollover presumably for a shot at the search team. Carl squeezed off another round and stopped any further movement. The additional shots must have attracted the attention of the compatriots of the fallen men. The motionless prostrate men apparently inflamed their compatriots. Six men, in succession, shot at their original antagonists, as they ran from their cover positions toward their fallen comrades.

"Let's see if these guys choose to pursue the search team," Carl said softly.

"I'm watching."

The men checked on their two fallen friends. When they confirmed the two men were dead, they appeared agitated and pointed to the street the search team had disappeared down. They moved to pursue.

"I'll take the first one. Let's see if that slows them down." Carl concentrated on the lead man advancing with a semi-automatic pistol in his right hand. He momentarily disappeared behind a corner building. When he reappeared on the south side of Washington Avenue, he raised his right hand, as if preparing to shoot at the retreating search team. Carl squeezed off another round. The shot missed just to the left of his torso and kicked up a cloud of snow and ice, and probably made a ricochet sound off the pavement underneath. The confusion and uncertainty of what had just happened caused the man to pause and turn to assess what happened. That hesitation proved fatal, and the second round impacted the center of his chest and killed him instantly. The next man appeared and displayed signs of shock on seeing the blood and his prostrate, motionless colleague. The next round impacted the center of his abdomen and knocked him back, bouncing him off the corner of the building. By the time he hit the ground, he was struggling to find cover. Carl considered a kill-shot, but decided the man was on the path to a slow death without a second shot. Saving the ammunition seemed more important.

"The others are backing away," Pete whispered.

"Let's watch them. We might want to take action." Carl found the team. They were crossing the Blue River at the Lincoln Avenue – 4 O'Clock Run Road Bridge. "The team is across the river. Where are the bad guys?" Carl asked, as he searched the streets.

"At Ridge and Adams. It looks like they are having a conference, trying to figure out what happened."

"I doubt they heard the shots."

"Yeah. They seem to be confused."

Carl found the four men talking together in a small shop entry alcove on the east side of Ridge Road, not quite to Adams Avenue. *This is the perfect shot.* All four of them were clearly visible and surrounded on three sides by the shop's entrance. "I've got 'em. Should we take them out?"

Pete did not respond promptly. He was probably considering Carl's query. "Let's see if they try to follow the search team."

They watched. Snowflakes began to fall—very light at the moment, and the snow was not falling vertically. The group looked around their surroundings. The men were still trying to figure out what happened. Then, Carl saw one of them pointed almost directly toward their perch. They were trying to figure out where a sniper would be perched. "Did you see that?" Carl asked softly.

"Yeah. I think they've figured things out."

"We'd better take them before they come searching up here."

"Agreed."

"Let's go together. I'll go left to right. You go right to left. Ready?"

"Ready."

"OK. Here we go. Three, two, one." Pete's rifle shot report was the only sound and it was very loud in the apartment bedroom, especially compared to the dull thud of the Remington. Two men fell. The other two hesitated in the confusion, just a moment too long, as the second shots struck home. Both Pete and Carl chambered their next rounds. "I see only one moving."

"Yeah, me too."

"Let's see what he does." Without taking his eye out of his sight, Carl asked, "Larry, can you see the team?"

"Yes sir."

"Where are they?"

"They are on 4 O'Clock Run, nearly behind the building."

"OK." Again, without taking his eye out of the sight, Carl continued, "If you're OK with it, Pete, let's send Larry to meet the team and tell them what has happened. I think we need to stay here and make sure no one tries to follow or find us."

"Agreed."

"Are you OK with that, Larry?"

"Yes sir."

"Then, tell the team we are making sure the scene is safe before we return to the apartment."

"Yes sir," Larry responded. "I'm off."

They heard him depart.

"You've raised a good boy, Pete," Carl observed, as he reloaded the internal magazine of the rifle.

"Thanks. I could say the same for your children."

"Thanks. Now, let's close this out, so we can both get back to our families."

"Aye aye, sir."

Carl smiled at the nautical response. "Let's search the streets and buildings for anyone who may be watching or moving to follow the search team."

"Got it. As before, I'll take the south of Washington."

"Yep."

Carl methodically searched from the near field, across the river, to each street. Each window and door in every building he could see. The sky was darkening substantially. Snow was falling more heavily. The buildings on French Street, and then Ridge Road were no longer visible, even with the optics of the rifle sight. "Did you see anything?" Carl asked.

"Nope. Just snow."

"I've seen nothing either. We'd better get back to base before the snow gets too deep."

Without a verbal reply, Pete laid his rifle on the chest, closed the window, and then closed the curtain. With the darkening outside, the interior became nearly pitch black. Carl allowed his eyes to adjust. He retrieved the M1A. They made their way out of the perch apartment and back to Building 3 and the base apartment. By the time the two fathers reached the warmth of the home base, everyone was inside. They quickly figured out that Nick had been wounded in the left arm. Barb and Janet were tending to the treatment of his wound. Barb was stitching up the wound, while Nick bit down on a rolled dishtowel. The muffled screams illuminated Barb's needlework without anesthesia and vodka as a disinfectant. Once they were finished and had cleaned his wound, they carried out a mission debriefing.

The Heartstone Restaurant had not yet been disturbed when the team entered. Unfortunately, the eatery did not have a deep supply inventory. They had nearly completed their search of the premises when the shooting started. They talked about the risk of exposure and decided to make a break for home, rather than risk being in the restaurant when one of the belligerent teams came to them. Nick had been grazed in the arm during their escape. The team managed to return with modest size canned goods and several loaves of frozen bread that appeared edible.

"Did you get 'em, Dad?" asked Nick, gritting his teeth in pain.

"Yep, Mister Higgins and I dropped all eight of them."

"We only heard two shots from across the river," observed Alex.

"Those were the 1903. Nice to know the Remington cannot be heard in town," Carl added.

"Are we going to go back into town tonight," asked Mike, "like we did yesterday to collect up their weapons?"

"We don't need more guns," interjected Janet. "We have enough, already." She was probably more worried about the risk than the quantity of firearms in the arsenal.

Carl ignored his wife's admonition. "I suspect we may have to pass on that one," he said, and then he went to the blackout curtain over the balcony window. The snow was so heavy the adjacent buildings were nearly obscured by blowing snow. Carl replaced the curtain and turned to the group illuminated by the modest fire. "With snow like that," he said, gesturing with his right thumb over his right shoulder, "we are not likely going anywhere soon."

"When the snow stops . . . ?" Alex asked.

"We will evaluate our situation through the storm and reassess a possible recovery mission when the snow begins to let up. Until then, I suggest we rest as much as we can."

Several of the boys did just that and laid down on their mattresses, probably the descent from the adrenaline rush of the engagement in town.

Before Nick moved, Carl looked to him. "How's your arm, Son?"

"Hurts like hell . . . but at least, the bleeding has stopped."

"Good. It's going to be sore for a week or so."

"Have you ever been wounded, Dad?"

"Yes . . . a couple of times . . . shrapnel from anti-aircraft fire . . . a little more serious than yours."

Just then, Lisa winced in pain and called, "Oh!" She grasped the bottom of her distended abdomen.

"Contractions?" asked Janet.

"It felt like a severe cramp, and then went away."

"Your water has not broken, yet, has it?" Barb asked.

"No. I'm still . . ." Another contraction stopped her reply, and she groaned with the pain.

Barb placed her hands just above Lisa's hands and felt the contraction. "Probably Braxton-Hicks. The birth is not far off."

Lisa began to cry.

"What's wrong sweetheart?" asked her mother.

"I'm scared, Momma. Childbirth up here . . . in these conditions . . . I'm scared."

"We will just have to do this the old fashioned way . . . the way humans have delivered offspring successfully for millennia."

"What if something goes wrong?"

"Then," Barb answered, "we will deal with what comes, just as we did with Nick's wound. Humans survived and prospered without hospitals and doctors. We will get through this, perhaps not without struggle, in fine form."

Another contraction tensed Lisa's body, and she groaned again against the full pain.

"You should lay down, sweetheart," Janet said. "I'll get a cold compress. It will help." Janet helped her daughter to her feet and to her mattress. She assisted her daughter to lie down. Janet went to the bathroom, found a fresh washcloth, dampened it in the ice-cold water, and returned to the living room. Lisa was on her right side in a semi-fetal position. Barb had covered her with a blanket. Janet touched the cold, damp cloth to her forehead, which caused her to suck in a deep breath.

As Lisa adjusted to the cold compress, she said, "That actually feels good." She closed her eyes and seemed to relax a little.

Carl watched until things calmed down, and then laid down himself. Sleep claimed him quickly and lasted for an unrealized amount of time, until Janet woke him.

"We need to eat," Janet said.

"Sure."

They ate another rare sumptuous meal of grilled venison, green beans and new potatoes. Carl wanted some wine to go with the meal, but water had to do. Lisa's cramps had disappeared and she was back to herself. Nick had come to grips with the pain of his wound. Carl noted a sense of refreshment in the banter. He finished quickly, excused himself from the table, and went to the blackout curtain. Darkness made visibility nearly zero, yet, there was no escaping the heavy blowing snow that continued unabated. The drift on the balcony was already more than a foot deep in places. He restored the curtain and turn to the group.

"Still snowing heavily," Carl announced.

"Too bad we can't be skiing in this fresh powder," Alex commented.

"Yeah," added Larry, inducing several of the younger ones to laugh.

"So no recovery mission?" asked Mike.

"Not tonight. Now, the question is, how long will this storm last and how much snow will we have to deal with on the other side?"

"But, we are safe," Janet added.

"Yes, for now. We should enjoy whatever respite we can find. Things are going to get worse before they get better."

"You said that before, Dad," Nick said. "Where are the people? Where is the worse?"

Carl smiled and scanned the family looking to him. "To be blunt, I have asked myself the same question several times a day for the last week or so. We have only seen a mere fraction of the people who had to be in the valley when the power went out. Some of them have already perished for one reason or another. Others are probably holed up to avoid any conflict. As food becomes scarcer, people will become progressively more desperate and aggressive; it is the nature of survival. We must be prepared to fight for survival."

"Should we reach out to some of the other people," Pete asked, paused, and then added, "at least to some of those in our condo complex?"

Carl considered the aspects of Pete's query. "There are positives and negatives. Having more eyes and more defenders is certainly a positive." Carl stared at Pete. "My primary concern is thinning our food supply. We have been extraordinarily lucky to collect sufficient food to make it to spring. To be painfully harsh, unless new members bring a comparable food supply, I think the negatives seriously outweigh any positives."

"That is indeed a bit harsh, Carl," Janet said.

"It is!" Carl asserted. "I don't really care about nice in times like these. I am only interested in the survival of our families. We've got to make it to spring, when the roads clear, with sufficient supplies to defend ourselves on the trek out of these mountains."

"I'm afraid I'm with Carl on this issue," Pete contributed. "I am grateful . . . we are grateful," he said, pointing to Barb and Larry, "you welcomed us into your family."

"Your contribution to our collective defense has been invaluable . . . a mutually beneficial relationship."

"OK," interjected Barb. "Enough lovey-dovey bro-mance stuff. We have a birth to prepare for." Everyone looked to Barb Higgins without words. "I don't want to presume, Janet, that since I have the only medical degree in this august group, the birthing will fall to me."

"We will look to you, Barb," responded Janet.

"There is going to be lots of fluids and blood. We will need the shower curtain. We'll put a clean sheet over the shower curtain. If I may ask a rather intimate question, Lisa . . ." Barb asked. Lisa nodded, somewhat reluctantly. "I do not know how modest you may wish to be."

Lisa seemed puzzled. "What do you mean, Mrs. Higgins?"

"Depending upon how the birth progresses, you are going to be in various positions and potentially exposed. We all should do our best to respect your wishes and desires. This is your moment, no one else's, Lisa. I suppose the most discreet way to ask this is, do you want the family to watch the birthing process?"

"If they want to watch, I have no problem with that."

"OK. Then, we will not worry about a modesty curtain or covering you up. We will need to orient your pelvis toward the fire for the best light we can get in these circumstances." Lisa nodded her head in acknowledgment and consent. "We will do our best to make you as comfortable as we can. Whom would you like to cut the chord?"

"My Dad," Lisa answered without hesitation.

Carl smiled and nodded his head.

"Once her water breaks and labor begins, we will need a pot of boiling water to wash and sterilize towels and clothes to avoid infection."

"I'll take care of that," Janet volunteered.

Barb nodded her agreement. "Once the baby is out, I will need to focus on the baby. Janet, if I could ask you to tend to Lisa. She may need assistance in delivering the placenta. I do not mean to be crude, but given the state of things, frankness is warranted. Lisa will likely need assistance getting her milk to let down. The baby is going to be hungry fairly soon after birth and will need nourishment. The only source that will work for the next few months will be your breasts," Barb said, looking to Lisa.

"We will do what needs to be done," Janet said.

Carl went to the blackout curtain, again. He checked the weather conditions outside and turned back to the group. "It's dark, now. From what I can see, the storm is still raging. It may last for hours or days. We have no way to know. Childbirth could come any minute, now. We all better get as much sleep as we can with what time is left. We have an opportunity. Let's take it." Carl did not wait for a response. He went to their mattress and laid down. Janet joined him and snuggled to his left shoulder and the crook of his neck. They kissed, and then fell asleep together. Tomorrow would be another day, undoubtedly full of more challenges.

—

13

Lisa's muffled scream woke everyone. Janet and Barb were on either side of Lisa.

"What happened?" Carl asked.

Without taking her eyes off Lisa, Janet answered, "Her water broke an hour ago. It looks like her labor contractions have begun."

Carl checked his wristwatch—01:13. It was the middle of the night. Although he would not be able to see much outside, Carl felt the urge to look. He could not see anything, but he did hear the wind blowing. *The drifts for this storm are going to be worse than the last few.* Carl restored the curtain and went to Lisa.

The boys were awake and had gathered in the kitchen area well behind Lisa, as if there was something contagious with their sister.

Carl looked at the boys and recognized what was about to come. "I need two volunteers to stand guard in the lobby. This is going to be very noisy, and I do not us to be surprised."

"I'll go," offered Dave.

"I'd like to go with him," Larry added.

"OK. Grab your weapons of choice. Don't engage anyone, just alert us if anyone approaches this building."

"Yes sir."

"I'll go with 'em," Pete said.

Pete and the boys went to the arsenal room, grabbed shotguns, and departed.

The mothers had moved the couch toward the wall and positioned Lisa's mattress directly in front of the fire for the best light they could obtain. Their daughter had only a thin white T-shirt on her torso that was already damp. Her pelvis and legs were bare. Her knees were spread and raised. Lisa held the bottom of her swollen and tight abdomen. Barb was positioned between her legs, slightly to the right side to use the light she had. Barb probed Lisa's birth canal several times in between contractions.

"I cannot see much, but the best I can determine, she has effaced. I cannot see how much. I am fairly certain the baby is properly positioned."

Lisa was panting and she was clearly sweating. The pain had probably become more persistent between the heavier contractions.

"Try not to push until you get a little farther along. Let the contractions do the work for now."

Lisa screamed loudly and a strong contraction racked her body. "Oh God . . . it hurts . . . so much," Lisa choked out between her panting for air.

"Do you want the towel to bite down on?" asked Janet, ". . . like Nick used."

Lisa could only feebly nod her head. Janet got the rolled towel just in time. Lisa lurched to bite down on the towel that muffled her scream as the contraction hit full force. Barb watched Lisa's pelvic muscles contract and pulse.

Janet held a washcloth. "Get this wet with cold water," she commanded.

Alex jumped forward, took the washcloth and disappeared down the hall. He returned quickly with the refreshed washcloth. Janet took it without words and wiped Lisa's face.

"Can I see?" Larry asked surprisingly.

Barb looked to Lisa, who was in between contractions, and gestured as if to say your call dear. Lisa looked over her shoulder briefly and nodded her head without letting go of her pain towel. Barb gestured for Larry to come forward and directed him to the precise spot she wanted him to stand, so he could see but not interfere with her available light.

Another contraction racked Lisa's body as she raised her head until her chin contacted her chest. She screamed against the towel. Janet dabbed Lisa's forehead and cheeks.

"Don't push, yet," Barb commanded. "Let the contractions expand your vaginal muscles. We want to try and avoid tearing any tissue." Lisa nodded her acknowledgment as the contraction subsided.

"Four minutes," Carl announced. The women understood his statement as the frequency between contractions.

As the birthing progressed, Barb kept up with the approach of the baby. "The head is well positioned. We just need to get through the stretch."

The frequency of contractions increased a little with each event. Lisa became irritated with the now soaking wet and virtually transparent T-shirt. She wanted it off and started to attempt the removal on her own. Carl supported her head and torso. Janet joined her husband in the removal of her T-shirt. As Lisa laid back down, Janet used the cool washcloth to wipe down her torso. Carl and Janet rolled her slightly between contractions to wipe her back as well. Carl noted the deteriorating impact of the pain on Lisa's dulling alertness, attention and focus. She was slowly retreating into a fog. They all worked to make her as comfortable as they could, but the pain of her body's enormous exertion was taking her deeper into the fog.

"She still has a few centimeters to go," Barb announced, regarding the effacement of Lisa's cervix. "Carl, Pete, each of you take a leg. Support her knees and legs." The two fathers did as they were commanded.

Carl felt his daughter's leg tense, as another contraction hit her and she strained against the pain. He twisted his left wrist to check his watch. "Two minutes, 30 seconds," he noted.

They continued their efforts to give Lisa the most comfort they could. She wanted ice chips. Mike and Nick went to the task without being asked. The boys returned with a glass of small ice chips, almost like crushed ice. They also helped their sister get the cold chips in her mouth. The eyes of both boys widened substantially as they absorbed the scene before them.

"How are you doing?" Barb asked Lisa.

"I'm so tired. I just want this done."

Barb chuckled softly. "As your Mom will attest, that is a very normal feeling."

"The pain is too mu . . ." A scream stopped her reply and filled the room before she could return the bite-down towel to her mouth. Lisa's breathing became short and pulsey. Her screams transitioned to deep, guttural growls, as she fought and strained against the pain. The heavy contraction lasted for nearly a minute, but seemed like hours and eventually subsided.

"Deep breaths," Carl said.

Lisa tried feebly to breathe as deeply as she could to clear her lungs and oxygenate her blood.

"OK. That one did the trick. It appears you are now fully effaced. It's time to push."

"I can't," Lisa cried. "I'm too tired. It hurts too much."

"We know, Lisa. You are not the first woman to birth a child."

"I'm too tired. Just get it out."

"You are nearly there. The baby wants out. We all want to help you get the baby out, but we cannot push for you."

"You can do it, sweetie," Carl said softly.

"The next contraction will be coming shortly. When you feel it begin, I want you to bear down like a bowel movement. The baby is doing its part. Now, you must do yours."

Lisa nodded her head in what appeared to be resigned consent.

Nick left without being asked and returned with a fresh cold washcloth. Janet smiled at Nick, took the proffered cloth, and wiped down her daughter, again. Lisa took some more ice chips, while her mother finished swabbing her body.

The next contraction hit. Lisa screamed against her bite-down towel.

"Push!" commanded Barb.

Lisa grasped the top of her abdomen in response. She grunted hard as she tensed her already stretched, painful and tight abdominal muscles.

"That's it," Barb commented.

Lisa continued to strain and groan loudly, as she huffed hard for air. When the contraction subsided, Lisa fell back to the mattress with a thud.

Carl could see the crown of the baby's skull protruding ever so slightly, but definitely closer. Progress was being made.

Nick offered his sister some more ice chips that she gratefully consumed.

The birthing process continued with slow but steady progress for another hour. When Carl glanced at his wristwatch, it was 05:37—pretty good progress by contemporary birthing standards . . . well, at least to Carl's knowledge and awareness. Lisa felt no sense of time—only the pain consuming her body.

Then, Barb surprisingly announced, "You're very close, Lisa. I think the next contraction may well do it. So, prepare yourself. I want you to push nice, hard and steady." Lisa feebly nodded her head in acknowledgment with her eyes closed. The exhaustion of her exertion and debilitating pain dulled her face. Her hair was as wet as if she had just come out of the shower. The contraction hit hard and sharply, and seemed to surprise even Lisa. "OK, Lisa push. Let's get this baby out."

Pete and Carl held her knees up and out, and supported her shoulders to assist Lisa in her effort. She was straining so hard, like she was forcing her guts out.

"That's it! Here it comes." Carl saw the baby's eyes—still closed, and then the nose. "Almost here. Just a little more. Keep pushing, Lisa. Yes, yes . . . that's it." Then, the baby virtually squirted out of Lisa's body and into Barb's waiting hands.

Carl gestured to the boys for a pen and paper. He checked his wristwatch—07:16. Carl noted the time. *I have no idea what the date is.* He would have to do his best to calculate the birth date, once the dust settled from the turmoil of birth. For the sake of the historical recording, Carl noted Barbara Higgins as the midwife, and both families as witnesses. No name, yet.

Barb's attention immediately turned to and focused on the baby—a girl. She quickly wiped the baby to evaluate the infant for any injuries or abnormalities. Without the normal tools of childbirth, Barb resorted to the only method she had and covered the baby's mouth and nose with her mouth, and sucked to clear the mouth, nose and throat. She spit the extracted mucous into a separate, used towel. Barb repeated the procedure several times, until she removed as much as she could get. She rolled the baby slightly and smacked her back a couple of times. The second strike caused the girl to cough and suck in a big breath. Her skin instantly turned from light blue to bright pink and she let out an impressively healthy cry, for being disturbed from the comfort of her mother's womb. Once the girl was breathing and crying, Barb grabbed two pieces of twine. She tied off the umbilical cord at the baby's heaving abdomen, and then tied the other piece about an inch away from the first tie. Barb then grabbed a waiting pair of scissors and handed them to Carl.

"The honor is yours," Barb said to Carl.

Carl lowered her knee and placed her foot close to her buttock, leaving her groin still open. Pete did the same. Janet took Barb's place between Lisa's knees. The new grandfather took the scissors, placed them between the two ties, and cut the cord. Just about the only blood in the process so far squirted out onto the sheet. Janet pulled gently on the cord to see if the placenta was ready to release. It was not.

Barb finished cleaning up the infant girl, and then lay the baby face down on Lisa's bare chest. Mother and child were skin-to-skin. The contact stopped the baby's crying instantly. Carl grabbed a couple of pillows and propped up Lisa's head, so she did not have to strain to hold eye-to-eye contact. Barb placed a small, soft blanket over Lisa's torso, more to keep the baby warm rather than for whatever modesty Lisa may have felt. Mother and daughter stared into each other's eyes for several minutes, until the baby began to stir and whimper.

Without prompting, Barb uncovered Lisa's right breast and squeezed her right areola several times to express the colostrum and open her milk ducts. She massaged her right breast. Lisa winced several times—her breasts were clearly swollen and sore. Barb gently shifted the baby's position to touch Lisa's nipple to her mouth. Instinct worked precisely. The child found the nipple, took it in her mouth, and began to suckle. Barb did not wait for progress and immediately went around to Lisa's left breast. She repeated the process of stimulating Lisa's milk to let downfrom her left breast. Lisa winced a few more times, as Barb massaged her left breast. Barb achieved successful. Lisa's left breast was ready.

"How is the baby doing?" Barb asked Lisa.

"I think she is getting something. The pressure is decreasing."

"Excellent."

"Thank you," Lisa answered.

"You are most welcome. I am just so glad the birth went well." Barb looked at Janet. "Placenta delivery should be nearly there."

Janet continued to periodically press on Lisa's lower abdomen and tugged gently on the cord. The placenta eventually detached and was expelled. Lisa wrapped the expended tissue in a soiled towel and set it aside for disposal. The associated bleeding was minimal, and Janet readily mopped up what blood did appear. Barb rolled up a fresh, small towel, placed it vertically between Lisa's legs, and then gently lowered and closed her legs to hold the towel in place.

"You need to rest, Lisa," Barb said. "Let Mom see if she can get a good burp, and then we can see if she will take any more from your left breast." Lisa nodded her head, barely alert. Barb lifted the baby from Lisa's chest and handed her to Janet, who placed the baby on her left shoulder and gently patted her back. A good, audible belch marked success.

Barb covered Lisa with the blanket. They would clean up Lisa later. "Do we have any diapers?" Barb asked.

"No," answered Janet. "None of us expected to be delivering a baby in the mountains."

"I'll have to fashion at least a makeshift diaper. The baby will be passing fluids soon."

"We'll have to add that to the list for our searches," noted Carl.

Janet placed the baby at Lisa's left breast. New mother and child were both asleep. Barb found a small, fresh towel, folded it into a triangle, and tied the towel around the baby's pelvis. She also found a small sheet to swaddle the infant. They fashioned a small bumper bed and lay the baby down.

Carl looked into the eyes of both Janet and Barbara. "You ladies need to get some rest. The boys will clean up what we can and let you sleep as long as you can." He went to the blackout curtain. It was daylight, but still quite dark. The snow continued to fall heavily, obscuring virtually everything. The adjacent buildings were barely visible. "Looks like this storm is going to be a doozy." He checked his wristwatch—08:56. Carl turned back to the ladies. "Please get some rest while you can. Lisa is going to need your help. We'll take it from here."

The ladies knew Carl was correct and gave in to their exhaustion.

The boys quietly collected the towels, sheets and other paraphernalia utilized for the birth. Alex and Nick jumped into washing the utensils. Carl and Mike took turns with Pete and Larry carefully washing the cloth items to avoid contaminating their water supply. The remainder of the hot water from the fireplace made the process easier. They used a makeshift washboard that had been an oven rack in the days when the oven worked. It was not an ideal set-up, but it worked. They managed to clean the cloth items surprisingly well. The men and boys wrung each cloth item to remove as much water as they could into a waste bucket. Their situation left them with no choice but to dry the items in the already crowded living room kitchen area; if they tried to use the bedrooms, the wet items would simply freeze, not dry. The women and the baby were still asleep. They spread everything out on chairs, the table, the available counter tops and any piece of furniture that would not absorb the dampness.

When they finished the clean-up task, Carl checked the exterior, again, and then motioned for the males to follow him to the arsenal room. He wanted to talk without disturbing the sleeping women. Once everyone was inside, Carl closed the door. "The storm is still in full form and may well continue for the next day or more. I'd suggest everyone get as much sleep as possible. I'm going to stand watch, so to speak, to tend the baby when she awakes."

"When do you want relief?" Pete asked.

"Don't worry about it. Things will start to happen soon enough." Pete nodded his recognition. "Any other questions?"

"I'm not sleepy, Dad," Alex said. "I'd like to stay up with you."

"That's up to you, Son. I'm good with it . . . the same for anyone else. We just need to be quiet . . . to let people sleep as much as they can. Anything else?" Everyone shook his head in the negative. "OK. Let's get to it, just remember . . . be quiet."

The male group filed out of the arsenal room. While most of the boys descended to their mattresses, Carl went again to the blackout curtain and Alex followed. The already heavy snowfall appeared to increase in intensity, darkening the sky even farther.

"Can I see, Dad?"

"Sure," Carl answered and stepped back, allowing his youngest son a view.

"Wow!"

"Yeah. This one is a serious storm. The drifts are going to be difficult to deal with in the first few days after the storm ends." While Alex continued to peer into the raging storm outside, Carl added, "We need to keep our guard up. Moving around in a storm like this would not be easy and would inherently make anyone more vulnerable. Yet, on the flipside, people would not expect anyone in their right mind to be out in this stuff."

"Then, shouldn't we be on guard?"

"I've seen no signs of movement—human or animal—since the snow began. So, the risk is low."

"What should we look for?" asked Alex.

"Tracks . . . disturbances in the snow . . . like brush marks . . . attempts to cover tracks."

"When you see 'em, would you show me what they look like?"

"Sure. But, I hope we don't see those signs for quite some time."

"What will they mean?"

"In one word . . . danger. It means people are becoming more desperate, willing to take progressively greater risks to survive. That is the point when people will kill for food."

"You've killed quite a few people so far."

"Yes, I have, but for purely defensive purposes. We have not killed to take."

"But, we have stolen other people's stuff."

"Yes, we have, Alex, for our survival and to prevent anyone else from taking the stuff. The reality is, no one is coming here and getting us out of here until spring, or later . . . potentially much later."

"It is a fine point. You're splitting hairs, don't you think, Dad."

"Perhaps, yet, that is how I see it. In these circumstances, I have only one job, one task . . . protect our family. That means providing sustenance and getting us out of these mountains when springtime comes."

"I have so much to learn."

"I am sorry you have to learn these lessons, in this way. At least, you are able to . . ." They heard the baby whimper. "I better check on her. See if you can find one of those cloth napkins. The baby probably needs a diaper change . . . and maybe a snack."

They left the curtain. The baby was awake and fidgeting. She did need her diaper changed. Carl waited for Alex to return with a cloth napkin—the perfect size. *At least we have a few more.* Carl changed the baby's makeshift diaper, and it did indeed need to be changed. The doubled up napkin fit perfectly. Carl re-swaddled the baby. Her mouth opened and her eyes squinted, as is she was winding up to cry. *There is probably only one other thing a baby this age would want.*

Lisa was sleeping soundly. She had not moved. She was on her back and so still, like she was laid out on a morgue preparation table. Carl very gently and slowly uncovered her left breast, and positioned the infant's mouth at her nipple. The baby eagerly took to the task of feeding herself. A pillow propped her up in position. She suckled for several minutes, and then detached. Carl lifted the baby to his left shoulder and patted her back until she burped without expelling any of her consumed milk. Carl returned the baby to her momma's breast, until she was sated and fell asleep. Carl felt her makeshift diaper. She was dry. Carl returned the baby to her pseudo-crib and covered his daughter's chest.

By the time Carl finished his grandfatherly tasks, Alex had gone out onto the balcony, using the small provided shovel to clear the deepening drift. The younger Parks was nearly done with his task, although the snowfall remained

heavy and the wind rather brisk. Snowdrifts would continue to accumulate
. . . at least until the wind shifted direction. As Alex finished one portion of
the balcony, the other side had accumulated snow. The youngest of the Parks'
children cycled a couple of times before he had had enough and came inside.

"A never-ending task," Carl chuckled softly. ". . . at least until the snow
stops. Thank you for doing that."

"You're welcome."

"Have you seen or know where Mom's purse is?"

"I think so."

"See if you can find her day planner."

"OK."

While Alex hopped to his task, Carl found his previous note on the time
of birth. He moved to the fireplace, poked the wood to stimulate a flame. It
was not yet time for a new piece of wood. At their rate of consumption, they
still had a month's supply—not enough to make it to springtime. No need to
consume more of their scarce candles, when the fire would give him sufficient
light. Alex returned with Janet's day-planner.

"What are you doing?" asked Alex, as he handed the small booklet to
his father.

"While I've got a moment to think, I need to calculate the baby's birth
day . . . to make a quasi-birth certificate."

Alex smiled and sat down on the hearth on the other side of his father
from the modest fire.

Fortunately, the planner had an extra month. Carl started at December
19th—the day they arrived. He remembered the nightmare. The crisis began
during the night with the realization of the situation on the 20th. Carl then
noted the day events in a few words and conferred several times to make sure
he remembered events on a particular day.

"Well, by my calculations, today is the 4th of January. We missed our
New Year's celebration."

"Not exactly a time to celebrate. Seems rather frivolous in these conditions."

Carl chuckled softly. He rechecked his calculations. "OK." Carl recorded
the date calculation on the paper and in the planner. He wrote a space for
the baby's name and left it blank with a female gender. Carl also added the
mother's full name, father unknown, and the names of all witnesses in addition
to Barb and Janet, as midwives. Carl added his signature next to his name, and
handed the paper and pen to Alex, who signed next to his name. "We need
to have the others sign when they awake." Alex nodded his head. Father and
son sat in silence by the fire.

After an unrealized amount of time, several of the boys began to stir.

Mike was the first to speak. "We missed our morning meal," he observed.

"Yes, we did . . . but, to stick to the rules, we must wait for everyone to be awake."

"I'd like some fresh air," Nick stated.

"Alex cleared the balcony some time ago."

"No . . . out front or out back . . . to walk around a little."

Carl thought about the situation and conditions. He went to the curtain. The snowstorm was still raging at full intensity. Turning back to the boys, Carl said, "OK, but do not go far. There are certainly difficult drifts that could strand you."

"OK," responded Mike.

"I'll go, too," Dave added.

"If you see any signs of tracks or other human activity outside, come back immediately and tell me what you saw."

"Should we be armed?" Mike asked.

"Better safe than sorry."

Mike, Nick and Dave nodded their heads and headed to the arsenal room.

"Be observant. Don't take any chances. Move away from the building and stay on the trail. Don't stay out too long."

"OK, Dad," Mike responded. "Stop worrying."

"Never," Carl answered and smiled. Carl gestured a knock, pointed at the door, held up two fingers, and then two more fingers.

The boys held up their right thumbs. Carl nodded. The boys departed. Alex locked the door behind them and braced a chair under the doorknob.

Larry and then Pete were the next to rise, followed shortly thereafter by Janet, who approached her husband and kissed him.

"Thank you," she said.

"You are most welcome, my darling."

Janet looked over to see their daughter was still asleep, as well as the baby. "What happened while I was out?"

"We cleaned everything except what is under Lisa. We also calculated the birth date as the 4th of January."

"We missed New Year's."

Carl laughed softly. "We figured that out, too."

"Where are the boys?"

"They wanted some fresh air and went for a short walkabout."

"Did the storm end?"

"Not yet."

"Carl, why are they out in a storm?"

"They are not going far. I told them to stay on the trail."

"Carl, really? Was it worth the risk?"

"You'll have to ask them. They handled themselves quite well on the mission into town yesterday. A few days ago, you argued to let the boys do more. This is part of that process, Janet. They wanted fresh air. With all this snow, they can't go far."

"I sure hope you are right."

"Me too, Janet, me too."

They noticed Barbara stirring, and then sitting up. Janet clearly wanted to talk to her, but knew enough to let her awaken as she chose, at her pace. After several minutes, Barb looked over her shoulder and waved feebly. She crawled over to check on Lisa, who was still asleep, and then to the baby. Satisfied that all was well, Barb stood and hobbled toward Janet and Carl.

"How are you?" asked Janet.

"Tired. That was pretty intense."

"You handled it extraordinarily well," Carl added.

"Thank you, but I will confess that I was scared out of my mind."

"Why?" asked Carl.

"The reality that it was just us. There was no back-up, no hospital, no doctors, no blood supply, no EMTs, nothing . . . just us . . . scared the hell outta me."

"Well, put in that context, your feelings are quite understandable."

"And, we are most grateful for the skills you brought." Janet turned to Carl. "Has Lisa awakened?"

"To my knowledge, she has not moved. The baby did wake several hours ago. I changed and cleaned her diaper. I put her to breast, and she ate well. Lisa never even twitched during the process."

"The birth must've been very hard on her," Janet said.

"That was my opinion, which is why I was not going to disturb her."

Two knocks on the door were followed after a pause by two more knocks. Alex looked to his father, who nodded his consent. Alex went to the door, checked the peephole, and then went through the process of opening the door. All three boys entered.

"How did it go?" Alex asked.

"Beautiful . . . if you like snow," answered Mike.

"How is your arm?" Janet questioned Nick.

"Sore, but it's OK."

"We probably should change your bandage." Nick nodded his head in agreement.

"We missed the morning meal," Mike observed. "I think we are all hungry."

"I am as well, but we agreed to the process, so everyone saw for themselves that apportionment was equal and fair. We do not want anyone to feel they are being treated unfairly."

"But, Lisa has always gotten a double portion," said Nick.

"Yes, she has, because she was carrying a child, and now she has given birth, she must feed the baby. She is the only one who can. Do you really want to make that a point of debate?"

"No, Dad . . . I understand . . . it's just . . . I'm hungry. I think we are all hungry."

"Oka . . ."

"How about this," interjected Janet. "We can all witness the portions, and we will set aside Lisa's double portion until she wakes up. We will collectively attest to the equality, so that we do not violate our agreement. Does that work, Carl?"

"If everyone agrees, then yes, that is a reasonable compromise given our current circumstances."

Janet did not wait. "Is everyone agreed?" Each of them checked each other. They all nodded their concurrence, except Carl who only shrugged his shoulders in resignation. "Very well. We are agreed to the amendment to our food rationing policy." Again, Janet did not wait. Carl went to check on the weather, while Janet collected the meal from the stores.

The storm still showed no signs of abating. Carl scanned the exterior as best he could and saw no indications of human or animal activity . . . just a lot of fresh, virgin snow. Vehicles in the parking lot were no longer recognizable; they were just mounds of snow now.

Janet returned to the kitchen. Carl stayed at the window. When Janet finished establishing the portions, she called Carl over so they could all witness the portions. She separated 10 portions with Lisa's double. Each of them had three roughly equal strips of jerky, five Ritz crackers and a glass of water. They ate in silence. None of them noticed Lisa.

"My breasts are so sore," she pronounced softly, as she sat up.

"They are producing milk the baby needs," Janet answered, as she moved toward her daughter.

Barb joined her. "I need to check your vagina, Lisa. Are you OK with that?"

Lisa lifted the blanket off her lower body. "I'm naked already, so yes I'm OK."

Janet checked on the baby, who was still asleep and not stirring.

Barb attended to Lisa. She checked the crotch towel first. There was some additional blood, but it appeared to be comparatively old and partially coagulated—a positive sign. Barb had Lisa lie back, and raise and spread her knees. Barb used a candle to illuminate the focus of her examination to the best extent possible. She asked for and received a damp washcloth to gently clean the residual dried blood and fluids. Barb pronounced, "For a woman who has given birth just this morning, you are in extraordinarily good shape."

"I certainly don't feel that good. I am so sore . . . everywhere."

"Even though your mom and I are the only two other mothers, I cannot imagine how you must feel without the benefit of modern medicine. Your birth was textbook and a comparatively short delivery process. We did the best we could to help you, but my dear, it was all you. The pain will pass in a week or so, and diminish in a few days." Barb looked over her shoulder to Janet. "How is the baby?"

"Good color, quiet for the moment and peaceful."

"As long as she is in good form, I'd suggest we let her sleep." Janet nodded her consent. "The baby will let us know when she is hungry or uncomfortable." Barb looked back to connect with Lisa's eyes. "For the next few weeks, your breasts will produce at their pace, not necessarily at the baby's consumption rate. We can help as you wish, however, in such circumstances, you must express your milk to relieve the pressure, since the timing between the baby's consumption and your production are not yet in synch. We have a larger freezer in the back, so we can save your expressed milk."

"How do I do that?" Lisa asked.

Barb retrieved the largest glass she could find in the apartment, and then began teaching Lisa several methods of manually extracting her milk. She learned quickly and at least achieved a point of more comfort. Once the lesson was completed and the milk covered and stored in the back bedroom, Barb encouraged her to don a large T-shirt and stand to walk around the room a little. Lisa started to sit on the couch by the fire. Janet quickly placed a folded towel beneath her, and then brought her meal portion to her.

As Lisa consumed her allotment, Janet asked, "Inquiring minds want to know, have you decided on a name for your baby girl?"

Lisa finished chewing the chunk of jerky in her mouth before answering. "Yes. I think Breckyn Lee seems most appropriate."

"Breckyn for Breckenridge?" Janet asked.

"Yes . . . B-R-E-C-K-Y-N and Lee for Grandma."

"That's a beautiful name, Sweetheart," Carl injected from the kitchen. "So, is it settled?"

"As far as I'm concerned," Lisa answered.

"Very well. I'll record the chosen full name. I've prepared a birth certificate." Carl checked the paper. "Everyone has signed the certificate, except Janet, Barbara and Lisa. Once it is signed and fully completed, I'll place it in a safe place. We'll just need to remember to take it with us when we leave this coming spring." Barb and Janet added their signatures. Lisa wanted to wait until she finished eating. Carl went to the balcony, once again. "It's nighttime and still snowing. The baby will awaken anytime now. Perhaps, we should take single, internal watches to tend Breckyn, so Lisa can sleep."

"Great idea," said Janet. "But, it is probably not fair to the boys, since they have little infant care experience."

"They need to learn," Carl stated.

"Yes, they do. How about we stand regular watches inside. Each one of the adults has one of the children with them. We can teach as we go."

Carl turned to the boys. "Does that sound reasonable?"

"Sure," Mike responded. The other boys nodded their agreement.

"Very well, then. Who wants to go first?"

"I'll volunteer Nick and me," Pete said.

"Any objections?" Hearing or seeing none, Carl said, "Very well, then. Let's do it. I will only ask each team to periodically check on the weather outside. If anything changes dramatically, we may need to reexamine our watch standing."

The group calmly dispersed. Several of the boys decided to do a little reading before sleep. Several others took to sleep directly. Carl laid down on their mattress to think and allow sleep to claim him slowly.

—

14

Breckyn's cries awakened Carl. He looked toward the baby. Janet and Mike were tending to the child, so he was confident the cries would vanish shortly. Carl laid his head back down to get whatever sleep he might be able to gain. He knew the Team Four watch cycle was due up next. Sleep swiftly claimed his consciousness.

All too soon, Mike was wiggling Carl's big toe. "It's your turn, Dad."

"Thanks, Son."

Dave was already awake and standing with Janet in the kitchen. Mike and Carl joined them.

"I woke up when the baby cried the last time, I think," Carl said very softly. "When was that?"

Janet answered, "I don't know. I don't have your wristwatch . . . but, I think an hour, maybe 90 minutes."

"OK, so Breckyn should be good for a while longer."

"Probably so."

"Anything else happened, or we need to know?"

"Nope," she said and looked to Mike. "Can you think of anything, Son?" Mike shook his head in the negative.

"Very well. We have the watch."

Janet saluted rather crudely and went to the mattress. The lack of a kiss from his wife struck Carl as odd. *What could she possibly be pissed off about? I need to remember to talk to her at the next opportunity.* Janet and Mike laid down for rest. Dave saw the need and took the initiative to add another split log to the fire. He brought the fire back to a moderate level. Carl went to the balcony, as had become his practice. It was still ink-black outside, although blowing snow was still falling, but barely detectable.

"How's it look?" Dave whispered.

"Black." They both fought to stifle a hearty laugh. When they regained control, Carl added, "It should be a quiet watch and a quiet night." The hard part of Team Four's watch period was staying awake. Nobody moved. The baby did not cry. The fire remained modest and adequate. Nothing happened. Team Four passed the watch to Team One, and then they both went back to sleep.

The cycle continued through the morning and into the afternoon. Lisa was moving a little more in between feedings for Breckyn, which was a very positive sign. The snowfall began to taper off and the sky lightened, although the storm was not entirely done. They cleared the balcony and prepared to resume their exterior watch duties.

Carl asked for the group to gather up in advance of their evening meal. "We have at least a couple more months of winter to deal with, probably more. Come spring, we are going to hike out of these mountains."

"Where to?" asked Mike.

"Based on what we know now, I would say our best shot is south, toward New Mexico. We can reach lower elevations sooner in that direction."

"But, that does not get us home," Lisa observed.

"No. Our first, most immediate, objective is to survive the winter. Our second objective, which is what I wanted to talk about is, preparation for the journey out of the mountains. We really need to start exercising, as best we can."

"Like what?" Janet asked.

"Well, anything to work our muscles and heart that does not make noise, so push-ups, sit-ups, squats, stretching and such. Running in place, or jumping jacks, stuff like that will make too much noise. The walk out of these mountains will be at least 40 miles, and given our lack of conditioning, may well take us a long day or two to make that distance, maybe more. We will all be loaded with full backpacks, since we will have to carry our food and weapons."

"Exercise," protested Lisa.

"Yes, my dear. If we don't, we take the risk of becoming crippled, which in turn would make us a burden to the rest of the team. We will try to pick a good window for the trek, to avoid getting caught in the open during a storm. In the spring, we could face more snow, ice, sleet, hail, thunderstorms, lightning and the like—none of it good without tents or protection of some kind."

"Won't someone come get us?" Alex asked.

"We cannot depend on that possibility," replied Carl, "but, it is always possible . . . especially if I have overestimated the seriousness or totality of our situation."

"When are we supposed to exercise?" Larry asked.

"I would suggest for 30 minutes before or after our respective watch periods."

"Then what?" asked Pete.

"Well, my suggestion is our next objective would be Cañon City, Colorado. Hopefully, we will find some semblance of civilization, and if we are lucky, some news about what happened and what is happening beyond this valley." Carl thought for a few moments. No one interrupted his pause. "There are many options from that point and the choice depends upon what we find. At least we would be out of the high mountains."

"Like what options?" Janet asked.

"One would be to make our way to Pueblo, heading back to Wichita for us and back to Denver for Barb and Pete. The second option, depending upon what we run into and learn, would be Albuquerque."

"And, perhaps more desperate than we are," Pete added.

"Yes, there is that; but, we are learning nothing up here and we cannot stay, which is exactly why I suggest we set our sights on Cañon City, to get out of the mountains. We'll figure things out from there."

Breckyn began whimpering as part of her effort to demand attention. Lisa jumped up and tended the baby. Janet helped Lisa clean up the baby and put their first recycled diaper on her. Once Breckyn was clean and dry, Lisa fed her.

"OK," Janet protested. "Enough of this doomsday crap. How about I heat up a couple of those big cans of beef stew, and Carl, you can grill up some additional meat."

"As you wish, but before we close this discussion, I just want to remind everyone that we have a very long, hard, foot journey ahead in a few months. Hoosier Pass is 11,500 feet. It will be really thin air up there and most likely cold. We really must prepare for that hike."

"Understood, Carl," said Janet. "Now, let's get our families fed." She did not wait for approval and went to the supply room to retrieve the cans she wanted.

Carl went to the curtain first. The snow had stopped. He saw a patch of blue sky to the west. The sun was perhaps an hour past the western ridgeline. He asked the boys to clear off the last remnants of snow from the balcony and prepare for exterior watch standing after their meal. Nick and Dave took that task. Carl went to their freezer room, found a package of buffalo meat, and returned to the kitchen. The meat was frozen solid. Fortunately, the previous owner has sliced the large, loin roast into 18, fillet-size pieces; they would have extra, but he would cook the whole amount. Carl used a strong knife to chisel apart the fillets of dark brown meat. Pete had already used the fireplace tongs and poker to place the grill rack at the highest level they could in the fireplace, to allow them to slowly cook the meat above the pot of stew. The preparation process took an hour or so to complete.

Breckyn was awake and alert through the meal preparation phase. They each took turns holding her and connecting with her absorptive blue eyes. She had her mother's eyes.

They all ate together as one large family. The evening meal conversation focused on the good memories from before the crisis. Laughter spotted the remembrances. For the first time, they learned that Pete was a successful, practicing, corporate attorney, and Barb had been working at a local hospital in Denver. The conversation was collectively light-hearted and airy, until Pete looked to Carl and asked, "Should we check on the other apartments?" The conversation stopped and everyone looked to Carl.

"What do you mean?"

"Well, as I recall per your survey chart, we have searched each of the unoccupied units in this complex, but we have not tried to make contact with other survivors who may be out there. There are probably others . . . at least there were from your survey."

"Yeah."

"Opening or closing a curtain, or the flicker of a fireplace had to be done by humans . . . survivors."

"Good point. How many of those do you know?"

"I'd have to look at your chart, but we must know some. The problem is, we probably know the owners, but they may have rented out their apartments during ski season."

Carl found the chart they had created and used during their initial searches. He placed it on the table in front of Pete. "Can you mark any of the year-round residences?"

Pete found a pen and studied the chart. He circled three units: 111, 421 and 512. "The Bensons live below us in this building. That's 321. They are regular residences, but the last time we saw them was . . . what Barb . . . a week before the blackout."

"That's about right," Barb added.

"We haven't really checked this building, since we could not observe the units below us. It's too late for that kind of reconnaissance tonight. So, as long as the weather holds, we can make that outreach tomorrow. My concern is and remains, what do we do even if we find others? We probably have sufficient food for our two families, but if we start dividing it up, we will place ourselves at risk . . . at the very least, weakening ourselves before the long, hard march out of the mountains." *I am not going to mention the reserves outside, stored along the trail. They may never be needed.* "We don't know what condition they might be in."

"True. We will never know unless we try."

"Agreed, but we must have a plan. The best case is they have their own supplies and they wish to join us. The worst case is they have no supplies or very little. What do you propose we do when they plead for assistance?"

"I had not thought of that . . . but, I can see it is a serious concern and worthy of our contemplation."

"We just need an agreed to plan for possible outcomes."

"Let me think about that. We'll talk later." Carl nodded his head.

They cleaned their bowls and utensils as best they could with the limited water allocated to the task.

"Where did we leave off on the watch rotation?" asked Carl.

"Team One finished theirs," volunteered Pete. "So, Team Two is up next."

Carl passed his wristwatch to Pete. "Better bundle up good. It's probably going to be a very cold one tonight."

Pete took the proffered watch. They had about ten minutes to go. He kissed Barb on the lips and kissed Larry on the forehead, and then started to suit up. Nick suited up as well.

Since the Team Four watch period was four hours off, Carl decided to set the example. He chose exercises that did not impact the floor, walls or furniture. His muscles were tight—a sign of disuse. Stretching of various forms worked all the skeletal muscles he could get to with his contortions. He tried a series of modified yoga and Pilates routines. Carl also did push-ups of several forms and sit-ups combined with leg-raisers and bicycling motions. He was satisfied with his heart and respiratory rate increases. Perspiration felt good. When he was done, Carl drank a good size glass of water and eventually went back to the bathroom for an adequate sponge bath.

When Carl returned to the living room, Janet and Barb appeared to be sleeping. Alex, Dave and Larry followed Carl's example, which rendered a brief smile of satisfaction. Carl lay down beside Janet, carefully trying not to disturb her sleep. Surprisingly, sleep claimed him quickly.

The night remained stone cold quiet. Nothing was seen or heard by any of the watch teams. The most excitement occurred after Dave's eyes adjusted to the darkness. The three-quarter waning moon descended behind the western ridgeline 30 minutes earlier, leaving the clear sky very black.

"I never knew there were so many stars," observed Dave.

"Yeah . . . amazing what no lights allows us to see. The astronauts have reported for decades the dazzling array of stars that become visible in total darkness."

"That band is so bright."

"That's the Milky Way, our home galaxy." Carl pointed to the sky above them. "That's the center of the galaxy. The astronomers tell us there is a massive black hole entity at the very center."

"I've heard of black holes, but I've never understood what they are."

"They are the collapsed remnants of old stars that have condensed to such a degree that nothing can escape the enormous gravity, not even light or radiation. Everything that comes within its gravitational pull eventually disappears and becomes part of an even more massive black hole."

"Wow!"

"Some theorists believe the universe will eventually collapse down to a single entity that will initiate another Big Bang and a new universe."

"I can't imagine."

"Way beyond me as well, but still fun to contemplate."

They lapsed back into silence and returned to observe what they could see or hear in the darkness. The starlight offered surprisingly better illumination than expected. Nothing moved. I know this calm and quiet is not going to last. I just hope it lasts as long as possible. The remainder of the Team Four watch remained uneventful and cold.

When twilight returned before local sunrise, the group gathered for their morning meal. Lisa fed Breckyn, as they ate their modest meal in silence.

As they finished, Alex was the first to break the silence. "Are we going to venture out today?"

"Based on the amount of snow we got in this storm, I'd recommend we do not go outside for a day or so. We don't have a compelling reason to go outside. Let's allow others to pack down the snow, and watch where they go and what they do."

"Can we go outside for some fresh air?" Alex pressed.

"The balcony should be OK, as long as you stay low . . . below the covered railing. We do not want any potential observers to be attracted to us. The desperate or bad people will come."

"But, Dad, you've always told us not to live our lives in fear."

Carl smiled. "You are quite correct. That is what I always say. My primary caution is, these are not normal times. To be perhaps overly blunt, we have had to kill more than a few people who threatened us. There are no second chances. I admit that I may be overly cautious, but it is the risk of misstep that makes me so cautious."

"I'm with your dad on this one, Alex," Pete chimed in to reinforce Carl's words. "In situations like this, there is no law—only survival."

"Two peas in a pod," Janet mumbled.

Carl glared at his wife for several seconds, and then said, "May I have a word, please." He did not wait for an answer and walked to the hallway, past the blanket barrier, and to the back bedroom. Janet was a half dozen steps behind and eventually joined her husband.

"It's cold back here," she observed and crossed her arms over her chest.

"Yes, it is." Carl looked into Janet's unemotional eyes. "What the hell is going on?" he asked softly.

"What do you mean?"

"Don't be coy with me, Janet. I recognize your passive-aggressive behavior. This is not our first rodeo."

Janet mocked her shock, placing both her hands over her mouth.

"Well?"

Janet stared at her husband for a dozen seconds or more with a stone sober expression. "I've had about enough of this damn macho-male bullshit, Carl. You've made your point. These are not normal times, but the message repetition is getting old and tiresome."

"I'm sorry you feel that way. I will gladly relinquish our protection to you, if you think you can do better."

"No martyr crap either. You are my husband and the father of our children. They understand. We understand that we are in a bad situation."

"Apparently, they don't . . . and neither do you?"

"You don't have to be an asshole. Things are bad enough as they are. None of us need your doom and gloom bullshit. We have all taken our turns standing these bloody watches in the cold, watching nothing while we freeze. We have been at this for nearly three weeks and we probably have another eight to twelve weeks ahead of us. Alex just wanted some fresh fucking air, damn it!" Janet said, allowing her voice to rise more than she wanted with her exclamation.

Carl stared into Janet's anxious eyes, as he considered his words. "I'm not going to argue with you. I will only say that I have regrettably had to kill more than a few men who were threatening me or one of our family. I accept that the danger may not seem as close to you as it does to me. I also respectfully submit that I have been exposed to the animal side of mankind far more than you and far too many times in my life. I have been trained well to do what I do, and it is all to protect our family. I have no interest or desire for the macho-male bullshit, as you call it. I have only one interest today—survival, plain and simple."

Janet actually smiled ever so slightly, for the first time in many days. "I may not show it, Carl, but I truly appreciate your skills and your efforts to keep us safe. My only advice is, try to tone down the negativism. We know our situation is bad. We do not need to be reminded of that fact in every other sentence."

Carl nodded his head and chose not to speak further. He held out his arms. They embraced and kissed, at first just a peck, and then passionately. "I love you."

"I love you, Carl." He gestured toward the door. Janet did not hesitate. Carl followed.

The boys were not in the living room—only Pete and the other females. Carl gestured his query to Pete, who in turn pointed to the balcony. Carl nodded his acknowledgment and went to the blackout curtain. He peeked out to see all the boys. Mike and Nick were on the watch stools, while the other boys were sitting behind them, leaning against the glass. Carl did not want to disturb them and turned away.

"They took what they could get," Pete volunteered. Carl nodded. "Are y'all OK?"

"Yes," answered Carl and glanced to Janet, who was sitting and talking to Lisa, holding Breckyn. "She thinks I'm being too negative, so I'll try to soften my words. Things are not hopeless, just dangerous.

"I'm with you, brother. We've seen situations too often—no law."

"Yeah."

"Hopefully, they all understand."

"She says they do. Have you and Barb talked about all this?"

"Not really. She just hunkers down like a turtle."

"Maybe we should all do that."

"No, you know better. Marines attack."

"You got that right. Semper Fi!"

"Semper Fi."

Carl took a moment to think. "I'm surprised we have not seen more bandits."

"We certainly have seen more than we wanted as we were making our way back to Breckenridge. They are out there. It is only a matter of time."

"Yeah. We've seen some . . . just not as much as I expected."

"The people who were trapped up here, like us, may just be foraging elsewhere."

"Possible. I checked the main grocery stores a few days after the lights went out, and they had already been looted and picked clean. I found nothing useful."

"Yeah, like the check we did on the Wellington Road Market."

"City Market was the same." He paused for thought. "I was only looking for food. Do you remember seeing any baby things . . . diapers?"

"No. I was not looking for that stuff either."

Carl held up his right index finger for a moment. He went to the arsenal room to retrieve the range chart. Back in the living room, he checked the two main grocery stores. "I covered Wellington easily at 550 meters. City Market is right at 900 meters—a long shot that needs a more static target."

Pete chuckled softly. "For being a flyboy, you're a pretty damn good shot."

"Every Marine is a rifleman."

"Ya got that right, brother."

Just then, the balcony door opened and Mike peaked past the lower corner of the blackout curtain. "Dad," he said softly, "you need to see this."

Carl and Pete both went to the balcony, crouched down, and went outside, closing the door behind them. They carefully looked over the covered railing. Several groups of people, mostly men with a few women, were trudging down 4 O'Clock Run Road toward town in the thigh-high deep snow. Another group of four men was coming down King's Crown Road, toward 4 O'Clock Run Road, behind the other two groups. None of the groups appeared to be interested in their home base apartments. Carl carefully scanned the complex. There were no tracks in the fresh snow between any of the buildings. "Stay down. Keep an eye on 'em. I'm going to get the rifle, just in case." Pete nodded. Carl made his way back inside.

"What's going on?" Janet asked.

"People."

Carl grabbed the Remington 700, checked to make sure the safety was engaged, the magazine was full and a round was in the chamber. He also opened the ammo box and put a handful of rounds in his pocket. By the time he made it back to the balcony, the first group was no longer visible, apparently moving south down South Park Avenue. Carl kept the rifle muzzle low behind the railing. The other two groups appeared to be aware of each other, but were not interacting. None of the people exhibited any threatening behavior, so Carl kept the rifle hidden. *There's no reason to use the sight.* They were content to observe. Carl looked over his shoulder on the now crowded balcony deck to Pete. He noticed Barb and Janet discreetly peeking out the edge of the blackout curtain. "Where do you think they are going?' Carl asked Pete quietly.

"I've no idea, but they are tamping down the snow . . . at least on the road."

"Yeah. That they are. Whatever they are doing, they only have a few more hours of daylight."

"They might try something on their way back . . . if they go back."

Carl turned, sat on the deck and leaned against the railing. "This is what I have been expecting for some time now, boys. This," he said softly, jerking a thumb over his right shoulder, "is why we have watches."

"We don't want anyone sneaking up on us," Pete whispered.

"Exactly."

"Dad . . . ," Mike whispered.

Carl cradled the rifle, turned and peered over the railing. The third group stopped at the road, in the track of the previous group, and looked at the apartment complex, as if they were deciding whether to enter. "Stay down," Carl whispered. He moved slowly and precisely, to allow the boys to shift their position without exposure, to take up a prone position on the deck. Carl very slowly fed the rifle's muzzle under the sheet cover and the railing, making sure the sheet remained closely draped over the sight and barrel. The magnification of the sight enabled him to see extraordinary detail, but only parts of one person at a time. Carl could make out a few words by reading their lips—search, look, find. The leader of the group became quite apparent; he was doing all the talking and pointing. Carl flipped off the safety and placed his right index finger on the trigger, but did not apply pressure, yet. Apparently, several others were objecting to the deep, undisturbed snow, as an obstacle to their effort. The group eventually decided to head into town. Carl looked up at Pete, kneeling beside him behind the railing. He pointed his right index finger to Pete, to his eyes, and then downrange. Pete knew exactly what Carl signaled and slowly rose to look over the railing. Carl went back to the sight and reacquired the group. They were moving away. Carl laid the rifle down where it was and joined Pete, peering over the railing. He scanned the whole scene from right to left in an effort to detect any additional movement. They could see more movement in town. Carl signaled for the boys to move up and observe the movement, as he reengaged the safety and withdrew the Remington 700 from under the railing and moved back to allow the boys to take his place. Carl gestured with his head to Pete, to lead them inside.

Once they closed the door and restored the curtain, Carl cradled the rifle in his left arm and said to Pete, "I think we may have passed the threshold of tolerance."

"People are getting desperate."

"Yeah."

"Action is coming."

Carl nodded his agreement. "It also means, what we have is what we have. Searching for more is going to be riskier."

"How important are diapers?"

Carl chuckled. They walked back to the arsenal room to deposit the Remington 700. "Important for the baby, but not worth a life."

"We could strong arm it."

"Yeah, we could . . . but, looking at those groups this afternoon, I suspect other people are going to be doing the same thing . . . like that group of six men a few days back." Carl paused for thought. "We're past the full moon, so a night mission becomes more problematic." Carl remembered their last night mission. "It's almost impossible seeing anything inside a building without lights . . . even with a full moon, and we are a few days short of a waning half moon."

"What did they do with babies a century ago . . . before plastic pants and disposable diapers."

Carl chuckled again as he sneaked a peek out the bedroom window. "Good question. I wish I knew. Napkins contain most of it, but they leak."

"Yeah, and we gotta clean those nasty things." They both laughed.

"Tracks in the snow on 4 O'Clock Run trail."

"Any people?"

"No, but people have been moving through the snow."

"Anyone approaching the building?" Pete joined Carl at the window.

"No tracks, yet."

"We should post a watch back here, too."

"Yeah. I was hoping to avoid it. Splitting the watch has its own risks, and we don't have enough people to warm and rest our watchstanders."

Pete stood back and said, "We can't just hole up for two or three months."

Carl restored the curtain, leaving the room dark. Neither man moved to allow their eyes to adjust to the dark. "I guess the time has come to reach out to our neighbors."

"Now?"

"No, no, too late in the day. The sun is nearly to the ridgeline. We should lay out a plan before we set the evening watches."

"Are we going to cover the back?"

"Yeah. You're right. We'll have to risk the split and see how that goes."

The two men slowly shuffled across the floor to the dimly lit doorway. The boys had returned to the interior, except for Nick and Dave. The two friends volunteered to keep an eye on things. Carl went to the balcony door and peaked out. The scene appeared peaceful and evening twilight was nearing completion. He tapped on the glass. The boys looked to the sound. Carl gestured with a thumb's up and thumb's down. Both boys raised a thumb's up. Carl signaled for them to come inside.

"Before we eat our evening meal," Carl announced, "we need to adjust our defense plan." Everyone remained attentive and unanimated. "We have now seen several groups of people outside in the fairly deep snow, which suggests the threshold of desperation has been exceeded for a growing number of people trapped up here with us. Fortunately, no one has challenged us, yet, but Pete and I both agree those challenges are inevitable and looming, as hunger and hopelessness mount." Carl paused to allow for reaction. There was none. No response whatsoever. "We," said Carl, nodding to Pete, "have seen evidence of people moving down the trail, in addition to those the boys noticed on the street. Beginning after we eat, we are going to try splitting the teams. One will stand watch on the balcony as we have been doing, and the other will stand watch in the arsenal room to keep an eye on the back door and the trail."

"Doesn't that defeat the purpose of standing together?" asked Janet.

"That is the risk, but, Pete and I feel we've got to cover the back door, and we don't have enough people to have four people on watch at a time."

"Who goes to the cold?" Alex asked.

"Each of us. We'll rotate outside on every other cycle. Depending upon how that goes, perhaps we can try splitting each watch period, but let's try the first approach."

"At least the back bedroom won't have any wind to deal with," observed Mike.

"True. I don't have a strong justification for either approach. Do you, Pete?"

"Nope."

"OK. How about we put it to a vote. How many want to split the watch period?"

Everyone raised their hand, except for Pete and Carl. "OK. It's settled, then. Whoever has my wristwatch will initiate the switch at the one-hour mark. We'll continue to stand two-hour watches. No matter what the time is, if you see people moving around or approaching this building, please wake either Mister Higgins or me. We have been trained in such things. Let us handle the initial defensive actions. Are we agreed?"

Half the group nodded, while the other half voiced various forms of affirmative responses. They ate a simple, small meal of jerky and canned new potatoes. Team Three picked up the watch. Carl went with Janet to the balcony. Pete went with Mike to the arsenal room.

Janet sat on the box stool. Carl knelt beside her. They scanned the scene as best they could in the darkness. The waning moon was just above the eastern ridgeline and did not provide sufficient light; however, the parking lot was pristine—no tracks. Neither of them saw any movement.

"Are you OK with this?" Carl whispered.

Janet nodded her head. "I'll just be glad when all this is behind us."

"Me too, sweetheart. Me too. I'm going to go check on Mike." Again, Janet nodded her head. Carl kissed her on the cheek and said, "I love you." She only nodded.

Carl left his wife alone on the balcony and went directly to the arsenal room. Pete was still with Mike. They both were under the curtain, rather than pulling it back. Pete backed out. Carl signaled for him to go to the balcony, while he would take his place with Mike.

Carl waited for Pete to disappear out the door, and then went under the curtain beside his oldest son. "Anything interesting?" he whispered.

Mike shook his head in the negative.

"Light should improve as the moon moves up," Carl added.

Mike nodded and kept scanning the exterior. There was not much space between the building and the trees along the trail, and there were no tracks they could see in the snow between the building and trees.

"Mom has my watch. She'll come get you when it is time to switch."

Mike nodded his head, again.

"Any questions?"

Mike shook his head, no.

"Stay vigilant," Carl commanded and left his son to his task.

When Carl returned to the living room, Pete was back inside and in the process of laying down. Several of the children were sitting by the fireplace and reading. Lisa was rocking Breckyn in her arms. Carl smiled and laid down himself. Sleep quickly claimed his consciousness.

—

15

"It's a perfect day outside," observed Mike, as Team Three joined the group for their morning meal.

"Except for the cold," Janet added, having just completed her balcony watch.

"Would be a great day for snowboarding," interjected Nick, "with all that fresh powder."

They all joined in the laughter.

"If . . . only . . . ," Carl said.

Barbara Higgins had recommended they switch their "big meal" from evening to morning, and they all had agreed. They grilled steak for each person, along with several scoops of sweet corn. It was certainly not a gourmet meal, but it was satisfying, especially given their conditions.

As they finished their meal, they refined their plan.

Pete began, "I think our best shot for peaceful contact would be Barb, Larry and me making the contact attempts. If there are residents, they should recognize us. Appearing as a family should be less threatening to visitors."

"There is going to be risk no matter how we cut it," Carl observed.

"I propose we search this building first, then you should be able to watch us from the balcony," suggested Pete.

Carl thought for a moment. "More people seem to be moving on the street rather than the trail. Perhaps we should use the back entrance to access each building."

"Good point. We'll move along the backside to avoid tracks that might be more observable."

"OK. You're sure about this?" Carl asked, for reassurance.

"No," Pete responded succinctly. "Do you have a better idea?"

"It's difficult, if not impossible, to predict how an initiative like this will turn out."

"Action is better than inaction," Pete noted.

Carl chuckled softly. "Indeed! The best defense is a good offense. So, let's take the offense."

"Very well."

"Since we can't observe this building, let's do this one first and regroup back here with the findings, before we go to the other buildings."

"Sure. Agreed."

Pete, Barb and Larry suited up and armed themselves. Carl checked the exterior from the balcony door—all clear, so far. He turned and gave Pete a thumb's up, and then gestured the knock signal—one, three, two. Pete held up his right hand and gestured, one, three and two. Carl acknowledged with a thumb up.

Pete left with his family. Alex locked and braced the door behind them. Breckyn let out a short, robust cry. Lisa jumped to tend to her daughter.

Carl looked at Mike. "Please keep an eye on the back door. I'll watch the front." Mike nodded his consent and went to the arsenal room. Nick and Dave followed Mike to the bedroom. Carl went to the blackout curtain and pulled it back from a low point to keep the line of the curtain straight and less of an attraction to potential observers. His observation point and technique were not ideal, but they were sufficient to observe the parking lot entry. Alex joined his father at the balcony door. More people, smaller groups of two or three appeared on the street. None of them showed any signs of entering their apartment grouping. He pointed them out to Alex. Carl also listened carefully to detect any sounds of difficulty below them in Building Three.

The Higgins' search took surprisingly few minutes, as the agreed to knock sequence announced their return. Carl gestured to Alex to recall Mike and the boys, so they could hear the results. He went to the door, checked the peephole, and then opened the door. He chose not to speak with the door open.

Once everyone was back in the living room, Carl asked, "What did you find?"

"Actually, nothing," responded Pete. "We checked both first and second-floor apartments. We got no answers. I watched the peepholes to have some indication of presence. Nothing. No sounds, nothing. I even felt the door to feel any warmth from the interior, as a sign of occupancy. Neither Barb nor I can remember or are we aware of any occupancy before we left town. My guess, the apartments are either empty or the occupants have frozen."

"I suppose that is good news in a form."

"Yeah. Should we search these apartments before we check the other buildings?"

Carl considered the query for a dozen seconds or so. "There is no immediacy. They are not going anywhere."

"Unless others get to them first," Pete responded.

"True, but we can handle that aspect by our protective observation of your searches of the other buildings."

"Sure. That works for me. Are you ready?"

Carl chuckled softly. "Y'all are the ones going out. Are you ready?"

"Yep. Let's do it," responded Pete, as he looked to the others. "Depending upon the progress we make, we'll take Building Two first, and then One. We'll come back here with the findings on one or both buildings. We'll signal either way from the near, rear corner."

"OK. Good plan."

With everyone's eyes on him, Carl gestured the new re-entry knock sequence—two, two, one. Pete gave him a thumb's up acknowledgment. The Higgins family headed out on their mission. The remaining males took up their previous posts. On this one, Carl and Alex assumed the normal position of watch on the balcony rather than peaking out the glass; it was cold, but gave them a better field of view.

While the Higgins family remained out of sight on their task, two strangers approached Building Five.

Carl whispered to Alex, "Any sign of the search party?"

"Not yet, Dad. I've not taken my eyes off of Building Two."

"Let me know as soon as you see anything. I may have to engage these guys."

Carl could not see the building well, as the two men moved the snow from the front door and entered without obvious caution. *These guys are far more confident than they should be, or they may be so desperate they just did not care.* Carl carefully laid the rifle down on the deck, ensuring it was stable and safe. He rose up on his knees to peer over the railing at Building Five.

"Anything, yet?"

"Nothing."

"The two men have gone into Building Five." Three muzzle flashes and muffled shot reports changed the situation. "Shots fired," Carl announced softly and went to the rifle. He flipped the safety off, placed the crosshairs of his sight on the front door about chest high and took up the slack on the trigger. The first man appeared, carrying a small bag he did not have going in and the shouldered rifle. He turned, raised a pistol and fired past his colleague into the building. Carl squeezed off a shot. A dull thud marked the discharge. The bullet hit the first man center chest and knocked him into the snow. He operated the bolt to chamber another round and went back to the trigger. The second man saw his friend and looked in the direction of Building Three just in time for the next round to strike him center chest as well, knocking him off his feet and into the snowdrift next to his buddy. Both men were dead, or would die quite soon. Carl knew there were only two outsiders going in, but he watched the door to see if anyone would appear. He noticed the barrel of a shotgun appear first, pointed at the two fallen intruders. The person quickly deduced what had happened.

"Duck down," Carl whispered. Alex immediately did as he was instructed. "Stay down for now."

Carl watched carefully, motionlessly and quietly. The barrel disappeared. The dim shape of a man appeared in the dark interior with the shotgun raised and pointed toward Building Three. *He knows generally where the shots came from and undoubtedly recognized they were intended for the intruders, not him.*

"Don't move," Carl whispered, as he concentrated on the shape in the doorway shadow. The person chose not to expose himself further. He reached out and closed the door. Carl could detect no motion or other signs. He waited a few more minutes before he said, "OK. Check on Mister Higgins."

Alex moved to the edge of the balcony to minimize his exposure angle and peered over the railing. Carl watched for any observer from Building Five and did not take his eyes off that task. Alex returned to his stool and said to his father's head, "Mister Higgins was standing at the corner. He signaled complete and moving to Building One. He's waiting for an acknowledgment."

"Give him a thumb's up."

Alex did so. "He acknowledged and moved out."

"OK. We'll need to get them back here after the next building, so we can talk about what happened."

"What happened, Dad?"

"You heard the gunshots?"

"Yeah."

"The two men we saw across the road went into Building Five. There is at least someone defending that building, now. There was apparently a shoot-out, which is the shots we heard, and I had to drop the two men."

"What about the guy in the building?"

"Well, he knows there is at least one shooter in our building, and he probably knows it is a silenced weapon that hit the two intruders. We need to be careful, if we go into that building."

Satisfied there was no immediate threat, Carl slowly lay the rifle back down, to minimize the detectable motion of the protruding barrel. He returned to his stool. They picked up their alternating observation. Neither of them picked any additional movement within their field of view. They continued their scanning for uncounted minutes, until Alex detected Pete halfway along the north wall of Building One, chest deep in a snowdrift.

"Mister Higgins signaled complete."

Carl shifted his attention to Building One and quickly picked up Pete. He signaled for them to return. "OK. They're coming back. We need to keep watch until they are back inside."

"Sure."

The process of moving back to Building Three took less time, as the search team utilized the path they had packed down on the way out. The soft knock on the glass door marked their return. Carl gestured with a head nod for Alex to go inside, and he followed.

The other boys were already back in the living room when Alex and Carl joined them.

As the search team warmed themselves at the fire, Carl asked, "How did it go?"

Pete took off his ski jacket and pants. "Well, we learned a lot. We saw the two apartments that y'all searched earlier in Building Two. They appeared to be undisturbed. Only one unit was occupied in Building Two—unit number 221—a middle-aged couple from England. They are scared, but they appear to be doing OK. They had a whole bunch of questions, none of which we had any answers for—the same questions we all have. They said they are safe for now. I have no idea whether they can defend themselves, or how long they have supplies to hold them. I hinted at our probe for information, but they were not willing to tell us anything about their condition. The other units—212, 222 and 231—had no response or even sounds that we could detect." Carl noted the findings on their survey chart. "Those units are candidates for search, depending on what other indications we may have."

Carl did not want to get into all the aspects of the problem. "What about Building One?"

Pete continued, "We got no response from 121 or 132." Again, Carl marked the chart. "We made contact with occupants in 111, 112, 122 and 131. By the way, when we were in 122, talking to the Manson family, we heard the fracas in Building Five. The lot of us happened to be looking out the balcony window, when we saw the two bad guys fall without a sound. I knew it had to be you, but I did not say anything to them. They were surprised and curious, but not enough to do anything about it."

"I'll fill in the details after you are done. What did the occupants say?"

"A mixed bag," Pete responded. "Two of the responses—112 and 131—told us to go away and do not come back. In both those cases, they were male voices. We must take them seriously and avoid any further contact. There is a small family in unit 111. They are nearly out of supplies. They are in trouble. They were begging for help. I think both Barb and I agree, it was heartbreaking to hear their story and see their condition. They appeared to be too weak to take action. We might consider searching the no contact units and passing whatever food we find to the family in 111."

"That's a possibility. Let's come back to that. What about the last unit?"

"That one—unit 122—was more productive. Middle-aged parents and two, early teenage children, a boy and a girl, from Santa Monica, California. They appeared and claimed to be in stable condition, but they are concerned about what lays ahead. They were the ones who witnessed the Building Five action. They were reluctant to disclose their supply status and rightly so. They have set up a similar arrangement as y'all have done here, consolidating their living space around the fireplace in the living room – kitchen. I saw no weapons, and I chose not to query them, to avoid making them feel nervous or threatened. They are clearly in far better shape than the folks in 111. So, Building One yielded one potential merger group and two potential search units. I have no way to assess the aggressiveness of the "go away" units, so we must consider them as possible aggressors, as this situation continues."

"Well done," Carl said. "Any questions?" he asked the group.

"How old are the boy and girl?" asked Nick.

"Well, I don't know. I didn't ask. Based on my short visit, my guess is mid-teens, perhaps a year or two apart." Nick nodded his head.

Carl looked at each person. There were no other questions for Pete. "So, back to Building Five."

"Yeah, what happened?"

Carl recounted the Building Five engagement. Satisfied the situation was stable with the new normal, they agreed to tackle Building Four and postponed any contact with Building Five, for the time being. They returned to their positions, as the Higgins headed out to Building Four.

Alex, Mike and Carl maintained their overwatch continued for uncounted minutes. The sound of the sliding door opening behind attracted the attention of all three of them.

"Dad," Nick said in a louder and more excited voice than expected, "there's a man at the rear door."

Carl looked back to Mike and Alex. "Give Mister Higgins the stop signal."

"What is that?" asked Alex.

"Crossed arms. If he gestures, why, give him danger signal." Carl drew a flat hand across his throat. He decided to leave the rifle. "Watch the rifle. Use it if you need to, but do not leave it out here." Carl did not wait for an answer.

Carl moved swiftly through the living room to the arsenal room. He tossed the Remington 1100 to Nick, picked up the conventional Mossberg and headed for the front door. Carl felt for and confirmed the M1911 in his jacket pocket. Before he opened the door, he signaled Nick—one, two, one. Nick nodded. Carl unblocked and unlocked the door, and then signaled for Nick to lock the door behind him.

As he stepped out on the landing, Carl cleared the landing and waited to hear the door lock behind him. He kept the shotgun to his shoulder and pointed at the stairway. Carl stepped quietly toward the stairway, and then stopped to listen. The sound of several attempts to open the rear door was easily heard and persisted. *He's not being very careful.* Carl used the intruder's struggle presumably with clearing the drifts from the door to enable him to move precisely and rapidly down the stairway. He carefully cleared the second landing and moved quickly to the mid-landing to the ground floor. He held back in the corner to give himself as much cover as he could. The man was inside the ground floor lobby and jiggled the doorknob on apartment 311, but did not try to break in. The fellow appeared at the apartment 312 door and in Carl's sight. He did not even bother looking up the stairwell. Big mistake.

"Freeze!" commanded Carl. "Do not move." The intruder did as he was ordered and did not submit to the urge to look at his challenger. "Do not twitch, or you will die. What are you doing here?"

"Looking for food, man. Don't shoot," he said, under the correct assumption that a firearm was pointed directly at him. "We're very hungry. We need food."

"This is not the place to find it. Where are you from?"

"Sawmill Road Apartments."

"You have a choice. You can go back from where you came, or you can d . . ." The man turned sharply and raised his right hand.

Carl fired a single shot to his chest from the 12-gauge shotgun. The blast knocked him completely off his feet and away from the door. Carl moved smoothly toward the man without taking the barrel off of him. He was still alive and gasping for air with fresh, frothy blood bubbling from his mouth. He did not have long to live. "Big mistake," Carl said to the dying man. The fellow moved his mouth without sound beyond the gurgling of him drowning in his own blood. Why, he seemed to be asking. Carl looked to the man's right hand and lifted the semi-automatic pistol above his head. "This is why." The man tried to say something else, but Carl could not ascertain what he was trying to say. The man's breathing attempts stopped. His eyes remained open and his pupils dilated fully. He was dead. Carl leaned the shotgun against the wall, and quickly searched the man's clothing and body. He had only the pistol—one he did not immediately recognize. He put the pistol in his left jacket pocket. Carl could not find any additional magazines or ammunition.

Concerned for the blood as a marker, Carl quickly removed the man's jacket and stuffed a sleeve into each large hole—front and back. Once satisfied he had curtailed the draining of the man's blood, Carl checked outside the rear door. He saw Pete's packed paths left and right, as well as the footfalls of the fallen man. The path from the ski trail was not yet packed, and he was not keen on dragging the body and making an obvious trail. Carl went outside, careful to use the intruder's footprints in the snow. He saw the man's track from the east and across the 4 O'Clock Run ski trail. Carl searched up and down the trail to find a reasonable spot to stash the body. He considered preparing the body, as he had done with the boys several weeks ago, but decided he did not have time. Pete was likely complete and waiting to return to base, and the ladies would be worried given the shotgun discharge along with his protracted absence. Carl found a spot in some bushes at the base of a small clump of bare deciduous trees. He returned to the building lobby by the same process. Carl grabbed the dead man's right arm and jerked him up, and then dipped down to put his left shoulder into the waist area, lifting the body in a fireman's carry. He carried the body outside to the spot he had selected and deposited it with a thud. Carl made a modest attempt to camouflage the corpse.

Carl returned to the lobby, retrieved the shotgun, checked the area and went upstairs. The agreed to knock sequence opened the door. Alex closed the door and locked it.

Janet was standing near the door. "What happened? You scared the hell out of us."

"A single intruder searching for food. He tried to draw down on me, and I had to eliminate him."

"Did you really have to . . . ," she stopped when Carl raised his right hand.

"I'll answer all your questions, but first, we must get the Higgins back here." Carl did not wait for a response. He went to the balcony. Mike remained in a watchful position. "What's our status?"

"I heard the shot."

"Yeah, we'll talk about it later." Carl looked over the railing, but saw nothing. "Where is Mister Higgins?"

"He is there, just not near the door. He has signaled repeatedly, so he is waiting for the all-clear from us."

"OK. I'll watch the building, so he can see me. Please watch everything else."

"Sure, Dad."

The sun had descended beyond the western ridgeline. The reappearance of Pete took several minutes. Their eyes connected immediately. Carl gave him a thumb's up and waved for them to return. Pete acknowledged the signal. Carl leaned out more than he wanted, but he felt compelled to observe their passage between the buildings—Pete, Barb and Larry, all's well. He gestured for Mike to follow him inside. Nick and Dave returned to the living room indicating the Higgins had entered the building. The contact party arrived a few minutes later. They waited patiently for the Higgins family to warm themselves.

Pete opened this discussion. "What happened?"

"An intruder searching for food. He tried to draw down on me."

"I saw the fresh blood by 312."

"Yeah. That is where he died."

"Was he breaking in?"

"No. He tried the door on 311, and then went to 312, where the confrontation occurred."

"What did you do with the body?"

"I carried it up the trail a ways and did the best I could to cover it." Carl paused. "Any other questions on what occurred downstairs?"

Lisa raised her hand. Carl nodded to her. "Did you really have to kill him, Dad?"

"He left me no choice. I was in the process of telling him to leave and not come back when he turned on me with a pistol in his hand, so yes, he left me no choice." She shook her head. Carl did not want to challenge his daughter's disagreement at this moment and saved it for a later day. He felt for and confirmed the confiscated pistol in his left jacket pocket. Carl withdrew the pistol. The etching on the side of the pistol body indicated the weapon was a 9mm *Fabrique Nationale* FNS-9 Compact semi-automatic weapon. He held up the firearm. Carl looked back to Pete, who nodded. Carl asked, "What did you find in Building Four?"

Pete smiled. "Some good news for a change. You will recall our previous discussion. I had mentioned the Johnson's in 412. They are there. They are safe and apparently well provisioned. To my surprise, Vicky and Bert Johnson recognized us and allowed us into their apartment. They have a similar set-up and are professed survivalists. I did not offer much beyond our effort to reach out. Barb had a nice chat with Vicky, which really helped the connection.

"Vicky is a non-practicing nurse," Barb volunteered. "I met her the first time several years ago at a hospital in Denver. My take is, and I think Pete agrees, they are open to a coalition, if the terms do not compromise their safety."

"Good news indeed," said Carl. "I think we have the same condition, Barb. So, the Johnsons in 412 are also candidates . . . and from what you've said, perhaps the best candidates so far. Are they armed?"

"Not that I could determine, but I didn't ask. Bert did mention that they heard the shootout in Building Five. Bert witnessed the end of the fight and was puzzled as to where the shots came from? He said he could tell by the way the bodies fell that that shots didn't come from inside. He also did not hear the shots that dropped the men and tried to find the source, without success. So, I know he is sensitive to firearms. I did not divulge our participation. I think we should trust them, as it will likely enhance whatever agreement we can attain."

"Anything else?" Carl asked Barb and Pete.

"Not as good as that, but yes. As we found in the other buildings, there was not full occupancy. We got no answer or other indications from 411, 421, 431 and 432. We got another 'go away' from 422."

Carl checked the survey chart. "Well, then, we have circles on 411 and 432, so that would suggest those units are unoccupied. Were any of the doors compromised?"

"No."

"Good, so they have not likely been searched, yet. We have asterisks on 421 and 431, which would suggest the occupants may have perished or taken flight."

"I would agree," Pete responded.

"Did you tell the Johnsons what we were doing?"

"In a general sense, yes . . . reaching out, but nothing more."

Carl thought for a few moments. "Breaking down doors makes a lot of noise, so we should probably reach some agreement with the Johnsons before we breach those doors."

"Agreed. And, regardless of their response, we need to be prepared for armed confrontation when we do. The person—a definite male voice—in 422 may not take kindly to the intrusions, just as you did not earlier today."

"Quite so. We also need to think through how we proceed from here."

"We still have Building Five out there," Pete added. "Like I said earlier, Bert Johnson was aware of and witnessed the end of the confrontation. I asked them if they knew who it might be in Building Five. He felt fairly certain the two bad guys were eliminated by an external source. From his expression, I think he suspects us. But, he did not know the Building Five person."

"Well, we can eliminate his suspicions, if we establish a coalition."

"Sure. It's getting late in the day. I'd recommend we complete the search of this building, and then we reconnect and make the pitch to the Mansons. Depending upon how that goes, we can tackle Building Four, and as you say, we should isolate Building Five for now."

"I'm good with that. Agreed."

"So, we should secure for the night and reset the watch?"

"Yes."

Pete nodded his head and they were done. He stepped to Carl and extended his right hand. Carl knew what he was suggesting and placed the confiscated pistol in Pete's hand. He examined the weapon, and then said, "I've never seen one of these."

"Me neither."

They admired the pistol. The boys examined the weapon as well. Carl showed them the significant features. When everyone was done, Carl placed the weapon in the arsenal room, next to the M9 Beretta. He kept the M1911 in his jacket pocket, just as Pete kept the 44-Magnum with him. Lisa fed Breckyn, and the whole group of two families enjoyed light-hearted conversation about earlier days while they savored the earthy flavors of venison jerky strips.

Carl checked his wristwatch. Team Four suited up, since they left off with Team Three this morning. Dave and Carl executed five rounds of Rock-Paper-Scissors to decide who took the first balcony cycle, or rather who avoided the last balcony watch. Dave won. Carl headed to the arsenal room for his first watch, and Dave took the balcony. So began the night's watch.

—

16

The search of Building Three had gone well. Three of the four remaining units had been unoccupied. The fourth unit—321—had a deceased, middle-aged couple; they appeared to have succumbed to the cold. No physical injuries or signs of violence were detected. While they did yield some additional foodstuff, the primary acquisition from the four, lower, Building Three units was firewood—already split and sized for the modest apartment fireplace. The wooden furniture might well serve as a reserve in case sufficient firewood might not make it until their spring departure. The men and boys moved the wood to their base in 332, and stacked it with their supply. They were getting closer to an adequate stock. The bodies of the frozen couple were stable at least until warmer weather arrived, so they decided to leave them in place. They could easily move the bodies outside, if they ever needed the additional space. After they had completed their search and stowed the acquisitions, they gathered back in the living room.

Carl turned to Pete. "Y'all have been the ones out making contact. How do you want to proceed?"

"With the assumption we will hold on Building Five, my recommendation is to start with the Johnsons in Building Four. Depending upon how that goes, we should search that building with the Johnsons' support."

"I'm OK with that, but there are some practical questions we should have pertaining to a reasonable idea of how to proceed. For example, do we remain spread out, or do we consolidate? We have empty apartments in this building."

"With broken doors," Pete interjected with a chuckle—several others laughed as well.

Carl smiled. "True. We would have to provide security, but communications would be infinitely easier."

"There is that. They may not want to consolidate and leave their belongings."

"As you say, there is that. My point is, without radios, coordination and mutual protection becomes exponentially more difficult, not impossible, but quite difficult. There are only two of them, correct?"

"Yes, that is correct."

"It is their choice entirely, but I think the risk-benefit options should be placed before them."

"Agreed. To that end, I'd suggest you and I both go have those discussions with the Johnsons. Once that is done, if we have sufficient light remaining, I would recommend we have the same or similar discussions with the Manson's in

122, and then the English couple in 221. From there, depending upon how it plays out, we need to search the unoccupied or unresponsive units. We have no way to differentiate between the unoccupied and unresponsive apartments, so we will need a different search process . . . to be prepared for armed confrontation with unresponsive occupants of one or more of those units."

"Carl!" protested Janet. "Don't do this?"

"What . . . don't do what?"

"Armed confrontation?" Janet pressed. "You two are describing a shootout at the OK Corral. Why? Why do you or we need to take those kinds of risks?"

Carl looked to Pete, as if to say, you answer this one.

Pete took the cue. "We are stronger together than we are separate."

"Oh, don't give me all that art of war crap. We are doing pretty good as we are. Why take the risk? It will only take a mere instant to change our situation."

"True, Janet, but I think Carl and I both believe it is a risk worth taking, that we must take, for several reasons. One, the collective for protection, as I mentioned. Two, knowing the lay of the land better, so to speak. Our defense and survival will be marginally easier if we know where our friends are and where the risks are. Three, until we check with those friendly folks within our reach, we will not know what assets or skills others might offer to our survival. We never know unless we ask. We are talking about the asking process . . . to better understand our situation."

Janet shook her head, and then looked to her husband. "If you get yourself killed or seriously wounded, I will never forgive you." Carl chuckled. "This is not a joke, Carl. I am afraid. I'm scared of what might happen."

Carl's smile disappeared in an instant. "There is no question of the seriousness, which is why we are talking about the process. We recognize the risks. Yet, in some ways, the risks of not reaching out to our *de facto* neighbors represent greater risk. I think both Pete and I can and will assure you that we will be as careful as we can. We do not want anyone injured or worse."

"Killed?" Lisa chimed in.

"Yes, Lisa . . . if necessary. I appreciate the reality that those of us who have not witnessed the worst of humanity are revolted by the violent and final means of rectification."

"Dad, stop!" Lisa interjected. "You have told us all about that nastiness, but we are concerned. You are ending lives. This is not how civilized people conduct themselves."

Carl smiled. "If the stakes were not so absolute, I would agree with you. My only point is, these are not . . . not . . . civilized times. There is only survival. None of you," Carl said, looking from the attentive and critical eyes of his wife and daughter, and pointing his finger at everyone except Pete, "have had your finger on the trigger. I hope and pray you are never called upon to do so. Taking a man's life is always serious and must never be taken lightly."

"Carl, please," protested Janet. "Enough of the lecture. Lisa is concerned about the killing because it is wrong. I am just as concerned as Lisa, but I am also very worried about taking unnecessary risks, especially where you get shot. I love you, Carl. I am not ashamed to proclaim that fact on the stump. I appreciate," she waved her arm to the whole group, "we all appreciate your efforts to keep us fed, warm and safe. We truly do, but the potential for a shootout is not a reasonable risk."

Pete jumped in. "The plan we have proposed calls for us to approach the least risky of all our neighbors. How about let us start with the amenable neighbors first, for the least risk, and then we can reassess our situation and the approach to further contacts. Is that reasonable?"

Janet nodded her head in agreement. Pete gestured to Lisa, who also nodded her consent.

"That works," Carl stated. One step at a time."

No one spoke or moved for several minutes. Barbara broke the silence. "Do you want me to go on the next step?"

Pete and Carl looked at each other. Neither reacted, as if to say, your choice. Pete smiled and looked to his wife. "I don't think that will be necessary. From here out, I think it is tactical integration rather than friendly contact." Barb nodded her head. "We're burning daylight. Let's get on with it."

Carl did not wait for a response and began suiting up for the cold. Pete did the same. They both stayed with their basic arms. When he returned to the living room, he gestured for the boys to gather around him. "While Mister Higgins and I are out doing these negotiations, I would like at least one of you on the balcony and each of the lobby doors. Arm yourselves with a pistol or a shotgun, or both for that matter. We will use the back route, since it is already tamped down. Any questions?" Each of the boys shook his head. "Fine. If you're ready, Pete, let's do it."

The contact team returned with a medium height, well-built man roughly the same age as Carl and an attractive, auburn-haired woman of about the same age, who was an inch or two shorter than her husband and in excellent shape and appearance, especially in the austere conditions of their present situation. Pete introduced Vicky and Bert Johnson to the group. Through mutual discussion, the group collectively agreed to reactivate the Higgins apartment. The Johnson would join the Higgins in unit 331. The boys helped move the Johnsons.

Carl noticed boxes of freeze-dried meals among the Johnsons' possession. "Lurps!" Carl pbserved. "You saved up that much stuff?"

"I've heard that term, but what does it mean?" Bert responded without answering Carl's query.

"When they were originally developed and introduced, they were called Long Range Patrol rations, since they were initially introduced during the Vietnam War to Special Forces, Recon and other deep penetration units to save weight and eliminate the canned rations of the World War II and Korean War era."

"OK. Now I know. It is my understanding that what we have is the commercial version. We started some years ago. We did not anticipate this kind of a disaster, but we wanted to be prepared for any eventuality we could imagine."

"You've done well," Carl commented.

"Thank you. We could stand some real meat, so perhaps we can share, once we combine our stores."

Carl looked at Pete. Both men nodded. "Do you have weapons?" Pete asked.

"We have one pistol . . . a .357 magnum revolver, and a12-gauge pump shotgun."

"OK. We have a small arsenal of weapons of all kinds that we have collected to deny them to the bad guys. You will have your choice. Do you have experience with firearms?"

"Not a lot, but some," Bert answered.

"Pete and I can help with that and build on what you have."

Once things were settled a little, Pete and Carl sat down to compare notes on the intelligence they held.

"Whoever is in 422, above you, is alive," Pete said, "but they gave us a 'go away' when we tried to make contact. Have you heard anything? Do you know who they are? Have you made contact with them?"

"No to all. We thought we might have heard a bump here or there, but nothing definitive. It is a rental, I do believe, but I do not know the owner."

"The other four units in this building are on our unoccupied list," Carl said.

"So, you want to search them?" Bert asked.

"Yes."

"We can help with that, but what happens after that?"

"Well," began Carl, "as with your choice, there are at least two options. One is, remain as is, and two is move to Building 3 and consolidate with us. Option one makes defense coordination far more problematic, since we do not have radios for communications. Option two makes defense much easier, however moving to Building 3 could become a problem."

"What about the watch schedule you mentioned earlier?" Bert asked.

Pete raised his hand, but did not wait for recognition. "Perhaps, before we decide the watch integration, we should complete the known contacts, like the Mansons in 122 and the English couple in 221, so we know how many we have."

"Good point." Carl glanced at his wristwatch. "We still have several hours of daylight. Let me ask," Carl said, looking to Bert Johnson, "do you know the Mansons?"

"Yes, we do."

"Perchance, do you know the English couple in 221?"

"No."

Carl shrugged his shoulders and looked at Bert. "It would probably be most efficient if you and Pete run the contacts.

"So," Carl said, "we have the beginnings of a plan. Let's see how many others wish to join us."

Everyone stood and began their preparations. The contact team headed to Building 2 and 1, with Carl and the boys standing overwatch for them. The process took the better part of an hour.

"How did the contacts go?" Carl asked Bert and Pete upon the contact team's return.

"Mixed results," answered Bert.

"Yeah," Pete added. "The Mansons are willing and I think they qualify, although perhaps not in total."

"How so?"

"They have food and firewood, but not enough of either to make it to spring. They have two children with them—a teenage boy and a pre-teen girl, probably 14 or 15, and 10 or so, respectively."

"Oh."

"The English couple is from Cornwall, England," Bert said. ". . . middle-aged, perhaps early 50s—man and woman, no children. Their family name is Armstrong. They arrived two days before the blackout for a long-planned ski holiday."

"They're scared outta their minds," Pete added. "They've managed to stretch their food, but they are running low, and they've begun breaking up furniture for firewood. They tried very hard not to appear desperate, but they clearly are."

"Yep."

Pete continued, "I don't know if they have any skills, but they are looking for help and safety. Bert and I talked to the Mansons first, and then the Armstrongs. We knew it was getting late and we would not have enough daylight for anything we decided to do. So, we told both families we would be back in the morning to let them know what, if anything, we could do."

"They know there are more of us," Bert contributed. "They both want to join our group, even though they do not know exactly what they are joining. Both families heard yesterday's Building 5 gunfire, and they both sense danger is closing in. The Armstrongs did not beg, but they came pretty damn close."

"We don't have time to set up your condo, tonight," Carl said, looking to Pete, "so, we should at least get settled in here for tonight. I would suggest we prepare your condo for cold weather occupancy first thing in the morning. We should talk through tonight what to do with the possible integration of the Mansons and the Armstrongs, and then implement whatever we decide after sunrise tomorrow."

"Vicky and I will do our part," Bert said. "How do you want us to blend in?"

Carl nodded his head, as he considered the question. "Well, since tonight may be a one-off, how about we make room for y'all here tonight and both of you stand watch together as Team Five. You will stand watch after Dave and me."

Carl covered their watch procedures, including the actions should they notice anything during their watch. As a gesture of goodwill and celebration, Carl proposed and they all agreed to a grilled meat supper with kernel corn. The change felt good. Laughter brought a measure of optimism to the group, as they shared stories from the days before the crisis began. The brief respite from the ordeal in which they were all immersed recharged their hope. As darkness enveloped the valley, they set the lookouts for the night with Team One taking the first watch period. Bert and Vicky blended in quite well. Vicky tended to Breckyn, as though the infant care was a missing part of her life . . . well, except for the feeding of the baby girl, which only Lisa could perform. Carl and Janet took the opportunity to cuddle a little and reconnect with what little intimacy they could manage in a crowded room. *Another good day*, Carl told himself, as the embrace of slumber approached. *I wonder how many more good days we might find?*

—

17

The night had passed quietly, and in fact, uneventfully. They collectively consumed their modest morning meal before they began the day's events.

The first order of business was the configuring of the Higgins condo for cold weather occupancy. They started a modest fire in the fireplace to begin warming the apartment, as they set up similar arrangements of blankets, sheets and curtains to light and thermally isolate the living room. They inventoried the contributed supplies brought over from the Johnson's apartment. They had all been impressed by the quantity and variety of food packets the Johnsons has accumulated. They also moved the appropriate mattresses and bedding from unit 332 to unit 331, and arranged them as directed by the two families.

Once complete with the physical setup of the Higgins' condo, Carl asked for Vicky and Bert to observe their inventory of canned and frozen food, so they had a clear concept of what was available. Carl also showed them the impressive accumulation of weapons and ammunition in the arsenal room. They agreed upon the redistribution of weapons, although the bulk of the firearms remained in the unit 332 arsenal room.

Through various discussions, they collectively agreed to absorb the burden of integrating the Armstrongs, if the couple agreed to the established rules. They all felt compassion for the plight of the older English couple caught in this crisis a long way from home. The Mansons were expected to be easier to integrate, as they had at least a portion of the necessary supplies. At least their opening plan was to set up unit 322, below the Parks' apartment, for their joint occupancy.

The logistics of watch standing and defense were getting more complicated, as the communications difficulties increased. They provisionally agreed to a four-person watch procedure—two high and two low. Once they had collected the additional team members they were going to get, they would collectively decide how best to defend the building and ensure survival.

The plan for the day entailed Pete and Bert going back out to bring first the Armstrongs, and then the Mansons to Building 3. If the initial visit went well and they agreed upon the integration plan, they would then use the same process to move both families to Building 3, with Carl and Larry maintaining overwatch, armed with the same weapons as yesterday.

Carl had observed Pete and Bert moving on the tamped down path to the back of Building 2, but it was not until Janet knocked on the glass door that Carl knew something had changed.

"The Armstrongs are here," Janet whispered.

"Thanks. I'll wait until everyone is here before I come in."

Janet nodded her head and closed the door. Again, Carl saw Bert and Pete pass between Building 3 and 2. He could not see the gap between Buildings 2 and 1. They would know soon enough.

The movement of the Mansons took appreciably longer than the Armstrongs, presumably because there were more of them, and thus more preparations were required. The second phase consolidation took a little over 30 minutes. Carl first saw Pete leading the single file group, followed by the father, daughter, son, mother, and finally, Bert Johnson bringing up the rear. Carl waited for Janet's notification.

The knock on the glass caught his attention. Carl quickly glanced to the sky. The sun was near local zenith, and he also noticed high cirrus clouds moving toward them from the southwest. *Another weather system*, he told himself.

Carl looked back to the door. When he did, Janet cracked it and whispered, "The Mansons are here as well." Carl nodded his head in recognition and moved inside.

Carl cradled the rifle in the crook of his left arm. The living room was very crowded with the whole group—all 19 of them including Breckyn. "Welcome," he said with buoyant confidence. "I'm Carl Parks," he said, raising his hand and signaling for everyone to do the same, as they were introduced. "My wife, Janet; our oldest child and only daughter, Lisa, with her newborn daughter, Breckyn; our oldest son, Mike; middle son, Nick, and his buddy, Dave, and our youngest son, Alex. Like most up here this time of year, we came up for our annual pre-Christmas skiing vacation, and arrived the night of the event. Pete, would you be so kind to introduce your family?"

"Sure. I'm Pete Higgins," he said, raising his hand as well. "This is my wife Barbara, and our only child and son, Larry. We were on our way out of the valley back to our home in Denver when the event occurred. We were near Dillon Reservoir when everything went black."

Vicky Johnson jumped in. "I'm Vicky," she said and gestured to her husband, "and my husband Bert. We own unit 412 and usually spend the holiday season up in these mountains. We love skiing. We expected our two adult children and their families to join us for Christmas. That did not happen and we've heard no word on their situation. So . . . here we are."

Carl nodded to the Mansons. The father took the task. "I'm Oscar Manson. This is my wife, Emily; our oldest and only son, Aaron; and our youngest and only daughter, Melissa. We had been up here for the whole week prior to the blackout. In fact, we were going to leave that Saturday. Does anyone know what happened and why it has taken so long to get the power back on?"

Carl answered, "None of us knows what happened. I will confess I had some kind of premonition that night. The Higgins were on the road and witnessed the high altitude flash, and their automobile went dead simultaneously. From the evidence we do have, I suspect this country was attacked, and a high energy, Electromagnetic Pulse event was what the Higgins family witnessed. EMP, as it is called in the military, causes electronic circuits, especially microchips and other small circuits that are common to virtually every device in modern society, to fuse and short-circuit, rendering them permanently inoperable."

"Damn!" Oscar exclaimed. "If I understand what you've said, electricity is not likely to be coming back on anytime soon."

"Correct. Those circuits compromised by the EMP are toast. Repair is not possible. Replacement is the only option, and even some of the replacement parts may have been compromised. Clearly, remedy is not likely for a mountain resort village like Breckenridge. There is a possibility electrical equipment that was *de facto* shielded from the source might be operable, or older equipment like vehicles that did not have microcircuits and switches. If I had to decide, I would focus our recovery effort on the population centers like Denver, assuming they still exist, and work out from there."

"Damn. That is rather bleak," Oscar offered,

Pete jumped in. "Yes, for the moment, which is precisely why we see this as a survival situation. We must remain calm and try our best to remain safe and healthy. In the spring, when the roads and mountain passes are clear of snow and ice, we plan to hike out of the valley," Pete paused and looked to Carl, who nodded his concurrence. "Our expectation is, once we reach lower elevations, we will encounter more people and perhaps some form of normalcy. If we are lucky, those people will be closer to the recovery efforts and can inform us of what happened and is happening."

"As Americans," Carl interjected, and looked to Anne and George, "we must apologize to our visitors. I am terribly sorry y'all got sucked up into whatever this is," he said, waving his hands all around. "Please introduce yourselves."

George Armstrong nodded his head and stood. "I'm George Armstrong, and this is my wife of 30 years, Anne," he said, gesturing to an attractive middle-aged woman, who in turn raised her right hand. "We live, or at least used to live," he said with solemnity, "in Cornwall, England—the southwest of England and across the Severn Estuary from Wales. Like the Parks family, we arrived the day before the blackout befell us all. I must thank Janet and Barbara for feeding us." George looked directly at Janet and Barbara. "That was the first meal we have had in nearly three weeks. We are grateful beyond expression for your generosity. If I understand what you've told us, Mister Parks, it may well be even longer, if ever, that we return home."

Carl nodded his head slowly and reluctantly. "I do not want to be a pessimist, but the reality is, if I am correct, all commercial aircraft are quite likely to be in the category of inoperable without replacement of their electronics. Military vehicles and aircraft are generally hardened by design to withstand EMP, but no commercial aircraft, to my knowledge, are comparably hardened."

"Oh dear." A long silent pause absorbed all sound including the occasional crackling of the fire. George looked up from his feet and smiled. "Well then, we must make the most of what we have. After all, we are alive, and with profound gratitude, we place ourselves at your mercy."

Carl immediately changed the subject. "Do any of you have military experience in any capacity?"

"No sir," George responded. Oscar shook his head to the negative. Neither of the new women reacted in any manner.

"Do any of you have firearms experience?"

The response was the same.

"OK," Carl continued. "We will have to teach you quickly, as it is necessary for our mutual protection. Also, I am mindful of the time. If we are going to do this, we need to complete the moves before sunset," Carl said, paused, and then continued. "Because we are nearly doubling in size, we also need to restructure our watch organization and implement what we agree to before we get too deep into twilight."

"Watch organization?" asked George.

"Yes. We stand watch, mostly at night, so that everyone can get a decent night's sleep, and we do not get surprised by any marauders."

"Very well."

"As far as the living arrangements," Carl pressed on, "my suggestion is we set up unit 322, as we have done here and in the Higgins' apartment, for cold weather living. In case you might be curious, unit 321 has a deceased couple still in it . . . frozen to death."

"Dear God," gasped Emily Manson.

"It is a bit macabre, but it is the reality we are living. They are not the only ones."

"Dear God," Emily repeated.

Carl chose to move on without dwelling on the negative. "Our pack mules..."

"Oh great," Nick protested. "Now, we are simply pack mules." Quite a few in the room laughed, as did Nick.

"As I was saying, before I was so rudely interrupted, our sons can help move what supplies you have, as well as your belongings you wish to protect, while Pete and the ladies help configure your new residence. Larry and I will assume the overwatch, as we have done."

"Was that you who terminated those two robbers outside Building 5?" asked Oscar.

"Yes," was Carl's succinct response. Oscar did not pursue his inquiry. Carl looked to his sons. "Mike, you and Alex go with Oscar and Aaron. Nick and Dave can go with George."

"I can help," young Melissa chimed in.

Carl smiled. "Very well. Why don't you go with your dad." Melissa nodded her head. "OK, folks, let's get 'er done."

The crowded living room became an instant beehive of activity, as each member of the expanded group went about preparing for and tending to their assigned tasks.

As the move proceeded, Carl kept track of several groups across Four O'Clock Run Road. Several episodes of gunfire along with a woman's screams in the distance heightened his attention.

Janet opened the door and joined her husband on the balcony. "322 is ready," she whispered.

"Good." Carl continued his scanning of the field of view.

"They've already moved in some stuff."

"OK."

"The door is busted up pretty good."

"Yes . . . nature of the beast," he responded without taking his eyes off the scene around them. Carl occasionally looked through his rifle sight to evaluate details of points of interest. Trees obscured his clear view, but gave him enough direct sight, to assess the situation. So far, what was going on across the road posed no threat to the move teams. "We'll figure something out to ensure they have security."

They sat quietly and observed. Janet did tap Carl on the shoulder several times to point out the boys carrying out the transportation task for the consolidation. It appeared they were making good progress. The sun was approaching the western ridgeline. They had perhaps another hour of sunlight, although high cirrus clouds were thickening and dimming the sunlight, and then they would have a couple of hours of diminished geography-induced twilight.

Carl took a few moments to re-assess the two bodies in front of Building 5. Neither body had been disturbed, which likely indicated their stolen items were still there as well as their weapons. Perhaps when the moves are complete, with any daylight left, a couple of them could venture out to search the bodies for anything useful to the group's survival.

Barbara tapped softly on the glass door. Both Janet and Carl looked to the sound. Barb cracked the door and whispered, "The Armstrongs are complete." Carl nodded his acknowledgment. "The Mansons should be finished in 20-30 minutes, by their estimate." Again, Carl nodded his head. Barbara closed the door.

"I think this is a good idea," whispered Janet.

"Yeah," was Carl's succinct reply.

"You won't have to take on so much."

"Yeah."

Janet abandoned her observation task and turned her head to look at her husband's right ear. "What are you concerned about?"

"Many things, my darling."

"Like what?"

"It only takes one thief to sour the whole pudding."

"There is that risk. What else?"

"The more people we have on the inside," he said quietly, without taking his eyes off the scene before them, "the more variables we have to contend with at any one time. Our situation is going to get more confounding and threatening, as our supplies dwindle. Protecting our group is difficult enough without the threat of looking over my shoulder. I just hope nobody betrays us."

"Do you think that is possible?"

"It is always possible with human beings. Desperate times lead desperate people to do desperate things. That is what I worry about."

"Hopefully, it will not come to that in any form."

"Yes, well . . . it will be what it will be."

Janet returned to her observation task and thoughts, until the knock on the glass door attracted their attention, again. Barbara did not bother opening the door and simply gestured for Janet and Carl to come inside. Carl nodded his head and secured the watch station. He took one last look at the sky. The sun was not yet beyond the western ridgeline, but it was nearly obscured by the thickening high clouds.

Again, Carl cradled the imposing rifle in the crook of his left arm. The living room was once more filled with now four families.

"How did it go?" asked Carl, as he put his arm around his wife's shoulders.

"Everything is done," answered Oscar. "We still need to settle in, but at least we are here."

"As are we," George added.

"Excellent. We still have some daylight left, although the clouds are thickening. We may well get another storm tonight or tomorrow, and while I was watching, I noticed the two intruders we dropped outside Building 5 have not been disturbed, as far as I could tell, which means their loot and weapons are likely still there. Before it gets any darker and especially before the next snow comes, I would recommend Mike and I go out to recover what we can from the bodies." Carl looked at Pete. "You could do the overwatch for our short excursion."

Pete chuckled. "I could and would, but you are pretty damn good at it. My suggestion would be for Mike and me to do the search, and you perform your exceptional overwatch."

"Thank you for the vote of confidence, but I need to get out and move around a little."

"OK . . . totally understand," Pete said and reached for the Remington rifle. Carl checked to make sure the safety was engaged, and then passed the weapon to Pete.

Carl and Mike went to the arsenal room. Carl chose the Tactical Mossberg since it has a large, robust, shoulder strap. Mike chose the other Mossberg, as well as the other M1911 plus two loaded magazines. Carl still carried his M1911 and the holstered PPK. He handed Mike a set of shoulder bags and took another set for himself, just in case they found more to carry than they could observe.

They returned to the living room ready to go. Carl stood before the expanded group. "Why don't y'all work on 322, to get ready for tonight? This search should not take long. When we get back, we can have a collective evening meal and establish our new watch teams and procedures."

"OK," Oscar replied with an ebullient enthusiasm.

Carl looked into the eyes of his oldest son. "Ready?"

"Yes, Dad. Ready."

"For everyone's benefit," Carl said and waited for all eyes to be on him, "we've been accustomed to using a knock sequence upon returning after being outside. We hold up our hand and signal the sequence, rather than speak it." Carl held up his right hand and extended his fingers in sequence—three, three, one. "Does everyone have it?" Everyone nodded in the affirmative. Nick and Alex held up their hands and repeated the sequence. "OK. We're off."

"Good hunting," Bert said. Carl held up his extended right hand without looking back or verbally responding.

The Armstrongs and Mansons followed Mike and Carl down one level, and entered their new residence.

Carl stopped at the rear lobby door and connected with Mike's eyes. "Here we go."

Their movement from Building 3 along the now tamped down path through thigh-high snow was comparatively effortless to the Building 4 rear lobby door. The virgin snowdrifts beyond the door made their movement more problematic.

Carl and Mike took turns being the snowplow, while the others kept watch. Mike developed a method of turning and falling backward to tamp down snow, after he handed his shotgun to his father. The technique worked surprisingly well. Carl considered going through the Building 5 lobby, but ultimately he decided the risk was too great. They crossed from back to front between Buildings 4 and 5. When they reached the northeast corner of Building 5, Carl looked back to the balcony of unit 332 and received a hand wave from Pete. He returned a thumb's up. Carl carefully checked the ground floor windows and balcony of unit 511. There were no signs of inhabitation or disturbance. They moved as quickly as they could between the building wall and the hedge.

When they reached the bodies, they were both frozen solid in their final positions. Before stepping in front of the lobby door, Carl leaned to Mike's ear. "Keep a close eye on the interior without exposing yourself. We don't need any surprises." Mike nodded his head. "I'll search the bodies." Again, Mike nodded his head. Carl signaled to go. Mike nearly jumped across the door, took several quick glances into the lobby, and then signaled his father that it was clear.

Carl stood over the first body. Up close, he was a 20-something man with a dark brown beard and was oddly not well dressed for the cold. The shot hit him center torso, directly at his heart. Two days exposed to freezing temperatures had rendered his clothing very stiff, almost solid as well. The bag he had been carrying contained a dozen or so cans of tuna, salmon and perhaps some other meat. He broke the bag free of the thin ice entrapment and placed it in one of his shoulder bags. The pistol—a Smith & Wesson, Model 36 Classic, 38-caliber revolver with a just under two-inch barrel had fallen not far from his right hand. The heat of having been fired several times melted some of the snow into ice, capturing the weapon. Carl used the stock of his shotgun to break the pistol free, although it still had chunks of ice stuck to the metal and handgrip. He placed the pistol in the bag, as well. Carl did the best he could to search the body for any extra ammunition or other weapons. He found none and had gone as far as he could go short of thawing the body, which was fairly well frozen in place. Carl went to the second body that was also a 20-something fellow, short and with a slighter build than his compadre, but at least he had ski clothing. The bag of the second man contained nearly the same number of canned meats that were about twice the size of the other cans. Carl placed the heavy bag in his other shoulder bag. The second man's pistol appeared to be a Glock Model G36 subcompact 45-caliber semi-automatic with an extended magazine still gripped and frozen in the dead hand. *Maybe I should just leave this one,* he thought to himself. Naw, I just can't do that. *Someone else might go to the effort to refurbish and use the weapon.* Carl tried to twist and pull on the pistol, but it would not budge. He withdrew his hunting knife, flipped open the blade, and tried to pry the pistol loose without success. Carl resorted to a combination of cutting, hitting and prying the pistol out. It was a rather grim appearance with ice and parts of the dead man's fingers still stuck to the pistol grip. Carl placed the gruesome item in his first bag with the other pistol. He felt the exposed clothing, which was more malleable than the first man's clothing. Another folding knife he would have to check out later, and three loaded magazines for the Glock. The recovered items went into the first bag. Carl quickly checked both bodies, again, just to make sure they had recovered everything of interest they could. Satisfied, Carl signaled for Mike to precede him back to Building 3. The return trip was much easier.

Carl decided to stop at unit 322 to check on progress. He knocked – 3-3-1. The door opened.

Oscar said with a smile, "Welcome to our new abode."

Carl nodded. "Are y'all comfortable with this arrangement?"

"We are," George replied promptly.

Oscar looked to his family, and then replied, "Yes, we are as well."

"Thank you, Mister Parks," young Melissa interjected.

"You are quite welcome. This is a mutual relationship. We protect and support each other."

"We will do our share," added George. Emily nodded her head in agreement with her husband.

"We recovered a fair amount of canned meats from the two intruders that we would like to contribute to your stock." Carl removed his shoulder bag and handed it to Oscar. "This is a rather indelicate question, but a necessary one in our circumstances." Oscar and George displayed somewhat puzzled expressions. "What is your food and firewood inventory state?"

"How about we show you?" Oscar said. He did not wait for a reply and led Carl and the whole group to the first bedroom. Carl liked how they had deployed their thermal curtain. On the lower bunk bed, they had arranged a sizeable inventory of canned fruits, vegetables, potatoes, and some meats. "We have a good amount, but it is not enough to make it to spring."

"This addition will help," Carl said, gesturing to the shoulder bags.

Emily took the bags from Oscar's hand and unloaded the first bag. "Good . . . chicken and salmon . . . excellent . . . large cans, too." She opened the second bag, gasped loudly and dropped the bag.

"Oh, sorry, Emily. I forgot about that," Carl said and reached for the bag.

Oscar took the bag from his wife and looked inside. "What the hell!" he exclaimed, as he lifted the semi-automatic pistol with the finger parts and ice still attached.

Anne covered her mouth and stifled her scream, as she turned away. Emily stretched her arms and stepped in front of her children to block their view of the gruesome item, and then ushered her children out of the room. Anne left the room as well.

Carl looked at Oscar. "I am sorry for that. It was frozen in place and had to be broken free."

"Looks like they were cut free," Oscar said.

"Yes . . . cut," answered Carl. "A little warmth will clean up the pistol. If you don't want the pistol, I'll take it, if you wish."

"That's OK. Thanks Carl. I'm not quite so sensitive as my wife is. I'll clean it up."

"As you wish. There is also a snub-nose 38 and a folding, hunting knife in there. In fact, I did not have time to examine the knife. Would you mind?"

Oscar put the Glock on the bed, withdrew the knife and handed it to Carl.

Carl took the knife, spun it in his hand several times to feel the balance, and then flipped the blade out and in a half dozen times. "Impressive. I've seen these advertised, but I've never held one. If I remember correctly, this is a KA-BAR Warthog, I think they call it, not exactly like the military K-Bar I carried in the Marines, but still an impressive knife." Carl re-folded the knife and handed it to Oscar.

"You can keep it," Oscar said and held it out to Carl, who held his right hand, vertical, palm out.

"May I?" asked George. Oscar handed him the folded knife. George flipped the blade out and in a few times, and felt the edges of the blade. "Dear me, that is a very sharp blade."

"High-quality steel, I suspect," added Carl, and looked to Mike. "Would you like to handle the knife?"

"Sure, Dad." George handed the knife to Mike. "It's heavier than it looks. I like your K-Bar better," he proclaimed.

Carl chuckled softly. "But, my K-bar does not fit in your pocket easily."

Mike handed the folded knife back to Mister Manson.

Carl looked at Oscar. "You did not mention your attempt to leave in your introduction. Did you attempt an exfiltration, as we call it in the military?"

"Yes," answered Oscar. "We moved on during the introductions, and it did not seem relevant."

"Pete and Barb were on their way out in the car, when the event occurred. It took them a horrific week to make it back here. Fortunately, their condo had not been compromised. Knowing what we are up against is important."

"We loaded the car that Saturday morning, expecting to drive out. The car was stone cold dead . . . not even a flicker of light. We noticed all of the streetlights, the store lights in town, everything electrical were out—black. We knew something bad had happened. We waited another day and night to see if the lights would come back on. I thought we might get out if we made it to I-70 and Silverthorne. We didn't even make it to the reservoir. It wasn't so bad going out, but trying to get back was a nightmare. We were extraordinarily lucky. We saw other groups out there with the same objective, apparently. A couple ahead of us by a hundred yards or so were killed by a sniper—first the man and then the woman. We found a small maintenance shack near the road and hid there until nighttime. The smell of gasoline was terrible. I saw four men search the bodies of the dead couple. They stripped them and took everything they had. We had no weapons. That night, we tried to continue, passing by the naked bodies and came upon more dead people. As best I could tell, all of them had been shot—a single, well-aimed shot I must say. They had all been stripped of everything. It was rough on Emily and the kids. We had to find places to hide during the daylight hours and moving at night was quite difficult, with lots of stumbles and falls. After seeing the first couple killed just ahead of us, I was very cautious, which made our progress even slower."

"So, there are snipers out there picking off people trying to escape?"

"Yes. We saw perhaps a dozen people killed, and left on the road or beside the road. I don't think they were killing to kill. They were killing to take what the people had without confrontation. Like us, I imagine they all carried food and perhaps other supplies to survive in the open during winter. It was very brutal out there . . . one of many reasons we were most grateful for your offer to join your little band of happy campers."

They all chuckled briefly at the spot of levity.

"The Higgins family did not see slain people that I'm aware of, or perhaps they just did not mention what they saw. It may well be worse out there than I figured. Those incidents you witnessed were not robberies; they were murders and looting."

"I would agree. The first couple that we saw was not threatening anyone. They were simply walking down the snow-packed road, just like we were. They weren't warned or challenged that we could tell. It could have been us."

"A very sobering reality."

"Gun violence seems to be so bloody common in the United States," interjected George.

Carl smiled. "Not really. These are times without law and order, and are quite chaotic and anarchistic. Desperate times . . . and all."

"We shall have to rely on your judgment and protection. I have no experience with firearms."

"We are comparatively safe here . . . as long as we maintain vigilance. Between Pete and me, we should be able to deal with intruders, short of a full-scale assault, which we will strive to avoid." Carl checked his wristwatch. "We have another hour before local sunset. We really should confer with the group and agree upon our revised security procedures."

"How do you wish to proceed?" asked Oscar.

"Well, we need to gather the whole group and talk things out."

"We have more room. Perhaps we should gather here, then." Oscar paused, but received no response. "Plus, the extra bodies will help warm our living room." They all laughed.

"There is that," Carl added with a smile. "That is fine by me. Plus, it will be a little easier to keep an ear out for the doors." Oscar and George nodded their heads. Mike just shrugged his shoulders. "OK. I'll go gather up everyone and be right back."

Carl and Mike entered the living room, followed by Oscar and George. The women and children looked at the men with an odd expression of puzzlement and disgust. "I'll let Oscar explain," Carl said, as he passed through the living room and departed.

Carl knocked first on the Higgins' door. Barb opened the door. "We're going to have a group meeting in 322 to decide on the security plan." Barb nodded her head and closed the door. Carl gave the knock sequence on their apartment door. Nick opened the door and stood back, allowing Mike and Carl to enter. "Let's get everyone in," he commanded. Before Pete and Larry returned, the knock sequence announced the arrival of Barb, Bert and Vicky. Once the remainder of the group was present, Carl informed them, "We're going to gather up the whole group in the apartment below to settle the watch make-up and schedule."

"Do you want me to come too?" asked Lisa.

"You are part of the family, are you not?"

Lisa sneered at her father and prepared Breckyn for the cold . . . not that they would be exposed that long. Those who were not appropriately dressed did so. Carl decided to keep the shotgun with him, just in case something happened while they were downstairs. He gestured for Mike and Pete to retain their weapons.

"Should we be armed?" asked Nick.

"Not necessary," Carl answered. "Mister Higgins, Mike and I should be able to handle things, if something happens."

Once everyone was ready, Janet held up her right fist and flashed, three, three, one, with her fingers, as she held her husband's eyes. Carl nodded his head in acknowledgment. Janet led the group down one level and connected with the Mansons. Carl was the last to enter the 322 apartment. Vicky had already taken Breckyn from Lisa and was rocking the baby girl in her arms.

Carl whispered to Mike, "Guard the door. Let us know if anything changes out there." Mike nodded his concurrence. "Remember, better safe than sorry." Again, their oldest boy nodded his head. Carl turned to the whole group and remained standing. Except for Mike, Pete and Vicky, everyone was seated on chairs, couches or the floor. The modest fire had warmed up the living room nicely. Carl kept the Mossberg cradled in his left arm. "With us somewhat spread out on two floors, communications will be a little more problematic."

"What does that mean?" asked Larry.

"Difficult." The boy nodded his head. "We need to keep our doors locked." Oscar raised his hand. Carl knew what he was going to say. "Or, braced closed . . . for those who do not have functional locks." Oscar smiled and Carl nodded. "Because we will inherently be moving around more, we should confine ourselves to one knock sequence per day. We'll change the sequence each morning at zero eight hundred, when everyone should be awake; it is twilight out; and, the beginning of another day. I want to remind everyone to do your daily exercises. We must remain fit for the arduous journey out of these mountains this coming spring. Without implying a *dictum*," Carl stopped when Larry raised his hand, "meaning not an order." Larry nodded his head and lowered his hand. "If anyone has s better idea, I urge you to speak up." Carl paused to scan the audience. Nearly everyone nodded their heads. "Now, I think we will need to guard the lobby doors, to protect the building, and I think we must maintain the highest observation point we can. We have enough people for four teams of four members each, including all the women and Melissa, but excluding Lisa and Breckyn." Several people chuckled at the thought of Breckyn being required to stand watch.

"Larry will be the supernumerary, now, filling in for anyone not able to stand watch. I sketched out a team composition to spread out those who know the process, mixing older and younger adults, and males and females, and from each apartment, so no one apartment will be empty and no one will be alone. Each team will have an 'A' and 'B' section that will rotate between high and low."

"High and low?" asked Janet.

"Low being the front and rear lobby doors, and high being this apartment—the balcony and first bedroom, to observe the front and back of the building. So, each section will stand high watch and the next period stand low watch. The high watch will rotate split shift, as we have been doing, since the balcony watch station is the only outside position. For the time being, until we can get everyone trained better, if anyone sees any human being or animal that appears threatening or moving toward this building, wake me and/or Pete. We will handle the weapons for any contingency, until everyone is trained properly. Any questions so far?" Carl pointed to everyone, including Mike, and received a negative gesture or reply. "Is everyone agreed so far?" Carl checked everyone for an affirmative response. "The assignments I have sketched out as a starting point are: Barb and Aaron as Team One 'A' Section, and Oscar and Mike as 'B' Section; Pete and Melissa as Team Two 'A' Section, with Emily and Dave as 'B' Section; Janet and George as Team Three 'A' Section, and Bert and Alex as 'B' Section; and lastly, Anne and me as Team Four 'A' Section, and Vicky and Nick 'B' Section. Again, Larry will be the supernumerary for now. How does that sound?'"

"Good starting point, Carl," responded Pete. "We can try it for a day or two, and then make adjustments as we deem appropriate. Is everyone in agreement?"

"Anne and I are very new to this," George said. "We will need a little extra instruction, I'm afraid."

"Sure. That's why I put y'all with Janet and me."

Janet laughed. "You are giving me more credit than I am due, my darling." Others laughed as well.

"I don't know anything about guns," Anne stated. "I'm afraid of guns."

"No need to worry about that for the time being. I've taught my family the basics. But, for now, Pete and I should be able to perform the weapons work, unless the amount of activity we have to deal with gets to be too much. Until then, Pete and I will handle the weapons, and we will take the training more slowly . . . for better absorption."

"I just don't think I can do anything with a gun," Anne pressed.

"Don't worry about it, for now, Anne. There are enough of us, now, to take care of protection . . . at least until we have to begin the trek out of here in the spring. I've not thought through all the logistics of that, just yet, but all in due course. Any other questions or concerns?" Carl checked his wristwatch. "By the way, do we have any other mechanical watches?"

"Anne's watch is mechanical," George answered promptly. "Mine was electronic and stopped that night. We also have an old mechanical, portable, alarm clock that still works."

"My watch still works," Vicky added.

"OK," said Carl. "With your permission, George and Anne, how about we use your alarm clock as the master time and place the clock at the first bedroom watch station, so whoever has the watch station at the end of a cycle will have the responsibility of notification of the next watch team."

"How do we know who is next and where to find them if they are sleeping?" asked Bert.

"I will write the team assignments on the living room wall of our apartment in big letters, so it should be easier to read even in the firelight at night. There is a person from each apartment on every team. That person will handle the cycle notification for his or her respective apartment. It will be a little awkward, at first, but I think we can get the hang of it, soon enough. We can always tweak it, as we gain experience."

"Supper time," Janet said, sensing the end of the security discussion.

"Definitely," Carl concurred. "The first watch period is rapidly approaching. With your concurrence, Bert and Vicky, I would suggest a freeze-dried meal for everyone tonight. We have water. We can heat a pot of water for a warm, somewhat sumptuous meal, before we secure for the night."

"Agreed," Bert responded.

"Very well, then, let's hop to it."

Everyone began to move, initially to their respective apartments. Nick helped his mother with getting the large kettle filled with water and on the fire. Carl went to the blackout curtain. It was quite dark out and light snow was falling. They were not quite halfway through evening twilight, so the darkness suggested the flurries were the beginning of what probably was another large snowstorm.

"The snow is beginning," Carl announced softly and matter-of-factly.

"Does that mean no watches tonight?" asked Alex.

Carl smiled. "Perhaps. Let's get past our evening meal, and then we'll decide." The response satisfied Alex and anyone else who was curious.

The prescribed knock sequence heralded the first arrivals—the unit 322 folks. Carl found a fat marker in a utility drawer. He went to the wall opposite the balcony windows and door, and marked in large letters the watch schedule he had articulated earlier.

The unit 331 folks arrived a short time later. Bert carried a cardboard box nearly full of freeze-dried meals. They emptied the box, laying each packet flat on the counter top with the labels up and oriented in the same direction. Each member of the team examined the watch schedule on the wall to varying degrees. No one asked any questions.

"Water's ready," Janet announced.

Alex used the removal handles to lift the kettle of steaming water off the grill and carried it carefully to the inoperable stovetop.

"Is everyone familiar with these meals?" Bert asked.

"No," responded George. "I'm afraid not."

Bert nodded his head. He selected a meal. Looking to Janet, he asked, "Do you have a cup size measuring cup and spoon?" Janet went to the exact drawer, retrieved the proper size, measuring cup, and handed it to Bert. "It is really quite simple. Open the pack, remove the packet, unfold the sides," he paused to slowly demonstrate the opening process, "then, take a cup of hot water," which he did, "and pour water in it." Bert did so, spreading the water on the contents. "Stir it a little to make sure everything is equally hydrated . . . and *voilà*, a ready-to-eat meal. You can add seasonings to taste . . . like Tabasco, pepper, salt and such, as you wish. I would suggest you try it *au naturel* first, before adding to it."

"It is a little dark to read the labels," Janet said, and then lit one of the candles. "This should help." She did not select a meal and handed the candle to Melissa.

"Me, first?" she asked.

"Yes," Janet answered. "You are the youngest."

Carl looked at the labels as the team members made their selections and prepared their meals. It had been quite some time since he had used the meals during his military service days. He was amazed at the variety: Beef Stew, Beef Stroganoff, Chicken à la King, Chicken and Dumplings, Chicken and Rice, and he chuckled when he saw Chili Mac with Beef, and even Italian Style Pepper Steak with Rice and Tomatoes. "My gosh," Carl exclaimed, "even Pasta Primavera and Spaghetti with Meat Sauce. This is amazing variety."

"Yes," said Bert. "Incredible stuff, and this is just a small sampling. Even with our rather large inventory, we don't have all of them."

"Incredible!" Carl waited until everyone had made their selection. The last item remaining for him was Breakfast Skillet. "Even breakfast."

"Yep. We even acquired a few desserts, just for grins."

"I want one of those," Lisa said.

"You can have 'em whenever you wish."

"Sweet," she added.

They ate with surprising joviality. They were always hungry, but with these meals, just about everyone ate their modest meals surprisingly slowly, as if to savor the welcome change.

Carl enjoyed his Breakfast Skillet meal and the refreshing reminder of what tasty food meant to them. Several of the group expressed a yearning for an end to their ordeal, so they could appreciate a well-cooked, delicious meal without the drama that had enveloped their lives for the last three weeks.

Unusual contentment possessed most of the group, as they sat around the fireplace and shared their perspective of skiing Summit County—the five associated ski areas: Breckenridge, Keystone, Copper Mountain, Loveland and Arapaho Basin. Skiing was the one passion they all shared. Even Anne and George became more animated than they had been since they met them. Yes, skiing was important to all of them. The Armstrongs offered their observations of European ski areas versus Summit County, and they claimed they preferred Summit County to all the places they had been to date.

While the group shared their skiing experience, Carl went to the edge of the blackout curtain, but he could not see much. He quickly went behind the curtain in the hope his eyes adjusting to the dark might help him see what he wanted to see. That was not successful. Carl opened the door and stepped outside. An inch of snow had already blanketed the balcony. Snow was falling more heavily now. Fortunately, so far, there was little to no wind blowing the snow around. He could see nothing beyond the falling snow. In fact, he could not even see the ground below them. Carl returned to the warm interior.

"It is snowing quite heavily out there. We can suspend the watch standing until the snow stops, or at least begins to taper off. It is doubtful anyone will be moving around in this storm."

"What do we do next?" asked George Armstrong.

"Get a good night's sleep. I'm going to check the lobby doors to make sure they are locked and secure. Everyone is welcome to enjoy the moment of respite." Carl went to the door.

"I'll go with you," Pete said.

The dim firelight illuminated the landing as they stepped out and closed the door. Pete placed his right hand on Carl's left shoulder. Neither man spoke, as they waited for their eyes to adjust to the dark. Once they achieved most of the adaption they would obtain, they moved slowly and carefully, feeling their way down the stairs. The lobby remained clear and the doors were closed. They validated that both glass doors were closed, locked and secure. The two men made their way back up the stairs. The knock sequence opened the door to unit 332. Even the dim light hurt their eyes, as they adjusted to the light.

The whole group enjoyed the light moment, as if they wanted to preserve it. Eventually, they dispersed to their respective dwellings for the night. They wished each a good night's sleep, and so ended the day.

—

18

The snowstorm lasted three days and deposited more than two feet of new snow on top of what they already had on the ground. The inoperative automobiles left in the parking lot were no longer recognizable as anything other than mounds of snow. Drifts deepened to five and six feet, and in some cases even more.

They spent the days of quiet, cleaning their clothes and apartments, cleaning the weapons, and enjoying downtime from the intensity of their new normal. Carl and Janet even started reading one of the available books. He also tried to sketch out some notional approaches to the logistics of their eventual journey out of the mountains. Carl thought about sustenance en route, protection from the weather and bad men while they were on the road, and the practical question of their method of portage.

Periodically over the intervening days, Carl checked the exterior, as much as he could see at any one time, and found not a single sign that anything was moving outside. One positive facet of all this snow, it is hard to walk on snow without leaving telltale tracks that are very difficult to mask.

"It looks like the snow has stopped and the sky is clearing to the west," announced Alex after returning from the cold rooms. "Can we go outside?"

"I'm down with that, too," Lisa chimed in, ". . . if Grandpa or Grandma will watch Breckyn."

Carl smiled. "I think it is safe for now. I'll take Breckyn." All the boys and Lisa began to suit up. "I'd suggest y'all tamp down the snow on the trail behind the building and to either side of the building wall at least to the corners. Try to go as far up the trail as you are comfortable and down to Park Avenue. It will be constructive to getting fresh air."

"We can do that," Mike said.

"You can use your tamping technique," Carl said to Mike. "Between the bunch of you, y'all should be able to make quick work of it."

"Sure, Dad," answered Mike. "I'll show everyone."

"Also, one of y'all need to stand guard with one of the shotguns, while the others are playing in the snow."

Mike nodded his head, went to the arsenal room, and returned with the Mossberg Tactical shotgun. Carl smiled and nodded his head.

"Also, please stop at the other apartments just to let them know what y'all are doing."

"Sure, Dad," Mike said, again.

All five of their children departed with Mike leading the way, leaving Janet and Carl alone for the first time since the crisis began . . . well, except for the baby. Carl cradled his granddaughter in his left arm, approached his wife with a broad smile on his face, and leaned forward to kiss her.

"No, no, no you don't. I know that look. We're not doing any of that until we've both had a proper bath."

"Janet!" protested Carl.

She wagged her right index finger at him. "Not on your life . . . ain't happenin'."

"You can't blame me for trying."

Janet smiled, faced her husband, looked into his eyes, and said, "No, I don't. I appreciate the sentiment. I want our intimacy back as well, Carl. I truly do. But, these are not conducive times."

"You got that right."

The prescribed knock sequence took Carl to the door with the baby still in his arms, despite the urge to grab a shotgun. He quickly peered through the peephole and backed away. Peter stood facing the door like he was facing a mug shot. Carl unlocked and opened the door.

"Good morning to you, Carl."

"Mornin' Pete. Come in," he said and allowed Pete to enter, and then closed and locked the door. "To what do we owe this pleasure?"

"Just thought I'd check in for the day. The kids stopped by to inform us on their way out. They were kind enough to allow Larry to join them. I don't know if Melissa and Aaron joined them, but it should be a welcome break from the rigors of our situation."

"We need a break, now and then," Carl said, smiling and winking at Janet, who could only shake her head.

"Quite so." They all chuckled briefly. "With the clearing weather, what is the plan?'

"Well, we still need to search the remaining no-activity apartments, and we still have to deal with the Building 5 problem."

"How should we proceed?"

Carl carefully passed Breckyn to Janet and retrieved their survey sheet. "We've completed Building 3. By my tally, we have three remaining units in Building 2, two units in Building 1, and four units in Building 4. Building 5 remains more problematic, for the moment, but there are at least a couple of units that qualify there."

"We're not quite to mid-day, so we could search some today," Pete observed.

"I don't see any pressure to get these searches done. We still have weeks to get through, and we have not seen the intrusions that I expected . . . at least so far. I'm good with letting the kids have some playtime to relax a little. If they consume the daylight hours, I'm OK with that, too. So, when they return, we should evaluate the daylight we have remaining and decide to search the remaining units. If we don't get them today, we'll work it tomorrow as required."

The prescribed knock sequence announced a return or new arrival. Carl checked the peephole. "It's Oscar," Carl announced and opened the door. "Good morning, Oscar," he said and allowed their teammate to enter.

"It's a beautiful day out," Oscar said with a smile. "Melissa and Aaron joined the kids' group."

"That's quite a little army out there."

"Yeah, I watched them for a while from the back window. I guess you told them to pack down the snow on the trail."

"Yep. It was useful for all of us, as we move around; but, it would also burn up some youthful energy."

"Good point. They appeared to be attacking their task with vigor and élan."

Pete interjected, "We were discussing our plans for the next few days of good weather." Oscar nodded his head with an expression of curiosity. Pete continued, "We were going to let the kids have their day. We have a number of units to search . . . to clear the whole complex. I think our plan is to work our way through the remaining units, until we've cleared this complex."

"What about beyond these buildings?"

"Good question," answered Pete.

Carl picked up the topic. "It all depends upon what we find, and what our food and wood supply status is when we complete the exploration. We have searched and recovered as much as we can from town, and there is certainly more risk with forays into town. We have a number of options, depending upon what we face ahead."

"That sounds reasonable . . . no need to take more risk than necessary."

"Exactly . . . to survive the weather and to ensure we are prepared—physically, mentally and emotionally—for the arduous journey out of these mountains."

"Certainly," Pete said and turned his attention to Breckyn. "How is the baby doing?"

"She's doing quite well in these medieval conditions, wouldn't you say, Sweetheart," Carl answered to the backs of Pete and Oscar, as the two men moved to Janet, who was bouncing the baby on her lap.

"Quite well, actually," Janet responded, "although Momma will need to bring back lunch here pretty soon." They all laughed. Breckyn began to fidget more as Grandma's attempts to distract her became less successful.

Carl checked his wristwatch. More than an hour had passed since the youth of their group had gone outside. Carl went to the arsenal room and looked outside only to see Lisa leading the group off the one-time ski trail and to the rear door. He returned to the living room and announced, "Looks like they've had enough cold to satisfy them for a while." Carl considered whether to just open the door, but decided it was better to exercise their security procedures, even though there was no threat. He watched at the door's peephole.

Lisa knocked three times, as if these were normal times. Carl did not respond in any manner. Mike reached around his sister and delivered the prescribed daily knock sequence. Carl smiled, unlocked and opened the door. Lisa passed right by her father without even a glance or apology for not providing the proper knock sequence. Lisa went directly to Janet. As the boys filed in, Carl heard Lisa say, "Breckyn must be hungry. My breasts are about to explode and hurt like hell."

The last of the children entered. Carl closed and locked the door.

"How did it go?" Carl asked to no one in particular.

Nick answered for the group. "We managed to tamp down the fresh snow from the street to not quite the next apartments to the west of us."

"We found several bodies among the trees," Alex announced. "One of them had apparently been discovered by a wolf or wolves."

"Which one?" Carl asked.

"The one to the west . . . up the trail."

"We also found three other bodies that appear to have been slaughtered—prepared, butchered, if you will—before being placed out there and buried in the snow."

Carl glanced to Janet, who was helping Lisa with Breckyn and staring at him. "How did you find them?"

"I was looking for a branch to use as a broom. I uncovered a foot."

"What do you mean . . . prepared?" Oscar asked.

Alex jumped in before Carl could respond. "They had been sliced open and their organs removed."

"Who would do that?" pressed Oscar.

Carl glanced again at Janet, who nodded her head for him to answer. "I did."

"What!"

"Before we get judgmental, perhaps we should gather up the whole group, so everyone hears the same thing and can ask questions," Carl said.

"OK," Oscar said and left to retrieve the remaining 322 folks. Peter did the same for 331.

Once everyone was present and the door closed, Oscar gestured to Carl, as if to say explain yourself.

"About a week after the crisis began, I was returning from town with several bags full of jerky I had purchased in town."

"How did you purchase them?" Oscar asked in a rather accusatory tone.

"With cash, which the keeper was all too eager to take. Anyway, on the way back, up the ski trail, three young men confronted me. They appeared to be late teens . . . early adult age. I asked them calmly to move aside and leave me alone. They made a move . . . ."

"Were they armed?" asked Bert.

"Yes, a large hunting knife, a baseball bat and an ax."

"They did not have a chance, did they?" asked Oscar.

"I gave them every chance possible, but I was not going to hand over the jerky, and I was not going to debate them."

"You killed them?" asked Vicky.

"Yes."

"What happened after that?" pressed Oscar.

"I saw no reason to let their deaths to be wasted. I removed their organs to prevent spoilage, and I packed them in snow to freeze and preserve their bodies. I tried to cover them as best I could, but apparently not good enough."

"For what purpose?"

"To be direct and blunt . . . as insurance," Carl answered with solemnity.

"Insurance? Insurance for what?" Bert asked.

"Against starvation."

"What the fuck!" Bert protested. "You're kidding, right?"

"No, I'm not."

"We are not cannibals!" protested Vicky, as Emily ran to the kitchen sink to vomit.

Carl waited for emotions to calm down. Barb went to help Emily clean up. "I share your concern and apprehension. I hope our situation never comes to that point. Those men chose a violent path. They met a violent end. I saw no reason to waste their deaths. I am far more driven to ensure our survival during the winter months in these mountains than I am in propriety."

"No way," muttered Emily, as she paced back and forth in the kitchen. "No way, no way," she repeated several more times, more strongly.

"As I said, I hope it never comes to that, which brings me to a more pertinent and now moment. We still have quite a few apparently empty apartments to search. It is better that we search them and control whatever useful contents we find than to let others do so."

"That's robbery," protested Vicky.

"Not in these circumstances. It is survival."

"Don't we have enough food?" Bert asked.

"I think by everyone's calculation, we have enough to make it to April, and perhaps enough to sustain us on the trek out of the mountains, but more is much better than not enough . . . and that is quite a bit better than tapping our insurance."

"I get your point," Oscar said, with a tone of acceptance rather than resistance. "What do you suggest?"

They discussed options and agreed to use their numbers to search the "unoccupied" apartments simultaneously with separate teams. The multiple teams made security overwatch more complicated, but do-able. On Peter's recommendation, Carl took the overwatch duty, as he had done previously. Janet agreed to take the rear overwatch to allow Larry to go with his father. Bert, Vicky, Nick and Dave searched Building 4 with four inactive, unsearched units on the survey sheet. Pete, Larry and Alex cleared Building 2 with three unsearched, inactive units. Oscar, Aaron and Mike handled Building 1 with two inactive units. They agreed to maintain their standoff stance regarding the search of the Building 5 "unoccupied" units, for the time being. Each search team armed up and dressed. Additional shoulder bags were created to ensure each team member had a set; it seemed oddly optimistic to Carl, but better prepared than not.

Oscar's team confirmed the two remaining families in Building 1 maintained their independence and at least apparent stability. They could detect no response from the folks in unit 111, but Oscar chose not to investigate more deeply than repeated knocks on the door and listening with an ear to the door for any activity.

Bert reported Building 4 cleared as well, and more notably the only remaining occupants, a young unmarried couple by the names of Reynolds and Baker, both in their late 20's or early 30's, were stable for now and open to joining the group at some future point, as yet unspecified.

Before their evening meal, the existing group gathered in unit 332.

"A good day," Pete declared.

"Yeah," added Bert.

Janet stood and moved next to Carl. "OK, so my question is, do we have enough now? Can we avoid the risk of armed confrontation?"

Nearly everyone looked to Carl, as if it was his question to answer. Carl felt the anticipation. "I am only one opinion. The direct answer, by my calculation, yes; we have enough. However, we cannot absorb any other mouths to feed without comparable food supply. So, I would say we are in pretty good shape, but our margins are not comforting."

"What the hell does that mean, Carl?"

"We still have two months, or more, to go before the roads clear enough for us to make it over the pass. A lot can happen and go wrong. We have been blessed to avoid illness or injury . . . well, other than Nick's wound, which by the way, we should check."

"Barb and I have checked his wound every day since it happened a week ago. He is healing quite nicely, especially considering our rather primitive circumstances."

"The acquired medications," Barb interjected, "although some appear to be expired and possibly of reduced efficacy, have improved our situation."

"Thank you for that, Barb. Anyway, the answer to Janet's query directly, we can take a more reserved stance for a few days or weeks, to see how things go."

"That's a start," Janet snickered and sat down.

"Let me ask, Bert," Carl said, looking to Bert Johnson, "what do you think the couple in 422 is going to do?"

Bert stood, cleared his throat, and answered. "My guess is, they intend to stay to themselves. I don't know how they are feeding themselves, and their food supply is probably thinner than they would like. If I read between the lines to their words, they are still hoping for rescue from the outside. Do you agree, Vicky?"

"Yes."

"I think they sense they may need help. We tried to convince them of the virtual permanence of the current situation, but they still hold onto hope for rescue."

"Agreed," Vicky added.

"They are potential joiners, most likely without bringing sufficient food supply with them. That would add stress and consume margin for the rest of us."

"What are you suggesting?" Vicky asked. "Should we reject them?"

"That is a hypothetical that . . . that . . . we are not to that juncture, yet."

"But, it is a worthy 'what if,' is it not?" Vicky pressed.

"The only thing I feel safe in predicting is, we will have many hard days and hard choices ahead, before we can extricate ourselves from this predicament,"

Carl responded and began pacing. "We have been extraordinarily blessed and lucky to have made it this far without serious injury or illness, except for Nick's wound."

"You paint a rather dark picture . . . ," Vicky continued.

"Yes, he does," added Janet.

Carl felt bombarded by friendlies. "Look outside!" he protested. "It's dark!"

"Vicky," said Pete with uncharacteristic strength, "Carl has done an extraordinary job protecting us, keeping us safe, fed and warm in the High Rockies during the middle of deep winter with no electricity whatsoever. I know what has been discussed over the last couple of days is disturbing and unsettling, but I can attest to the considerable thought Carl has invested in our survival. The Parks did not have to accept our family," he said, gesturing to Barb and Larry, ". . . or any other families. We joined Carl and his family to make our family stronger. We invited your family," Pete paused to hold Vicky's eyes, "and the others, to join us for our collective security and survival. There is no restriction or hold on your participation. You are free to leave anytime you wish, if you are not comfortable with the group."

"Wait a second," Bert interjected. "No one is talking about leaving. Vicky is only voicing her apprehension regarding the violence on our part."

"Understood, Bert," Pete continued. "I dare say a lot of this discussion is the shock of being confronted by the violence of this crisis. Again, I can assure you, Carl has tried to avoid the violence, but many of us, in his family and mine, owe our lives to his skills and confidence to act."

Carl decided to pick up the discussion. "This is not a dictatorship. I have no more authority than anyone else. Yet, what I do have to offer are certain skills . . . as does Pete . . . from our service as Marines. I am doing the best I can in often very dicey situations that leave little margin for error. As I have said from the beginning of this ordeal, if anyone thinks they can do better, you are quite welcome to do so. We have in the past, and we most likely will in the future, encounter bad people, who in their desperation, will hold no compunction with killing any one of us to take what we have. There are no do-overs in times like these."

"I second Carl's words," Pete added.

"I'd suggest we take a day or so to process the information and discussion of the last two days. We can discuss any aspect, at any time anyone may wish to do so. We are in comparatively good shape." Carl glanced at his wristwatch. "It's getting late. I imagine more than a few of us are hungry. We need to get everyone fed and set the watch for the night. It is getting quite dark out and twilight is nearly done."

People nodded and began standing without further discussion. The process of selecting and dividing up the food for preparation and consumption was also getting more complicated, and accentuated by the paucity of preparation facilities. However, working together, they managed to get everyone fed, including little Breckyn. The conversation during preparation and the meal fortunately stuck to more mundane aspects of their circumstances from yesterday's playing in the snow, to the gorgeous but cold weather outside. When everyone was fed, and the utensils cleaned and put away, they set the night watch with Team 3 taking the first shift.

The others dispersed. Pete was the last to leave. "Keep the faith, Marine," he said. "They'll come around as they experience things."

"Thanks buddy."

Once he closed and locked the door, Carl went to each of his children, hugged and kissed them on the cheek. He took Breckyn from Lisa's arms, kissed her sweet smelling forehead, and stared into her inquisitive, blue eyes, before handing his granddaughter back to her mother. Janet and Alex were on watch, so their hugs would have to wait. He then changed his mind and went to the arsenal room, where Alex was standing watch as the Team 3, B section. Carl hugged Alex from behind and kissed his cheek.

"What was that for?" Alex asked.

"Just because . . . I love you."

Alex returned his eyes to scanning the scene outside the window. "It's OK, Dad. I don't think they mean any harm. It is just a lot for them to process. Give them time."

"Wise words, Son."

"You'd better get some sleep. Your watch is up next."

Carl smiled, patted his son on the shoulder and left the room. He checked on Bert to make sure everything was OK out front, and then returned to the relative warmth of the living room and laid down. His mind churned over the discussion of the last two days. He did not like killing, but he knew it had to be done and should not be wasted. Their very survival through the lethal cold of the high mountains just outside the walls and windows depended upon not making any mistakes.

Blessedly, Carl was not aware of his drifting off to slumber. He only recognized some amount of sleep when Alex wiggled his big toe, bolting him upright in an instant.

"Dad, there are two men on the trail. They appear to be interested in our building."

The commotion woke the others. Carl did not wait for Alex to explain. He flew to the back window. Several seconds passed as he allowed his eyes to adjust to the darkness. A sliver of the moon, two days short of a new moon, and starlight were the only illumination. Carl saw them. Two men, moving carefully, inching closer. "Come with me. Grab a shotgun." Carl lifted the loaded tactical Mossberg off the bed.

Before he reached the front door, the knock sequence announced one of the watch team at the door. Everyone in the living room was standing. "Arm yourselves and lock the door after we leave." Carl opened the door. Janet and George entered.

"There are two men at the back door," Janet announced, somewhat breathlessly.

Carl went to the balcony door. He got behind the blackout curtain, knocked and opened the door. "Have you seen any activity?"

"No," whispered Bert. "What's up?"

"Two men at the back door. Keep a close watch. There may be others. Do you have a weapon?'

"No."

"We'll get you one."

Carl closed the door. He looked to his oldest son. "Get a rifle and shotgun, and join Bert on the balcony." Mike did not hesitate. He turned to Alex. "Follow me," he repeated. "I need you to cover my back. Below the next floor, everyone is bad. Do not hesitate. These are not good people."

"Got it, Dad."

"Let's go." He reconsidered and looked to Dave. "Get Mister Higgins up and armed. Tell him what is happening."

"Sure, Dad."

Carl unlocked the door, opened it quickly, cleared the landing, and stepped outside with the shotgun shouldered and aimed at the stairway. Alex followed him and closed the door. They heard the lock engage and what was probably a chair being placed under the doorknob. They waited for their eyes to adjust to the darkness, again.

Without lowering his weapon, Carl reached and tapped Alex softly on the hip to signal their movement. The darkness of the stairwell forced them to carefully feel for the steps. They moved smoothly, evenly and quietly down the first set of stairs. Pausing at the mid-landing, they listened for any sound of entry. Hearing none, they continued to the next floor, repeating the listening process. The distinct sound of someone jiggling the rear door told them the intruders were close. Carl and Alex continued to the ground floor. Alex tapped his father on the left shoulder to signal he had his back.

Carl swung 180 degrees to face the rear door. Sufficient illumination silhouetted a man-size figure. There was no shape of a weapon of any kind detected. Carl considered a preemptive shot, but he waited and did not move with the shotgun aimed at the center of the man's chest. He jiggled the door, again, and then the man apparently decided to try the windows and make their way to the front door. The shape moved to the left beyond view. The second man, less distinct in the starlight illumination, followed the first man. Carl reached back and tapped Alex's hip, again. They moved to the rear door. Carl quickly scanned both directions; he detected nothing untoward.

Whispering to Alex, Carl said, "I'm going to unlock the door as quietly as I can. Wait a couple of seconds and open the door as quickly as you can. I'm going to step out and engage. I want you behind me to cover my six," he added, knowing his son would recognize the aviator's form of cover my back. "Ready?"

"Ready."

Carl felt Alex's hand on the door handle. He grasped the lock tab and slowly turned the lock until he heard the soft click. Carl stepped aside, raised the shotgun vertical and heard the door open as well as the air movement as the door passed him. He stepped out into the cold, heard the crunch of the snow beneath his feet and leveled the shotgun at the two retreating shapes. "Freeze. Do not move or you die," Carl said firmly. Both men froze. "You do not belong here and you are not welcome."

"We mean no harm," one of the men said.

"Then, what are you doing here?"

"We're hungry, man. We're just looking for food."

"In the dark of night?" Carl challenged. Several seconds passed with none of them moving or making a sound. *I should drop both these guys right now. They are not just looking for food. I should disarm them, but the risk is too great in this low light.* "Are either of you armed?" Neither man responded nor moved. "Answer me or die!"

"No, man. We're not armed. We are just looking for food," one of the men repeated.

Damn it! I really should drop them both. Carl shook his head against his own doubts. "Leave now," Carl commanded. "Get out of here and do not come back, again. The outcome of another appearance will not be so merciful."

The frontman raised his empty hands and slowly turned to face Carl, presumably to evaluate his situation. The following man did not twitch. Even in the dim starlight, Carl could see the lead man had white skin and a peculiar full beard—a two-horned rendition with a white, nearly bare chin between the two horns. "We're sorry to have intruded. We will leave peacefully and not return," the man said.

"Be gone."

The leading man kept his hands raised and again turned carefully. He gestured for his companion to follow. They moved slowly, struggling through the snowdrift in a gap in the hedge, eventually reaching the trail packed down by the young folks, and disappeared among the trees. Carl remained in position, moving only his aim point tracking of the two retreating intruders. When several minutes passed after they disappeared and their crunchy footfalls in the snow and ice were no longer detectable, Carl lowered his weapon and turned to his son.

"Are you OK?" Carl asked.

"Yes. That was pretty scary."

"Yes, it was, and I suspect confrontations like this are going to increase in frequency and escalate in intensity. Are you OK temperature wise?"

"I'm shaking a little, but that is probably the adrenaline," Alex said, as he began to shift his weight from leg to leg.

"Yeah, quite normal. It would be a little warmer inside . . . in the lobby; but I need to stay out here, so I can hear anyone approaching, especially if those two bozos decide to make another attempt."

"I'll stay here with you, Dad."

Carl smiled and patted Alex on the shoulder. The sliver of the waning moon began to appear above the neighboring trees, adding a little more illumination. Alex's shifting weight made a few crunches in the packed snow. Carl held his now gloved left index finger to his lips.

"Sorry."

Again, Carl quietly patted his son on the shoulder to reassure him. They stood watch outside for several minutes more until a soft knock on the glass door behind them attracted their attention. They both looked to see Pete Higgins standing just inside. Carl and Alex stepped to either side. Carl gestured that it was OK for Pete to join them.

"I watched from the window," Pete whispered. Carl nodded. "Everything OK?"

Carl nodded his head in the affirmative and again held his index finger to his lips. Pete nodded. The three men listened another ten minutes or so, and then Carl signaled for them to go back inside. Carl relocked the rear door and motioned for Pete and Alex to precede him upstairs.

The whole group waited in the Parks' apartment. The word of the threat had spread quickly. The three reaction men were bombarded with questions even before the door was closed and re-locked.

Carl held up his hands with the shotgun grasped in his left hand. Everyone quieted down. "Please call in Bert and whoever is in the arsenal room." Carl leaned the shotgun against the wall and small end table near his mattress. Bert joined them. Everyone was present. "The threat is gone . . . for now. We have a long night to get through, and rather than keep everyone up to discuss what happened, I will only say we confronted two men who claim they were unarmed and searching for food. They've gone now. I believe they both understood they were not welcome here and to stay away. I think we handled the potential intrusion well. I'd strongly recommend we reset the watch." Carl glanced at his wristwatch. "Team 3 has another 35 minutes to go, before Team 4 takes over. Let's try to get back to sleep. Staying up serves no purpose other than exhausting all of us."

"We did not hear any shots," observed Oscar.

"Because none were fired."

"And, you just let them go?" asked Janet with a measure of incredulity.

"Yes, my darling. I did."

"Why?" Mike asked.

"Neither of them appeared to be armed, although I did not search them, but I did ask. And, they made no threatening moves beyond skulking around the building in the dark. They rattled the rear door, but they did not break the glass, as they could have, if they were truly being aggressive."

Mike nodded his head, accepting the explanation.

Carl waited for a few seconds. "We can and will discuss what happened tonight during the light of day."

More than a few nodded their heads in agreement. Alex went to the balcony, since his conscription as Carl's backup had caused him to miss the planned switch with Bert. Janet and George returned to their lobby watch stations. Pete was the last to leave.

"Thanks for getting me up to cover you," Pete said.

"Could you see us out the back window?"

"Only partially . . . like half of you at the door. I could see more of them than you."

"OK. At least you could see some of us."

"Do you think they will be back?"

"I've no idea, but from their words and reaction, I would not be surprised. If they do, they will not get another chance, and if it is me who decides, they will not be asked to leave, again."

"I will do the same."

"Good."

"See you in the morning. Good job."

"Thanks, buddy. Good night."

The watchstanders were posted. Their children not on watch were all laying down. Carl did the same, although he did not find sleep before Bert reappeared to begin passing the watch to Team 4. It was time. Anne joined him as Team 4 Section A in the ground floor lobby. The excitement of the night's event subsided.

—

19

Three days and nights passed without incident, challenge or even concern. They watched and listened. They all agreed activity in their area remained surprisingly quiet. Sure, an occasional gunshot in the distance and at least one multi-shot firearm exchange were heard, but nothing close or protracted. They could see people moving around, but none of those people came close to their home complex. The excitement of the evening three days prior had subsided into a more routine existence.

The relative tranquility was destined not to last.

When Carl regained consciousness, Mike was standing over him. "Dad, I spotted the horned beard guy by Building 1. I've seen two others." Carl shook his head as he digested the information. "They are armed and appear to be maneuvering toward us."

Carl jumped to his feet. As he headed to the arsenal room, he said without looking at Mike, "Get Pete up, first . . . then everyone else. Everyone needs to be armed." Carl considered grabbing the Remington rifle to pick off one or two, but decided it was probably too late for that. He instinctively knew this was the moment he feared—a purposeful assault on their position. The two men he had allowed to leave three days ago had developed a plan, found the courage and arms they needed, and were now determined to take what they believed Building 3 held. Carl grabbed both Mossberg shotguns. The door was open when he got there.

Carl tossed the Mossberg Tactical to Mike, who caught it firmly. "Give that to Pete. Ask him to join me in the lobby, as quick as he can. Grab the Remington Auto and go to the second-floor landing. Don't let anyone up those stairs unannounced. I will call out, when I need to come up. Listen for my commands."

"Sure, Dad."

Carl descended the first set of stairs with his weapon raised and safety off. As he started down the last set of stairs, the door to 322 opened. Oscar quickly looked and darted back in. Satisfied that it was Carl, he looked back out, again. Carl said firmly, "Bad guys. Probably many. Get everyone up and armed." Oscar nodded his head and did not verbally reply.

Carl quickly cleared the front door, but left it locked. They would not likely approach the front door—too exposed. Carl first scanned what he could see out of the closed rear door. The quick scan revealed nothing. A second, more careful scan also revealed nothing peculiar. He unlocked the door. A pistol shot popped close by but he could not tell exactly where or by whom.

Carl opened the door and stepped out, leading with the shotgun, first to the left, and then quickly to the right. *Clear. I can't wait for help.* He moved down the length of the building to the east. *Thank goodness the kids tamped down the snow. The horn guy was at Building 1, so he was on the eastside.* Carl repeatedly spun to check behind him, as he moved to the northeast corner. The last time he checked his six, he saw Pete moving swiftly to the northwest corner. *Damn, he's good.* Carl raised the shotgun, so as not to expose himself to the other side with the barrel. Carl took a deep breath to clear his lungs with the cold fresh air. He instinctively thumbed the safety to ensure it was off. Carl quickly glanced around the corner and back. *Damn!* He did not hesitate. This time he spun around the corner as the barrel dropped. Carl heard the zing of a bullet pass by his head. He fired at the center of mass of the horned beard man, and pumped another round into the chamber, and fired again. The red cloud around his chest and head marked the hit with the second shot.

Carl heard another shotgun blast behind him. He spun to see Pete at the far corner, still standing. The sharp report and a spray of splinters just above Carl's head startled him and caused him to spin away and drop to the snow. He quickly felt his scalp—blood and embedded splinters. *At least it's not in my eyes.* Carl promptly gyrated around to stay as low as he could. He peered slowly around the corner. A man was moving with difficulty through the snowdrift outside the hedge and his pistol was aimed at the building corner. *Thank God, the kids had not packed the gap between the hedge and the building wall.* The drift inside the hedge was deeper than outside. Several pistol shots and another shotgun blast occurred close by, but Carl had a more immediate threat. He rolled over on his back slowly, trying to minimize the noise of crunching snow. Looking through the hedge, Carl could see the shape of the man approaching, still struggling through the snowdrift. He placed the weapon on his chest with the muzzle next to his head and slowly extended it out, and then around the corner. Carl aimed upside-down through the hedge. As soon as the muzzle was pointed at the man's chest, Carl squeezed the trigger, took the recoil, and scrambled to his feet, as he pumped and ejected the spent shell and load another round into the empty chamber. Needles and twigs were still floating to the ground when Carl stepped through the hedge. Both men were clearly deceased as a halo of blood circled their bodies.

Movement immediately attracted Carl's attention. He stepped a little farther out and saw the back of a man bounding like a wolf through the deep snow of what used to be the parking lot. Carl sprang for the path and ran as best he could for the door. As Carl entered the lobby, Pete was already in the lobby with his shotgun on his right hip. "Hold the lobby. One getting away."

Carl turned to the stairway and began shouting, "It's me. Get the Remington rifle, now! I'm coming up." He heard heavy steps up the stairs and repeated his shouted command several more times. Carl passed Oscar, Nick, Dave and Bert on the second-floor landing, as he bounded up the stairs two at a time. "Help Pete. Cover the lobby doors," Carl shouted, as he ran up the last set of stairs. By the time, Carl entered the apartment, Mike appeared holding the rifle vertical. Lisa was holding the baby and standing behind Janet, who was clearly holding a Glock pistol, down and away from her body. Carl grabbed the Remington holding it vertical with the barrel up and tossed the Mossberg with the barrel down to Mike. "Come with me," Carl commanded. He threw the curtain aside and opened the door. Carl did not bother kneeling behind the railing and lowered the barrel. The man had made it nearly to the street when Carl fired a single shot bursting the man's head and leaving his body in a mound, partially buried in the snow. Carl worked the bolt to eject the spent casing and pushed the bolt home and locked it, chambering a fresh round.

As Carl scanned the scene, he said, "Search for any others. No one should escape."

Mike did not respond verbally, but looked out as far as he could to comply with his father's command.

Carl sat down on one of the stools and rested the rifle on the railing. More than a dozen people—male and female, young and old—were detected outside, moving around on various indeterminate tasks, none of them that appeared to be associated with the assault.

"Over there," Mike said and pointed at the gap between Building 4 and 5.

Carl snapped his head to the right and saw just an arm disappear into a tree line beyond Building 5 and along 4 O'Clock Run Road. Carl used the riflescope to detect any sign of the retreating man. He saw a patch of blue, put the reticle on that patch and fired. The dull thud and recoil marked the shot. The swatch of color disappeared. He ejected the casing and chambered another round. Neither of them could tell whether he hit the target nor any additional movement in the area.

Carl stood and gestured for Mike to lead him back inside. All of the females had gathered in the apartment, sitting and standing near the fireplace. Larry and Aaron stood with their mothers. Alex cradled the M1A rifle, just inside the door. George stood by the door, now closed and presumably locked, and brandished one of the other Glock pistols. Carl looked at George. "Post the watch, top and bottom. I've got to go after at least one of the attackers." George nodded. "I'm going to take Mike and Alex with me," he announced, and then looked directly to Alex. "I'll trade you," Carl said and reached for the

M1A rifle as he handed the Remington to his son. "Drop off the Remington. We don't have time to mess with the ammo. Grab the MAC-10 and the extra clips. We may need the firepower." Carl connected to Mike's waiting eyes. "Top off the Mossberg. Grab the M1A magazines and a box of each ammo type for the weapons we have. Make sure each of you has a pistol. Oh, also, grab the snowshoes. We'll need them. Meet me in the lobby. I need to brief Pete." The boys jumped to their tasks. Carl looked to see Janet's apprehensive and concerned gaze. He nodded his head to her. As Carl approached the door, he looked to George, "Lock the door after we leave and brace it with a chair. Do not let anyone through that door without the knock sequence."

"Yes sir," responded George.

Carl left. The doors to 331 and 322 were closed as he passed them. The front and rear door guards alternated sides of their respective doors for some cover and remained vigilant. Pete was pacing between the two doors.

Pete stopped at arm's length in front of Carl. "What now?" Pete asked.

"I think at least one may have escaped. Mike and Alex will be here shortly. I'm going to take them and track down that one and any others we might find. I've asked George to set the watch. We need eyes out. I'd like you to take one or two with you to confirm the kills. There are two on the east of this building."

"One on the west side."

"There is another one out by the parking lot entrance. Make sure they are dead. Search the bodies. Recover the weapons and anything else of value to us." Pete nodded his head. "We must do what we can before sunset. I want to be back here before twilight gets too deep." Again, Pete nodded his head. "We'll debrief when we get back."

"What do you want to do with the bodies?"

"Leave 'em. The snow is too deep and they will probably freeze before we have the cover of darkness."

"OK."

"How many were there?" asked Bert from the left side of the front door.

"At least, five by my count and perhaps a sixth. The shot we heard from the vicinity of Building 5 may have tapped another. There could be more. We're going out that way to follow the tracks. If there is another one out that way, we'll search him. Don't worry about that one."

"Sure. Anything else?"

"Hold down the fort."

"Got it, *el Jefe*," Pete said, winked, and chuckled softly.

Mike and Alex cautiously descended the stairs. Carl looked over his shoulder and asked, "Ready?"

"Yep," the boys said in unison.

All three of the search party strapped on their makeshift snowshoes.

"OK . . . for everyone to hear," Carl began and quickly checked each set of eyes, "we're going to track down one of the attackers that might have gotten away."

"Why not just let him go?" Oscar asked.

Pete jumped in. "Because one survivor might bring others. Five or six of them chose to assault our dwelling, presumably thinking there was only two of us here."

"But, it's just more risk."

"Indeed it is," Pete continued. "However, the risk of instigating an even stronger attack is far greater. We have no choice."

"Everybody satisfied?" Carl asked. He received affirmative responses in various forms. "OK, then." Carl faced Mike and Alex. "I will lead. I will be focused on what is ahead of us and on following the tracks. Make sure you keep our flanks and rear cleared. There may be others out there laying in wait to ambush us. Remember, better safe than sorry. If you see anything other than structures and vegetation, tap me on the shoulder and point out your suspicion. Let's be careful."

"You got it, Dad," Alex responded.

"Yeah," added Mike.

"Off we go," Carl announced. "Keep a close eye out."

Pete went to the rear door, unlocked it and held it open. Carl began scanning the scene, looking for any signs of threats. He could see Pete's tracks in the packed snow that stopped at the northwest corner. He quickly cleared the corner. Virgin snow filled the space along the west side of the building.

Carl climbed up on the snow. With the snowshoes, he only sank a few inches into the fresh snow and movement was considerably easier. As he approached the body, the amount of splattered blood indicated the target had not likely survived. When he reached the mound sunken into the snow, Carl saw that Pete's shot had hit the man in the upper chest and neck area, opening the carotid arteries and nearly severing his head. *No need to check for a pulse. Pete will search the body.* The large shallow tracks indicated the man had snowshoes and probably professional versions. Carl tried to pull at least one of the legs free. Mike and Alex both joined in to help. They managed to drag one leg with the snowshoe attached into the open, so it would be obvious to Pete and his team. Carl motioned for them to continue. He used the footfalls laid down by the attacker. Abreast Building 5, another body was discovered. Carl quickly scanned the building. No signs of human occupation could be detected. Looking back to the body, there was no bloodstain obvious, which suggested it was probably a pistol shot. The body lay away from the building, likely meaning the fatal shot had come from the building. *Another intriguing clue.* He reached for and pulled the winter, knit mask off. It was a female and a fairly young, attractive woman at that. He checked for a pulse—none, and the body was cold. Again, they pulled a leg free, so that one of her snowshoes was easily visible. Against his earlier thinking, Carl chose not to take the time to search the body. If Pete did not pick it up, they would search it on the way back.

Three sets of tracks had come out of the trees. Two of the three sets of tracks terminated at the bodies. The third set of tracks had hurriedly turned and made for the tree line from which they had come. *So, there were only three on this side.* Carl signaled for them to proceed and kept his rifle pointed ahead. The line of trees, all conifers, was about 10 meters wide. They made their way through, knocking accumulated snow off the bows—a nuisance but not an obstacle. As they approached the edge of the tree line, Carl could see the road shoulder. The roadway was now packed down, but there were perhaps a dozen sets of tracks going in both directions. Carl scanned the far side of the roadway in both directions. The trees were just as thick on the far side; it would be a perfect ambush site. Carl recognized there was no way to clear the roadway. They had to take the risk. Carl stepped out from his cover. No humans were seen. Then, he saw it.

An indentation in the snow about six meters to his right suggested a person had knelt at that spot. Small red spots indicated the person had been wounded at that spot and was bleeding. Carl pointed to the signs as they passed the spot. Both boys nodded. The blood-drip-accentuated tracks made following the path comparatively easy.

They followed the unique track another 20 meters up the road to the first right bend in the road, before it crossed and headed to a fairly new, lodge type dwelling of two floors of about 30 units each. As far as he could see, the tracks went directly to the front door. *This just got exponentially more difficult.* Following the trail to the front door was foolish, verging upon suicidal. The man had to know he might be tracked, and the front door would be the best ambush point. Carl turned, as if he had lost interest, and walked back to the cover of the roadside trees. He stepped into the tree line, just far enough to give them cover. The boys came close.

"The tracks look like he is seriously wounded and made it to the lodge. We cannot approach directly—too risky. We have at least two primary concerns. First, the wounded man may be desperate to gain separation, and protect himself and any others in their group. Second, unrelated people in the lodge may see us as intruders or attackers, and engage us . . . like we did them. Based on what I saw, I think our best approach is along the service road on this side of the building. The rather narrow tree line will offer us the only cover we will have. We need to get to the point closest to the southeast corner, which should be a blind spot, if he is waiting at the door. We need to get across the open ground as quickly as possible and against the wall, and then unstrap from our snowshoes. I'll go in first and hopefully deal with the attacker, if he's there. I'll take the MAC-10." Alex handed his father the machine pistol along with two extra, loaded magazines. Carl gave the M1A rifle to Alex with his two, loaded magazines. "Are we good so far?"

Both boys nodded their heads in agreement.

"If he is at the door and we eliminate him, we may be done. There is no way to connect him with a particular room . . . unless he has a numbered room key. If we find a room, we need to search it like we have the other apartments."

"What if there are people inside?" asked Alex.

"And women and children?" Mike added.

Carl thought about not answering, but decided it was better to be forthright. "If they are aggressive, they die . . . simple as that."

"Dad!" protested Alex.

"I know this is hard, but there are no genders or ages in these circumstances. There are only threats and non-threats."

Alex nodded his head more in acquiescence rather than agreement. Mike did not react.

"Once inside, I need each of you to cover both directions down the hallway, as we move." The boys nodded. "Ready?"

". . . as we will ever be," Mike responded.

Carl moved to the edge of the tree line. He pumped his fist up and down, and then pointed to the designated building corner. They made it to the building wall without incident. They checked all around them. *So far so good.* Carl quickly looked around the corner. Clear. Carl pointed at their snowshoes and began unstrapping his. They left their snowshoes where they lay. Carl gave and received a thumb's up from each boy.

Carl sidestepped with his back solidly against the building wall and MAC-10 held closely across his chest, aimed at the door. He knew breaching the door would be one of the riskiest tasks, but it had to be done. They simply could not leave a survivor. Carl sidestepped back a couple of meters, forcing the boys back as well.

Carl leaned close to Mike's left ear and whispered, "Find a rock or brick chip. I'm going to get low, as close to the door as possible. When I signal, throw the stone at the upper panel of the door, and then stand back."

Mike nodded his head.

The process took several minutes. While the boys were searching for a rock, Carl continuously scanned the area around the lodge. Luckily, no identifiable observers or potential threats were detected. Mike and Alex sidestepped back to Carl. Mike held up a small corner chip of brick. Carl gave him a thumb's up and moved into position about a meter to the left of the door. He took a deep breath, clearing his lungs.

Mike stepped out, away from the wall and tossed the brick piece, hitting the glass panel with a characteristic clink. Carl lunged at the door with the machine pistol aimed up into the door. No reaction could be seen, heard or felt. Carl jumped up on the landing, slipped a little, and quickly pulled the door open. No one was there. A small lobby was empty. Carl signaled for the boys to follow. They entered and quickly cleared the whole lobby. The dark interior added a daunting dimension to the task ahead. *We'll try this as far as we can take it.*

Carl pulled the boys to a corner away from the hallway and grasped both their heads, pulling their ears close to his mouth. "I'm going to have to get down on my hands and knees to see if I can track him." They both nodded. "Stay close to the wall and cover the opposite wall both directions as best you can. If you see something you don't like, stomp your foot . . . not hard." Again, the boys nodded.

The entry mat, just inside the door, was wet with chunks of snow still present. Carl found several drops of blood close together. The man had stopped at the door to see who might be following him. The drops were still liquid but just barely. He picked up the trail as the line of drops moved farther into the interior of the building. Fortunately, the building was quiet but dark. The glass doors at either end of the long hallway offered some light. As he suspected, Carl had to crawl on his hands and knees along the short strand carpeting in order to hold the trail. Several times, Carl looked over his shoulder to check on the boys, who were performing exactly as he suspected. The blood drip trail turned right up the central stairway. The light from the stairwell window offered at least a short respite from the difficulty of tracking the drops. The trail stopped at room 203. Carl took the time to confirm the destination. He stood, signaled at the door, and then gestured for Mike to move beyond him and take the far hallway. Alex would remain on the short side and take the hallway in the opposite direction. He got a thumb's up from each boy.

Carl stood back to allow him to put his full weight into kicking the door in. The crack of the wood doorframe was loud. Female screams bloomed shortly thereafter. Carl burst into the room. Three women, one man. His target, the wounded man was laying on one of the two king beds. The man was being tended to by one of the women and tried to scramble off the bed. Carl fired two single shots in quick succession into the center of the man's chest. The woman who had been tending to the wounded man stood shaking vigorously and screaming like she was having a standing convulsion. One of the other two women lunged for a pistol laying on the end table. Carl fired two shots into her chest and chose not to deliver a third headshot. The third woman held up her hands. The first woman continued screaming, as she looked back and forth between Carl, her man friend, and the shot woman.

"Shut up!" commanded Carl. The woman did not comply and persisted in her expression of horror. Carl pointed the MAC-10 at her face. She reflexively put both hands over her mouth and she tried to control herself. The terror in her wide eyes indicated she was not accustomed to such confrontations. "Mike," Carl called. Both boys appeared in the broken doorway. "Alex, keep watch in the hallway." His youngest son went back out into the dark hall, away from the door. "You two," Carl said with a stern voice, "get over there. Place your hands on the table and do not move even a twitch." He gestured with the machine pistol to a corner table. "Wait!" Both women froze. Carl thoroughly searched their clothing and bodies. Neither woman protested the immodesty of Carl's search. "Sit!" he commanded. "Hands on the table," he repeated. Without looking at Mike, Carl said, "Guard them. If either of them moves, shoot them both."

"Yes sir."

Carl allowed the MAC-10 to dangle from the shoulder strap with the butt of the extended wire stock just below his right armpit. Carl first checked for a pulse on the man, and then the woman—both were dead. The dead man's unzipped, blue, ski parka confirmed him as the sixth attacker. He retrieved the two obvious pistols, placing them in his left jacket pocket. Carl went about methodically searching the room. He found a dozen cans of tuna, considered confiscating them, but ultimately decided to leave them. One full and six partial boxes of ammunition were collected up from the closet. The only other weapon he found was a pocketknife. Carl put the closed knife on top of the chest of drawers. He could not find a set of snowshoes he expected to find.

Carl turned back to the two women. The first woman had calmed down.

"Why did you do this?" the other woman asked with a condescending sneer.

"I think you know why. Your friends are not going to return. You are on your own. I cannot allow you to have any weapons . . . the price of attacking us."

"How are we supposed to protect ourselves?" she pleaded.

"Not my problem. You chose to attack us. My family was threatened. I had to eliminate that threat. We are all trying to survive this crisis. Enough questions. I need answers. Where are the others?"

"What do you mean?" feigned the second surviving woman.

"I am not going to play games. Tell me or you die right now," Carl said, as he grasped the handgrip of the machine pistol and raised the barrel.

"Across the hall in 204," the first woman said with an air of desperation.

"Are they everyone, or are their others beyond that?"

"That's everyone."

"How many are in 204?"

"Two."

"Not three?"

"No. Hank was alone. His girlfriend could not make the trip," the first woman responded.

"OK. We can do this the easy way or the hard way. I am going to search that room for weapons. You can help me, and we can do this peacefully, or I will use a more aggressive method. What will it be?"

Both women responded in unison, "We'll help."

Carl gestured for both of them to move. They stood and walked slowly out of the room and to the room 204 door. The second woman knocked.

"Go away," the muffled voice of a woman responded.

"Janie, it's Meg. You need to open the door . . ."

"No!"

". . . or he will break it down."

"No," the woman answered with a tremor of fear in her voice. "I saw what happened."

Meg looked to Carl, who only motioned for her to continue, and then held up one finger. "Please Janie. He just wants to search for weapons. He won't harm us, if we cooperate."

Carl allowed silence to give the occupants time to think about their untenable position. The sound of the door locks announced their decision. The door opened. Carl motioned with his weapon for the two surviving 203 women to enter first. They both went to the table and sat down. Only two other women occupied the room as they had been told. The 204 women started to follow, until Carl commanded them to stop.

"I've got to search you first."

"Want a cheap feelie, do you now," one of the new women said with a tone of defiance.

"Think as you will, but both of you are going to be thoroughly searched."

Both women spread their legs and held their arms out horizontally without being commanded to do so. *These two have apparently experienced this process before.* Neither of them twitched as Carl completed his body searches. Carl gestured for them to join the other two. They followed the lead of the first two, placing their hands on the table. "Don't move!" Carl commanded.

Mike moved into position with the shotgun pointed at the center of the table. Again, Carl worked through a complete search of the entire suite. He found a small caliber, pink, semi-automatic pistol buried in one of the women's purses, as well as a can of Mace in each purse. Carl also discovered five more partially filled boxes of ammunition that he removed from two drawers and handed to Mike for portage.

Again, satisfied neither room contained any additional serious weapons, Carl stood back from the table and signaled for Mike to leave, which his oldest son did. He left the barrel down but kept his right hand on the handgrip, just in case. "All five of your male friends and two females are dead." One woman audibly gasped and muffled a soft scream, as Carl waved the barrel of the machine pistol at the two bodies. "Two of them tried to enter our building three days ago. Those two plus four others came back armed and intent upon taking whatever they could find. I had to protect my family and our survival."

"What about us?" pleaded one of the new women.

"I am truly sorry for your loss, but they made their choices, and they were the wrong choices."

"We are just trying to survive . . . like you," she continued.

"Understood. I wish y'all luck. I mean you no harm, as long as you do not threaten my family."

"You took our men," the fourth woman said. "Can we come with you?" She did not wait for an answer. "You need to take care of us, now."

"No. We don't. Other options might have been available, but you attacked us," Carl responded calmly. "We had to end it."

"You killed our men," the third woman shouted angrily.

Carl held up his hand to stop, and then raised the machine pistol. "I can end your uncertainty right now, if you wish."

"No, no," the first woman interjected. "We'll figure it out."

"OK. As I told the man with the horned beard three days ago, if I see any one of you, again, there will be no discussion, and it will not end well. Do you understand?"

One woman answered yes, while the others nodded their heads in the affirmative.

"I'm going to leave you. Make no attempt to follow us. My admonition and warning starts now," Carl said and slowly backed out of the room. He closed and latched the door. Carl backed down the hallway several paces and stopped to see if they might try to follow them. He heard the door locks engage. Carl motioned for them to leave.

They moved quickly, making sure they remained prepared, in case they were challenged. Outside, they strapped on their snowshoes. Carl signaled for them to proceed back into the narrow tree line, in reverse of how they had entered. The long axis of the lodge pointed right down 4 O'Clock Run Road. Carl repeatedly searched behind them, walking backward, to make sure they were not being followed. He kept them on the south side of the road until well past their complex. He knew there was a tree-lined service road, leading to the ski trail. At the service road, they crossed and made their way over the trackless service road. They were all grateful for the packed snow on the ski trail. As they approached the rear door of Building 3, Carl slowed their movement and looked intently at the rear door.

Barb was standing watch at the rear door and eventually recognized Carl. She waved her arm for them to come ahead and opened the door before they arrived.

"How did it go?" Barb asked.

"Mission accomplished," announced Carl. "Is Pete finished? Anyone else outside?" He began unstrapping from his snowshoes. The boys did the same.

"Yes. He's finished and everyone is inside now that you have returned."

"OK. Make sure the doors are locked and let's gather in 332."

Barb nodded her head and called to Aaron. They led the search team up the stairs to the top floor. Barb delivered the prescribed daily knock sequence. The door unlocked and opened.

As soon as Janet saw Carl in the doorway, she walked quickly to her husband, embraced him tightly and kissed him passionately. "I'm glad you're home safely," she whispered.

"I'm glad to be home," Carl whispered back. Standing side-by-side with his arm around his wife, Carl said to the group, "Let's gather up, so everyone can hear the debriefing."

Larry came in from the balcony, and Oscar appeared from the arsenal room.

"Well, I imagine there are a lot of questions, but before we get to your questions, please allow me to summarize what happened today. It has been a very busy day. First, one of the men who we confronted just outside the rear door three nights ago came back with five other people—all armed. He had been warned three days ago that he should not come back. He chose to ignore my warning. Our security system worked as intended. We confronted the attackers before they were able to breach our building. At this juncture, Pete, you and your team searched the attackers. What did you find?"

Peter Higgins stood and moved next to Carl. "First, the five bodies we found were deceased. They were all armed. Several had multiple pistols. My conclusion, they acquired their weapons from other attacks." Carl began unloading the confiscated weapons from his jacket pocket onto the kitchen counter, and then gestured for Mike to unload the boxes of ammunition. "So, you found more?" Carl nodded his head and gestured for Pete to continue. "We also recovered the snowshoes . . . very high quality, professional grade, I must say."

"So, obviously better than our makeshift versions?"

Many laughed. Pete answered, "Yes, much better . . . much," he repeated.

"Would you say those snowshoes belong to them?" Carl asked.

"Impossible to say for sure, but my guess is no. Most folks come to Summit County to ski, not go traipsing through fresh snow."

"Valid point," added Carl. "So, they probably acquired those snowshoes like the weapons."

"Exactly."

"We did not get back to the fifth body behind Building 5. Did y'all manage to search her, too?"

"Her?" interjected Vicky.

"Yes," Carl answered. "The fifth person was a woman."

"Yes. Thanks for reminding me," Pete said and looked to Carl with a smile. "Yes, we searched her like we searched the others. As we were searching the fifth body, we found one pistol, and then we heard a tap on the glass of the rear door to Building 5. We saw a hand holding up two fingers, followed by a quick glance. The three of us stood straight up, pocketed our weapons, and held our arms out to appear as least threatening as possible. Without being obvious, I noticed the curtain pulled back slightly on the second-floor apartment on the left. The door unlocked and opened. I told the boys to finish searching the body and removing the snowshoes. I went inside. It was Betsy Mossman. She recognized me and wanted to reach out to us."

"Excellent," Carl responded.

"We need to discuss their proposal," Pete said and waited for a response, but Carl only nodded his head.

"Did you find any other tracks not accounted for?" Carl asked.

"Only the set that you followed."

"The best shot I had," began Carl, "wounded the sixth man. We picked up the blood trail on the road. We followed the trail to the lodge up the road. We broke into the suite where the trail led. I finished off the wounded guy and had to terminate a woman who went for a pistol. The other two wisely chose to help us enter the other room across the hallway peacefully. We searched that room as well." Carl gestured to the pistols on the kitchen counter. "Those are the weapons we confiscated. I warned the women about showing up here. I think they understood, but we need to be vigilant."

"Did they have any food?" Barb asked.

"Yes, a little, but not enough to make it to spring. I chose to not confiscate what food they had."

"So," Pete said and paused, "is this incident closed?"

"I believe so. They appeared to be acting out of necessity. I'm afraid we are going to see more of these assaults."

"I certainly hope not," interjected Lisa, rocking Breckyn in her arms. "That was way too scary."

"Nature of the beast, I'm afraid," Carl responded. "I have tried to prepare everyone for this eventuality. Regardless, each of us must gird ourselves against the trauma of such episodes that likely lay ahead before we can extricate ourselves from this situation."

Breckyn began to fidget, presumably from discomfort, since her cries followed shortly thereafter. Lisa and Janet tended to the infant.

"We are beyond dusk and twilight is deepening," Carl said. "I'd suggest we suspend our exterior work for today, have a nice supper, since at least some of us did not get our morning meal." Carl paused. Lisa held Breckyn, sat back down, and arranged herself to begin feeding her daughter. "Unless anyone has something else to discuss, let's get everyone fed and the watch set for the night. Who's up first?"

"I think we are," Pete answered. "Team Two."

Barb and Janet had anticipated the meal situation and selected sufficient beef to thaw for everyone. They also thawed a couple of medium-size cans of kernel corn. The tension of the day's events slowly subsided, as the group tried to enjoy some refreshed camaraderie. They discussed the approach to the Mossman's tomorrow and their potential integration in the group. An undercurrent of sadness from the loss of life around them could not be denied, but a modest celebration of their safety dominated.

—

20

Two quiet days and three nights passed with no activity. Carl remained cautious about leaving the women at the lodge. The feisty woman's confrontational stance in the face of immediate threat bothered him. Carl chose to keep his apprehension to himself.

The newly acquired weapons from the engagement with their attackers three days ago were checked, made safe, and left in a bag in the arsenal room. Their growing inventory of weapons already seemed excessive. None of them could imagine reaching a point where they would need the additional weapons. At least others could not use any of the firearms against the Building 3 group. Where there was ammunition compatibility, they unloaded the associated weapons and added the rounds to their stock. The discharged weapons were all cleaned and reloaded. Carl carefully evaluated the compatibility of the 7.62 x 51mm, NATO equivalent rounds with the Remington 700 sniper rifle. Satisfied with compatibility, Carl reloaded the rifle's magazine.

Around mid-day of the third day, a single woman appeared at the rear lobby door, knocked and waited for her knock to be answered. Emily saw the woman on the other side of the locked, glass door and held up one finger signaling for her to wait. The woman nodded her head in agreement. Emily went to unit 332 and delivered the daily knock sequence.

Mike answered the door after checking the peephole.

"There is a woman at the rear door," Emily announced.

"Come in, Mrs. Manson. I'll get my Dad." When Emily stepped inside, Mike closed and locked the door. He went to the arsenal room and came back with Carl.

"Did she say anything?" asked Carl before he reached Emily.

"No. I asked her to wait with a gesture. We did not talk."

"I suspect it may be the Mossman woman," said Carl. Emily nodded her head. She had no reason to disagree. Carl instinctively felt for the pistol in his jacket pocket. He gestured for Emily and Mike to follow him. Carl knocked on the door to 331. He informed Pete. It was best to let Pete do the talking, since he was most likely to be the most recognizable.

As they descended the stairs, Carl noticed that Mike had picked up the Mossberg Tactical. Carl gestured for Mike to keep it down, so as not to appear threatening. Carl stopped and held back Emily and Mike, as Pete approached the door with both of his bare hands at shoulder height, palms out. A trim woman with an attractive, bright face smiled, apparently recognizing Pete. He unlocked and opened the door. "Come in," Pete said.

The woman did not move. "Good to see you, again," she said.

"Great to see you, Betsy. How can we help?"

"Hank asked me to be our emissary. We would like to talk about joining your group."

"OK . . . here or your place?" asked Pete.

"Our place, if you don't mind . . . so the girls can listen."

Pete looked over his shoulder to Carl, who nodded his concurrence. "Y'all are in 521, as I recall?"

"Correct."

"Fine. Let me get Barb, and I would like to bring along Carl," he said gesturing with his thumb over his right shoulder, "who is our leader."

Betsy nodded her head. "Thank you, Pete."

"Sure. Do you want to wait and go back with us?"

"If you don't mind, I'll go back and await your arrival with my family." Pete nodded. Betsy Mossman departed. Pete closed and locked the door. When he no longer could see Betsy's retiring figure, Pete turned and stepped a couple of paces toward Carl. "I'd suggest, you, Barb and I go, discuss options, and get their proposal."

"Yeah," Carl responded. "We'll need to vet their proposal with our whole group and gain concurrence before any action on our part." He looked at Emily. "Would you be so kind to inform everyone else what we are doing?"

"Sure," Emily answered and headed upstairs.

Carl looked first to Pete. "Why don't you get Barb, and we'll go now. Do you still have the 44 Magnum with you?"

Pete patted his left chest to indicate the big revolver was in its makeshift holster under his jacket. "I'll be right back," Pete said and left as well.

"I'd like you to stand guard in the lobby, at least until we get back," Carl said to his oldest son.

"Sure, Dad. No problem.

Barb and Pete returned, along with Alex carrying the Remington shotgun.

Looking to his youngest son, Carl said, "Stay here and help your brother. We should be right back in an hour—plus or minus." Alex nodded his head and went to the front door. He checked to make sure the door was still locked. "Ready?" he asked Barb and Pete.

"Let's get 'er done," Pete responded and smiled.

"Lock the door once we're out," Carl said and opened the door for Barb and Pete. The snow had been packed down enough so they did not need the snowshoes, although it was tempting to use their newly acquired versions. Pete led the way with Barb in the middle.

In front of the door with the polished brass numeral '521,' Barb stood in front with Pete on her right and Carl behind her to the left. Carl instinctively had his right hand in his jacket pocket, wrapped around the grip of the M1911 pistol . . . just in case. Barb knocked.

Carl noticed the peephole darken, and then the door deadbolt disengaged and the door opened.

"Please come in," Betsy said.

The introductions were made, namely for Carl and the Mossman family. Henry 'Hank' Mossman presented a common, confident and large image—a good head taller than his wife. Their adult daughters, Helen and Holly, both youthful versions of their mother, were equally elegant in their appearance, even in the primitive conditions of the crisis. Everyone found a seat around the modest fire.

"I would offer you a drink," said Hank, "but, these are not normal times."

"It's quite alright," Pete responded. "We are far more interested in your proposal," Pete looked and nodded to Betsy, "as you have suggested."

"First, allow me to be direct. I do not know who the shooter was, but I have admired your work and the characteristics of your weapons. The shots that killed the two intruders two weeks ago were delivered with no rifle report . . . even at a distance, which means a suppressed weapon. We also witnessed the assault two days ago. I tried to help."

"The attacker behind your building?" interjected Carl.

"Yeah. I took him out about the time the shooting started."

"That him was a woman," Pete added.

"Oh my," Betsy exclaimed.

"She was well armed and part of the assault team," Carl said.

"I saw that you went back on their tracks. I imagine you wanted to track down one of the attackers trying to escape," Hank stated.

"Yes," answered Carl. "There were six of them. We dealt with four. You got the fifth. I wounded the sixth person and tracked him back to the lodge up the road. He was not cooperative." Carl decided to leave the recounting at that level. "There were four surviving women in their group. I don't think they will be a problem, but in these trying times, we never know."

"Therein lies the essence of our proposal," Hank said. "As this situation continues, others out there will become progressively more desperate . . . and more aggressive. We have arms and ammunition, but the four of us could easily be overwhelmed. We have also watched some of the others moving to Building 3. We imagine you have collected a group."

"Yes, we have," Pete responded. "There are five families . . . 19 of us, including a newborn girl."

Betsy gasped audibly. "Incredible. How old? Health?"

Pete looked at Carl to answer about his granddaughter. "Yes. Both our daughter and granddaughter are doing well, so far, and Breckyn is only two weeks old."

"Thank goodness," sighed Betsy. "Beautiful name."

"So," Hank said, to return them to business. "What would it take to join you, and is there room?"

Again, Pete looked at Carl to answer. The Building 3 leader nodded his head. "I will speak frankly and directly, so as not to waste your time. We have been and will most likely remain in a survival situation, until winter breaks and we can walk out of these mountains. There are essentials necessary for our survival: 1.) Warmth; 2.) Water; 3.) Food; and 4.) Weapons for defense. The families that joined our group brought a degree of self-sufficiency. By joining together, we are collectively providing for our mutual defense. Water has not, is not and most likely will not be a problem." Carl felt no need to explain. "In the process of defending ourselves, we have accumulated sufficient firearms and ammunition, so our needs in that area are not great. Our principal concern would be that whatever firearms and ammunition you may have are secure and not obtainable by potential marauders. That brings us to warmth. We have prepared three apartments in Building 3, essentially sealing off all of the rooms and consolidating our living space down to the living room around the fireplace. We have sufficient firewood for those three apartments to make it most of the way to spring. I point this out only to say that living accommodations and the provisions for warmth are an issue to be resolved." Carl paused. Hank nodded his head in agreement, but did not speak. "Lastly, food. We have enough for the families we have, but not enough to absorb others. So, I must ask about your food status."

"Thank you for your frankness, Carl. It is appreciated. For now, let it suffice to say, we have done largely the same things. We have enough to make it to spring and beyond. What we do not have is numbers; thus, our approach to you. I believe we are going to see more assaults like we," Hank said, pausing to gesture to everyone in their apartment, "have experienced over the last few weeks. It is probably going to get worse, before it gets better." Carl and Pete both nodded their heads in agreement. "I assume you have some security plan. We can contribute to that plan. Betsy and the girls are all accomplished hunters. If one of the apartments in your building is open, we would propose to occupy one of the open units and join your defense scheme."

The group delved into specifics of occupancy, their watch provisions and mutual protection procedures. Searching the "inactive" units in Building 5 was agreed to, since no one had yet disturbed the other units. Oddly, none of the Mossmans even hinted at awareness of Pete and Carl searching the Kramer condominium—532—early in the crisis and none of the Building 3 trio raised the topic. They also discussed the general plan to hike out of the mountains in the spring. Everyone agreed there was little hope of rescue and self-reliance was their only means of survival. As trust began to grow, Hank described the specifics of their firewood, food and weapons status. The Mossmans had saved a combination of dressed meats from their hunting before the crisis, along with canned, preserved and freeze-dried meals. They also offered to contribute several traps they had acquired over the years. Several rifles, shotguns and one pistol would add to the substantial arsenal already held in Building 3, but more importantly, they possessed more ammunition.

Carl looked at Barb and Pete to receive gestured concurrence, before he spoke. "We are satisfied. We are a mutual group, so if you would be patient with us, we need to present your proposal to the rest of the group and gain their concurrence, as well, before we can formally agree. Is that acceptable?"

"Yes, of course," responded Hank.

"Well, then, if you will excuse us, we will do just that and return with the answer as soon as possible."

Hank stood and extended his right hand. Carl, Pete and Barb stood as well. They shook hands. The Mossman ladies also stood and shook hands with the visitors.

The Building 3 trio made their way back to their base, gathered the entire group up and presented the Mossman's proposal. Appropriate questions were asked and answered. They were unanimously in agreement, well, except for Breckyn, who could not comprehend the matter. Even Larry, Aaron and Melissa were asked for their opinions. With the group's agreement, the trio returned to 521 and informed the Mossmans.

Carl returned to Building 3 and sent back Mike, Nick, Dave and Alex, all armed, to guard Building 5 and allow the whole Mossman family to meet the Building 3 families and survey the available accommodations. None of the Mossmans were particularly pleased with the frozen, deceased couple in apartment 321, but they eventually agreed their occupancy of unit 321 was the best option.

While the Mossmans returned to their condominium to prepare for the move, the negotiated solution provided for Carl, Pete, Oscar, Bert and George to move the 321 couple outside next to the accumulating bodies up the trail.

They also moved that mattress outside as well. The remaining mattress was moved into the living room along with a mattress from one of the lower units. The men prepared the thermal barriers, as they had in the other units, and started a fire in the fireplace to begin warming the living room of 321. With all the helpers they now had, the move was completed in a couple of hours. The Mossmans settled into the new group quickly and in fine form.

One of the first orders of business for the expanded group entailed restructuring the watch teams to reflect the additional members. They also walked through the whole process of standing watch, so that everyone knew their place and responsibility in the defense plan. They added another watch team, interspersed the Mossmans and redistributed existing members to maintain their basic principles. The group collectively agreed that since Melissa Manson was the youngest at 12 years of age, she would be assigned as the watch supernumerary, replacing Larry, who joined the regular watch teams. They gathered in unit 332 to reorder the watch assignments on the wall, as they had done earlier. They were approaching standing room only numbers in the modest size living room. The new assignments on the wall spread the available people across five teams with an 'A' Section and a 'B' Section, so that each team had members from each apartment to make the wake-up call for the successive team.

With the numbers they had now and the consolidated group in Building 3, they could make it through the night with only one two-hour watch period for each team, and they had longer undisturbed sleep. Everyone seemed to be in a better mood.

The following day enabled them to search the remainder of the Building 5 units. Blessedly, they found no more dead people. They collected canned foods, not a lot, but anything was better than nothing. They also found several first aid kits, including a defibrillator that was no longer functional. This time, they also gathered up cleaning supplies to make things a little cleaner, if not live a little better. They did not discover any additional weapons in the building. What they did find when they finally went back to the 532 unit was an unlocked metallic compartment in the gun case they had broken into during their last search. To Carl's delight, they found full-up ballistic charts for both the .308 (7.62 x 51mm) round and the Springfield .30-06 (7.62 x 63mm) round. Of perhaps more significance, they discovered a LASER rangefinder that was battery-powered and surprisingly was still operable, having been shielded from the EMP attack in the metal box.

That night, Carl compared his memory-derived ballistics chart with the real deal. He had not been far off, but Carl's estimated chart was long, meaning he had predicted a longer range than actually achievable at a given elevation setting. The next day, Carl took the range-ring map, the ballistics charts and the rangefinder to the sniper's perch they had used during prior missions into town. Carl smiled when he validated that his map rings were as close to accurate as the width of the pencil he had used. He checked the range to three locations they had searched before. Carl did not want to do more and use more battery life. They would likely need to use the rangefinder during their exfiltration.

Another modest snowfall came on the third day after the Mossmans joined that offered the group more rest. Several of the young folks found some board games and actually took pleasure in the diversion from the protracted crisis. During the off-day of the snowfall, while the kids were playing games, Barb and Pete approached Carl and Janet with a suggestion.

Pete began, "I probably should have thought of this earlier when we first joined up and while we were scavenging in town. Barb brought up the point that we have few medical supplies. We were lucky with Nick's wound and your wounds that they did not get infected. We might not be so lucky the next time."

"I think we really should take the risk of searching the pharmacies in town," Barb interjected.

"How many pharmacies are there?" asked Carl. "We've never had to use them."

"There is only one in Breckenridge—the City Market Pharmacy. There are three larger ones around Dillon Reservoir—Walgreens and CVS in Silverthorne and the Safeway unit in North Frisco, just off the interstate, which we've used."

"The City Market is within reach. The other three are quite a distance out . . . probably several days to make the round trip in these conditions. Y'all saw the risk on the road north."

"Yes, we did," Barb responded. "We will not be an unarmed family this time. I think the benefit warrants the risk."

"We could probably handle the City Market, but we will expend considerable effort, exposed to incalculable risk, to reach farther. What do you think, Pete?"

"I understand Barb's proposal, but I also feel the risk. How about we tackle the City Market, first, and then reassess an attempt at Frisco."

"If we do decide to attempt a foray to Frisco and Silverthorne," Carl paused to think a moment, "we should probably make it a night operation to minimize the reach of any snipers. We have a waxing moon with a full moon in a week. We only need the weather to cooperate."

"That sounds reasonable," Pete said and turned to his wife. "Is that OK?"

"Anything is better than nothing," said Barb.

"The best defense is a good offense," added Carl. They chuckled and several of the listeners joined in. "We will need to organize, ensure everyone volunteers, and gain consent from the whole group."

"Agreed," Barb said.

"I concur," contributed Pete

"One last thought for now, since you've been into town," Carl pressed. "Virtually every place has been pillaged . . . probably scoured since we made our last run in town, and we did our part of pillaging. And," he paused for emphasis, "the risks will be substantially higher, now."

"There is no disagreement," Barb said. "I just feel the need for some form of medical protection . . . whatever we can find. Better to search now than later, when we get closer to spring."

"True," Pete added with a head nod.

With the basics of a proposal, they asked everyone to gather in 332 to consider the operation, at least in part. Barbara Higgins presented her case for the objective—both part one and part two, if there was going to be a second part. Carl and Pete added the basic operations plan to achieve the objective as well as the necessity for volunteers. The debate concerning risk was understandable. Surprisingly, Janet, who was usually risk-averse, argued the risk for part one was worth taking. They definitely had to improve their medical supplies situation.

Hank, Pete and Carl debated the overwatch task and collectively agreed that Hank would man the overwatch perch with his Winchester Model 70, bolt-action rifle, chambered for a .308 round (7.62 x 51mm NATO) with matched 10x scope. He had his ballistics chart and would use Carl's range ring chart for his sight settings. Carl and Pete would use the rangefinder, if they needed it. Pete chose the 1903 Springfield. All three of them had their pistols. Hank's youngest daughter Holly volunteered to backwatch with him in the 232 perch unit. Alex and Nick volunteered to backwatch for Pete and Carl.

The late morning sun gave them plenty of daylight. The sky was generally clear and bright with scattered altocumulus clouds and little to no wind. The search team suited up for the cold air. Aaron and Dave manned the lobby doors, as the team departed by the rear door and headed down the trail. A box of four protectors surrounded Vicky and Barb, as they moved north on Park Avenue. Their transit to the City Market Mall complex was comparatively swift for packed snow and icy ground. The stores were in worse shape than when Carl had last visited the mall shortly after the crisis began.

The condition of the pharmacy was comparable to other stores. Barb and Vicky brought candles to help with the low light of the interior. The women went directly to the controlled substances, prescription medicine area. The security screens had been torn, twisted and bent away from the once-secure area. Carl and Pete stood watch inside and partially behind a wall adjacent to a broken window. Alex and Nick searched the ransacked store shelves for any remaining and usable medical supplies like bandages, antiseptics, protective ointments like lip balm and sunscreen. The search proved more difficult with the low light conditions, and all of the merchandise had been swept from the shelves, strewn on the floor, in simple destruction rather than purposeful search.

From what Carl and Pete could see at the front of the store, the searchers were actually finding useful items in the debris of the wrecked store. Neither of them could ascertain the yield of the nurses at the back of the store and behind the counter. They watched the exterior carefully.

People were moving around outside. Two men approached the pharmacy with no apparent objective. They did not notice the rifles aimed at their chests until they came within ten meters of the storefront. Both men did not speak and raised their empty hands. An expression of shock and fear etched their faces. Neither Pete nor Carl moved or gestured to the men. No one spoke. When the men realized they had survived, they backed away slowly and kept their hands raised until they disappeared around the north corner of the last shop.

The search took several hours, much longer than any of them expected; however, the bulging shoulder bags indicated they also found more than they expected. No words passed between them—only hand signals. They would wait until they returned to Building 3 to inventory and consider what they had collected. With their transit formation reestablished, they headed out by the same route, toward Park Avenue.

The group had not reached halfway to the southwest corner of the mall complex when the zing of a projectile near Carl's head and the impact slightly behind him startled Carl. Impact debris and perhaps shrapnel hit Vicky behind Carl. "Down!" Carl shouted, as he dove for an open doorway and heard the crack of the muzzle report maybe a second later. Vicky was screaming in obvious pain. Another shot impacted very close and again the crack of the shot came about a second later. "Are you OK?" shouted Carl.

"I've been hit," Vicky screamed, "not serious, but I'm bleeding."

"She's covered," shouted Nick.

"We're all covered," Alex added, anticipating the next question.

"The shots came from the southwest. Stay covered. Watch for a ground contact party," Carl commanded. "Shout out if you see anything. I'm going to find the shooter. Stay covered. This may take a while."

Carl and Pete had made it to the first shop—a curio store before it had been ransacked. The others were behind them. Carl and Pete low-crawled through the debris on the floor, deeper into the interior. No signs, and far too close. At the back, in the dark, they moved to the north wall and slowly began the process of checking the field of view to the west, working their way to the south. At first, all they could see was hillside, snow and conifer trees. The closest buildings they could see were only 200-300 meters away—too close for the separation between impact and report. Nonetheless, Carl and Pete used their riflescopes to search every window they could see, working their way out.

Pete was the first to spot him, after 20 minutes of the search process. "He's in the right window on the second floor of the green house between the two white ones."

Carl tried to find the point of reference, Pete indicated and asked in a lower voice, "Do you have the shot?"

"I have him in the optics. He's searching and waiting for us. I do not have my sight dialed in."

"Where's the rangefinder?"

"In my backpack," Pete said and did not move from this sight position. "He's maybe 500 meters out."

Carl laid his rifle on the floor, moved behind Pete, and very carefully and slowly opened his backpack, so as not to disturb or shake his sight position. He felt the unique plastic box shape and slowly removed it. Carl felt for the switch and initiated the device. He moved deliberately back to his position and exposed only enough of the rangefinder to see the building through the optics. The illuminated reticle and symbology indicated the device was working. Carl reacquired their target, placed the rangefinder reticle on the building wall just to the left of the shooter's window. Depressing the activation button produced the needed numbers—623 yards.

"Hang on. I'll get us an elevation setting." Carl deactivated and switched off the rangefinder, and placed it on the shelf next to him. He removed his backpack, felt for the newly acquired ballistics charts and removed them. The interior darkness prevented him from seeing the range lines. Carl crawled toward the storefront until he had sufficient indirect light to see the charts, and crawled back to Pete. "Fourteen clicks for you; sixteen clicks for me. Do you want me to dial in your sight?"

"No. I'll feel it. Get your sight set. We should fire together to ensure we get this guy."

"OK."

"He's still looking for us. He's not moved since we acquired him."

"He may not be working with others."

"Uh-huh."

Carl heard the soft clicks of Pete's sight elevation knob. He lifted his rifle, but waited to dial up his sight setting. *Firing together is a really good idea.* When Pete dropped his right hand back to the trigger, Carl dialed in his sight setting and slowly returned the big rifle to its resting place on the top of the medium height, now barren, store shelf.

"I'm dialed in and ready."

"Sure. I'm ready."

"So am I. I'll probably fire twice, if I can see the impacts. You call it."

"OK. Here we go. Three, two, one." The crack and flash of the pair of virtually simultaneous shots rang out. Carl heard Pete work his bolt to eject the spent cartridge and chamber a fresh round. The two spent cartridges hit and bounced off something. The pink puff mist in the window and the immediate disappearance of the sniper suggested that one or both of them hit their target. Both men watched the window. A torso appeared in the interior. They could not hear anything. It was a female torso from the chest bumps of her sweater and she was clearly agitated. Carl took up the slack on his trigger for another shot, but he held short. The woman disappeared. Carl released the trigger slack. "Search the other windows," he said softly.

"Did you get him?" came a muffled male voice from next door.

"Looks like it," Pete answered.

They continued to assess the house for any additional threat. "Looks like we're done," Carl said without looking to Pete. "Are you ready to move?"

"Yeah. Let's do it. Maybe we should be using bounding overwatch until we get to the street," Pete added, referring to the military technique of one segment covering another segment advancing quickly, and then alternating that mutual coverage.

"Good point and agreed."

They both stood. Carl stood watch at the door, while Pete moved quickly to the adjacent store. Once he disappeared from his peripheral vision, Carl did the same.

Inside the store, Carl found the boys in good watch positions and the two women farther into the store. Barb appeared unharmed and held by Pete. Carl looked to Vicky, who had several bandages on her face and scalp, and a noticeable bulge under the bloody hole in her jacket. "Are you OK to move?" Carl inquired cautiously.

"I can run just fine. Barb bandaged me up well, and we think she stopped the bleeding. I'm still shaking."

"I'll bet. Never a good thing . . . getting shot at. If it is any comfort to you . . . that shooter will not be taking another shot."

"Good. Thank you."

"Because there is potential danger out there, we are going to move in bounds. Vicky . . . you and Barb stay together and always be the second group to move. Nick, you will be with Pete, and Alex with me. You'll get the handle of it pretty quick. As soon as the next bound watch is set, move quickly to that position and take cover. The following group will then bound past the other two groups, and so forth. Any questions?" Carl scanned all five other members. Several nodded without speaking. "OK. Let's get to it. The sun is nearly to the horizon. We need to get home before we lose the light."

Pete gestured for Nick to follow him. Carl and Alex scanned the viewable scene, as Pete and Nick moved two stores down. Once Carl saw both weapons point out, he turned to the ladies, "OK, move as fast as you can without slipping to the next position." Neither of the women hesitated and off they went. When they made it safely to cover at Pete and Nick's position, Carl nodded for Alex to follow. They ran as best they could beyond Pete's position to the next overwatch cover place. They made it to the trees along the street in short order without interference from anyone else. Carl checked both directions and the hillside. He gestured for them to cross to the west side, since that offered the least exposure.

The sun descended below the western ridgeline before they made it to the trailhead. The cover of the trees on both sides of the trail offered some comfort and enabled them to move collectively, more quickly. As the rest of the group moved up the trail, Carl stopped to scan one last time to make sure they were not being tailed.

Hank and Holly joined Carl at Building 3 for the last dozen meters to the door. Hank said, as they walked, "I happened to see the original shot hit the wall behind your head. I searched for the shooter, but I could not find him."

"His perch was facing us . . . away from you . . . no way for you to see him."

"Where was he?"

"Two-story house . . . at the end of Woods Drive or on Ski Hill Road. I haven't looked at the map, yet. Pete found him. Rangefinder showed 623 yards. We should be able to find the house easy enough, if we want to follow-up."

Bert was at the rear door by the time they arrived. When he saw the bandages on his wife, he burst out of the building and embraced Vicky. "What the hell happened?" he asked.

"A sniper attacked us as we were trying to leave. Debris fragments or shrapnel ricocheted at me. Barb patched me up. I'm OK."

"Anybody else hit?" he asked.

"No."

"He missed me," Carl added, "and, the spray got Vicky."

"Thank God you are not seriously wounded." Bert looked to Carl. "We were really starting to worry. Oscar heard shots, and you took a lot longer than we expected."

"Let's go inside," Carl said. "We need to debrief for the whole group."

"And, check what we recovered," Barb added.

They went upstairs. Carl was the last to follow, after he had checked both doors.

Before Carl shut the apartment door, he was bombarded with questions. He held up his hands with the rifle still grasped in his left hand. "Pete, why don't you take this one?"

"Sure," Pete said and shifted his position, standing next to Carl at the now closed and locked door. "Our transit to the City Market Mall was uneventful. The pharmacy store was a mess. Carl and I stood guard while Nick and Alex searched the store in general. Everything had been pulled off the shelves onto the floor. Vicky and Barb took the medicine." Pete looked at his wife. "What did you find?" he asked.

"We have to more carefully count and evaluate what we found, but we managed to find several forms of antibiotics, antihistamines, strong antiseptics, anti-inflammatory agents, and such. We did not find any pain meds."

"I might have found a few," interjected Vicky. "We need to check more carefully."

"Then, perhaps we found some. We'll know more once we can inventory what we collected. We've also checked what Nick and Alex collected—bandages, wraps, quite a bit of sunscreen, surprisingly, and Chapstick, along with several bottles of Betadine and tubes of Neosporin. Anyway, I think Vicky and I agree that our medical supply state has substantially improved. We'll take the time to list and count what we have, so any of us can find what they need."

"Why did they shoot at you?' Janet jumped in.

"We have no way to know," Pete responded. "Once we had collected up what we have, we began the return transit. Shortly after we exited the pharmacy, the sniper fired at Carl. The impact debris from the first shot struck Vicky. We took cover in two abandoned stores—Carl and me in the southern, and the others in the adjacent store to the north. The sniper got off a second shot with less effect. After checking that Vicky's wounds were not serious and there were no other injuries, Carl and I began searching for the shooter. We needed to neutralize him, before we could move. We found him . . ."

"Pete found him," interjected Carl.

Pete smiled and nodded his head. "As I was saying, we found him. Carl used the rangefinder. He was at 623 yards. We dialed in our sights with the elevation settings for the range. We fired together to ensure we got him. We were successful."

"There is at least one woman in that house and perhaps more people," Carl added. "They did not try to follow us, and there was no way they could track us; so, I do not think follow-up is warranted."

"Good," muttered Janet. Carl noticed Vicky was the only one who smiled, or showed any reaction to Janet's utterance.

"Once we eliminated the sniper, we used a leap-frog bounding technique to make it back here without further incident. Questions?"

"Does the yield of this mission preclude having to make the protracted journey to Dillon?" Betsy inquired.

Pete looked to Carl for the response. Carl cleared his throat. "Unless anyone else has input, I think it appropriate to leave that decision to Barb Higgins and Vicky Johnson—our medical experts." Carl nodded to the two women, who bobbed their heads in acknowledgment. "I think Pete will agree, we have a workable technique for moving in potentially hostile country, and we are prepared to perform the mission, if our medics think it is necessary for our protection. For reference in that decision process, I think it will take a small team two to three days transit time in clear weather to make the trip each way, and another day or two to search the two pharmacies in two different towns."

"So, you'd be gone for over a week," Janet noted.

"Yes. I think that is a fair estimate." Carl paused. No response. "And, if we are going to attempt it, sooner rather than later would be better. Whatever might happen, we must consider recovery from injuries or wounds, which means we should complete a mission like this before mid-February."

"Well," Barb said, "we have plenty to think about, don't we?" She stood from her seated position on the floor against the wall. "Vicky and I need to assess what today's yield brought us, and what our needs for a long walk out of these mountains might require. Anyone else who would like to help or know what we have is welcome to join in. Give us a day or so to figure things out, and then let's reassess the answer to the question."

Carl went to the blackout curtain, glimpsed out, and then announced, "Twilight is nearly ended. We need to get everyone fed, Vicky's wounds properly cleaned and dressed, and set the watch for the night. I do not expect any intruders, but vigilance is our watchword."

Without the slightest grumbling or further discussion, the group moved with surprising unguided purpose born in the routine they had established.

Team Two would take the first watch period. Carl was more than ready for at least a couple of hours sleep before his watch duty arrived. They ate quickly, tended to their cleaning, dispersed, and settled into their nightly routine. Day 35 in the cold mountains was near an end.

—

21

Carl chose to let the sleeping dog lie. The apartment remained quiet, not even the dwindling fire offered any crackling. Janet slept peacefully. He stood slowly and carefully, so as not to disturb Janet, and added a log to refresh the fire and warm the living room. Oscar remained dutifully alert on the balcony and did not notice Carl's discreet peek. Twilight was breaking the darkness. The day would begin soon. Carl went to the front (warmer) bathroom and tended to his daily personal hygiene. When he was done, Carl went to the arsenal room. Only Holly's bottom half appeared beneath the curtain, as she maintained her watch station, observing the rear of the building.

No purpose would be served in startling her. Carl stood in the doorway for a moment, and then softly said, "How's it goin'?"

Holly's legs shifted, so she heard Carl's words. "All quiet, Mister Parks." Holly did not move from her watch station and duties. *She has been taught well.*

"Excellent. Any movement out there?"

"I actually saw a squirrel about . . . oh . . . 45 minutes ago. Is something wrong?"

"No. As you say, all's quiet. I woke up while the rest of the house is still asleep. Best to let them sleep as long as they can." Holly did not respond or move. "I'll leave you to it. I'm going to the back bedroom to see what I can see."

"OK," was the only response that Holly offered.

What once was the master bedroom and now was their cold storage room kept the wind out, but cold was still cold. Carl pulled the curtain back and around him in similar fashion as Holly stood watch in the arsenal room. The Earth's rotation brought them closer to local sunrise and a brightening day. The view out to the west proved not so encouraging. The entire western sky reflected the high altitude sunlight, but darker lower down. The leading tongue of a high cirrus shelf thickened to the west. "Another storm's a'comin'," Carl said aloud, only to himself. *We often experienced snowfalls in previous weeklong ski holidays in these mountains, but this is verging on relentless. I had no idea these storms came this often. Skiing up here is great, but there is no way on God's little green Earth I would live up here year around.* Carl examined the buildings above them that were not obscured by evergreen trees. The sunlight hit the western ridgeline and the snow-covered peaks took on an almost painful brilliance that visually darkened the western sky beyond the peaks. The clear ski trails looked so inviting. *How great would it be to make a couple of runs through the untouched powder snow on those trails?* There were no signs of humanity—none, not one.

Damn, this could almost be a winter version of Stephen King's *The Stand*, or Philip Wylie's *The Disappearance*, except the women were clearly still here.

Muffled, unintelligible words suggested the occupants of the apartment were beginning the process of animation. Carl scanned the scene one more time—no change—and then, ducked under the curtain to extricate himself and checked to make sure the curtain was fully in place before he left.

As Carl stepped into the living room, Mike was holding and rocking Breckyn in his arms. Janet and Lisa stood at the kitchen counter with Barb and Vicky. The women were working together organizing, noting on a paper tablet what they were learning. Oscar and Holly sat near the fire, still warming themselves, having concluded their watch period. Carl saluted the watchstanders, who both nodded in acknowledgment.

Carl looked to Vicky. "How are you feeling?"

Vicky Johnson smiled appreciatively. "A little sore frankly, but I think Barb has done a professional job of treating my wounds." Barb nodded her recognition.

"How's the inventory going?"

"Pretty well, actually," answered Barb. "We are about halfway through, and it appears we may have been quite lucky."

"Better lucky than good," Carl added.

"Yes, then lucky is the word. I suspect many people before we chose not to spend the time to search through the refuse of the pharmacy after it had been ransacked. I must say, the store looked like it had been hit by an angry mob rather than pillaged for valuable contents. Anyway, we are the beneficiaries of those mistakes."

"Excellent." The boys—Nick, Dave and Alex—gathered around them to observe the efforts of the ladies. "There is no rush. It looks like we have yet another storm coming in probably tomorrow, would be my guess based on the clouds to the west."

"Wow! We don't need more snow," Nick said and made several simulated snowboard turns, "since we can't use what we have now."

"Yeah, just more snow to melt," added Alex, "before we get out of here."

"Well, boys, unfortunately, we do not and cannot control the weather. We are confined to playing the cards Mother Nature deals to us. My only point is, we will probably have a day or two, maybe longer, before we can act on anything."

Others began to arrive. The ladies suspended their inventory tasks. The morning meal was prepared and consumed in comparative silence. The inherent chitchat of social gatherings did not involve yesterday's operation or even their status. Carl chose to just listen and let things settle. By mid-afternoon, the ladies completed their meticulous inventory and written listing of the yield. Carl's curiosity drove him to examine the list that did show better than expected acquisitions. So many people must have passed over this stuff . . . too lazy to examine what was in that store, or perhaps not able to recognize what was there. They decided to store their medical supplies on the closet shelf in the cold storage room—out of the way.

Everyone avoided pressing for more action, as if each in their own way sought a down day from the close call they faced yesterday. Even within the Parks family, no one pressed their curiosity. Each chose their particular distraction. Nick and Dave played several games of competitive chess. Lisa and Alex read books, even some they had already read, more than once, as if they might find new meaning in the words. The family took up the task of tending to Breckyn—cleaning, entertaining and stimulating her. Only Lisa could feed her daughter, and she was doing quite well at that task. Breckyn displayed all positive signs of good health and growth. They gave Lisa as much of a break from motherhood, as they were able. Carl tended to the weapons they used yesterday, and even Janet helped him.

The snowstorm began shortly after noon the following day. They observed the rapidly accumulating additional snow. The kids took it upon themselves to perform sessions to tamp down the snow, as they had done before, except on a more frequent and periodic basis. Carl even took an opportunity to join them, both in the tamping process, but also in the local overwatch security task.

The storm lasted longer than previous storms, and Carl suspected two or more storm systems had combined by the time they reached the eastern Rockies. The snow did not diminish until nearly sunset on the third day. One last tamping session on the fourth day proved sufficient.

The return of direct sunlight seemed to inspire more than a few of the group. Barb, Pete, Vicky and Bert raised the question of continuing the potential medical supplies acquisition task. Carl tended to agree with their assessment; however, he knew the task should be a group decision. Carl called for a group meeting to discuss the medical supply status before the evening meal.

Once everyone was present and settled, either standing or sitting, in the living room of unit 332, Carl opened the discussion. "Thanks to the knowledge and expertise of Vicky and Barb, we have substantially improved our medical supply status. Is that safe to say?" he asked, looking to the two nurses. Both nodded their acknowledgment. "They have also raised the question of continuing our search for medical supplies."

"After what happened the last time?" protested Janet. "How many more times are you going to get shot at," she said rather forcefully to her husband, "before your bag of luck runs out?" Janet had heard his aviator mantra far too many times—you take an event from your bag of experience and place it in your bag of luck, as well as his incessant use of the phrase, better lucky than good.

"Janet!" chided Carl.

Pete decided to jump in. "We can have Carl do the overwatch duties that he does so well."

"Fi . . ."

"No! Janet, darling, I appreciate your concern for my well-being, but we all must take risks together to get us out of these mountains."

Janet was not satisfied. "Show of hands, how many of us have been shot at or wounded since this crisis began?" Nick, Pete, and Vicky raised their hands. "Raise your damn hand, Carl," Janet commanded. Carl reluctantly did so. Janet stood and paced a few times, and then faced the group. "I know Pete and Carl have skills imparted by their service to the nation, but our security cannot fall to them alone."

"They are not alone, Mom," responded Mike in an unusual contribution. "We have been out there, too."

"I've never handled firearms," George added. "Nor served in the military. I'd have no idea what to do or what to look for."

The debate continued for another hour, until Janet finally accepted with trepidation the reality that all risk was not equal. The best chance they had to minimize the risk from being realized was to deploy the best skills they had, to anticipate and deal with threats to their safety.

They collectively agreed to search the ransacked stores for overlooked first aid kits and supplies. They would also visit the ski patrol stations they could reach at lower elevations as well as the medical services clinics in town that might yield specialty items like tourniquets, simple inflatable splints, or saline drip bags to at least lessen the risk of any potential blood loss. Over the next two weeks, they took on limited, specific, targeted searches in the early morning, before local sunrise, to collect what they could. They contained their ambition to do more on any given day, primarily to reduce their exposure. They were not always successful, but they did find accomplishment and added to their stock of supplies. They also recovered two ski sleds from one of the ski patrol stations that incredibly had not been ransacked, or even touched from what the search team could determine. Two stock carts found at the nearly bare Wellington Road Market were the best they could find with wheels to haul their cargo out of the mountains. They used the ski sleds to move the carts. The process of moving the carts was a bit of a struggle. Just transferring the heavy carts from the sleds into the protection of the building lobby proved to be quite the challenge; but, most importantly, they accomplished the task. Moving the carts convinced them all that they should keep looking for better, wheeled conveyance and kludge up some kind of harness to make haulage easier and leave their hands free for weapons.

The forays were not without danger. The show of force for the few confrontations that did occur curtailed any violence. The deployed teams were extra careful to watch for tails on their return and to mask their movement as best they could to avoid any direct observation of their base of operations. Fortunately for everyone, no shots were fired. Several of the teams even began to feel the threat might be diminishing in that the violence-prone or desperate people had been culled from the population in the stranded mountain town, and the remainder were more self-sufficient. There was always hope, but none of the Building 3 group let their guard down. They remained constantly vigilant and suspicious of any human being they encountered for any reason and in any circumstance.

Day 58 was the 15th of February and a new moon. The Building 3 group spent the clear, sunny, cold day inside, collectively taking stock of their food, water, firewood and supply status. By late afternoon, the group completed the assessment process and gathered for the conclusion.

"We have done well," pronounced Carl. "As we agreed all those weeks ago, this is the moment we transition from search and acquisition to preparation." Carl paused and scanned the group. Head nods and thumb's up gestures displayed unanimous agreement. "We need to take our exercising a little more seriously. We have six to eight weeks or so of time remaining before we abandon out safe abode for the rigors of the road, and the hike out of these mountains." Several cheers and handclaps complemented Carl's statement. "We also need to prepare our food supply for the journey."

"What do you have in mind?" asked Oscar.

"My suggestion, we should set aside . . . say . . . six weeks of food at our normal consumption rate, and then take the remainder, especially the meat, and make jerky."

"We don't have a functional oven," Hank observed.

"No, we don't, so we have to engineer a makeshift oven to enable drying of the meat without cooking it. I've got a couple of ideas. Who has experience making jerky?" The whole Mossman family along with Oscar, Emily, Pete and Barb raised their hands. Carl smiled. "I think we can manage this task with all this expertise. I must say I have never made jerky, so I am looking forward to learning."

"It's really pretty simple," Hank added. "We'll figure it out."

"I would also suggest we hold off consumption of more freeze dried meals, since they are light and not perishable, and we really should consume the remaining canned goods. They are too heavy, cumbersome, and difficult to deal with on the open road." Carl noted general agreement, but not unanimous concurrence. "Are there any objections?" Twelve-year-old Melissa raised her hand. "Yes Melissa."

"I really like the corn," she stated. Several of the group chuckled. Melissa seemed a little embarrassed at the reaction.

Carl smiled and answered, "I'm with you, Melissa. I love the corn . . . and green beans, too. We can enjoy the vegetables while we are here, but the journey out of these mountains is going to be difficult. It is going to be very hard to carry what we need for the hike. I just think the cans are too heavy for us to carry out."

Melissa nodded her head and said, "OK."

Carl nodded his head in agreement. "We have other, more practical, logistics tasks to complete before we move, not least of which is the haulage harnesses for the carts. We also need to sort out how we move our cargo through the various conditions we are likely to encounter during the journey . . . from dry roads to ice and snow covered roads. The snow and ice may well not be fully cleared, especially over the high mountain passes we must cross to get out of this valley."

"We can divide up some of the physical preparation work," Pete added.

"That would be most appropriate," Carl said. "We should also begin thinking about organizing our group for the road trip and what firearms to take and such."

"Perhaps," Pete said, "Hank, you and I can make a first pass at that plan."

"Agreed." Carl looked around the dimly lit room and the attentive faces all watching him. "Now, before we adjourned for our evening meal, is there any new business?"

No one responded. They began to stand and jumped into the routine that had sustained them through two months in the cold and challenge of the high Rocky Mountains. The group set aside the business before them and kept their discussions to the routine, the mundane and the passion for skiing they all shared. They lingered in social discussion, while the first watch team took their positions to protect the building and its residents through the night.

Another glorious, clear day in the cold mountain air with light breeze to add some additional chill greeted the Building 3 group the following day. After their morning meal and local sunrise, Helen and Holly eagerly leapt to their volunteer task and most of the children joined in the new adventure and learning new skills for their survival. They took several breaks to warm up and stayed at their task of devising and setting animal traps with the appropriate bait until dusk.

The evening meal discussion centered upon the day's activities. The setting of the traps garnered the most enthusiasm and understandably so. No one asked about the jerky experiment. Only a few of the group stopped to examine the first trial batch of jerky.

As they lay down on their mattress to begin the evening routine, Janet and Carl softly assessed the day's accomplishments.

Janet began, "Sounds like the kids had more fun in the process than in any sense of accomplishment."

"A good thing, at this stage. Any harmless distraction has to be positive."

"I sense a positive-ness building in the group," Janet said and turned her head to kiss her husband on the cheek. "Everyone seems to sense the end of this nightmare."

"We're not out of the woods, yet."

Janet chuckled softly. "Oh, don't be such a stick-in-the-mud Debbie-downer."

Carl joined her in the lighthearted moment. He smiled and looked into her loving eyes. "I just worry."

"I know you do, but there will be a time . . . 'a time to every purpose, under heaven,' as the old song goes."

Carl rose up on his elbow, leaned over and kissed his wife as loving husbands do. Holding her eyes, Carl smiled and said, "Ecclesiastes 3:1-8."

Janet giggled, "I was thinking the Byrds' '*Turn! Turn! Turn!*' and written by Pete Seeger."

"All one and the same."

"I love you, Carl."

"I love you, my darling," he said, as he lay back down beside his wife, and then whispered, "This will all be over someday."

Janet let the moment pass, as rejuvenating sleep rapidly claimed them.

The following morning, after the meal, those who wished to do so participated in the tasting of the newly produced jerky. While the preparation was good and acceptable, no one liked the plain or salted samples. A few others actually thought the peppered and rubbed samples were edible.

The young Mossman ladies and their pupils checked their traps a couple of times during the day with no sign of any interest or nibbles. Rightly so, Helen and Holly cautioned patience. *Yes, these young ladies have been taught quite well*, Carl told himself.

Holly and Mike checked the traps one last time after sunset and midway through evening twilight—still no nibbles.

During the early hours of Day 61, the night watch detected a sufficient scare to scramble a reaction. On the balcony watch station, Janet saw movement along 4 O'Clock Run Road. She could not see enough detail to describe the movement other than it was a human form and not moving casually. Carl got Nick up, armed and down to the lobby to reinforce Betsy and Alex. He chose the Remington 700 to minimize his signature, if he had to shoot and joined Janet back out on the balcony. From his odd, instant concern, Carl looked back to reassure himself he was not silhouetted by light leaks. *Clear!* They watched carefully for the remainder of the Team Three watch period. Team Four assumed the watch. They remained vigilant, but saw no further evidence of movement or intruders making an attempt on Building 3.

As dawn brought another cold sunny day, a renewed jitteriness returned to the group with the specter of more confrontations and perhaps violent conflict. The unease dampened the enthusiasm of the previous few days. No one chose to raise the topic for discussion, after the few known facts about the early hours scare were disclosed to the group.

As soon as they finished their morning meal and the fire was allowed to burn down to the desired level, the jerky-makers put the new batch of meat into the dehydration process. The anticipation of the tasting among the group was palpable. Those who chose to participate agreed the rub version offered the best taste, so far, and looked forward to tasting the day's test strips. In another experiment for clarity, half the marinated strips were embedded with the rub seasonings, to see how that would mix.

While the latest jerky experiment progressed, Helen, Holly, Mike, Nick and Dave went out to check the traps. When they did not return in a quarter of an hour, Carl retrieved the Mossberg 500, made sure the magazine was full, and then felt for his M1911 and the PPK. He went out to see what was taking the group longer than usual to check the traps and found them up the trail.

"We caught two squirrels, Dad," announced Nick with more excitement than he wanted. "Sorry," he continued with a lower voice. "It's just really cool that we finally caught something."

"Congratulations to all of you. Well done. A skill that will likely serve you well in life." Carl looked directly to Helen and Holly, who were by now supervising the dressing of the two squirrels. "You had an excellent teacher," he said directly to the young women.

"Thank you, Mister Parks," Helen responded. "That credit goes entirely to our Dad."

"It appears y'all are nearly finished with your task. I suppose the next question is, do y'all want to cook your squirrels, or jerky them?"

"Good question," Holly answered promptly. She looked to the others. "Should we take a vote?"

"Yeah," Mike said.

"Those for cooking?" Everyone raised their hands. "Then, it is decided."

"Very well. We'll roast 'em for supper . . . unless y'all would rather have them prepared another way."

"Roasting is the quickest and easiest," said Holly.

"And, it may be the only practical method we have on the road, should the need arise."

"Done," pronounced Mike.

"Now," Helen said with a commanding voice, "we need to clean up, cover the area, and reset the traps."

"Excellent. Then, I shall leave y'all to it."

Carl returned to 332 and happily reported on his findings. Not everyone seemed to be impressed with the acquired squirrels, but no one objected. Carl made a point of a personal conversation with Hank and Betsy to convey his thoughts about how well their daughters performed. They reacted with discernible pride.

Several of the men and women chose to contribute to the evaluation of the preparations for the impending hike out of the mountains. Everyone thought the twin harnesses for the two haulage carts would work, as long as they did not encounter appreciable snow. Ice might work, although control of the cart could be questionable. Pete Higgins had also taken on the task of sketching out the organization of the group for movement, including the criteria for rotating the scouting, security and logistics tasks, as well as a notional distribution of weapons. All of the long guns and shotguns were allocated and assigned members who had some experience with rifles. He had little labels with each weapon and distributed the pistols to minimize the types of ammunition they would carry. Carl felt Pete's sketch of the movement formation offered a great starting point from which to build and adjust.

The interim results discussions to date illuminated one major gap in their preparations so far—protection from the elements during transit. They would be on the road for several weeks, which meant they would most likely encounter inclement weather at some point. Even if they were lucky with the weather, they would have to deal with the cold at night when they needed to rest. They also had to find a way to carry, keep warm and protect Breckyn, who was the most vulnerable among the group. More work to do!

As Holly led the trappers back into the building, Carl noted the time and suggested the group gather to assess before a good meal. Once everyone was present, Carl began the status report. "First, I want to acknowledge the exceptional work of Helen and Holly Mossman. They demonstrated their skills and trapped two squirrels that will be roasted tonight as we prepare our evening meal." The young women appreciated the group recognition. "Our preparations are progressing well. Better to get them done early rather than wait until the last minute. I think most of us are agreed the harnesses for the carts and sleds will do the trick. Kudos to Pete for putting together a notional plan for our movement out of these mountains when spring arrives. Well done, Pete!" Several of the group clapped in approval. "I should say at this juncture, any contributions anyone wishes to make are always welcome. Also, no one is required to make this journey. If anyone wishes to opt out, the sooner we know the better we can adjust our plans." Carl paused, scanned the group, but no one responded. Breckyn also began to wind up her crying. Emily took the opportunity to change the baby's diaper, and then gently laid Breckyn in her mother's arm for her feeding. "We still have several notable gaps in our preparations, so far. One," Carl said looking to his granddaughter at breast, "we need to develop the means to carry, protect and care for Breckyn on this move. Two, we need to figure out our nighttime procedures, specifically how we are going to protect the group from the cold and the elements. We are likely to face rain, snow and ice, since the passes are so high. For several days during the transit, we may be above the tree line, so firewood will be scarce to non-existent. Anyway, these are just thoughts to stimulate any contributions to help resolve these gaps." Carl paused for anyone to speak. No one did. "Now, to more immediate items, we have the latest samples of our jerky experiments. We are going to have limited production capacity, and by my estimate, we have more meat to jerk-i-fy than the likely time we have to complete the task. We have enough samples to evaluate and agree on preferences. We cannot afford trying to transport and use the amount of frozen meat we have. I am happy to report that we have done better than expected in our consumption of meat. We will need to rely on jerky and our remaining freeze-dried meals during transit. So, anyone who wishes or has an opinion, please taste the samples and let us know your preferences tonight, so we can all agree on the process. We need to start dehydrating our excess meat tomorrow to have a shot at completion."

"Do you want to do the taste test, now?" Barb asked.

"Well, actually, I'd suggest we do it after our evening meal, so hunger is not a factor." Carl paused, again, for comment. "Are there any questions, or items of new business?"

The group began to move to the now well-established evening meal selection and preparation process. The lightness of spirit that had been stifled early in the morning began to return. The positivity felt good. The meal went well. Laughter seasoned their sustenance—a rare occurrence in the crisis.

The jerky sampling added to the lightheartedness they all felt. Members compared their impressions and acknowledged they did not use the best cuts of meat for the process experimentation. Near universal acceptance confirmed the marinade. They agreed to use the marinade as long as supplies lasted. A half dozen of their number volunteered to press the search for fresh supplies to extend the application of the marinade and to find additional, appropriate pans and pots to expand their capacity. At the end of the evaluation, the whole group agreed that half of the production should be marinated with half of that adding the rub seasonings, a quarter using rub alone, and the remaining quarter using pepper. They also agreed to and ordered the sequence of meat entering the dehydration process—bison, elk, venison, beef, pork, and fowl. They had consumed all of the available lamb and only a little chicken or turkey remained. The fowl included duck, goose, and dove. They still had some of the jerky that Carl had acquired early in the crisis, and they further agreed to preserve what was left for the journey.

Oscar prepared the first full batch of marinade, and several of the group helped to thinly slice the first package of buffalo meat. Per the agreed to process, half the sliced meat entered the soaking process for the night. The remainder of the first production batch was also prepared. The production dehydration process would begin in the morning. The jerky team did not finish until after the first watch was set—Team Four—to begin the night's routine.

As Carl stared into the night from the front lobby door, he thought, *things are looking up. We might actually get out of here. And . . . we might eventually learn what really happened. I just want this part of our living nightmare to be over.*

Carl and Helen switched places several times, just for a switch of scenery, not that they could see much. The time passed much faster than expected. Hank and Anne arrived to assume the lobby watch for Team Five. Carl bade Helen a good sleep. He joined Janet on their mattress, under the blanket. He kissed her on the cheek. She did not stir. Carl lay down and quickly achieved sleep in the quiet apartment.

—

22

The ensuing two weeks yielded good results, adding to the slowly growing optimism. They might actually make it out of the mountains. The trappers picked up several more squirrels, a chipmunk, and a mature, healthy snowshoe hare. The young folks took on the additional task of making jerky of their catches. The conversion efforts of the frozen meat to stable jerky progressed slightly ahead of plan. The group scrounged up three additional dehydration ovens—one in each habited apartment. They considered adding dehydration teams to the bottom two apartments, but decided their current production pace had adequate margin, not great but sufficient. The food preparation task seemed to be well in hand.

The group began to separate and arrange the goods and equipment they thought were needed for the journey out of the mountains. They had also agreed to the guidance on the selection and limitations of what to take. They had even tried loading one of the carts and evaluating the means of securing their cargo. The haulage would be bumpy and everything other than smooth, and they had to find some means to retain their cargo during the bumps and bounces of a difficult transit.

The cart cargo retention system attempts failed a dozen times over the weeks of experimentation. Carl desperately wanted to weld a strong railing on the sides of the flat cart. They even tried making a crude net to drape over the cargo, but the mass of cargo just overcame everything they tried.

Just after noon on Thursday, Day 76, the trapper team joined the logistics experimenters in the Building 3 lobby—an unusual excitement filled their eyes. Mike was the first to speak. "Dad, we saw an elk on the slope."

Carl, Pete, Hank and Bert stopped their cart, cargo retention, engineering task to listen.

"Well, how about that," Carl responded.

"Holly thinks we can track it for fresh meat," Mike continued, as he shifted his weight from leg to leg in a rather nervous, antsy manner.

"A big male," added Nick. "A really big male . . . huge rack."

"Not yet shed," Holly contributed.

"Do we need the meat?" asked Carl.

The young folks looked puzzled, like the question had been asked in some strange foreign language. Then, they looked to each other silently asking who was going to answer.

Mike turned to his father's waiting eyes. "No. I suppose not." He then smiled. "Extra is always good."

"Yes, I suppose so," Carl said. "Extra is much better than not enough. But, in all such situations, is the risk worth the potential benefit?"

"What is the risk?" asked Alex.

"Well, as an instructive moment, allow me to articulate the risks. Tracking an elk is never an easy task. The snow is still deep and snowshoes would be required."

"We have snowshoes," interjected Nick.

"Clearly, y'all want the challenge," Carl paused to search each set of eyes. "If you saw the elk, others probably saw the animal as well. They may well be far more hungry than we are, and that will make them more desperate and willing to kill."

"We could use one of the long guns," Alex said.

"Yes, but I suspect the window of opportunity may well have passed. A bull elk is not going to stand still waiting for you. Even if that worked, there is still the task of recovering the carcass, dressing the meat, and returning without being interdicted by one or more hungry people."

"Good point, Dad," Mike said. "Holly and her sister have helped us feel more confident in our hunting." Mike smiled and nodded his head to Holly. "Seeing that bull elk inspired us."

"Quite understandable, but the risk is far greater than the potential reward," Carl said. He turned to the other men. "That's just my opinion. What do you guys think?"

Pete was the first to respond. "I'm with you, Carl. The risk is too great."

"If these were normal times," Hank added, "I would say Holly is good and could readily lead the hunting party, even if it took days to track down the bull." He paused and looked to his daughter. "But, these are not normal times. I'm afraid I must agree with Mister Higgins' assessment."

"I agree," said Bert.

All four men looked to the young folks. No one spoke in the long pause.

"Well," Holly said, finally, "I suppose this is an opportunity lost by now."

"True," Hank added. "The bull has moved on."

"What are y'all workin' on?" asked Alex.

"We're still trying to solve the problem of securing our stuff on these carts for the journey out of these mountains," Carl answered and gestured toward the carts. "We've got to secure stuff on these slippery carts, or we'll be constantly chasing fallen items. Some of the trip out of these mountains will be rather steep and bumpy."

"What about boxes? They would be easier to strap down," Alex responded.

"True. But, we don't have any boxes of that size or even close to that size," Carl said. "Plus, we need a means to protect the contents from the elements. We'll undoubtedly face storms while we're out there."

Alex turned back to Mike and Nick. "Didn't we see some storage chests at the restaurant we searched weeks ago?" he asked his brothers.

"Yeah, I think we did," Mike answered.

"Should we go back into town," Alex asked with a degree of anticipation, "to see if we can find some large chests to store our items and secured them to the carts?"

Carl looked to the other men, who nodded their head in consent. He considered the risks. "OK. I guess we are in agreement," he said and again looked to the other men for concurrence. "We need to stay pretty close to the cart dimensions. Any overhangs will have a tendency to grab things and get hung up."

Mike held his father's eyes as he thought. "I think we can stay within those constraints, if those boxes are still there."

"So," said Pete, "how do we want to organize for this mission?"

Carl looked at Hank. "The ranges are in the 400 to 700-meter bracket. We used apartment 232 as our perch, which gives us the best field of view to cover most of the town. Do you feel comfortable handling the sniper overwatch task?"

"Sure," Hank responded, "especially with the rangefinder still working. The Sharps will work just fine at those ranges?"

"Sharps?" asked Carl with a tone of incredulity.

"Yeah, my other long gun is a Sharps 1874."

"I'll be damned . . . 45-110 cartridge, as I recall. How do you find ammunition for that thing?"

"That's the one. All special made these days, ordered from a supplier in Montana, which is now impossible. I've got a partial box of about 18 rounds left."

"That's a freakin' elephant cannon."

Hank chuckled. "Well, kinda, but it does have some stopping power."

Carl laughed heartedly. "A serious understatement, I should think."

"Why don't both of you stand the overwatch?" Pete suggested.

After some debate, they agreed upon Pete's suggestion and organized two search teams to alternate missions. The one common point remained Hank and Carl with the long gun overwatch, with Helen and Larry as backwatch for the sniper team. The plan was presented to and approved by the rest of the group. The waning moon, three days past full, precluded practical night foraging missions. Over the following two weeks, they made a dozen trips into the town. At this stage of the crisis, virtually every store, restaurant, shop and boutique in town had been ransacked or pillaged. The target objects of their searches were more difficult to find. They also passed by intact residential structures and more homes that had been broken into and looted. They chose to stay away from the residential buildings, especially those that had not been ravaged by others. They also rechecked the apartment complex they had already searched to see if they had overlooked any items that might qualify under their new search criteria.

A moderate snowstorm split their search process and slowed their return to searching. They used whatever downtime they had to continue working on the travel configuration of the carts, including a makeshift single, dual, and quad harness to haul the carts up the steeper sections of the roadway out of the high Rockies. The harnesses allowed hands-free operation for weapons use, if necessary. Progress with the carts was slow but positive. The carts were actually beginning to take shape. They organized their storage into compartments for food, some split wood, medical supplies, reserve water, cooking items, blankets, tarps and even one, six-person, collapsible tent contributed by the Mossmans. The wood they could carry was to be used as reserve in case they could not find dry wood and kindling while they were on the road. They wanted to have enough essentials for any particular item they could not forage for, while on the road. They would use their backpacks to carry a day or two of rations, an allotment of ammunition for the weapons they would carry, and dry underwear & socks, to avoid trench foot if they got wet.

The casual, meal conversation of these days reflected the thoughts of younger and older alike on what to carry during their trek out of the mountains. The positive views, devoid of the negativism that would be understandable in their predicament, added an upbeat mood to their days of preparations. The older folks chose to simply absorb the upbeat words rather than dampen or quell the brighter outlook of the younger folks. Optimism is useful in hope, and there would be plenty of time for the reality that would come their way regardless of their wishful thinking.

As they observed the darkness of the new moon, Carl consulted his created calendar. The 87th day of their ordeal calculated out to be March 16th and brought the first of three days with brilliant, cloudless sunshine and daytime temperatures sufficiently above freezing to begin melting the snow. Unfortunately, the nighttime temperatures froze the snowmelt at night, making even simple movement treacherous since they had no ice cleats.

Pete joined Carl in the 332 living room after Team Five set the evening watch. "Nice to feel the warmer temps of the last three days."

"Indeed."

"Not much we can do out there with sloppy conditions during the day and ice at night"

"Yeah, lousy skiing conditions . . . well, except for higher up on the slopes."

"True."

Carl sensed that Pete had something on his mind and wanted to talk. He looked around the room. Mike was on watch with his section in the ground floor lobby. Janet was lying down to get some sleep before her watch cycle. Lisa had just finished changing and feeding Breckyn, and was now immersed in another book. Nick, Dave and Alex were preparing for sleep. Dave was next up on watch from the 332 people, and had a little less than four hours for sleep before the Team Two duty period. "If you want to talk, Pete, let's go to the back room. We can add our eyes to look out, while we talk."

Pete nodded his agreement and followed Carl past the thermal curtain to the back storage room. They retracted the window curtain, since there was no light to give away their position or occupancy. The sliver of the waxing moon had just risen above the eastern ridgeline. The clear sky offered a brilliant array of stars above them. *It never ceases to amaze me how many stars are visible with no ambient light to affect our eyes*, Carl thought.

"What's on your mind?" Carl asked eventually to open whatever they needed to discuss.

"The warmer weather of the last few days seems to signal our departure time is approaching?" Pete paused. Carl chose to listen—nothing new in Pete's observation. "I think we have a workable solution on the carts with the boxes and straps the boys found. I've been thinking about our movement procedures."

"What do you have in mind?" Carl asked.

"We have decisions to make, and at least two main aspects of our movement process that need to be settled: organization and training. Most of our group have never had to make tactical movements, and we will need to do some training to make sure everyone fits."

"I could not agree more," Carl responded, as he continued to scan what little he could see with the starlight and a thin moon. "Do you see any reason to continue the searches of town?"

"Not much. The last few runs into town yielded nothing substantive. Weeks ago you mentioned that our day of transition would eventually arrive. I'm feeling that day is very close."

"Yeah. I share your assessment. Unfortunately, we do not have weather forecasts to at least get an impression of what lays ahead . . . weather wise. I've never been in these mountains this late in winter, so I have no idea what spring looks like, which makes me more conservative."

"We have . . . and I suspect the Mossman's have as well," Pete replied.

"Spring equinox comes in a couple of days," observed Carl.

"There is that—a marker for sure. We will see warmer days and snow melt. This is the mushy time . . . or some call it the ice rink . . . difficult skiing."

"Yeah, which is why we have avoided late winter, early spring skiing."

"Well, once you've done it a few times, you adapt to the changing conditions."

Carl chuckled, but did not look to Pete. "How confident are you in judging the spring weather up here?"

"All I have is my experience, off and on, over the last decade," Pete answered. He shifted his weight a few times. Carl waited for Pete to continue. Several minutes passed. "How long do you figure it will take us to make it out of the mountains?"

Carl chuckled, again. "Like most questions, so much depends upon definitions."

"Like what?"

"Well, like when will we be out of the mountains?"

"Pick a definition."

"Since we have not decided on a chosen route, yet, I would suggest we use that marker as the first inhabited town on the other side of the pass that is clear of snow and at a lower elevation."

"That works. So . . . ?"

"Taking my suggested route south, rather than east or west, I figure it may take us a week or two to make it over Hoosier Pass. Going should be easier on the other side—less snow, better footing and downhill . . . perhaps another couple of weeks or so to make it to Cañon City. They had a population of about 20,000 before the crisis, and more importantly, the town is 4,000 feet lower in elevation than Breckenridge. Hopefully, in addition to being warmer, we can find some humanity and news of what happened." Carl paused to think. Pete did not disturb his thinking. They both stared out the window into the dimly lit darkness. Their eyes had adjusted to the darkness as much as they were going to adapt. "From there, we can decide what each of our families wishes to do. Cañon City is probably our decision point. So, that's a long-winded answer to your query, but I'd say we have a couple of hard weeks to get over the pass and out of this valley, and perhaps four to six weeks to our decision point."

"OK," Pete responded with an airy, distant, almost distracted tone.

Carl chose not to intrude upon whatever it was that concerned him. Instead, he went to a related but different topic. "Based on your experience, when do you think the roads will be clear?"

Pete looked to Carl, who did not meet his eyes, and then returned to the outside scene. "Good 'Q.' I've no idea. We've always had snowplows and road treatment." Pete thought about the question for several minutes. "The best I can do is guess."

Carl interrupted his reply with an audible chuckle. "Sorry. Guessing is all any of us have been able to do for the last three months."

"True. Anyway . . . as I was going to say . . . based on conditions we've seen for the last few days, I'd say four weeks . . . plus or minus. If we get lucky with the weather, maybe sooner. We can only hope."

"Yeah. Hope is about all we have these days."

The two men stood at the window, gazing at nothing in particular and mostly admiring the array of stars spread across the visible sky.

His curiosity finally stimulated Carl to break the silence. "You seem to be concerned about something. Anything you want to talk about?"

"Not particularly. I'm just trying to get my mind around the process of walking out of these mountains with a group of 23 people, half of whom are not yet adults. It is not going to be easy."

"Of that there should be no illusion," Carl responded with solemnity.

"Yeah . . . no illusions. I suppose the paramount element beyond the mission plan is training the group to move with discipline, purpose and attention. It sure would be nice to have a rehearsal or two before we attempt the real journey."

"Good point. A rehearsal is a good move, except it will also expose our general purpose and intentions. Such exposure might attract the wrong element still alive up here."

"True." They both lapsed into thought, again. "It was just thought."

"We'll see what we can do. We need the plan first."

"Yeah."

"We can start working on it anytime, but I think you may need to get some rest before your watch duty."

This time Pete laughed softly. "Now, there is that, isn't there?"

The two men closed the curtains, returned to the firelight and warmth in the living room. Team Five had indeed completed their watch period, and Team One was roughly 30 minutes into their cycle. Pete whispered good night and departed to their apartment. Carl lay down beside Janet, who was sleeping soundly. He wanted to feel her skin and kiss her cheek, but he also did not want to wake her up. Carl pulled the rest of the blanket over himself and soon drifted off to sleep.

Five and a half hours later, Janet woke Carl for the Team Four watch. He swung his right arm in a broad circle to signal his request for their condition. Janet shook her head that there was nothing to report, and then she gave him a thumb's up. Larry departed. Alex arrived, nodded to his parents, and went directly to his mattress. Helen arrived. Carl gave her the choice of initial station—inside or outside. She chose outside, so she could finish inside. Carl kissed Janet and went to the arsenal room with its scent of gun oil, to assume his Team Four, Section 'A' watch position.

As had become their new normal, the night was quiet and the day uneventful. Carl felt they were nearly as ready as they were going to get. He was heartened by the pick up in exercising. Even Lisa began exercising while carrying Breckyn, making a game of it with her daughter. Carl felt an undercurrent of anticipation in the group that their long ordeal might well be approaching a final phase.

It had been eight weeks since their last armed engagement with other people, and nearly ten days since they last came in contact of any kind with other human beings. The calm often led to complacency, so Carl, Pete and Hank softly and consistently cautioned the group against letting their guard down. The positive attitude and spirit were good for everyone, but they needed to remain vigilant and cautious. Mistakes were easy to make and might dampen the encouraging outlook shared by the group. They felt the end was near.

—

23

A day past half moon in the waxing gibbous phase, the 96th day of the crisis and 25th of March on Carl Higgins' tally sheet that served as a calendar, appeared as another bright and comparatively warmer day. The icicles hanging from the roofline were beyond the dripping stage, verging upon a steady stream, as the melting continued. It was also the day the group had agreed to for decision time. They needed to start solidifying their egress plan.

After the group morning meal, those who wanted to listen to or participate in the planning process stayed in apartment 332. The younger children—Larry, Aaron and Melissa—wanted to go outside to enjoy the sunshine. Mike agreed to provide security for the younger ones.

"OK," Carl said loudly to quiet the side discussions. He waited for silence and the attention of the group. "Has everyone reviewed the maps?" Various forms of affirmative responses gave Carl the consent he was looking for. "Do we need to review the details of the route choices?" Hank raised his hand. "Yes Hank."

"The maps give us the physical routes. I think we are all agreed, there are only three choices out of the valley." He paused. Several people nodded their heads. "Going overland, or attempting to use secondary or tertiary roads or trails is simply not practical." Again, affirming head nods signaled general agreement. "My point is, before we decide, I wanted to suggest there are other reasons for selecting a route."

"Such as?" asked Pete.

"Well, we live . . . ," Hank paused to swallow, "perhaps I should say used to live . . . in Golden. We have a big home and more supplies, and Boulder is the largest city, close to us."

Carl wanted to respond, but looked to others to weigh in first.

"Given our experience up here over the last nearly one hundred days," Pete chose to respond first, "your home may not be there."

"We live in a gated community, so less likely to be looted."

"That may be," added Pete, "but, it is more likely your home is not physically standing, either."

"Why do you say that?"

"The evidence we have suggests this country was attacked in a major way," Pete continued. He paced a couple of cycles, and then faced Hank Mossman. "We have seen no indications—none, not one scintilla—that anything exists beyond this valley. We know we cannot stay here. The risks are simply too great. Frankly, I think we can only hope there is life beyond this valley. So, several factors enter into our decision."

"I understand that nothing electrical has worked up here," Bert interjected, "but, I do not understand this whole EMP thing you and Carl have talked about, and as a consequence, I do not understand the implications to what might be outside Summit County."

"Since our decision," Pete said, "or rather decisions plural, will be based on one predominant reality, perhaps we should reassess the basis of our situation. Carl has an engineering degree and understands Electro-Magnetic Pulse. The whole group, minus the young ones, was present. Maybe, we should examine the facts of that basis. Carl," Pete said and gestured to Carl.

"OK. That might be worthwhile," Carl began. "We lost more than just electrical service, which might have been explained by a serious power outage. However, we lost everything electrical—clocks, radios, our automobiles, everything. The only thing that survived that we have found so far is the rangefinder, which had been in a metal box and thus protected from an EMP surge. However, I must say, the damage we have seen is far worse than what I am aware of in my knowledge of EMP devices. Whoever did this may well have developed a significantly more effective device. Electro-Magnetic Pulse is an induced strong array of atomic particles that temporarily create magnetic fields and surges of electricity—electrons—that fuse or burn microcircuits, switches and any sensitive electrical component. The military often has circuits hardened or protected against EMP, but very few commercial devices are so protected.

"There are only a handful of countries on this planet that are capable of carrying out that level of attack, and one of those countries is us. We have no evidence that the EMP attack was coupled with the employment of more traditional nuclear weapons, but if an enemy went as far as vastly improved EMP devices, I cannot imagine why they would not go all the way with thermonuclear weapons to eliminate major infrastructure hubs . . . like Denver. If they did hit Denver with one or more weapons, Golden did not fare well, so from my perspective, east is not a good choice. West might give us a better shot at finding untouched or unaffected communities, but that leaves us in the high mountain and subject to the rigors of the high Rockies for a far longer time." Carl paused and regretted his words. "I'm sorry. I did not mean to commandeer the discussion."

Silence filled the room. Carl weaved his way to the blackout curtain and pulled it back to see the brilliance of a sunny, clear day in the snow-covered mountains. He did not turn around and continued to look out the balcony door glass, as Pete picked up the conversation.

"You said what needed to be said, Carl." Pete paused to see if anyone else wanted to speak. No one did. "I think the point is, we do not know what is happening beyond this valley. Heck, we barely know what is going on next door." Several among them giggled, lightening the conversation, just a little. "I think the point is, the risk-reward assessment appears to be the least negative taking the southern route out of the mountains. And . . . we can get to lower elevations faster by the southern route, which means warmer temperatures."

Carl remained at the curtain with his back to the group, wanting the conversation to broaden without further input from him.

Pete eventually picked up the conversation, again, and referred to his worksheet. "We have just three practical options to get out of Summit County and these mountains. After that, an array of options opens up. We have east to Golden and Denver, south to Cañon City, and west to Grand Junction. Looking at the details of each route, we have the east route with Loveland Pass at roughly 12,000 feet and Golden at 5,700 feet with a population before the crisis of something like 20,000 and a distance of I'd estimate 70 miles. Denver is another 10 miles beyond Golden. The south route has Hoosier Pass at 11,500 feet and Cañon City at 98 miles and 5,300 feet with a population of 16,500. Colorado Springs, Pueblo and Albuquerque are reachable that way."

"And, 13 prisons in and around Cañon City, as I recall," Hank interjected, "including the federal SuperMax prison in Florence. I heard an odd statistic somewhere that 16% of Cañon City's population are . . . or were prisoners. God only knows what they have done with those prisoners?"

Carl had not heard those details and did not know what to do with the information. They had no way to reconcile those facts, if they were facts, with what they might face en route out of the mountains. Carl continued, "Lastly, the west route has no significant mountain pass to contend with, but Grand Junction is 180 miles away. Grand Junction is at 4,600 feet elevation and once had a population of 62,000."

"There are smaller towns en route to Grand Junction," added Bert Johnson. "We lived in Denver."

"As did we," Pete added.

"If Carl is correct, there is likely nothing useable, and the roads may be non-existent, precluding easy travel beyond Denver."

"Furthermore, as I recall," said Pete, "Golden sits in a valley that faces Denver, so whatever happened to Denver probably affected Golden in similar fashion."

Bert stood and paced, or rather shifted his weight, since there was not much space to actually pace, but that is what it looked like. "We've driven south on Route 9. There are a few small villages along the road, Blue River before the pass, and Alma and Fairplay beyond the pass. The roadway is reasonably well maintained, not like I-70, but still good road. Further south, at Hartsel, Route 9 intersects US-24 before continuing south to Cañon City. US-24 heads east to Colorado Springs. US-50 goes east from Cañon City to Pueblo."

"Isn't Royal Gorge at or near Cañon City?" asked Emily Manson.

"Yep, sure is," answered Bert.

"What if the bridge is out . . . or blocked?" Emily pressed.

"Well," Pete started to answer and paused. "Route 9 pretty much disappears at Cañon City, and Royal Gorge is to the west and is more of a tourist attraction than a useful bridge. From Cañon City, we would have decisions to make. Pueblo is not far away. But, it is also not far from Colorado Springs, which is where Cheyenne Mountain is."

"What is that?" asked Janet.

Carl did not budge from his position.

"That is where the North American Aerospace Defense Command is located—NORAD."

"Holy cow!" exclaimed Emily. "I forgot all about that. If we were attacked, as Carl suggests, wouldn't they have hit that place first?" she asked with incredulity.

"I suppose so," Pete responded, and then looked to Carl's back. "Wouldn't you say so, Carl?"

Carl finally released the curtain and turned to face the group. "Yes, that is quite likely, but not a certainty, since it is well known that the Cheyenne Mountain Complex is buried deep in solid granite and seriously hardened against such attacks, which is the whole point of the facility—survivability. Denver is a soft target. Cheyenne Mountain is a very hard target."

"Good point," added Bert.

"I would like to add," Carl said, as he worked his way back to his spot at the end of the kitchen counter, "there are other options once we make it to Fairplay. One other aspect I like about the south route is fewer people to interfere with our movement and more open country."

"There is that," Bert commented with a particularly contemplative tone. "Fewer towns and villages than either the east or west routes."

"One last point," said Carl. "There are few to no worthy alternatives on either the east or west routes. Once we commit, we are in it to the end. Turning around, or at least attempting to turn around, would be a costly and risky action, as we will have limited supplies to extend our transit. I see this decision as a point-of-no-return judgment. We make the decision and commit ourselves to the end. Remember," Carl paused for emphasis, "our objective is to make it out of the mountains and hopefully to more survivable conditions and a more reliable food supply."

"So," interjected Hank, "if I read between the lines of your words, your mind is made up?"

"No. I am open to arguments for any option that is workable," Carl answered. "I've been thinking about this decision and its ramifications since the crisis began three months ago. Some of you have been in and know these mountains far better than I do. Plus, this is not a unilateral decision. It belongs to all of us. The collective is only by choice. I intend to get my family out of these mountains as soon as conditions permit."

"Carl, no one is seeking to break up the group," said Hank. "Our strength is in our cohesion and our ability to operate as a team. We entered into this discussion as a debate before we decide. I only wanted other factors to be considered."

"That's quite alright—no harm, no foul," Pete commented.

"So," Carl said and spread his arms, "like a jury, let's take an initial vote to see where we are." Carl lowered his arms.

"Good point," Pete added. "Let's see where we are."

"OK. Based on what we've discussed, who favors the east route?" Four votes. "Who favors the west route?" Two votes. "And, who favors the south route?" Carl raised his hand and five others joined him. "Wait. Unless anyone has an objection, our children have a vote in this . . . including the four outside."

"They haven't heard the arguments," protested Bert.

"True. We will have to bring them up to speed, but they are old enough to have an opinion and contribution to this decision. It affects them as it does the rest of us." Carl looked around the room. "Any objections?" Several shook their heads in the negative.

"Should we wait until everyone is present and had the opportunity to ask questions?" Pete asked.

"We have half the young folks with us, now," Hank said.

"Plus, this is not a final decision," added Carl. "I was only trying to get a view of where we are and what the issues might be. I believe we are all agreed that everyone, other than Breckyn, will have a say in the final decision."

"That works for me," Pete said. Hank and many of the adults nodded their heads.

"OK, let's try, again," Carl said. "For the east?" Six votes. "For the west?" Six votes. "And, for the south?" Seven votes. "Well, then, of those present so far, we appear to be roughly evenly divided."

"Are we seeking unanimity?" asked Bert.

Carl looked around the room, hoping someone else would answer. No one did. "In my humble opinion, yes, that is precisely what we should seek. This journey and effort are going to take a unified team. Preferably, there should be no doubts, once we commit to a route."

"Then," Bert continued, "how will we resolve the differences?"

Pete jumped in. "Perhaps, we can send out reconnaissance teams to evaluate each route."

"Good suggestion," Carl responded. "That would be the proper way to collect the necessary intelligence we need for an informed decision. My only concerns are time and communications. It would take several weeks to accomplish and the route recon teams would be out there without support. Further, a reconnaissance would either take too long or would not be definitive. They could disappear and we would never know it."

"True," Pete said. "The risk might well be excessive and we still do not have the intelligence we need."

"There is that."

Hank raised his hand, and Carl and Pete nodded to him simultaneously. "Let's try this, those who voted for east, what were your reasons?"

"Mine were simple," Vicky began. "East is the shortest distance out of the mountains . . . and part of the path is through the Eisenhower Tunnel."

"She has a point there," added Betsy. "We could hold up in the tunnel if the weather turned nasty."

"If we were close enough to reach the tunnel," mumbled Carl.

"What else?" asked Hank, ignoring Carl's faint words.

"There is only one way to find out if our home still stands," Betsy continued, "and that is to go there. And, if it is intact and untouched, we will have more supplies of all kinds. We have really nice neighbors, too. They will help, if we got there."

"Carl, you seem to see things in tactical terms, what do you think?"

"My principal concern is what next. If Betsy is correct, then it makes sense. East is the shortest distance, and the tunnel makes the pass less difficult. However, if she is wrong, where do we go after Golden?"

The question produced long seconds of silent contemplation. Betsy spoke first. "We will have to continue east."

"And, east may not be available due to damage and potentially radiation," Carl responded.

"There are other roads out of Golden," Betsy pressed.

"Back into the mountains."

"Yes."

"Are there any roads that go around Denver . . . to avoid perhaps . . . a ten-mile radius from the center of Denver?" Carl asked.

Betsy looked to her husband. Hank saw the signal, searched his wife's eyes, and looked back to Carl. "Not that I'm aware of," Hank answered with solemnity.

"Not to be antagonistic," Carl said, "you propose to use our one shot out of the mountains to check on your home?"

"Said like that, it does not sound reasonable," Hank said, as he looked back to his wife.

"As much as I just want to go home and get out of these mountains," Helen contributed, "I think Mister Parks is correct."

"I will add," Carl continued, "once we are out of the mountains, Colorado Springs is about 70 miles south of Denver, and Pueblo is another 40 miles beyond that, on much flatter ground. Approaching Denver from that direction retains other, more workable, options based on whatever is found. We might well learn more from locals to help guide our extended actions."

"Good points," Hank said and looked to Betsy. "Do you agree?"

"Yes."

Hank looked at his daughters. They both nodded their heads.

Vicky and Bert made eye contact, spoke in unspoken words, and then Bert said, "We agree as well. We want to see what has happened to our home, also, but it makes more sense to get out of the mountains, and then work our way home."

Carl chose not to react in any manner. Silence filled the room. Not even whispered discussions could be heard. Pete looked at Carl, who only nodded back to him. Pete took the cue.

"OK. Let's cover the west route. Those who voted for the west route care to offer your reasons."

Lisa jumped right in. "Less climbing." Several of the group laughed softly at her succinct answer.

George chuckled as well and spoke for his wife. "We are with Lisa. The thought of climbing these mountains at our age appears rather daunting to us. We have nowhere to go, so from what everyone has said, the west route appears to be the easiest."

"Hard to argue with that," Pete said. "Oscar, Emily, do you have anything to contribute?"

"We're from Los Angeles . . . Santa Monica, actually . . . so west moves us in that direction. Plus, as Pete summarized from his notes, Grand Junction is lower still in elevation than Golden or Cañon City. It seems like a more attractive route, since we have to walk out."

"Anything else?" asked Pete.

Oscar nodded his head, cleared his throat, and added, "From there, we could head south into Arizona, and potentially Southern California, and home."

George raised his hand, but did not wait to be called upon. "I must say, Anne and I wish to stay with the group no matter which direction is selected. We know so little about this part of your great country."

"Not so great at the moment," mumbled Alex.

"That may be," replied George, "but, this country inherited the same fighting spirit as the Motherland, so keep the faith. I imagine others beyond our little scenic valley here are tending to business."

"Hear, hear," interjected Pete.

Just then, the daily knock sequence—two, two, three—terminated the discussion. Carl went to the door, instinctively grasped the grip of the M1911 in his jacket pocket, and flipped the safety off. He looked through the peephole and confirmed it was Mike and the kids, and more importantly, no one else. Carl unlocked and opened the door. After the outside quartet entered, Carl closed and locked the door, and then thumb'ed the pistol safety back on.

"Wow!" exclaimed Larry. "What's going on? Everyone looks so serious."

The group contributed to informing the arrivals of the afternoon's discussion and where they were at in the decision process. Surprisingly, the young ones asked a number of cogent questions, and even more surprisingly, none of them sought guidance from their parents. Larry voted for east, Aaron and Melissa for west, and Mike voted for south.

"Very well," said Pete. "We are still split three ways on the second vote. May I suggest a third vote now that we are all together and after hearing the rationale?"

"Wait," Emily said, "we've heard east and west, but not south."

"I think Carl offered the essence of the south choice, unless you would like us to expand on those points."

"May I suggest," Carl finally began, "we take a day or two to digest what has been presented, and allow for families to discuss privately what matters most to them. We can reconvene whenever everyone is ready. We probably have a week or two before we need to make a decision. I think we have solved our logistics problems, as best we can. We are ready to go, whatever direction we select."

"We still need to get the group ready for the movement procedures," Pete added.

"Yes, we do . . . and do some training," Carl said, "so, everyone knows their job during the movement."

"When do you want to start that?" Pete asked.

"My recommendation . . . a week or two at the most before we leave, so everything is fresh. We probably have some refresher weapons training to do as well."

"So, to Carl's suggestion for adjournment, are we all agreed?" asked Pete. Several affirmative verbal responses and head nods conveyed general agreement. "Does anyone object?" No one offered a peep or gesture. "Very well, then, we are adjourned until further notice. Feel free to talk to whomever you wish. Thank you everyone."

The group dispersed. Barb and Larry left for their apartment. Pete remained to continue discussions with Carl, who wanted to check the exterior. Pete waited for Carl, who appeared to be thinking, more than evaluating the weather outside. Carl got a drink of water, and then he was ready to talk.

"That went fairly well," Pete said.

"Yeah."

"We are essentially evenly split. My question, what if we remain split?" asked Pete, as they both sat on the couch in front of the fireplace. Alex was freshening the fire.

Carl looked at Pete. "Then, we divide everything and split," he said with firmness. Carl found Janet's eyes and held them. "How do you feel?"

"I'm with you, babe. The kids and I are with you. We have faith that whatever you choose, you are doing the best for us."

"That does not help much, but thank you for that vote of confidence." Carl got head nods from the boys, including Dave. He looked to Lisa and waited quietly until his daughter looked up from Breckyn cradled in her arms. "You voted for west, Lisa. Are you against south?" When he did not get a prompt response, Carl added, "East is not a viable option from my perspective."

"No, I'm not against south. I will stay with the family, Dad, but I'm just concerned about climbing 2,000 feet in a few miles. It scares me." Lisa paused, glancing at Breckyn, who just gazed at her mother, as she thought. "I know I'm not in the best of shape after giving birth." She stared at her father. "I'm worried about disappointing you."

"Oh, Lisa, sweetie," Carl said with compassion. "I'm sorry you feel that way. You are not going to disappoint us. We will carry you, if you are unable to walk. Please don't worry about it. There are going to be many challenges out on the road. We will have to adapt and deal with whatever comes. We have tried to think of and prepare for everything we can anticipate, but there will be surprises. We'll deal with them. All any of us, including me, can ask is for you to do your best and be honest with us, so we can help."

Lisa smiled. "Thanks, Dad."

"Your first priority above all else is to take care of yourself, so you can take care of Breckyn. The baby is 100% dependent upon you. None of the rest of us, including Mom, has the milk she needs to grow and gain strength. So, when it comes to this journey, do what you can for the team, but never forget . . . your oxygen mask first."

Lisa smiled broadly at her father's consistent use of the flight attendant's safety instruction. "Thanks, Dad. I'll try to do the best I can."

"That is all any of us can ask."

After a pause of silence, Pete returned to his query. "What if we do not achieve unanimity?"

"I suppose that is an unavoidable question," Carl answered. "My first blush response is, we divide our supplies and go our separate ways," he repeated. "Everyone should have and retain complete freedom of choice. Whatever we commit to individually and as a group must be total—no doubts, hesitations or wavering. The trek will be hard enough without having to deal with divisions or doubts out on the road."

"Perhaps we should think about how we divide things, namely our food supply."

Carl considered Pete's suggestion. "One step at a time. I gave up a long time ago trying to predict the behavior of others. Each of us is driven by what matters to us. We still have several weeks to adjust to whatever the group decides. As for me, I am going to focus on a more detailed map study for the south route. I want to have a clear view of our primary path, each village on the way, and the secondary alternatives once we are across Hoosier Pass and out of the mountains."

"I trust your judgment on the route," Pete said. "I'll try to sketch out a movement formation definition and how to proceed. Barb and I are convinced the south route is the only viable option, so we are with y'all regardless. What we decide at Fairplay or Hartsel is a indeterminant at present in our mind, but as you say, one step at a time."

"I'm good with that, Pete."

"Hopefully, this latest obstacle will be resolved sooner rather than later. I don't like things being unsettled. We have had enough of that. I'm OK with any decision, as long as it is decided and we can move on."

"I look forward to seeing your formation proposal."

"Should I assume the whole group or just our two families?" Pete asked.

Carl smiled. "Let's think positive and say the whole group. That is our strongest position."

"OK." Pete turned his eyes to the fire. "I'd better get back to Barb and Larry. I might actually hear what Bert and Vicky are thinking, now."

"Sure. Evening meal is in a couple of hours. Who knows how everyone will feel? I'd suggest we not press the group, just yet. Let's allow this to play out naturally, at least for a couple of days."

"Agreed." Pete stood, gently brushed Breckyn's forehead a couple of times, and then departed. Nick locked the door after Pete Higgins left.

The Parks' middle son went to the fireplace and warmed his hands. Nick sat down on the hearth beside the fireplace, facing his father. "Do you think we really might split?" Nick asked.

"I don't know. I would like to say I don't care. Everyone is free to make decisions that are best for them, including all of you," Carl said waving his arm around the room. "Y'all may not be legally adults, but the law no longer applies. You are essentially grown, and as far as I'm concerned, you are adults and able to make your own decisions. I will respect you and love you no matter what you decide, so I encourage you to think about what matters to you and what the best choice is for you."

"We're with you, Dad," Nick said.

"Yeah," added Mike.

"Yes, we are," Alex said.

"You don't have to decide, just yet. Now, I'm tired. I'm going to take a nap before evening meal."

No one spoke. Janet did not move, presumably to allow her husband some undisturbed naptime. Carl managed a decent practice nap—not quite a power nap, but more than a combat nap. He took a few minutes to return to full alertness. They still had not quite an hour to the group evening meal.

Carl decided to spread out the Rand McNally map of Colorado. The road offered no topographic information other than the location and elevation of a few key mountain peaks, but it still provided important information. As he sat at the dining table with a large candle for illumination, Alex and Nick stood behind him to observe the map and any actions by their father. Carl stood, went to the kitchen counter and retrieved a large notepad along with a pencil. Using a piece of paper to measure distance, Carl began to jot down the distances between likely waypoints as well as the total mileage.

Breckenridge

Blue River =   6   6

Hoosier Pass =	*2*	*8*			
Alma =	*8*	*16*			
Fairplay =	*6*	*22*	*==> Colorado Springs =*	*63*	*85*
Garo =	*9*	*31*	*CMC − CS = 8 − P =*	*30*	
Hartsel =	*9*	*40*			
Guffey t/o =	*22*	*62*	*==> Guffey =*	*3*	
Cañon City =	*25+9*	*96*	*==> Pueblo =*	*38*	*134*

Carl stood, continuing to absorb the map.

From behind him, Nick asked softly, "Do you still see the south route as best?"

"Yes," Carl responded, recognizing the teaching moment. "I'm just checking distances and trying to imagine the travel time, and trying to see the difficulties we might encounter through each segment. I would feel better if I had aerial photography, like Google Earth, and proper topographical maps."

"What would they show you?"

Carl chuckled softly. "Topography," he responded with lightness.

"I don't know that term," Nick said.

"Topography is the depiction of terrain on a map. It uses lines of constant elevation to represent the ground, so the separation of contour lines shows us what the steepness or grade of the land was when the map was created."

"Can we get those maps?" asked Nick, as he continued his inquiry. "That seems pretty important, especially between here and Hoosier Pass."

Carl smiled. "Well, good question. They sell USGS topographic maps in outdoor stores, especially those that specialize in hiking or hunting activities."

"I think we've checked most, if not all, of those stores in town during our previous searches," Nick said. "As I recall, they have been pretty well emptied and destroyed."

"Nick's correct," added Alex.

Carl considered the boys' comments. "They might have a topographic map of the area at the city engineer's office, but it would most likely only cover the city limits and adjacent land in the valley . . . and the ski area, since the engineer had to approve structures in the area like lifts and lodges."

"I think I saw the Town Hall sign at a building on this side of the river at Ski Hill Road and Park Avenue," Alex contributed. Carl thought about his youngest son's observation. "Would the engineer's office be in there?"

"You know, Alex, I think you may be correct. That is the most likely location. Even if they have topo maps and only cover their jurisdiction, those maps would be useful as far as they go."

"When do you want to go?"

"Whoa dawgy, not so fast. Well, I mentioned the idea to Pete at evening meal, but the group needs to approve, as long as we remain together."

"OK. I'm ready, if you decide to go."

"Thanks, Son."

Carl sat back down and refocused on the map. He noted several additional details for alternate destinations on his notepad.

US-285S	*Fairplay–Alamosa, CO*		*132*
US-24W	*Hartsel*	*joins US-285 @ Trout Crk Ps (9345')*	*12*
US-50W	*bypass Cañon City*	*Texas Creek*	*17*
Route 69	*Walsenberg*		*87*
	Hillside	*11*	
	Westcliffe	*14*	
	Gardner	*34*	
	Farisita	*6*	
	Walsenberg	*22*	

"Those are some big numbers," Nick observed, "for a walk out of these mountains."

Carl chuckled. "Yes, they are, but we have to do what we have to do. The numbers to Wichita are far bigger."

"Yeah, but one step at a time, right Dad?"

Carl smiled. "Yes, Alex, long journeys begin with a single step, as the Chinese proverb goes."

The daily knock sequence announced the first arrivals. The apartment 331 portion of the group entered. Carl folded the map and returned everything to the drawer. They had thawed the beef for the evening meal. Pete, Carl and Mike jumped to cutting 23 portions of equal size and thickness. Bert stood on the other side of the counter—supervising. ;-) Carl recounted the map study conversation while they worked.

"What do you think?" Carl asked.

"Seems like it's worth a shot," Pete said. "Alex is correct. That is where the city engineer's office is."

"OK. I'll wait until after supper before I present the mission to the group. I want to leave plenty of space, if anyone wants to discuss the route decision."

"Sounds reasonable," Bert commented.

"Agreed," added Pete.

Janet, Barb and Vicky retrieved two medium-size cans of green beans. The men prepared the fire and began cooking the meat. The rich aroma of the beef offered an almost festive mood to the room. The others began to arrive, as the pot of beans went on the grill to heat up. The meal came together nicely, as the group reconvened.

The supper conversation focused on the children playing in the snow earlier in the day and the accumulating warmer weather. Noticeable snowmelt generated flowing creeks and the rising Blue River. No ice remained over the river. Most of the roof snowpack on the buildings in their complex and around them let go, and fell to the ground. Even the ice stalactites on the rooflines let go.

As the group finished eating their comparatively sumptuous meal, Carl presented his mission brief to the group. No one objected. They agreed that the weather looked reasonable for tomorrow and the mission had the unanimous consent of the group.

Six members volunteered for the search team. Hank and Holly would take the overwatch sniper task. Carl, Pete, Bert, Oscar, Nick and Alex would carry out the search.

The watch period arrived. Team Four was up first. Helen and Carl took their positions in the now somewhat crowded lobby. Vicky took the balcony first, while Nick went to the arsenal room. With Helen's concurrence, Carl stepped outside in the almost pleasant, vanishing twilight. He stepped far enough away from the building in the slush to check the roof. It was clear of any snow or ice.

Carl returned to the lobby and locked the door. "The roof is clear. The snow is melting nicely."

"Excellent."

"We may be able to leave early."

"That would be good."

She is not going to take the opportunity to discuss the pending route decision. They settled into their watch duties. It would be another couple of hours, after their watch cycle, before the waxing gibbous moon rose above the eastern ridgeline horizon. *This has been a full day.*

—

24

The search mission had gone well. They could not find a city engineer's office, but they did find a civil engineer's desk in the Public Works office. As luck would have it, the office was not locked and appeared untouched by looters or other assailants. It took nearly an hour of checking each of three large chests of a dozen, flat drawers each that contained building drawings, infrastructure layouts and a wide variety of physical documents to establish the organization of the community. In the last drawer of the last chest, they discovered United States Geological Survey maps—small scale for the detailed topography of the city itself and medium scale to cover a larger area. The maps represented all of Summit County and portions of adjacent counties, and as luck would have it, the southern-most map extended to Alma and not quite Fairplay—the most difficult terrain of the southern route.

Carl checked the terrain maps carefully with Pete and Hank to ensure he had considered the grade for movement. They recognized that they might have to contend with some residual snow or ice as they approached the crest of Hoosier Pass. Their experience indicated the climb would not be easy, but it was probably manageable in the six-man harness for each cart.

The Vernal Equinox had passed on the 20th of March—Day 91 of the crisis—so, they were astronomically a week into spring, when a moderate storm dropped rain, then sleet and an additional dusting of snow.

The group chose that weather day—Day 98—for their route decision meeting. The process and decision did not take long. The group unanimously agreed to the south route out of the valley. The consent was not all enthusiastic, but it was unanimous. They intended to remain together until they were out of the mountains. What would happen beyond the logical milestones—Fairplay, Hartsel and Cañon City—was agreed to be pushed off to the subsequent decision points, depending on the conditions at those points.

"OK," Carl declared once the decision was done. "We have the basis of a plan. The route is defined. Now, we really need to flesh it out to estimate our travel time and potential waypoints or campsites along the route. I have not traveled Route 9 south of the town. Several of y'all have at least driven the road. Perhaps collectively, we can annotate time to the only map we have—a 2D roadmap."

"Good point," Pete said. "We've traveled that road several times."

"So have we," added Bert Johnson.

"And us," Hank Mossman contributed. "That would be a worthwhile exercise."

"Yeah. Once we have that estimate, we can finalize the manpower part of our plan."

"Whoever would care to contribute is welcome to do so," Carl said, and then went to the kitchen drawer to retrieve his notepad, map, and pencils. He spread the map. "I think my crudely measured distances are probably close enough for our purposes. What I do not have a feel for is the condition of the roadway and more importantly the elevation—the steepness of the grade—between the waypoints."

Pete cleared his throat. "I doubt any of us has any meaningful appreciation for the grade, other than qualitatively. There is a huge difference between driving the grade and walking the grade, hauling a bunch of stuff."

"Agreed," Carl responded and looked everyone around the table in the eye, "but, y'all have the only intelligence we have and will have, so just give it your best guess."

"We'll give it a go," Hank added.

"On the city map, I put being out of Breckenridge at roughly the intersection of Boreas Pass Road, which appears to be a little less than a mile. We will have a lot of exposure at least until that point, not much elevation change, and good roads."

"That's reasonable," said Hank.

"The day we decide to launch," Carl said, "if we are lucky enough to have decent weather and a good moon, we might minimize our exposure departing before dawn . . . to get beyond the town before twilight."

"Good idea," responded Pete, "but we will have to be well organized and fully ready. I would not feel comfortable moving everyone in the dark without some good training, so everyone knows their part and what to expect."

"Agreed," added Bert and Hank together.

"I don't see a problem. Our supplies are ready to be loaded." Carl looked to the others. "When we are a day or so prior to our departure, we load everything, including our backpacks, so that we only need to get everything outside, form up and hit the road." Carl looked to everyone, again. "Agreed?" Everyone, including a few of the boys who were observing, nodded their heads in agreement. Carl consulted his makeshift calendar. "By my calculation, we have our next full moon on April 1st, and the next one after that on April 30th." Several affirmative gestures punctuated the observation. "It is probably a stretch to think we'll make the first window, but based on our thawing progress, we have a good shot at the second."

"The moon is predictable. The weather is not," observed Hank. Several chuckles were heard.

"Yeah," Pete said. "We'll have to make some difficult weather assessment decisions and watch the weather more closely from now on, since we are roughly a month away."

"We don't have to jump at the first opportunity," Bert said. "I mean, even if we waited until summer and virtually all the snow is gone, and the often volatile spring weather season is past, it won't hurt our prospects."

"All of that is correct," responded Pete, "but, we do not have limitless supplies. The sooner we go, the better our margins for success, given our finite supplies."

Carl held up his right hand. "We will have time for the necessary discussions on timing. We need to complete our route recon to the best of our ability to understand the value of the timing question, so let's get back to the task at hand." Everyone nodded their heads in agreement. "I noted the first milestone as Blue Valley on the road map."

Hank laughed. "There really is nothing there. What the map shows as Blue Valley is actually the junction of Blue Valley Road and Route 9. On the east side of the road, there is a small development of mostly rental homes to support ski season."

"I have that at about six miles or so . . . maybe a little farther, since I was not precise with my measurements on the scale of the map. How is the grade to that point?"

"Pretty shallow," Hank answered. "That intersection is up valley, but still comparatively flat."

"Given that will be our first day on the road, that may be our first waypoint."

"Surely, we could make it farther than that."

"We will be traveling in a fairly large group . . . with women and children . . . ."

"The women will manage," interjected Vicky. "We'll keep up!" she exclaimed. "Don't hold up for us."

Carl smirked slightly and searched for Lisa's face. Her head was down, sitting on the couch, looking at Breckyn, who was awake and flailing on her lap. *Lisa and the baby may be our shortest link. I can feel the need to defend her, but it is what it is. She has tried to exercise, but she has not done enough. There is going to be pressure to exceed her capacity.* "Let's take a conservative estimate, for now, so we're prepared." Carl did not seek agreement and continued, "At Blue River, we are closer to the fifteen hundred to two thousand foot rise to Hoosier Pass."

"Yeah," Pete answered. "Goose Pasture Tarn Reservoir and the headwater marsh end at Blue River. The road grade increases from that point. The switchbacks for the climb to the pass are not shown on this scale of map, but my guess is they begin at about a mile south of Blue River Road. Would you guys agree?" Pete asked, looking to Hank and Bert.

Both men thought about Pete's query.

"That's about right," Hank answered. "Maybe a little bit farther, but it's in the ballpark."

"We should make that point in less than a day. My impression is, perhaps we should layup, even if it is early, to rest up for the climb."

"That's probably a good idea," Pete said. "There are some other homes at Mark Court Road . . . before the switchbacks begin. We might find shelter there. Those homes are farther from the slopes and usually fill up last. The crisis began before the peak of ski season, so more than a few of those homes might be vacant. Or, if we get lucky, we might find a local or two to put us up for the night . . . maybe even trade food for shelter."

"I may know some folks up there," Hank offered.

"From that point, we climb and moving will be more difficult." Carl continued. "It may take us several days to haul our stuff up one or two thousand feet. I have no idea what's up there. We need waypoints to hold up for the night, eat and rest before continuing the next day."

Bert pulled a fresh sheet of paper from the pad. He sketched the road, as he recalled it. The three Coloradans collaborated on the configuration of the roadway to the pass. They also marked several potential waypoints on the ascent to the pass.

"To summarize," Carl said, "our best estimate is roughly a week to make the pass."

"That looks reasonable," Hank said.

"If we don't have any problems," Pete added, "we might do better than that."

" . . . or worse," Carl interjected.

"There is always that," said Pete.

"It will be what it will be," Hank contributed, "but that is a decent estimate. There is a good-size parking area at the crest, which should give us a worthy rest stop as we transition from pulling to restraining the carts on the downhill portion of the road," Hank said, pointing to the Route 9 road between the pass and Alma.

"How is the road on the south side?" asked Carl.

"Actually, fairly straight and moderate slope," Bert answered. "Certainly more manageable than the north side . . . no switchbacks, less steep, pretty straight."

"Yeah, I would agree," added Hank.

"Me as well," Pete said. "I think our system of using the harnesses in reverse should work just fine."

"How fast do you think we can move?" Carl asked.

"Faster than pulling uphill," Pete responded promptly. "If we move continuously during the daylight hours, we should be able to cover 2 to 3 miles per hour, conservatively. The days are getting longer. We should have something like 13, maybe 14 hours. So, if we can keep moving, we should be able to cover 25 to 40 miles in a day."

"That seems a bit much to me," Carl observed. "That movement pace does not account for distractions, rest stops, obstacles and such. We have to expect difficulties rather than easy going."

"OK. Let's half that . . . say 10 miles," Pete offered.

"For planning purposes, that should give us a little more margin," Carl said. "I crudely measured the distance from the pass to Alma at about 8 miles. At our planned pace, that would put us into the first real town in the afternoon. Do we take the time to make contact with locals? Do we stop there for the night?"

"Our task is movement to a safer, more sustainable place," interjected Vicky.

"True," Bert concurred with his wife.

"I could go either way," contributed Pete.

"Agreed," Carl said. "My only point of discussion is, that town may be our first opportunity to learn what happened. They are on the other side of the mountains, farther from the event, and probably experienced less damage. They may actually have some communications."

"Fairplay is larger than Alma," Hank said. "Perhaps, we can learn more there. The road is more flat from Alma on. We might, or rather should, make better time."

"Good," replied Carl. "We can evaluate both towns. Make those decisions based on what we find. Just to be clear, being around more people, who may or may not be more desperate than us, presents a palpable risk that might have to be dealt with . . . possibly with aggressive action."

"No argument there," Pete said.

"We do have choices."

"For example?"

"We could hold up a mile or so short of Alma, and pass through town at night, when there is less exposure risk. The moon should be full around that time, so illumination would be adequate . . . unless there is overcast or other obscurations."

"Sure, Carl," answered Hank. "There are options. People may be friendly, or they may be hostile. We have no way to predict what we might find. Heck, for all we know, the town may be abandoned."

"Then, what would you recommend for planning purposes?"

"Well, the conservative approach would be to assume we stop at Alma and Fairplay, to rest, recharge, learn what we can, and if we are lucky, even have a decent meal and a bath."

"Oh yay!" exclaimed Janet from the couch. Several laughed at the insertion.

"Alrighty then," Carl said, "we shall assume a stop at both and respond accordingly to conditions we encounter on arrival. That puts us at day seven in Alma and day eight in Fairplay. The next stop on the map is Garo at nine miles or so."

Hank looked at the map, ran his finger down the line that represented Route 9, found Garo, and began laughing. When he regained control, he said, "I'm not sure what the mapmakers were seeing or thinking, but there is no Garo. It is open country. There is certainly no town there."

"Hank's correct," added Bert.

"All I know is what the map tells me," Carl said, somewhat defensively.

"That is about where Route 9 crosses over the Middle Fork South Platte River," Pete contributed. "So, at least there is water there."

"I'm not so sure of the water quality, since there is farm runoff upstream," Bert said.

"We will probably be faced with boiling native water to at least deal with bacteria," offered Carl, "and whatever chemical exposure there may be, the risk should be minimal with the snowmelt runoff from the mountains. Dealing with dehydration is going to be far more challenging, no matter how we cut this journey up. Anyway, that point is roughly a day's travel by our metric."

"That should work OK, Carl. Let's leave the plan at that point," Pete commented.

Carl jotted down his notes. "The next point on the map is Hartsel, again, at roughly nine miles."

Bert and Hank both examined the map. Bert spoke first. "I'm afraid there is not much there either. At least there is a country store. We stopped there some years back. Depending upon how this electricity crisis has affected them, we may find support, or we might find nothing useful remaining."

"It is what it is," Carl said. "As with the other waypoints, we will have to adapt to what we find. So, if we are agreed, that should be our day ten waypoint." Heads nodded. No objections were voiced. "Continuing down Route 9, I measured 22 miles to Guffey."

"Another hole in the wall, I think," mumbled Hank. "I've never seen it or been there. Anyone else?"

Bert and Pete shook their heads. No one spoke.

"The map says it is three miles north of Route 9 at that point."

"That's why no one has seen it," Hank commented. "No reason to go there."

"Anyway, it would be two days to that point," Carl pressed on. "We'll call it another open country waypoint and split that leg at 11 miles, not that it will matter much in the grander scheme of things." Heads nodded conveying concurrence. "I will say one positive aspect of this route besides being comparatively flat beyond Alma is there are streams or rivers along nearly the entire route . . . at least according to the map; and, the snowmelt should mean they are flowing and fairly full."

"There is that," added Hank. "What's next?"

"By my simple map study, we have another three days to Cañon City."

"That city has a population of nearly 20,000," said Bert. "So, we should learn more and find more support."

"That is the hope," Carl said. "I would only caution against anticipating very much. We have no idea what has happened out there. But, one fact is certain, we will be out of the high Rockies and at least closer to more stable conditions."

"Quite so," Pete said.

"From there, I figure it will be another three days with two more nights in open country before we reach Cañon City."

"What then?" asked Bert.

"Well, if our estimates are anywhere close, we will have been on the road for two weeks, not counting any longer stops for problems, rest and such. I'd say we should take a break, find a place to shelter, recharge and assess our situation based on whatever information we collect en route. Depending upon what our supply status is, we can take a few days to rest up. We may even reach a stable location to remain indefinitely. We won't know until we get there. Pueblo is another 38 to 40 miles beyond Cañon City and had a population of over 100,000 before the crisis."

"There is no way to predict what we are going to find outside this valley," Pete said, as he stood and went to the balcony curtain. He discreetly peered outside. "Looks like the weather is clearing. I can actually see some of the car tops in the parking lot and all of the roofs are clear of snow."

"Spring is coming," Janet said.

"Indeed it is," Pete commented.

"I think we have completed what we needed to do. Let's let this sink in for a day or so. If anyone thinks of anything else or has any other ideas, we can reconvene." Several members stood and started to leave. "Oh, one more thing while I'm thinking of it, we might want to top off our water supply before the snow melts entirely. Also, the frozen meat is beginning to thaw, so we need to consume it, or make more jerky. Wasting good meat would not be smart."

"Maybe we should just jerky the rest of it to be safe," Pete suggested.

"Let's have a nice steak supper tonight and restart our jerky process tomorrow," said Carl.

"Full production or partial," asked Vicky.

"Let's assess our supply status tomorrow before we start."

"OK."

"Then, we are adjourned until the evening meal," Carl announced.

The various apartment groups departed, leaving the Parks family in unit 332. Carl laid down for a short combat nap while the opportunity presented, to freshen his mind. Even 30 minutes helped.

The group enjoyed another comparatively luxurious meal of grilled beefsteaks and a choice of green beans, corn, asparagus or Brussels sprouts.

After their evening meal, Team Five took the first watch period. Pete wanted to try out his proposal for their movement procedures. They sat at the dining table with their usual large candle. Most of the children sat around the fire reading. Alex joined them to listen and Janet chose to read by the firelight.

"We have two primary objectives in our movement procedure: security and haulage. We are the pack mules." Carl chuckled at the notion and nodded his head in agreement. "I've sketched out what I'm thinking," he said and placed a paper on the table in front of them.

Pete explained, "The haulage part will take the most manpower, until we make it to the south side of the pass. At the worst of the slope, we may have six people in harness for each cart. The number and position will vary depending upon the slope we encounter. As we've already prepared for, the cart haulers will likely vary from two to six for each cart, so in my sketch, I have assumed six. I have also assumed that all of us will take our turn in harness."

"That is a reasonable assumption," Carl affirmed. "The only exception I would recommend would be Lisa and Breckyn."

"I think the team will agree with that recommendation. Her first and only priority should be caring for her infant child."

"Thanks, Pete," Carl paused, clearly wanting to say something more. Pete respected his pause. "Even if the team does not approve of my recommendation, I will take her turn and double time, if it comes to that."

"I don't think it will, but you are a good father," Pete added. "It is a bridge we may never reach."

Carl wanted to move on and changed the subject. "What are you thinking about the point group?" asked Carl, pointing to the point group at the vanguard.

"We need a recce team to check the road ahead, look for potential ambush zones, find bivouac sites and such. I'm thinking you, Hank and me. We have the most experience with such things."

"True," Carl responded. "However, I sense from our time together that this whole journey will be an extended and frustrating exercise in herding cats." They both laughed softly. "I suspect our experience will be sorely needed to keep the main group cohesive and moving in the same direction."

"Then, who do you see as the point group?"

"My suggestion . . . Helen, Holly and perhaps Alex, or one of the older boys," Carl said, looking to his youngest son. Alex smiled in recognition. "They've demonstrated a good sense of conditions and sufficient skills to handle risk, danger, aggression, observation and anticipation."

"Good point."

"I think Holly will jump at the opportunity, and probably Alex as well. I'm not so sure about Helen. She is more reserved than her sister."

"Do you think we can teach them what they need to know in the time we have?"

"We will have to do the best we can. They will have to learn on the job and learn quickly."

"Perhaps one of us should be in the point group to teach them," said Pete.

"Sure. That makes sense. I suppose some of what we will be able to do will depend upon how things around us play out."

"OK," Pete said and paused to think for a moment. "I have assumed that we will only harness up when it is necessary, to reasonably pull the carts. If we are not in harness, then we are walking along beside the carts."

"That's about right. We need to stick together but not bunch up. This is not a tactical movement. I don't think we should assume we might be ambushed, but we should be prepared to deal with highwaymen who might seek to take what we have."

"A major concern, as such encounters have the potential to be fatal for our people. Although I suspect our greater challenge will be the weather. The thought of being caught in open country during a spring snowstorm is rather sobering."

"You got that right. For the most part, I think we should move during daylight hours—dawn to dusk. I also see our best protection by maintaining our night watch cycles. The duty watch would keep one or two fires going for several purposes—warmth, drying, light and perhaps even a little warning. We're here and we're strong."

Pete nodded his head in agreement. "We'll have to adapt as we go . . . to changing conditions."

Carl chuckled softly. "Probably an understatement."

"Perhaps. Anyway, we can and probably will shift positions as we go. Movement in open country will have one set of concerns, but we must pass through several towns that will present . . . potentially . . . entirely different threats to our safety and travel."

"Yeah. We may have to probe the towns with the group held up and secured outside of town."

"Part of our adaptation to changing conditions."

"Sure, Pete. As soon as we can move the carts outside, hopefully into the parking lot, we can do a little rehearsal training, to prepare everyone for what to expect."

"Sounds like a plan," Pete said. "I'd better get some sleep before my watch period."

Pete departed. Carl closed up their materials. The Parks family settled into the night's routine.

Their training opportunity window opened on the third day of warm, sunny days that Carl's makeshift calendar noted at Day 110 of the crisis or April 8th on the makeshift Gregorian calendar. The phase of the moon the previous night was a waning half moon. The light breeze and brilliant sunshine made conditions comfortable, as they hauled the carts outside and to the center of the parking lot. The group used Pete's sketch to form up in the one, two and six-person harnesses for each cart. Pete and Carl offered instruction regarding the point team, and the flank and rear guards. They switched places several times to feel the different positions. They also discussed defensive actions should a threat present itself. The group's mood made the training exercise almost enjoyable. Everyone was outside in the sunshine, enjoying the day, even Lisa joined them with Breckyn strapped to her chest in her makeshift carrier harness. They would repeat the formation training four more times on good weather days. In the last two sessions, they practiced their nightly bivouac procedures, although none of them thought a full cycle of watch periods were necessary for their training.

As they watched and waited for the weather to improve conditions sufficiently for them to launch their odyssey, Hank suggested they make several, swift, reconnaissance patrols out to at least see the pass. The group agreed.

Pete, Hank and Bert were the most familiar with Route 9 south, so they would make the recce patrols.

The first patrol occurred on Day 114. They returned without incident and reported the roadway was clear and in good condition to a point just past Mark Court Road junction. They attempted to go as far as they could beyond the clear point and abandoned the effort at the meadow near Blue Lakes Road, due to patchy ice and snow spots that blocked the road. The asphalt road surface began to show through the snow and ice in areas that picked up the midday sun. The recce team estimated another week or two of clear sunny days might clear the road.

The second recce patrol took place on Day 120 and validated the team's earlier assessment. By that time, nearly a week later, the roadway was clear past the meadow. They made it to within sight of the pass, but the road to the pass was obviously not clear and appeared to be an unbroken snowfield short of the crest of the pass. No one suggested or even questioned about attempting to move the carts through the snow.

Those of the group who had an opinion agreed to a third patrol that happened after a brief, spring thunderstorm on Day 123. The rain had washed away some of the road grit. The storm apparently missed the pass. The team found no new snow even at the higher elevation of Hoosier Pass. The roadway was not entirely clear to the pass, but a nearly clear path around the remaining icy patches gave the team sufficient indication the group could haul their supply carts through the pass.

The group gathered after the evening meal and the patrol's return on Day 123.

"We think Route 9 will continue to improve with each sunny day," Pete summarized, "and, is sufficiently clear for us to make it through the remaining ice patches. While we did not go all the way to the pass or beyond, the descending road on the south side will be facing more toward the sun and should be clear."

"So, what is the team's recommendation?" asked Carl.

"We think the time has come," Hank responded.

"Yeah, we do," added Bert.

"Does anyone in the group have any questions," asked Carl, "or, anything to add?" Most did not respond. Those who made a gesture shook their heads in the negative. "So, are we all agreed that we are ready to launch?" Various forms of aural and signaled responses suggested unanimous approval. "Any objections?" There were none. "Very well, then let me suggest we begin our journey out of these mountains," he paused to look at his constructed calendar, "on Thursday, day after tomorrow . . . Day 125 and April 23rd. We will have a waxing gibbous moon that night. That will give us a day to complete the loading of the two carts and preparations for the journey. One more thing," Carl paused, again, to ensure he still had everyone's attention. "Morning twilight comes around six. I'd suggest we get everyone up at five, have our morning meal, and hit the road before sunrise. That should give us a couple of hours before the sun breaks the eastern ridgeline. Does that sound reasonable?"

They all began looking around to see how everyone felt. Pete was the first to speak. "I'd say you have unanimous consent."

"So be it, then. Unless anyone has something else to contribute, I would say we are adjourned. I believe Team 4 is up first. Let's set the watch and get a good night's rest. Tomorrow will be a busy day."

To Carl's surprise, laughter and joking accompanied the dispersal of the group to their respective apartments. Helen and Carl grabbed their weapons and headed to the lobby. Before he left apartment 332, Carl kissed Janet goodnight and told her he loved her. The next to last night of their long challenge in Breckenridge, Colorado, began with peace and calm conditions. The beginning of the end was nearly upon them.

—

25

The Building 3 group formed in the parking lot, as they had rehearsed, except this time it was the beginning of morning twilight. Everyone responded to the wake-up call per the plan without a grumble. A handful, beyond the last duty watch team, was already awake.

The carts had been loaded and secured since yesterday afternoon. To Carl's surprise, the extensive accumulation of weapons over the last three months in the mountains had been evenly divided with the men holding either a long gun or a shotgun, and a pistol. Even the children carried the smaller pistols. They did not have to destroy, disable or dispose of any weapons. Only Anne Armstrong had refused to carry one of the firearms, and no one made any attempt to coerce her into doing so. The last thing they had done last night was top off their various water bottles, canteens, jugs and containers.

From their experience, they cooked up more meat than they could possibly eat. Nearly all of them ate too much. A small amount of meat remained. No vegetables other than what they carried on the carts remained. In the morning, the younger ones had consumed the leftovers from the previous night, while the adults consumed three strips of jerky, and water served as their morning meal. Few words were spoken by anyone.

Each in their own way bid farewell to the only sanctuary they had known for the last few months. Bert and Mike took to harness for cart one at the start, while Oscar and George took cart two. With a simple hand gesture from Carl, the vanguard team led the group out of the parking lot, down 4 O'Clock Run Road, and then south on Park Avenue. None of them detected any human or animal moving in the crisp, clear, morning air of Breckenridge.

By the time the sun peaked above the eastern ridgeline, the group turned right at the end of Park Avenue onto Route 9, and passed Boreas Pass Road at the southern outskirts of the town. They were moving well with no difficulty. The cart haulers did not feel particularly burdened, which was testament to the wheel bearing quality on the carts. The point group moved well ahead of the main group, and was in and out of sight, as turns and undulations in the road masked their position.

Carl began to notice people outside, watching the group move south on Route 9. Others began to notice as well. The group's movement remained steady and moderately paced. None of their observers appeared to make any move toward the two-dozen people walking out of town. Carl stopped on the shoulder to wait for the rear guard. He looked to Hank and said, "More than a few folks are watching us."

"I've noticed."

"Let's keep an extra sharp eye out for any followers or trailers."

"What's the difference?" asked Janet.

"Followers are people who are just doing what we're doing . . . leaving town. Trailers have a more nefarious intent," Carl answered, "like they are stalking us."

"What does nefarious mean?" Melissa asked.

"Bad, evil, criminal . . . they might want to harm us." Melissa nodded her head with understanding.

"Nobody has moved toward us, yet," Hank added.

Carl nodded his head and picked up his pace to return to his position in the formation.

Patches of water and thinning ice appeared across Goose Pasture Tarn reservoir to further indicate the spring thaw was well underway. They passed the Blue River junction by mid-day and took a comfort break shortly thereafter. Progress remained ahead of plan. The road grade had begun to increase. They switched out the in-harness folks and added a third hauler to ensure the carts moved easily without extraordinary effort. As they had practiced during their rehearsals, Lisa jumped onto one of the carts to feed Breckyn. When the infant was finished and Lisa had burped and changed Breckyn's diaper, Lisa put her daughter back in harness on her chest and stepped off the cart to walk like the rest of the group.

Tall pine trees lined both sides of the roadway. While the road shoulders and cleared space through the trees gave the group some observation room, the forest made Carl extra attentive. If someone or group of someones were intent upon an ambush, these would be near perfect conditions. Carl saw no signs that anyone had been along the road ahead of them. He had kind of expected to see an abandoned truck or automobile on the road, but the event had most likely occurred in the middle of the night, so less probable that anyone had been out on the rural mountain road. The full and heavy flow of the Blue River passed under the roadway numerous times and indicated the snowmelt at higher elevations had been progressing well. The road sign at a road junction said Whispering Pines Circle, and the small sign by the entrance to a paved parking lot and modest building said Town of Blue River Town Hall. When they passed a large road sign on the northbound side of the road that said Blue River City Limit Elev 10,000 Ft, the vanguard element appeared from around a left curve walking back toward the main group. They were walking normally and had no appearance of agitation. The main group stopped as the point group reached them. Some gathered to hear the information, while others sat to rest and drink some water.

"It's getting late," Helen said. "We have another hour or so of sun before twilight. The road remains clear. We've still not seen anyone. There is a large lodge ahead. The sign says The Lodge by the Blue. It's pretty good size and there are not many cars in the parking lot, so probably not many people there. It might be a good place to hold up for the night."

Carl retrieved their road and topographic maps as well as their plan worksheets. He checked the terrain and the map several times. "We are here," he said, placing his finger on the topographic map. "We are already ahead of plan. Did y'all see the pass?"

"No," Helen said. "Not yet."

"Too many trees," added Alex.

"How far is the lodge?" asked Pete.

"About a quarter," Holly said and paused, "maybe a half mile ahead . . . not that far really."

"We've had a good first day," said Pete. "Let's take advantage of the shelter at hand and rest up."

Carl looked around to those listening. He received head nods and other gestures of concurrence. "Very well." He looked back to Helen. "Lead on." The three-story lodge was just over a quarter of a mile ahead. "Before we try to enter," Carl said, "let's take a good look all around the building to make sure there is nothing untoward." Most of the group remained with the carts. Carl, Pete, Hank, Bert and Oscar moved to the building and split with one group going clockwise around the exterior of the building, and the other group going the other way. All five of them returned together. "It looks like the building hasn't been touched. The main entrance and lobby are on the east side, away from the street. Let's start there."

They pulled the carts up the paved path along the open parking spaces. Only six cars had been stranded in the parking lot. They stopped at the main entrance. The group was instructed to remain outside, around the carts, and to be vigilant for any threats. Pete, Hank and Carl would enter and ensure no threats existed.

All three of them traded their long guns for shotguns. Surprisingly, the front doors were open with no indication they had been compromised. A coating of dust on everything suggested human habitation had been a long way off. The three men collectively agreed the lobby was clear, and it was safe to get everyone and the carts inside. Hank remained inside on guard . . . just in case.

Carl and Pete returned to the group. Carl informed the group, "The lodge appears to be empty. Let's get everyone and the carts inside. While we check the rooms in the lodge, let's get a fire going to warm things up and get everyone fed."

With everyone inside, Holly said, "I'll tend to the fire."

Each of the men took one of the boys and divided up the search of each room, on each floor, in each wing of the lodge. They could not open the doors, since they had modern, magnet, electronic door locks. All of the doors were closed and locked. They chose not to break open the doors, but found no signs of occupancy. By the time they returned to the lobby, a good fire was burning in the large fireplace. Ample firewood had been carefully split, cut and stacked in a large, off-the-floor rack. It did not take long to be comfortably warm in the lobby. The search results confirmed, as best they could determine that the hotel was empty.

They ate their allotment of jerky and water. Two, sealed, five-gallon containers of water sat next to a water dispenser in the office. The group used a small amount of residual water in the dispenser to clean themselves and created some space on each cart to carry the jugs of water.

As darkness descended upon the exterior, the group set their normal watch with Team Two taking the first cycle. One member took each corner of the large lobby and maintained some cover, since they would be looking out of a partially lighted interior to a very dark exterior. They also collectively agreed to awaken, eat and prepare for the road during twilight, to be on the road no later than sunrise.

The night passed quietly and without incident. They ate and prepared for the road. Based on their rate of advance on Day T1, they might well get into the switchbacks for the climb to the crest of the pass. They agreed they would go as far as they reasonably could. The group made it out onto Route 9 heading south before the sun broke the eastern horizon. Scattered, fair weather cumulus clouds dotted the otherwise clear sky.

Several homes of modest form were close to the road. They saw more automobiles near the houses. Only one home appeared to be occupied, based on the steady wafts of smoke rising from the chimney. No one seemed to be aware of their passage. Larger, more elegant homes were situated farther back away from the roadway. The grade began to noticeably increase. They added a fourth person in harness on each cart at Mark Court Road. The switchbacks of the climb to the pass lay just ahead. As they reached the junction of Tordal Way and Route 9, a middle-aged man and woman stepped outside onto the narrow front porch of a rustic, two-story house that sat at the southwest corner.

Carl could not see any weapons. The couple watched the group as they passed and actually waved. Several in the group returned the waves. The roadway took a significantly steeper grade. Carl, Pete, Bert and Hank picked up the fifth and sixth harnesses on each cart. Carl looked over his shoulder to see the house couple at the property edge to the paved portion of the road, apparently fascinated with the effort of the passing group of refugees. Even with six in harness on each cart, moving the carts up the grade was no longer so easy.

"Let's pull off here," Carl shouted nearly breathless. They pulled the cart onto a comparatively level shoulder transition at what the signpost identified as Ellen Circle. "Block the wheels," Carl commanded to Mike and Nick. Once the carts were secure, everyone sat down to rest and drink some water. As their breathing rates returned to normal, Carl looked around to the group. "This is going to be a slog."

"Should we offload the carts, to reduce the weight?" asked George.

"A logical question," answered Carl. "We need these supplies to give us margin. I don't think we have a choice here. What does everyone else think?"

"I agree," said Pete.

"Me as well," Hank added.

"We knew this would be slow and hard. I think we need to get our strongest horses in harness and do the best we can. Others can help by pushing on the back end of the carts, but if we lose control, make sure you can jump clear. We do not want anyone to get hurt. Everybody ready?" One by one, everyone stood without responding. All of the males were now in the six harnesses per cart.

They pulled the carts back out onto the roadway. The males strained against the weight of the carts on the steep grade. A couple of women pushed on each cart. Every contribution helped. The going was slow but steady. The ground sloped off sharply to the left and rose sharply to the right. They were nearly at the tops of the conifer trees on the downslope. Carl pointed ahead to signal that he thought he could finally see the pass ahead and above them. The group took a break to rest every 200-300 yards.

The punishing stench of death carried on the breeze announced fatalities ahead. The first casualties the group had seen on the road lay ahead of them, clearly visible on the asphalt and gravel shoulder. The first body they passed had been an adolescent girl, and then a teenaged boy curled up in a fetal position 20 yards farther. A man and a woman, apparently the parents of the children, were just off the shoulder of the road. They could see no evidence of violence. The family appeared to have died during an attempt to escape the valley. Anne jumped to the opposite side of the road to vomit what little she had in her stomach and continued with the dry heaves. George tried to comfort his wife and offered her water, when she was ready. The group took a wide berth around the bodies and kept moving to attain some distance before taking their next rest break.

The sun fell behind the western horizon by the time they reached Mountain Kingdom Road. Carl encouraged them to press on a short distance more to the comparative flat meadow area that was depicted on the topographic map, adjacent to Blue Lakes Road. They pulled the carts off the roadway to the edge of the meadow. Once the carts were secure, they rested first and drank more water.

"Should we check out the houses?" asked Janet.

One modest house sat on the west side of Blue Lakes Road. Another larger house was located further away on the south side of Monte Cristo Creek that ran through the meadow. In the diminishing twilight, Carl saw no smoke, light or other evidence of occupancy.

"We might get lucky," Carl said, "if the house is open and empty. At least it would be shelter." He scanned the group. "Is everyone in favor of giving it a go?"

"What is the owner or someone else is already in there?" Alex asked.

"Therein lies the risk. I see no indications of occupancy."

"Well," interjected Hank, "we need to do something. We are running out of twilight and we need to settle in for the night . . . wherever that is going to be."

Carl scanned the group, again. He received various forms of concurrence. "OK." Carl removed himself from his cart harness. He looked over to the second cart. Pete was doing the same. "I'd suggest everyone stay here. Pete and I will check the house . . . less threatening. Stay on guard. This could go south quickly." Carl did not wait for a response. He traded the M1A rifle for Mike's shotgun. Pete did the same with Betsy.

Carl signaled for Pete to take the rear of the house. He carefully looked into each window. Several windows had shades drawn, which added uncertainty. Carl saw Pete in the living room. Pete signaled for the group to hold and for Carl to come to the back of the house. Carl nodded, and then he turned to the group and signaled for them to hold. He went around to the rear of the house. The door was still open. He carefully entered, and Pete joined him in the small kitchen.

Pete said, "The house is clear, except for a deceased, elderly man in the master bedroom."

The interior did not smell of death. Carl guessed the man was still frozen, or at least predominantly so.

"No one will want to use the house, if we leave him," Carl said.

"Yeah . . . exactly, which is why I signaled for the group to hold. I figured you and I could move the body outside away from the house. Better to have shelter."

"Agreed. Let's do it quickly . . . fewer questions."

The two men leaned their shotguns against the wall in the kitchen and went to the master bedroom. The man appeared to have been in his 70s at his passing and appeared to have frozen to death in his sleep. The body remained quite stiff and cold. Trying to lift the body was awkward and unmanageable. Pete found a spare sheet in the hall closet. He laid it out beside the body. They rolled the corpse onto the sheet, and then wrapped the corners around their hand—Pete at the head, Carl at the feet. Fortunately, the old man had been rather slight. They quickly carried him outside and laid him down behind a medium-sized workshop. They covered the body with the edges of the sheet. They returned to the house, picked up their shotguns to appear normal, and went to the front door. Opening the door, Pete and Carl walked toward the group.

"The house is clear," Pete said.

"We can stay here tonight. We'll have to leave the carts outside," added Carl. "I'd recommend we build a fire to keep the carts from freezing. Half the watch should tend the outside fire. The other half should keep watch, front and back, inside the house."

There was no discussion or disagreement. They pulled the carts up the road and driveway, past a disabled car in the driveway. The women went inside. Helen started the fire in the modest living room fireplace. There was not enough firewood for the night, so Helen asked for the boys to collect more. The boys went to the forest on the northeast side of Blue Lakes Road. They began returning with old fallen limbs. Carl went to the shed—a nicely equipped wood workshop. He found an ax, a hatchet and a couple of saws. While the boys continued to collect firewood, several of the men immediately took to sizing and splitting the wood. Mike stopped his firewood search and jumped into building a fire between the two carts. In short order, they had plenty of wood for the night, both inside and out. Carl stowed the ax on Cart One.

The group ate their evening meal. Trip Day 2 (T2) had been productive. They were a day ahead of plan.

Team Three initiated the watch. They brought mattresses, blankets, sheets and pillows into the living room—better to sleep in the living room warmed by the fire.

Carl felt like he had barely achieved sleep when Janet was waking him for Team Four to take over the watch. Helen and Carl took the inside watch first. They switched with Vicky and Nick halfway through their watch cycle. After ensuring the outside fire was going well, Carl told Helen what he was going to do and walked up Blue Lakes Road to get a little more elevation. As he scanned the visible terrain, Carl was surprised to see perhaps a dozen spots of light scattered around. The sources of light appeared to be other controlled fires. Carl returned to the carts.

"We are not alone," Carl said softly to Helen.

"Really?"

"I could see the light of probably a dozen other fires above and below us."

"Is anyone going to bother us?" Helen asked.

"I doubt it . . . too far away."

"Good."

"But, we need to remain vigilant."

The warmth of the fire felt good. They turned away from the fire periodically to warm their backsides. Carl and Helen turned the carts for the same reason. The last half of their watch cycle passed quickly. They woke up Team Five—Hank, Anne, Bert and Mike. Carl briefed them on what Team Four had done on their watch cycle. The Team Four members found spots and were swiftly into the embrace of slumber.

The night passed all too quickly. Before local sunrise, the group was back out on Route 9, continuing their trek out of the mountains. They chose to keep the males in harness on the carts and take rest breaks at roughly the same intervals. The grade of the roadway made the haulage more arduous. Fortunately, the condition of the road surface kept the wheels of the cart effective and efficient.

Carl noted the snow poles on both sides of the road that hinted at how deep the snow could get in the winter. Blessedly, the roadway was still clear of snow and ice, and the weather remained spring-like. They moved out of the forest into another high meadow. More prominent patches of remaining snow dotted the mountainsides ahead and above them.

By an hour after noon, they reached Carroll Lane that served as the entrance to a development with a dozen plus cabins scattered throughout the open ground. This was the last housing development before reaching Hoosier Pass. After another rest break and with several hours of daylight remaining, they agreed to press on. Carl was starting to feel the strain of hauling the carts up the slope. The thin air at this elevation did not help their capacity for exertion. He knew others had to feel the same, but no one talked about it. They inherently knew it had to be done.

The sun touched the higher peaks to the west. They were out of time. They stopped at a comparatively large and relatively flat turnout on the west side of the road that gave them another rest break. Their chests were all heaving, as their bodies struggled to oxygenate their blood in the thin air. They all drank more water to stay hydrated as best they could.

"We can't be far from the pass," Carl observed, as his breathing rate began to decrease. "Do we stop here, or press to the pass?" he asked.

The point group rejoined the group. They did not need prompting. Alex announced, "The crest of the pass is less than a half mile ahead, but still a good climb."

"We're all tired, Carl," answered Janet, "and hungry, and it's getting dark."

"We won't have moonlight for several more hours after evening twilight," Pete said.

"Let's camp here," said Hank, "so we can recharge for our push to the pass tomorrow."

"OK. So be it," Carl acknowledged.

They pulled the carts to the center of the packed dirt turnout. The carts did not like the change in surface bearing, but they needed to get the carts to a flatter position, closer to where their encampment would be. The boys did not wait for instructions. Gathering firewood was not going to be so easy this evening. While they still had twilight, the boys went to the steep slope off at the edge of the turnout and wisely chose to forego that direction. The upslope side of the roadway gave a better angle, but more than a few stumbles and groans indicated the difficulty of movement with the diminishing light and steep ground. While the boys continued to collect firewood, Holly and Helen set to the task of building their fire. Hank and Betsy got their tent off Cart Two, and set it up close to the carts and the fire. The fledgling fire offered some light for the wood gatherers on the upslope side of the road. It took until well after the end of evening twilight to collect sufficient firewood for the night. They ate late and set the watch. The warmth of the fire kept the cold at bay. The females arranged themselves with blankets in the tent for mutual warmth. The males would rotate a reduced watch around the fire.

Nick and Carl were the remainder of Team Four. They had to be near 11,000 feet in elevation. Several times during their watch cycle, father and middle son stood, walked away from the fire, defying the cold air, to the edge of the turnout, and gazed out to the moonlit terrain below them. They could no longer see the valley behind them, and this night, there were no other discernible light sources. Carl found himself yearning for the sun, just for the warmth.

Their third night on the journey also passed without intrusion by man or beast. The beginning of morning twilight backlit the eastern horizon. In their immediate location, the trees on the upslope side of the road were their local horizon. The men were eager to get moving for the warmth of their exertion, but the process of rousing the women proved a little sportier than they expected. The fire remained welcome and also kept the stored water from freezing. They ate, drank some water, and loaded the carts before the sun illuminated the western peaks.

As they began Day 128 (T4), the aches and pains of the previous days' efforts made their initial movements slow and more tortured. The audible and numerous groans punctuated the beginning of their fourth day on the road. The roadway felt steeper, although Carl knew it had to be perception rather than reality. Four hours and two rest breaks later, the group reached their first major objective. The large, brown and tan, bowtie-shaped, U.S. Forest Service sign on a stone pedestal, facing to the east, prominently proclaimed:

HOOSIER PASS

ELEVATION 11,539 FEET

CONTINENTAL DIVIDE

ATLANTIC OCEAN	PACIFIC OCEAN
PIKE	WHITE RIVER
National Forest	*National Forest*

The group halted near the sign. No one spoke until their heaving chests diminished in recovery. Melissa Manson was the first to speak. "What is the Continental Divide, Momma?"

"Good question, Sissy," Emily said and stood. "Come over here," she said and gestured for her daughter to follow her. Several other young folks joined them, apparently wanting to hear the explanation. Emily straddled a broad blue line painted on the asphalt across the roadway from margin to margin, with her back to the sign. "This line," she continued, pointing to the blue line between her feet that would bisect the sign, if extended, "marks the point at which water flows in this direction," pointing to her right and the south, "to the Atlantic Ocean, and this direction," gesturing to her left and the north, "toward the Pacific Ocean."

"Why is that important?" questioned Melissa.

"It's not. It's just an interesting fact of geography—a point of interest," Emily answered. Melissa nodded her head, apparently satisfied with her mother's answers. Emily and the young folks rejoined the group.

Carl checked the sun's position—near local zenith. He scanned the group to gain a quick assessment of the state. "We have just under half a day left of daylight," Carl said.

Several members of the group began to wander off to absorb the impressive vistas around the periphery of the large gravel scenic parking area on the west side of the road. The area could easily accommodate several dozen vehicles, but only two abandoned automobiles occupied the large space.

"What do you suggest?" Pete asked.

Carl smiled, even chuckled a little, and then said, "I'd suggest we take a half day's break. We could even call it a celebration of sorts. I think we just made it through the most difficult, physical part of our journey. We reached the pass two days ahead of plan."

"So, we could splurge and have a little extra of our food rations," suggested Pete.

"Yes. We will have to hit our water reserves. I suspect we won't be able to refill our water for another day or so." Carl paused, took a deep breath, and said, "Whatever we're going to do, we need to discuss our options and decide, rather than squander our daylight."

Pete did not wait for further discussion. He shouted, "Let's gather up folks." Once everyone was back together, Pete said, "We have a choice here. We reached the summit two days ahead of our original plan. We can press on. We have a day's journey to Alma, so if we do, we will probably have to find a campsite between here and there. Or, we take a break to rest, consume our extra food margin, and enjoy the scenery, as a little celebration of our achievement."

"I vote for the break," Janet promptly offered.

"This is not a stable site," Hank said, as he stood. "I'm inclined to use every available hour to reach whatever more stable point we can find. However, a short respite would be welcomed . . . perhaps by everyone."

"As Pete and I were discussing," Carl added, "we are two days ahead of plan, which in turn gives us two more day's rations with which to celebrate our achievement. Further, as Emily's explanation of the Continental Divide implicated, at this point, we must transition from pull to restrain."

"What?" asked Mike, for an explanation.

"Up to here, we had to pull the carts. From here, we will have to restrain the carts, to control the movement of the carts on the downslope. The restraint process should be easier than the pulling process, but it will still be a physical chore." Mike nodded his head in understanding. "So, what say you all?"

Unanimous consensus did not take long to achieve. A half-day hiatus on the trek would be welcome.

Carl looked around. "I'd recommend we pull the carts over there," he said and pointed to a Forest Service information kiosk across the turnout from the sign. "Let's setup over there, gather firewood for a day's consumption, and get the fire going."

No one felt the need for confirmation or guidance. They simply began moving the carts. The group's encampment was established in short order. The two abandoned cars were searched. Both were open and otherwise undamaged or disturbed. None of them found any evidence regarding the whereabouts of the owners or occupants of the cars. They found nothing useful beyond a couple of blankets.

Most of them took time to absorb the majestic scenery ahead of them. They could not see much of where they had come from. Carl remained gratefully surprised the western sky showed no signs of advancing weather. They had been lucky, so far.

Intermittently, people sat around the campfire, talking as though they were enjoying a more recreational time. The combination of the pine scent from the trees close by and the robust fire brought good memories of days gone by. More than a few times, one person or another voiced a pleasant wish for the goodies of roasted marshmallows, soft chocolate and graham crackers. They had to explain the camping delicacy of S'mores to George and Anne, to their demonstrative delight.

By mid-afternoon, several members could be seen napping in the warm sun and crisp mountain air. Motion to the north along the roadway caught Carl's attention immediately. He reached for the shotgun leaning against the cart and placed it across his lap, and then unzipped his parka to provide ready access to the holstered PPK under his left arm. Carl softly announced, "We have visitors."

Pete and Hank followed suit. They waited and did not feel it necessary to alert or alarm the others. The four young adult males made it to the northern edge of the turnout, clearly huffing and puffing with the climb at altitude. They did not seem to hesitate and turned to walk calmly toward the group. Carl could not recall seeing any of the four before. They all had full beards and wore ski bibs and parkas. Three of them had knit caps. The lead man did not have a head covering to mask his curly dirty blond or light brown hair and beard. None of them appeared to be armed, although that did not mean they were not armed. Carl, and then Pete and Hank stood—all three of them cradling shotguns in their arms.

"Good afternoon," the lead man shouted from a distance of about 10 yards. "It's great to see someone else on the road out of the mountains." The man paused, as if to encourage a response. They continued a slow pace toward them. None of the group responded. "Mind if we join you?" he asked.

Carl held up his right hand indicating for them to stop about five yards away. "Can we help you?" Carl asked.

"That would be most kind of you," the lead man said from his stationary, standing position, with his chest still heaving from lack of oxygen. "Do you have any food or water to spare?" The man's eyes were scanning the carts and the group in general.

"No, we don't," came Carl's succinct and commanding response.

The lead man's expression displayed his skepticism. He probably considered confronting the obvious bounty on the two carts. He wisely chose not to do so. "Would you mind if we warmed ourselves by your fire?"

"Yes, as a matter of fact, I would mind."

"Why?"

"These are dangerous times, I'm afraid." Other men in the group began to stand as well, perhaps sensing confrontation approaching. "I would suggest y'all move along. Alma is about eight miles ahead to the south. You can make it by sunset, if you do not dally. You might find shelter and sustenance there."

The four men did not move or react to Carl's words. Carl placed his right hand on the shotgun's stock grip and thumbed off the safety. The lead man understood the signal. He raised his empty hands to shoulder height.

"We mean no harm, man," the lead man said. "No need to be hostile."

"Best move along and leave us be," Carl commanded.

The lead man began to back up first. The other three followed suit and raised their hands as well. When they reached the roadway, they turned and began walking south. Within a couple of minutes, they disappeared, as the road sloped away from the crest.

Carl walked directly toward the south edge of the turnout. Hank and Pete moved along on each flank. They walked a little way down the road, just enough to see the four visitors with their backs toward them, walking down the road at a reasonable pace. They appeared to be doing as Carl had suggested. Without looking at his companions, Carl said, "How did you guys read them?"

Hank answered first, "Bad news."

"I agree," said Pete.

"Then, that makes three of us. I was sorely tempted to finish it right then and there, but the women would not have appreciated my caution."

"Yeah, Carl, you're probably right," said Pete. "But, I suspect we are going to see those four, again."

"My impression, as well," Hank added.

"If we do, I will not likely be so generous," Carl said.

"We're with you," Pete contributed. The four visitors passed out of sight, again. "Now, we'd better get back to explain what that was all about."

All three of them turned and began walking back to the group in silence. The rest of the group was gathered around the fire, half standing, half sitting. They were all watching the three men. The expressions of concern spoke volumes.

"What was that all about?" asked Betsy with the initial question.

"Four guys doing what we are doing," Hank responded.

"Then, why did you turn them away?"

"I did not like the feel," answered Carl.

"And, Pete and I concurred," added Hank. "They seemed like trouble."

"Do you think they were followers or trailers?" Janet asked.

Carl smiled that his wife remembered the difference. "My guess . . . trailers."

"They're ahead of us, now," added Janet.

"Yes, they are and they are off down the road to Alma," Carl continued. "If they are perfectly innocent, we will likely not see them, again. If they have other motives, we may see them, again. If anyone does see any one of those four men, please let Hank, Pete or me know immediately."

"So you can kill them," interjected Vicky with a noticeable sneer.

Carl stared at her, debating whether to answer.

Pete jumped in, "Yes," he said calmly. "All three of us feel they are bad men, who may well try to take what we have . . . and will probably have no qualms resorting to violence for that purpose."

"As if this journey is not hard enough," Betsy mumbled, and then said with more force and clarity. "Now, we have to contend with highwaymen."

"I hope not," Hank responded to his wife, "but we must be prepared and remain vigilant."

The visitors and the potential implications dominated the conversation for the remainder of this day. The group agreed to the usual four-person, two-hour, watch cycles were necessary. Several times during each cycle period, two of the watchstanders would go to the south edge of the turnout to check on the southerly approach. Team Four had the last watch this particular night. Helen and Carl made their checks. Satisfied they could not see any distant firelight or makeshift torches, they stopped to look up and marvel at the magnificent array of stars around them, even dimmed by the brightness of the waxing moon, not quite a week from full state. Twilight began to lighten the eastern horizon before Team Four finished their watch period. It had not been a restful night, but it had passed without incident.

—

26

As morning twilight pushed the stars away, the group prepared for their next day on the road. After they had eaten their morning ration and consumed sufficient water, they packed up their camping gear and secured the cargo on the carts. As the sky lightened, Carl noticed a broad swath of clouds across virtually the entire western horizon. *I need to keep an eye on that.* The boys dispersed the burning wood and embers, and then doused them with dirt from the nearby edge of the large turnout. They made sure the fire was smothered and not able to flare up. They moved the carts directly to the asphalt road. The air was still quite cold as they formed up for the day's journey.

Before they began the day's walk, Carl said to the group, "Let's keep our eyes out all around—left, right, forward and behind—for any people, close or far. If you see a human being, or animal for that matter, please speak up. Remember, better safe than sorry." No one responded.

The carts were reversed so that the harnesses and tethers were now on the backside. They decided to start with four in harness and two on each forward corner to steer or guide the carts on the descent grade of the road.

When they cleared some trees a half mile down the road, they saw a long view of the valley into which they were moving and it appeared in a magnificent vista. The roadway sliced smoothly down the eastern side of the valley. The road grade was not as steep as their ascent on the north side, and the restraint of the carts proved easier to manage. As they walked, they considered the possibility of reducing the number in harness down to three or even two, but they agreed four made it easy enough to maintain. They actually set into a well-paced routine for movement and were moving at a noticeably faster pace than they achieved so far.

Progress was surprisingly good, comparatively easy, especially with respect to their climb the previous two days. None of them detected human or animal activity . . . well, other than the occasional flock of vultures circling their next meal. They passed a rectangular, log, arch gateway with a large sign declaring Elk Ridge Ranch. The single-lane width, asphalt-paved roadway stimulated some distant curiosity about the other end of the road, but the curious moment passed with their progress. Just beyond the ranch entry road, another asphalt road heading downslope that was less developed than Route 9 and more substantial than the Elk Ridge Ranch access road. The green post at the intersection indicated they were on Hwy 9 and the other road was CR 4. Carl wanted to consult the map, but their progress was just too good and there had been no requests for a break. They passed several turnouts. Again, none of the group requested a break for any reason, not even from Lisa to feed or change Breckyn.

Sections of the roadway without obstructing trees gave them a nice, clear view of the valley floor. More than a few substantial homes were tucked into the edge of the forest on the west side of the valley meadow. The servicing roads appeared to be dirt or gravel, rather than paved.

After reaching a point that Carl mentally estimated to be halfway down the mountainside to the valley floor, they took their first break They all took water. Lisa tended to her daughter's comfort. Carl looked to the western sky. The high cirrus stratus leading edge of the approaching weather continued to advance toward them.

"There are some good-sized homes on the other side of the valley," Betsy observed.

"Are you hinting that we should go check them out?" asked Emily.

"No, no . . . just an observation. We've driven this road a few times, but I don't recall noticing those homes before," Betsy paused and continued to look off to the distant residential area. "It's amazing to me what you notice when we move slower through life."

"Fortunately," Janet interjected, "we've not seen those men, again."

"Yet," muttered Carl, more to himself. He scanned the sky, one more time. "We're burning daylight. We'd best move along." Pete looked to the western sky and nodded his agreement.

They switched out the in-harness folks and reduced the number to three. The wheels of the carts were unblocked as the slack in the harness tethers was taken up.

Smaller homes, more closely spaced just below them appeared as the trees gave way to the meadow. A modest sized reservoir occupied the center of the valley, almost from side to side. While they continued to move, they considered stopping to refill their water containers. The reservoir appeared healthy and was probably the water supply for the development. They still had plenty of water and agreed to press on and resupply later.

The road grade flattened out quite a bit as Route 9 reached the valley floor. They passed a large, green, road sign on the east side of the road that proclaimed HOOSIER PASS 4 MILES. They were about halfway to Alma and it was not yet noon. At the intersection of the valley road and Route 9, an identical street sign marked the rejoining of State Route 4 with Route 9. They had not seen abandoned vehicles on the road and not detected any human presence. Carl had not noticed any smoke rising from the chimneys of the homes in the development. They were off the mountain and in more open country, which gave them better margins with any potential ambush site. The roadway had flattened so much that gravity was no longer a propulsive force for the carts. They stopped just long enough to change carts to the pulling orientation and reduced the in-harness number to two. An occasional negative slope caused the tethers to slacken and briefly required restraint of the carts to maintain control.

When they passed the MILE 72 road sign, the point group had turned and was walking back toward the main group. They stopped near the edge of pine trees on the left. Buildings could be seen across comparatively open ground ahead and to the left. They did not need to block the wheels. The group took the opportunity to hydrate.

Helen reported, "There is a town a couple of miles ahead."

"That must be Alma," Hank observed.

"We still have several hours of daylight," added Pete.

Carl looked, again, to the western sky. "It looks like we've got weather coming in . . . maybe tonight or tomorrow."

"Are you thinking we should try to hold up at Alma?" Pete asked.

"Better to have shelter than not," Carl answered.

"How do you want to do this?" Hank asked.

Carl looked toward the town in the distance and the western sky. "We have no idea what to expect in that town . . . or any other. We need to reconnoiter the village to evaluate what residents remain, whether they are friendly or hostile, and assess what our options might be."

Hank looked at his oldest daughter. "Did you see people?"

"Yes," Helen answered, glancing at Holly and Alex. "We all did . . . not a lot, but more than a couple, and there is smoke rising from a few chimneys."

"So, Alma is populated?" Pete said, seeking confirmation.

"Yes."

"Then," Becky interjected, "why don't we just go into town?"

"Because," Pete said, "it is not wise to expose the whole group, if there are any hostiles."

"And, there is no way around the town," Carl added.

"How do you want to proceed?" Hank asked, repeating his earlier question.

"I'd recommend the group stay here and remain vigilant. Pete, you and I should scout the town, to see what we can find. Hopefully, at least one building is empty, so that we can use it for shelter. More importantly, we need to assess the friendliness of the inhabitants."

"How long will it take, and what if you do not come back?" asked Oscar.

"We cannot check every building."

"Pete's correct," Carl added, and checked the sun position and his wristwatch. "I would suggest we allot two hours to this task. We will try to return, or at least you should see us returning, within two hours. If something happens to all three of us, my recommendation is, stay here until about 22:00 tonight, and then pass through the town during the night. The waxing gibbous moon around midnight should give you sufficient light to make it to open country beyond the town. I strongly recommend you make no attempt to find or rescue us. If this goes bad, it will be bad in a big way."

"Pete, no!" exclaimed Barb. "Rather than risk something bad happening, why don't we just decide now to make the night transit and move on?"

"The risk has to be low, Barb, but there is still a risk," Pete responded. "We will be well armed, and we should be able to deal with any incident . . . short of being overwhelmed."

"I agree with Pete," Hank said.

"And, I concur," added Carl. "I will add, the upside outweighs the potential downside."

"How so?" asked Janet.

"There is more weather coming. Shelter would be better than being in the open. Further, we are not asking for anything from the town other than shelter."

"But, they might be desperate enough to want a lot from us," said Vicky. "And, we need our supplies to make it the rest of the way to some kind of civilization."

"True," Carl responded. "The risk is manageable, especially with the three of us. There is a possible positive outcome, as well. The town's people might be friendly and helpful. We're not going to scout the whole town. We simply do not have that kind of time. However, we should be able to acquire a reasonable assessment. Plus, the town may well be mostly deserted." Carl paused to allow anyone else to speak, if they wished. No one spoke or even twitched. "Then, are we in agreement?" Various forms of affirmation followed. Carl nodded his head and looked at Pete and Hank. "I suggest we take two shotguns and one long gun, in addition to our pistols, just in case."

Carl took the Mossberg standard grip and stock. Pete traded for the Mossberg Tactical. Hank traded Holly for the Winchester 70. All three of them ensured the weapon magazines were full with an additional round in the chamber and the safeties on. When they were all ready, they said good-bye to their wives and children, again, just in case.

The three men headed out at a faster than usual pace. They had quite a bit of ground to cover in the allotted time, and they would be near sunset before they could return to the group, which in turn meant it would be well into twilight to move the group, if they did find shelter.

The first development they passed was a large, cyclone fenced, self-storage facility, surprisingly large for a town of only several hundred inhabitants. No signs of human activity were detected. Just ahead, a small road sign on the right marked the Middle Fork of the South Platte River. Water was flowing well under the roadway and appeared to be clean and fresh. Two small homes next to each other and just before a wide left curve on the road showed no signs of occupancy. They chose not to them check them out. Halfway through the left turn more buildings appeared, this time on the right side of the road. They saw the large, colorful, custom sign declaring:

HISTORIC

ALMA

North America's HIGHEST Incorporated Town

10,578'

The sign also depicted the town's mining heritage with a pick and shovel prominently included in the display. The town was clearly proud of their claim to fame. However, to the scouting team and the group at large, the town was just another obstacle to be surmounted on their journey out of the Rocky Mountains. A hundred yards farther on a dozen or so arched, plastic covered, well-maintained, greenhouse growing sheds suggested productivity for whoever remained in the town. Across from the greenhouses along the northbound side of the road, a standard road sign said:

BRECKENRIDGE   16
DILLON   31

Carl smiled. His crude map estimates of distance had been pretty accurate so far. They had come a good distance already, but they still had so far to go.

Still, none of the homes or buildings showed any signs of occupancy or habitation, yet. Only the Route 9 roadway appeared to be paved in this area. The first sign of habitation came from the western upslope in the form of smoke wafting skyward from the chimney of a two-story, blue-gray, steep roof house. The three men stopped to look for any further signs from the home on the parallel dirt street, one block away.

"Do you want to check it out?" asked Pete.

Without taking his eyes off the house, Carl answered, "We have to come back this way. Let's do it on the way back, if we don't find anything else."

"Agreed," Hank added.

The town appeared to be almost deserted. Carl looked at his wristwatch. "It took us roughly 20 minutes to get into town. We've got about an hour to find what we are going to find." Carl looked south. "I see four or five more smoke columns. We have other options. Let's get as much done as we can in an hour."

The three men headed south farther into town. They passed a model, two-story, log cabin apparently built to showcase a local builder's expertise.

"Nobody in that one," Hank observed.

"Yeah," Pete said. "That would make a stylish shelter."

"So, that's one possibility," added Carl.

They did not stop to evaluate it further. What could be mistaken as the center of town had several shops for various purposes on both sides of the road. The first had what was once a lighted sign on the north-facing exterior wall that said: Al-Mart General Store. The sign on the east-facing exterior wall above the entrance doorway identified the building as: Carhartt Superstore. The windows were intact and the door was open. Hank started to head toward the door, but Carl signaled for them to continue.

"We'll search it on the way back, as well," Carl declared matter-of-factly.

Other stores appeared to be untouched and closed. One hundred yards farther on, they crossed over a nicely flowing, clear water creek passing through culverts under the roadway. The sign identified the creek as Buckskin Gulch.

"Looks like clear snowmelt runoff. We can refill here," Carl said without stopping.

They noticed for the first time that the ground on the far side of the Platte River had been cleared of all trees and vegetation for that matter. The evergreen tree line appeared to be straight and parallel to Route 9, which meant it was intentional . . . b*ut for what reason*?

The other, apparently, occupied houses were all on the south end of town. The southern extent of the town development was a short distance ahead. Carl signaled for them to continue to that point, and then they would double back.

They reached the south end of town, the city limit sign, and crossed over the Platte River, again. A short distance farther, another road sign on the southbound side stated:

FAIRPLAY   6

HARTSEL   24

Carl stopped and faced his companions. He checked his wristwatch. It had taken them 20 minutes to walk completely through the town of Alma. "I counted seven smoke plumes—five on the west side and two on the eastside. Where do you want to start?"

"I like that odd chartreuse house on the west side with the white picket front porch," Hank said. "It looks the most expensive, so perhaps the least threatened."

"What do you think, Pete?"

"Works for me," Pete answered. "We can start there and perhaps check a few others before we need to head back."

The high cirrus leading edge of the approaching storm was now overhead and the sun was dimmed. Whatever they were going to do, they needed to get it done to protect the rest of the group.

"OK. Let's get to it."

They walked back north and turned off on the dirt road that curved into a parallel dirt and gravel street. All three of them stopped in front of the chartreuse house. "Let's spread out, so one shot can't get us all, just in case." Pete and Hank did as they were directed. "Let's try not to appear threatening." Carl did not wait for a response and climbed the three side steps to the long porch. His footfalls on the wooden porch sounded a slow drumbeat. The windows had the shades drawn. The front door was nearly at the other end of the porch. Carl knocked on the doorframe.

"What do you want?" came a strong male voice from the interior.

"We mean no harm. We need information . . . just information . . . nothing else."

Hesitation suggested the man was considering Carl's statement. "What do you want to know?"

"We have walked out over the pass from Breckenridge. We are a group of 20 plus. Is there someplace in town we can shelter for the night, and we will be on our way tomorrow morning."

"Have your pick," the man said. "Most of the town folk are gone, left months ago when the power went out. You just can't stay here. We can't help you."

We . . . more than one. The man was probably protecting his family. "Understood," Carl answered calmly. "Thank you. God bless you," Carl added and turned to leave. The north end of the porch was fenced like the front. Carl walked back to the south end and signaled for Pete and Hank to head north on the parallel street. A mustard colored house was on the same parallel street, just over a small, narrow bridge across Buckskin Gulch. Carl estimated the house was just about behind the Al-Mart store.

Carl and his companions repeated the same process. He knocked on the front door. This time no response or sound of activity could be heard. Carl tried, again—same result. Carl turned and signaled for them to go.

As they walked, Hank asked, "Nothing?"

"Nope."

They turned down the next cross street that took them back to Route 9. The Al-Mart store was just ahead a short distance, on the right. Carl signaled for them to search the store.

Hank remained outside the store to guard against unexpected intruders. Pete and Carl entered the door, prepared to engage, if anyone was in the store. They took a few seconds to allow their eyes to adjust to the low light. The general store appeared to be empty shelving without signs of vandalism or ransacking. A large, antique, wood stove occupied the middle of the open space in front of the sales counter. Their quick search yielded nothing useful or usable; however, a half dozen, split logs were still in the adjacent rack, and appeared to be properly sized for the stove. Carl felt the cast iron stove. It was cold. Carl signaled for them to go.

Outside with Hank, Carl said, "Wood stove and some firewood, but nothing in terms of useful supplies."

"OK. Let's check that model home," Hank suggested.

Pete and Carl nodded their agreement. They continued back north. The model log cabin they had passed earlier was unlocked. The house was nicely built with a good layout for a vacation residence, but totally unfurnished. The house had been designed for electric heat like virtually all of the other homes in the mountains. The small fireplace in the modest living room had no firewood close by, or any sign that it had ever been used.

"We are going to be more crowded in here to be around the fire," Pete observed.

"Yeah," Hank agreed.

"Of the two options," Carl added, "I think the store would be the better choice for our group. Plus, the doorway looked wide enough to get the carts inside." Carl stepped to the northeast corner of the building and looked to the sky. The clouds were thickening. He checked his wristwatch. "The clouds are still OK for the time being. We still have 20 minutes for our return mark. Are we agreed on the store for our shelter tonight?"

"Yes," Pete and Hank responded in unison.

"OK. So be it. What y'all think of using the time we have left to check on that blue-gray house we saw on the way in?"

"That works," Hank said. "Who knows, we might find a more hospitable person."

They walked up the cross street just north of the model home, and then north on the first parallel dirt street. The house was halfway up the street. They stopped in front of the house. Carl noticed a curtain move. He signaled for them to spread, as they had done before. Carl took two steps toward the front door and the door opened. A middle-aged man, older than Carl, stepped one step outside with a 12-gauge shotgun lowered and aimed at Carl's chest. Carl raised his hands, trying not to be threatening.

"We mean no harm," Carl stated in a firm, commanding voice.

"Then, what do you want here?" the man said.

Carl repeated the explanation he had used earlier. "We are going to stay the night in the Al-Mart store and wait for the approaching storm to pass. Then, we will be on our way south."

"We have no objection to any of that," the man answered. *There was that plural pronoun, again.* "Just do not try to bother us."

"We won't. Can I ask a few questions?" Carl asked.

"Sure, that doesn't cost anything. I'll do my best to answer."

"Have other groups passed through ahead of us?"

"Yes. Four young men yesterday were not particularly respectful."

Those must be the four men who approached us at the pass summit. "Did they move on?"

"Don't know, but I came very close to pulling the trigger on this here scattergun," the man said, raising, and then lowering the shotgun muzzle.

"I'm sorry they were not respectful," Carl said, keeping his hands raised. "As I said, we mean no harm. How is the water in Buckskin Gulch and the Platte River?"

"Good. Clear. Clean. We use it. You can fill up your canteens in either."

"Excellent. We'll do that?"

"One last question," Carl said and waited for the man's head nod of consent. "Do you know or have any information about what happened last December to knock out the electrical power?"

The cautious man stared at Carl, glanced to Hank and Pete, made several unusual expressive scrunches of his face, before he answered. "We've heard nothing up here. Most folks in town, when the power went, left town within weeks. None of them have come back, to my knowledge. Only folks still here are the diehards like us. We love this country and this town, and we're not going anywhere."

"So, you are safe and stable. You can sustain yourselves?" asked Pete.

More facial expression gyrations came before he answered. "We're doin' fine, thank you very much. Now, best be on your way," the man said and waved his shotgun to the south.

Carl felt the need to make sure he understood what they were going to do, so there would be no misunderstandings. "We've got to go back north about a mile to bring the rest of our group into town. We'll stay in the empty Al-Mart store until the storm passes, and then we will continue south."

"That should be OK. None of us will bother you, if you stick to that plan," the man said. "Good luck on your journey."

Carl nodded his head and signaled for them to leave. He could not see another cross street to the north, so they headed back the way they had come. The man remained on the porch, watching them, until they disappeared from view, walking north on Route 9.

They had not noticed the MILE 71 road sign on the northbound side of the road on their way into town. They had about a mile to go, to rejoin the group.

They saw the group right where they had left them. Most of the group stood, as the search team neared them.

"How did it go?" Oscar asked.

"We found a place to stay," answered Pete.

The overcast was darkening and lowering. "Let's get everyone into town and sheltered. We'll debrief our search once everyone is inside and we have heat."

No one chose to press their questions. They efficiently arranged themselves for movement. Pete and Carl led the way. Hank took up his rearguard position. The movement into town and to the Al-Mart store was smooth and easy. The door was surprisingly just wide enough for the carts. They had to carefully align the carts with the doorframe to make it through the opening. Betsy and Barb immediately set to the task of firing up the stove. As they had done on the previous encampments, the boys set off to collect sufficient wood to sustain them through the night. Oscar and Bert split and sized the logs for the stove. Carl suggested they stock at least two full day's worth of firewood, just in case the storm lasted longer than expected.

Once the fire was going, the marginal light emanating from the stove enabled them to search the barren store more carefully. Melissa and Aaron found two, antique, kerosene lamps complete with wicks and nearly full reservoirs. The lamps lit easily and provided substantially better interior light.

Hank, Pete and Carl reported to the group on their findings while they ate their evening meal of jerky and water. There were few questions. The group was satisfied with their situation and thankful for the shelter. Team Two set the first watch. Before lying down for his rest, Carl stepped outside and away from the light to survey the darkened town. The detectable light appeared to coincide with the smoke plumes they had seen earlier in the afternoon. Content that the situation was calm and stable, Carl extinguished the oil lamps to improve the night vision of the watchstanders, and then laid down next to Janet, who was already asleep. He followed swiftly behind her.

His awakening came all too quickly. Alex wiggled the toe of his father's boot. Fortunately, this time, Carl did not awaken with a start. "Is it time already?" Carl asked sleepily.

"No, Dad. Lisa is missing."

"What!" This time he shot up.

"Lisa went outside perhaps 20 minutes ago to go to relieve herself. She's not come back."

"No one went with her?"

"She said it was not necessary. She was not going far."

Damn it all to hell! What the fuck was she doing, going out alone, and you let her? You know better. Calmly, Carl said, "OK. I'll go look for her."

Carl rose, felt for his trusty M1911 in his jacket right pocket, and then reached in and withdrew the PPK, before he zipped up his jacket. He pulled the slide back just enough to see the chambered round and twisted the silencer to ensure it was tight. "Do you have your pistol?"

"Yes, Dad." Alex produced the other M1911.

"Good. Trade your Remington for one of the Mossbergs." Alex did not answer, stepped away, and returned with the Mossberg Tactical. Carl saw Janet standing watch at the northeast window.

"Find her, Carl," Janet commanded with barely concealed emotion.

"I will. I'm taking Alex with me."

Janet nodded, and then said, "Be careful . . . and successful." Carl just nodded.

With the PPK in his right hand, Carl and Alex left the store and disappeared around the corner. He signaled for them to stand with their backs against the north wall, to allow their eyes to adjust to the lower light level. The overcast dimmed the nearly full moon intermittently appearing among darker clouds. The air smelled like rain. Satisfied they had sufficient vision, Carl moved slowly and quietly toward the back of the store, the most likely location of her destination. She was not there. He began to expand his search until he found what might have been staggered heel scrapes in the dirt road behind the store. The marks pointed north on the street. They had to retrace their steps several times to locate additional drag marks. The spacing and scuffing on the drag marks suggested the person was struggling and being mostly carried. As they reached the corner with the intersecting cross street, Carl thought he heard muffled grunts and scuffing dirt. He looked at Alex, pointed to his left ear, and then in the direction of the sound. Alex nodded his head; he had heard the sound, too. Carl held his left index finger to his lips. Again, Alex nodded. Carl thumb'ed off the safety on his pistol.

Carl moved more quickly, but still he was very careful with his footfalls on the dirt and gravel street. They moved up the cross street to the west, passing two dark houses, and came to an open lot. Carl saw a sight, as if under brilliant sunlight. Two men holding the feet and knees of the clearly white skin of a woman's legs wide apart with a bare, hairy, white buttocks pumping into the junction of the legs. Carl raised his pistol and fired two precisely aimed shots—one into the head of each man holding her knees and feet. As the men fell away, Carl saw the fourth man holding Lisa's hands and head. He aimed and hit the fourth man in the head, knocking him backward away from Lisa. The third man—the violator—rolled off of Lisa to her left and onto his back, struggling to crab crawl away against his partially lowered pants—his glistening erection waving like a metronome with his gyrations. With rage boiling within him, Carl calmly walked up to the man and fired one shot into the man's groin. The burst of blood from his genitals was punctuated with his wild screams in pain. Carl did not hesitate. He fired another round into each knee. The man's motion stopped. His screams continued and could probably be heard by the whole valley in the cold, crisp air. Carl recognized the man flailing on the ground before him—the curly dirty blond hair and beard from the pass. The urge to beat the man to his death welled up within him, but he had a better reaction. Carl fired another round into each shoulder. The metallic slide action of the pistol was almost louder than the muzzle report. The guttural groans of deep pain emanated from the writhing mound of flesh prostrated before him. Without taking his eyes off the immobile writhing man, Carl ejected the pistol's magazine and placed the empty clip in his jacket left pocket. He pulled the first of two spare clips from its holder on his shoulder holster, slammed the clip home, and released the slide to reload the pistol's chamber.

"Dad, that's enough," came Alex's voice from behind him and kneeling to help his naked sister remove her gag and rolled sock from her mouth.

"Oh God, oh God, oh God," Lisa groaned and cried.

"No . . . it's not enough. These shots are survivable," Carl said, waving the pistol at the man's body. "This despicable man," Carl virtually spit, "will not survive. He will die a tortured death." Carl fired two more shots on either side of his lower abdomen. "That's enough!" *If blood loss does not finish him, septic shock will surely do the trick . . . at a slower pace.*

"Finish me, man," the man screamed. He kept screaming the same thing, over and over.

Carl shook his head. It would likely take the man an hour or so to die; he would not see another sunrise. Carl looked around, could not see Lisa's clothes, reengaged the pistol's safety, and returned the PPK to its shoulder holster. He removed the M1911 pistol and placed it in the waistband of his pants at the small of his back, and then removed his warm jacket and put it around Lisa, covering most of her. Carl was fairly certain his initial shots were sufficient, but he felt the need to check for pulses in the other men. They were dead. Rain started to fall, initially at a light, drizzle level.

Carl turned, lifted Lisa into his arms, and began carrying her back to the store. Lisa leaned into her father's shoulder, still sobbing. Alex hesitated, raised his shotgun, as if to deliver the *coup de grâce* shot to the now whimpering man. The mortally wounded man renewed his demands for mercy, when he saw Alex with the shotgun aimed at him.

"Don't do it, Son. He does not deserve mercy," Carl commanded.

Alex lowered the shotgun, and joined his father and sister.

The rain grew harder as Carl carried Lisa into the store. Janet screamed. The whole group was awake and standing. More than a few had weapons ready. Barb and Vicky immediately jumped to the treatment of Lisa. As the two nurses worked on Lisa near the antique stove, Lisa's groans and cries diminished.

"Get those lamps on," commanded Barb. "We need more light."

"Oh, Carl," Janet said softly, "what happened?"

"Those four trailers we saw at the pass attacked her. One was *in flagrante delicto . . . .*"

"What the hell does that mean, Carl?" Janet asked angrily and in a demonstratively heavy tone.

"In the act," Carl answered calmly, trying to reduce the tension. "When I found them, three of them were holding Lisa down, and the leader was violating our daughter. I blew his fucking dick off." Carl growled. ". . . after I killed the three holders. I left the asshole to die a slow, painful death. The others are dead. They must have been watching us and were probably planning to rob us, when Lisa appeared and rape overpowered robbery."

"Oh, dear God, have mercy . . ." Janet said and did not finish. She went and knelt beside their daughter's head to soothe her, while the nurses tended to Lisa's wounds.

"We need clean water and some clean clothes," Barb commanded. "Get us some blankets."

The nurses covered the parts of Lisa's body not being treated. They handed Carl's jacket back to him. The light of the oil lamps enabled a closer examination. Lisa had been beaten. She had serious cuts, abrasions and deep contusions. A couple of cuts might actually need stitches or some binding for proper healing.

"We need to get out of this town," Emily said.

"Easy now," Carl responded in a louder voice to the whole group. "Lisa was attacked by the four trailers that we chased off at the pass. All four of them are dead." Neither Alex nor Janet sought to nitpick with his statement. "They were not town's people. It is raining, now, and we have shelter." Carl checked his wristwatch. "It's only 23:30. We still have the rest of the night ahead of us. I suggest everyone try to get some sleep. We are safe. We will tend to Lisa."

The group slowly began to disperse to the edges of the store. Satisfied the situation was under control, Carl leaned toward Alex. "I'm going back out to check on the bodies of Lisa's assailants. It's raining harder, now. Do you want to go with me?"

"Sure, Dad, I'll go with you."

Carl leaned forward to whisper in Janet's left ear. "I'm going back out to check on things. I'll be right back." Janet nodded her acknowledgment.

After donning his jacket and zipping it all the way up, Carl returned the M1911 to his jacket pocket. He intended to use the louder, bigger pistol, if necessary.

The rain was steady and moderate with almost no wind to drive the droplets. They moved quickly without allowing their night vision to adjust and worrying about the sound of their movement. All four men were exactly where they left them. There were no signs anyone tried to help them. The leader of the four trailers was no longer moving or making a sound. Carl check for a pulse—none. He was dead, as well. He quickly frisked the bodies. Each of the men had concealed pistol and several clips of ammunition as well as folding knives of various sizes. Carl removed the clips, ejected the chambered rounds, left the slides locked open, and tossed the weapons into different areas of the surrounding brush. He did the same with the knives.

Carl nodded toward the store, signaling for them to return. They moved quickly. The warmth of the store's interior felt good. They found what appeared to be a tablecloth for sale in the store to dry off. "Thanks for covering me, Son."

"You're welcome, Dad. I'm sorry I had to see that," Alex added.

"I know." *No one should go out alone*, Carl thought, but chose to wait for that lesson. "Go ahead and try to get some rest. I'll take the remainder of your watch. Team Four has the watch, now."

Alex followed his father's suggestion.

Carl said the same thing to the rest of Team Three—Janet, Larry and Betsy. Nick and Helen recognized the change. They chose to stand outside under the awning of the adjacent store. Carl checked on Janet, Vicky and Barb. They were nearly finished cleaning up and tending to Lisa's wounds. Lisa's eyes were closed. Her breathing was slow and restful. She appeared to be dozing. As the nurses finished, they covered up Lisa, rolled a jacket for a pillow, and extinguished the oil lamps. Carl placed another log in the stove to keep the fire at a modest level and maintain the heat.

—

27

The dull grey light of dawn under the thick overcast and steady rain heralded what would most likely be a whole day delay in their journey to lower elevations and whatever lay ahead. Blessedly, the precipitation remained rain and not sleet, ice or snow at the highest elevation of an incorporated town in North America. The air temperature hovered in the quite chilly region, but above freezing, which meant the group could hit the road as soon as the storm passed.

As members of the group awakened, they respected Lisa, who was still sleeping. The young folks—Melissa, Aaron and Larry—were purposefully quiet and subdued. Even Breckyn seemed to respect her mother's trauma in the middle of the night. Janet indicated she had tended to Breckyn before dawn and helped Lisa feed the baby. Everyone wanted to allow Lisa to sleep as long as she could.

As they ate their morning ration, they decided early to retain at least half the watch going during the day with the sections of each team standing their watch outside under the adjacent store awning for an hour. The 'B' Section stood the second hour, before turning over the watch to the next team.

Lisa woke on her own, shortly after mid-morning. She was quite sore, and rose and moved slowly and awkwardly to sit on one of four stools in the store. Barb checked her wounds and nodded her satisfaction with the early mending. Lisa ate her meal without inquisition. She had only consumed two of her ration allotment when she decided to talk. The group gathered around to listen. She was surprisingly frank. "I had just finished peeing when they jumped me. They had to have been close. I did not hear them. They hit me hard, knocked me down and stunned me. When I regained consciousness, they had stuffed a sock in my mouth, tied a gag to hold it in place, and were dragging me down the street. I tried to scream and fight them. They kept hitting me very hard. I was in and out of consciousness. They stripped me completely naked. It was so cold. They took turns on me. When I was awake, I fought them. They continued to hit me hard and hold me down. All four of them were on me. I think it was the third guy fucking me when Dad got there." Lisa started crying, tears streaming down her face, and her chest heaving with her sobs. She tried to regain control, as she recalled her sense of relief. Janet put her arm around their daughter. Lisa looked at her father, smiled broadly, her lips quivering and tears still streaming down her bruised cheeks. "Dad . . . Dad . . . Dad got them off of me," she sobbed. "He covered me up and carried me back here." Lisa cried hard, now. Janet held her and let her cry. Lisa stood uncomfortably and bounded to Carl's waiting embrace. Father and Daughter remained intertwined. Several times, she looked up to kiss his cheek. As her sobs diminished, she clearly said, "Thank you, Dad, for saving my life." Her chest heaved a couple of more times. "I thought they were going to kill me."

"You are safe now," Carl finally said. *I cannot chastise her for going out alone to relieve herself, at least not yet.* "They will not harm another person." Lisa released her embrace of her father. "Finish your meal. Breckyn will be hungry soon." Lisa smiled at her father, and returned to the stool and her meal.

Barb leaned toward Janet and Carl. "We have no means of preventing pregnancy," she whispered. "She had plenty of semen oozing out of her. Her lactating might protect her, but there is no assurance."

"We know," Janet whispered back. "She was raped previously, when she was just 13 years old. She dealt with that event fairly well, so she'll deal with this one as well. We'll have to deal with whatever comes."

"I'm so sorry."

Both Janet and Carl nodded their heads in recognition.

Again, whispering, Barb asked, "Where is Breckyn's father, if I may ask."

"Unknown, and Lisa wants to keep it that way."

Barb smiled slightly, more like a smirk, and nodded her head once.

Near noon, during a period of lighter rainfall, Dave, who was standing watch outside with Emily, entered the store. "A man is coming," Dave said firmly and returned to his station.

Carl went to the door. A man with a large, black umbrella and no apparent weapons walked toward them. Carl recognized the man they had talked to yesterday afternoon at the blue-grey house. With his hands in his jacket pockets and his right hand grasping the grip of the M1911, just in case, Carl stepped outside to greet the man.

"Good day," the man said.

"Rainy, but yes, and a good day to you, sir," Carl responded. "My turn, how can I help you?"

"You said you were going to leave this morning. I was just checking to see if you did."

"I hope you don't mind . . . we'd like to wait for this storm to pass before we leave."

"It's quite alright for me, for us I imagine. We were awakened last night by very loud screams."

"I'm sorry about that." *I want him to see Lisa.* "Would you care to step inside out of the rain?"

"Sure."

They entered the store. The man collapsed his umbrella before entering. The whole group was standing and facing the door. Carl faced the man after the door was closed. Again, he said, "I'm sorry for the screams. They came from a man who was raping my daughter." Carl turned to find Lisa's eyes and gestured for her to come forward. The cuts, bruises and abrasions on her face alone had darkened and swollen. She was carrying a swaddled and awake Breckyn.

The man audibly gasped. "Dear God above us. I'm so sorry, my dear," the man said to Lisa. She only nodded her acknowledgment. The man looked back to Carl. "What did you do to them?"

"I shot them."

"I heard no shots."

"I shot all four of them, nonetheless." *He does not need to know the weapons we hold.*

"Four?"

"Yeah. The same four I think you, and we, confronted a couple of days ago. I think they were preparing to attack and rob us, when our daughter went outside to urinate."

"Did you kill all of them?"

"Yes."

"Where are they?"

"I left them where they fell in an open lot up this cross street where the crimes occurred."

"Well," the man said and paused to hold Carl's eyes for several seconds, as he considered his words, "thank you for taking care of that menace. I was concerned they might hang around and cause trouble for us. We'll take care of the bodies when the rain stops. We've had to bury others during this situation."

"Thank you. I would not treat the bodies with respect. They deserve none from us."

Breckyn started to wind up. Lisa said, "I need to take care of my daughter." She turned and went to the counter by the stove.

The man asked more about what brought the group to Alma and where they were headed. Carl recounted their history since the event without the gory details as well as their plans in general. The man had not heard the term EMP. It was difficult for him to understand why the power outage happened, but he certainly understood what happened. The possible cause of such a complete electrical failure and its protracted endurance verged upon shocking to the Alma resident. He, as well as the others who remained in Alma, seemed quite content to remain in the town. Satisfied that his town's visitors were temporary and not threatening in any manner, the man said loudly, "Good luck on your journey," as he waved to the whole group. Many waved back and thanked him.

Rain continued all day, varying from light to moderate in intensity. Carl took the time to clean the PPK, after its use last night, as well as to reload the empty magazine and returned it to the shoulder holster holder. He also stepped outside several times during the afternoon to evaluate the clouds and the prospects of them clearing.

After his last check as dusk descended on the valley, Carl delivered his findings. "There is no sign of clearing that I can detect. We may be here another day or so. I still think we will do better dry than if we are all wet."

They all agreed and settled into their evening and nightly routine. The watchstanders detected no activity of any kind other than the rain during the night.

Day 130 (T6) passed inside the empty store with rain varying from light to moderate, and one episode of thunder, lightning and heavy rain. By dawn of Day 131, the rain had stopped and the overcast clouds began to thin and break up. Carl wanted to make sure they were not between bands, which delayed their departure from Alma until around mid-morning. They stopped at the swollen Buckskin Gulch to refill all of their water containers. The watering took just over ten minutes, and they were off headed south on Route 9, leaving Alma behind them.

The group passed the Mile 68.9 sign at 11:15. They were maintaining a good pace, now that they were on comparatively flat ground. Widely scatter homes appeared to be mostly inactive—no smoke plumes, no movement, no signs of human inhabitation. They did see less than a handful of occupied homes at least as indicated by smoke plumes rising from their chimneys. In one expanse of rolling grassland, Mike spotted a large bull elk grazing in the distance. The large animal appeared to be about 500 yards away. The group halted to consider dropping the animal for a fair amount of fresh meat. The general consensus rejected the attempt due to the time it would take to recover, dress and store the meat, plus they currently had sufficient food. They expected there would be other opportunities during their journey.

They passed through a patch of conifer trees that were quite close to the shoulders of the roadway. The Mile 68 sign marked their progress. The Speed Limit 65 sign caused many of them to laugh, as they were moving at a much slower speed. At Mile 67, the road sign said CR 14 and it was the first paved road other than Route 9 they had seen since Hoosier Pass. Just beyond the CR 14 junction, they negotiated a rise in terrain that required three in-harness men on the carts. At the crest of the rise in a curve to the right, a very large rock quarry west of Route 9 provided the first on-road, abandoned vehicle—a comparatively small dump truck on the northbound side of the road. Several members of the team speculated aloud why the dump truck had been on the road in the middle of the night four months ago. Several possibilities were offered, but of course, the answer was lost to the ether. The crest also yielded an expansive view of the valley ahead. As they descended from the crest, they noticed the first signs of a town roughly a mile ahead. They halted short of the town, as they had done before reaching Alma, to consider their actions. The group laid up to rest and drink some water, as they conferred.

Carl checked his wristwatch—13:22—and the sky—clear. "That must be Fairplay," he said, nodding toward the town ahead. "Prudence would dictate we scout the town, as we did at Alma, to avoid or minimize any problems. What say you?"

"We have several more hours of daylight," Pete said, "and, the sky is clear. We've made good progress, so far. I'd recommend we keep our pace up and move through town, and get as far as we can before dusk."

"I agree," Oscar and Hank said in unison.

"I suspect we may find the same result in Fairplay, as we did in Alma," Carl added.

"Mostly deserted," Bert said.

"The residents of Alma," Hank contributed, "at least those who were left, seemed to be largely, if not totally, self-sufficient and stable. There are no guarantees Fairplay will be the same. However, I believe we can deal with any confrontation or threat, which is why I vote for pressing on through the town."

Barb checked on Lisa. They could not hear the words exchanged, but Lisa shook her head.

OK," Carl said. "Are there any objections to moving through the town and going as far as we can before dusk?" Carl looked around the group. More than a few shook their heads in the negative. No one spoke or raised their hand. Carl stepped toward Lisa, and kissed the baby's forehead under the makeshift cap covering her head and safely secured in the harness on Lisa's chest. He whispered in his daughter's left ear, "Do you want to rest and ride on one of the carts?"

Lisa shook her head and whispered back, "No, Dad, I'm good so far."

"OK. Just let me know if walking gets to be too much." Lisa nodded her agreement. Carl turned back to the group. "Then, we are agreed. If everyone is ready, let's blow this pop stand."

They all rose and positioned themselves for movement. The group moved out down the modest downslope. "Don't get too far ahead, Helen," Carl called out to the vanguard group. "Stay close until we are through the town." Helen held up her right hand with her thumb up.

They passed the standard, state, highway sign that read:

FAIRPLAY
CITY LIMIT
ELEV 9963 FT

The group negotiated a descending, S-turn into the town of Fairplay. The town was more conventional than Alma. The streets were paved and had concrete sidewalks. More abandoned vehicles littered parking lots and several automobiles were stranded on Route 9 and a couple of the cross-streets. No human beings were detected and they were nearly through the town before they notice the first of a half dozen smoke plumes. Like Alma, Fairplay appeared to have felt the full effects of the electrical failure crisis. Commercial establishments lined both sides of Route 9, and none of them appeared to have been molested, as they had seen in Breckenridge. As Route 9 curved left, the road sign indicated:

◄   DENVER
SALIDA   ►
HARTSEL   ►

Just beyond that road sign, conventional signs alerted travelers that the intersection of Route 9 and US-285 was directly ahead. Route 9 joined the southbound US-285. A large, empty shopping center was directly across the intersection. Only one abandoned automobile occupied the large parking lot. In normal times, modern traffic lights controlled the intersection, but like everything else, the lights were dead. *No one sought to take the northbound direction.* As Route 9 crossed the Middle Fork South Platte River, the sign declared:

HARTSEL   18
BUENA VISTA   37
SALIDA   59

The river was flowing heavily and swiftly, but not broaching flood stage. The large overhead electronic traffic sign was stone cold. They were soon through town and back into open country in just under 35 minutes. Carl looked around the entire scene. The high mountains were now distantly behind them and the hills of various sizes poked up on both flanks and ahead of them. Carl noticed the vanguard group turn and walk backward, seeking a signal. Fifteen minutes later, they reached the sign that indicated:

▲   BUENA VISTA
◀   HARTSEL

They quickly approached the junction where Route 9 split off, heading southeast, while US-285 continued south. Carl felt no reason to consult the group, since they were still moving to plan agreed to weeks ago. Carl signaled for the vanguard group to take the left fork, which they did smoothly. As the group approached the junction, a large, south-facing, hand-painted sign advertised South Park City—a Restored 1880s Town in Fairplay. *In normal times, it would have been interesting to visit such an old west restored town, but these are not normal times.* The group followed the point team onto Route 9. The terrain continued to flatten out and the hills shrank. The barbed wire fences on both sides of the roadway suggested the associated fenced grassland was pasture for cattle or sheep. They passed the small, rectangular, Mile 63 sign—*good progress.* The whole group continued to move well over the nearly flat ground. The point group stayed a half-mile ahead of the main group. They passed another abandoned automobile in the northbound lane. At the Mile 62 sign, Carl checked his wristwatch. They were making about a mile every 30 minutes—not fast but steady.

Just past the MILE 60 sign, they passed from the east to the west side of the Platte River, and they went up a little incline to skirt the shoulder of a substantial hill. The idyllic scene of the river snaking through the green flat of the valley could be a postcard home. Healthy trees sporadically lined both banks of the river. Two nice ranch homes stood back from the river a mile apart, and both had plumes of smoke rising from two chimneys each. Several hundred yards south of the MILE 58 sign, another large, rectangular, log gateway stood on the east side of the road and a large sign hung from the crosspiece with two-foot high letters proclaiming the Platte Ranch. Carl removed the M1A rifle from his shoulder and cradled the weapon in his left arm with his right hand on the grip and his right thumb on the safety. Trees were now right up to the shoulder of both sides of the road. His military training made him extra cautious. *I don't like this . . . too close.* The closed in section did not last long, and they were back out in the open grassland. Carl looked back, saw Hank doing the same, relaxed a little, and returned the rifle sling to his right shoulder. As they continued south, the hills to the west retreated farther into the distance with broader expanses of flat grassland. The sun was getting low on the western horizon when they passed MILE 56. As the mountains retreated, so did the trees of the forests.

Carl picked up his pace to join Pete at the head of the main group. "It will be dusk soon, and we are running out of trees and likely sources of firewood. I think it might be easier, rather than tapping into our firewood reserve, to hold up back near that Redhill Forest development sign and the MILE 56 marker."

"Agreed."

Pete and Carl both signaled for the group to halt, which they did. Carl signaled for the vanguard team to come back. It took a minute to catch their attention, but the point team was soon headed back to them. The whole group gathered up.

Carl did not wait for Helen, Holly and Alex to arrive. "Looks like we are running out of trees, and as a consequence, we are losing our source of firewood. I'd recommend we backtrack a little to stop for the night, so we do not have to tap our firewood reserve." The point group arrived. Carl looked at all three of them. "Did y'all see trees ahead?"

"No," answered Helen. "There are a few, but no forests . . . mostly open grassland ahead."

"If there are no objections, let's move back about a quarter of a mile to the MILE 56 marker. There are more trees close by that location. We need to set camp before we lose the sun's warmth and light." No one objected. "I'm sorry we have to backtrack over ground we've covered, but we should be better off."

No one grumbled or complained. They turned the carts around and Hank, Janet and Melissa led the group back to the north. They reached the MILE 56 marker and the small Redhill Forest development sign. The dirt and gravel access road branched off to the right and rose over the shoulder of a nearby hill. Rather than try to pull the cart up the slope, over the rough ground and closer to the trees, they pulled the carts to the edge of the pavement and away from the grass. *No need to risk starting a brush fire.* All of the boys left their shoulder firearms and headed up the access road. Carl and Hank went with them as guards, just in case. The risk was low, but better to be prepared. The ladies and remainder of the men set to the task of setting up camp for the night. It did not take long to begin finding dry wood, big and small, among the trees. They did not have to venture far. By the time, Hank, Carl and the last of the collectors headed back to the group's encampment location, a good fire was already blazing away. *This group is certainly working well together without complaint or any discernible friction.* They were ready for the cold of the night when they consumed their evening rations and water. While they ate, the small talk seemed to be surprisingly lighthearted and positive, almost euphoric or joyous at their accomplishment, despite the journey still ahead of them.

"We did well today," Vicky said.

"Yes, we did," said Carl. "By my calculation, we moved better than 15 miles today . . . far better than any of our estimates. I figure we are back to two days ahead of plan, even after losing the rainy day yesterday and the late start this morning."

"It's amazing we have not seen more people," Bert observed.

"Everything is pretty spread out up here . . . not many people to start with," Pete added.

"We did see some smoke plumes, though," said Hank.

While they still had some twilight in addition to the firelight, Carl retrieved the maps and planning documents. They were off the topographic map they had, so it was of no value. Carl confirmed his memory assessment. They were indeed back to two days ahead of plan. Carl, Pete, Hank, Bert and Oscar conferred over the roadmap and milestone calculations.

"We should do better tomorrow with an earlier start," Carl said. "If we continue to hold our pace, we'll reach our first decision point at Hartsel tomorrow around mid-day."

"We're doing much better than I expected," Bert contributed. "The plan is looking better to me."

"Good," continued Carl. "I'm glad everyone is feeling better with this trek. No need to decide tonight. I will only ask everyone to consider their perspective, opinions, wants and needs, so we can make a quick, good decision for each of us at Hartsel."

"Agreed," everyone around the map offered in a staccato manner.

"OK," Carl concluded and began folding up the map. Let's set the watch for the night with the same process we used at Hoosier Pass, and try to get a good night's rest." Carl returned the papers to their safe, dry place on Cart One.

They scattered to find their spot for the night. They gradually found sleep at their own pace.

Carl saw that Lisa was finishing her feeding of Breckyn. He sat next to her. "How are you feeling, sweetie?"

"I'm pretty sore, Dad, but surprisingly feeling better. Walking has helped work out some of the kinks."

"Excellent. I am still very concerned about your health and stamina." Carl looked into Lisa's blue eyes. "No one will object, if you need to rest and ride for a bit. If you ever feel the need for a break, please just signal me. I'll take care of things from there."

"Thanks Dad. Now, I'd better get in the tent and settle Breckyn before it fills up."

Carl chuckled and nodded his head. "Good night, sweetie. I love you."

"I love you, Dad."

Carl waited for Lisa to disappear into the tent. He stood, found Nick, who was already pacing with the Mossberg Tactical shotgun cradled in his left arm, as if he was standing guard duty. Darkness had descended on the group's encampment. Carl scanned the entire vista—360 degrees. No other sources of light could be seen anywhere within the visible scene.

Nick joined his father standing on the other side of the road away from the fire. "You did good, Dad."

I'm not sure what that's for. "Thanks Son."

They stepped through each watch period and kept the fire at a comparatively high burn for the heat all night. The night passed calmly, smoothly and in fairly good fashion, as the day's exertion enabled their restful sleep.

Day 132 (T8) began before sunrise. They ate, tended their personal needs, packed up, extinguished the fire, and headed south on Route 9 before the end of morning twilight.

They reached the bridge over the Middle Fork South Platte River at the MILE 55 marker. They stopped to quickly top off their water supply, and then pressed on. Carl watched Alex go to a pole on the east side of the roadway. It appeared to be a solar cell-powered call box. He held the handset to his ear and replaced it. Alex looked back and shook his head in the negative. The main group reached the pole a few minutes later. It was indeed a roadside call box. A disused barn still stood on the right, and a particularly odd, kludged up combination of clapboard and corrugated tin buildings inside a wood slat perimeter fence sat across the road from the old barn. *I guess this is what was supposed to be Garo.* An old, green, '65 Pontiac GTO with a For Sale sign in the front windshield sat at what appeared to be the entrance to the strange compound. Alex checked the vehicle and again shook his head to signal the car was dead.

Five miles south on Route 9 and several hours after beginning the next leg of their journey, the vanguard team pointed to their right. Carl and Pete could not see what they were pointing at, but the three-member point team did not stop, so it was probably not that important. *I don't see any wildlife or domesticated animals in the wide, expansive, fenced grassland to the west.* Several minutes later, they reached the object to which the vanguard team had pointed. A crude, hand-lettered sign: HORSE RIDES AHEAD, along with a telephone number that was now worthless. Beyond the sign, perhaps a quarter of a mile, lay a half dozen scattered buildings of what appeared to be a well-kept range home and support facilities. The smoke plume rising from one of the large buildings near a solo, tall, conifer tree indicated human occupancy. Carl picked up his pace to join Pete at the head of the main group.

"Interesting sign," Pete said, as Carl came alongside, and they continued to walk.

"A horse would be nice," Carl commented.

"You want to stop to see what we can negotiate?"

"It might be worth a shot. They might have a horse-drawn wagon that could replace the carts and maybe even allow the ladies to ride."

"Good point. Let's stop at the ranch for a rest break, while we see what we can figure out."

The horse crossing caution road sign complemented the advertising sign. When Carl noticed Holly look around behind them, he signaled for them to come back to the main group. They stopped at a large, sawn log, rectangular gateway arch through the barbed wire fence along the roadway. *They went to a lot of effort and spent a lot of money for that portal in their fence.*

When the point team arrived, the group gathered around Pete and Carl. "Y'all may have noticed the sign a quarter mile back," Carl began. "Pete and I think it would be worth an attempt to see if we could procure a horse and maybe a wagon, to make our journey a little easier." There was unanimous, enthusiastic agreement with the potential. "Since we have Coloradans in our grand group, does anyone know these folks perchance?" Several laughed. No one responded in the affirmative. "OK. Let's take a rest break, while Pete and I see what we can determine here." They began to sit where they had stood and discussed the possibilities.

Pete and Carl headed through the gateway. There was no actual gate. Carl was somewhat surprised there were no cattle grates to discourage cattle, horses or any domesticated mammals from leaving the property. The first house on the right, the one with the smoke plume rising from its singular chimney, turned out to be a rather modest dwelling. The two men kept their long guns shouldered and their pistols concealed in an effort to appear the least threatening possible. Before they reached the steps to the front porch, a large middle-aged man about Carl's age stepped outside and closed the front door behind him. His bright red and black, checkered, flannel shirt with rolled up sleeves, well worn Levis, and western boots complete with shiny sliver spurs gave him a very rugged appearance. Yet, it was the black, pump, 12-gauge shotgun held in a ready position that was the most formidable. The two visitors stopped short. Carl and then Pete raised their hands to head height, palms out to show a non-threatening stance.

"There is nothing for you here," the man said in a deep, stern voice.

"We saw a sign just north of your ranch advertising horse rides," Carl said.

"So," the man responded. "We should have taken that sign down months ago."

Carl felt the need to explain. "We left Breckenridge over a week ago, walking out to Cañon City or Pueblo. A horse and wagon, if you have one you can spare, would make our journey less arduous."

"I'm sure it would. We do not have any spare horses or wagons," the man said without moving his shotgun. "Even if we did, you can't afford it."

"We never know unless we try," Pete added.

"Five thousand dollars."

Carl smiled. *That is outright circumstantial price gouging.* "We don't have anywhere near that amount of cash."

"As I said, you can't afford it."

"How about barter?" Pete suggested.

"You have nothing on those stocking carts of yours worth anywhere near that amount, either."

"Very well, then. You clearly do not want to help us." The man nodded his head. "May I ask you a few informational questions?"

"Depends on what your questions are?"

"Have you seen other people walking out of the mountains?"

"Yes."

"How long ago and how many?"

"Most tried months ago. There was still snow on the ground. I have no idea how many. My guess, since the electrical failure . . . perhaps a couple of hundred over the last four months. You're the first we've seen pass in more than two weeks."

"Any vehicles?"

"Not a one. None of ours, from cars to tractors, have even a spark."

"Have you heard anything about what happened last December . . . the electrical failure, as you call it?" Carl asked with his hands still held up.

"No, not a word . . . no radio, no telephone, no television . . . nothing. Now, let me ask you, do you know?"

"No," Carl said. *No need to attempt an explanation of my hypothesis.*

"Anything else?"

"No sir. We'll be on our way. Thank you for your time." The man simply nodded his head and did not move other than to track them with the muzzle of his shotgun as they departed.

The group stood as Pete and Carl approached. Carl reported, "No deal. We need to get going."

No one objected or queried Pete or Carl. They formed up and headed off down the road. An hour later, they reached the T-junction of Route 9 and US-24. The standard road sign prior to the intersection indicated:

◀   COLO SPGS
◀   CAÑON CITY
BUENA VISTA   ▶

They turned left continuing on Route 9 and US-24 East. The town of Hartsel lay just ahead. The map identified the meandering stream on the north side of the road as yet another branch of the Middle Fork South Platte River. Carl smiled. *There are a lot of branches of the same river.* Another, well done, custom sign on the westbound side of the road advertised South Park City, near Fairplay. They walked through an excavated gap in a small hill and the small town of Hartsel appeared ahead of them. A small sign proclaimed Hartsel and just beyond was a MILE 239 marker for US-24, which apparently took precedent. The Badger Basin convenience store and gas station appeared closed and vacant. No one made a gesture to stop and search the building. They kept moving. They were all looking for signs of human habitation. They saw no movement of any kind, and more significantly, no smoke plumes appeared in the small town. It took just a few minutes to pass through Hartsel. The signage indicated the east junction of Route 9 and US-24 was just ahead, although they did not need the signs to recognize the fact. A direction sign indicated:

COLORADO SPGS   ▲
CAÑON CITY   ▶

This is as good a point as any for their first decision milestone. Carl signaled a halt. He checked his watch—11:55. *We continue to make good time.* They waited for the point group to rejoin them.

Carl opened the discussion. "As we agreed during our planning stage, we agreed this point on our journey would be a decision point for those families that live in or near Denver. Let's take the time to make sure we get this correct for each family. I will say with enthusiasm that y'all are welcome to confer privately, so that you can have the frank discussions necessary to arrive at the best decision for your family. Our family," he said, nodding his head to Janet, "will continue on to Cañon City, which is probably two or three days ahead down Route 9."

They split into their family units, each walking off about 10 yards in different directions. The Armstrongs stayed with the Parks at the carts.

"We had decided," said George, "before that we will stay with you and the agreed to plan."

Carl smiled and nodded his head. He looked to each member of his family and Dave. "I should not have presumed your wishes. So, to be thorough and proper, do each of you want to press on to Cañon City?"

"Yes, Dad," Alex said, as if it had been a silly question. They all agreed. Carl sat down. The pavement was pleasantly warm in the mid-day sun. He retrieved one of his water bottles and took a good drink. The Higgins were the first to return. Carl stood.

"We're sticking to the plan," Pete announced.

A couple of minutes later, the Johnsons rejoined. "We will stay with the group."

"That is what we decided as well," Barb added.

Roughly five minutes after the Johnsons, the Manson family returned and confirmed their desire to stay with the group and the plan.

While they waited for the Mossman's decision, Carl moved to and sat next to Lisa. "How are you feeling?"

"I'm still sore, Dad, but moving helps."

"Good. I think we'll get moving soon. Don't forget you can ride anytime you wish, not just for Breckyn."

"I know, Dad." Lisa paused, and then kissed him on the cheek. "You may not have noticed, but I've jumped on the cart at least a couple of times each day to change Breckyn and feed her, while we continued to move."

Carl chuckled. "Yeah, you're right. I haven't noticed. I guess I've been more focused on what is beyond our group. I don't want us to be surprised."

"And, thank you for that."

"How is Breckyn . . . ," Carl paused when he noticed the Mossman's huddle breaking up for the return with their decision, "doing on the journey?"

"She is a perfect sweetheart. It's like she knows how important this is."

Carl stood, kissed his daughter on the forehead, and then returned to his center position.

Hank looked to the whole group before he spoke. "We want to go home." Several people in the group gasped, like something tragic just happened. "Heading back from here shortens the distance to home. However," he paused to gesture to Betsy, Helen and Holly, "we do not want to go alone. So, what has everyone else decided?"

Carl looked at Pete and nodded to him. "We're staying," Pete said.

"As are we," added Vicky

"And us," Oscar and Emily said in unison.

Carl looked at George and Anne. "We see no other options for Anne and me," George added.

Hank looked to his wife and two daughters. All three nodded their heads. "Then, we are staying as well."

"Very well then," Carl said matter-of-factly. "We are decided. Now, it is after noon. We have a choice. We can probably find shelter here. The town appears to be abandoned. Or, we can get another seven or eight miles down the road." Everyone appeared to respond in different manners, but the consensus was to move on. "Just to be sure, any objections to continuing?" No one took the opportunity to object. Carl looked to Helen, Holly and Alex. "This is going to be pretty empty country. When we get close to sunset, look for ample trees for firewood and our encampment." All three nodded. "OK then, let's move out."

The point team began their advance as the rest of the group stood and formed up. Fifteen yards later, they turned right, heading southeast down Route 9.

Just after they continued on a freshly paved section of Route 9, the road sign said:

CAÑON CITY   58

Carl did a quick mental calculation. *The distance would take them roughly 30 hours, so two plus more days, without any problems en route.* Shortly thereafter, they passed over whatever branch it was of the Middle Fork South Platte River. The road was straight as an arrow. They saw their first cattle grazing in the grassland beyond a well-maintained, barbed wire fence. The thought of roasted fresh beef made Carl salivate and induced him to swallow several times, but they walked on and the temptation passed. The next mile marker they came to was MILE 46. Alex checked another roadside call box and signaled that it was dead as well. The barbed wire fence and paucity of trees through these high grasslands did not bode well for a firewood supply at their next encampment. As the sun approached the western horizon, the temptation to stop began to grow at a modest size clump of conifer trees ahead just for firewood. As they reached the south side of that group of trees, Carl noticed more trees, farther back from the roadway, but still within reach, down the road. They kept going. Carl noticed there was not a single building of any kind within sight. *Not many people up here. Heck, not many cows either, but the fences on grasslands mean they are out there somewhere.* The half dozen, left arrow, yellow caution road signs directly ahead marked the first turn in the roadway in the last bunch of miles since the Hartsel junction. The first buildings, crude as they were, appeared well back from the road and beyond the road signs. At the MILE 39 marker, they passed the culvert for a dry streambed, *unusual for this time of year*. They also added two people in harness on the carts for an increase in grade. Fortunately, the perfect road surface made the haulage fairly easy. The point team had stopped at what appeared to be the crest ahead. As the main group neared them, they turned and continued ahead for about a quarter of a mile to a dirt road and metal gate through the barbed wire fence. There were plenty of trees close by, although certainly not a dense forest.

"The MILE 38 marker is just up ahead," Alex announced, as they stopped.

"Good choice for our night's encampment," Pete declared.

They were well into twilight when they completed their set up for the night and the fire was going. *It was another good day—18 miles today—pretty impressive for a group like this.* The absolutely cloudless sky would treat them to a brilliant full moon on the last day of April.

—

28

May Day began as Day 133 of the electrical crisis and the 9th day of their trek out of the Rocky Mountains. The chilly air before dawn made initial movement a little creaky, but the still blazing fire's warmth soothed the stiff muscles and joints. Again, they prepared for the day's movement during morning twilight and hit the road before dawn. The sky looked like they would enjoy another near perfect day for their walk through the Colorado countryside.

They were still moving upslope when they passed the MILE 38 marker. They began with three people in harness. The roadway upslope continued for several miles before they reached the summit of the high ground they were passing over. Roughly a half of a mile beyond the MILE 36 marker, they reached the apparent summit, which was actually a cut in the terrain, and they could see well down the road and switched to restraint of the carts rather than pulling them. They appeared to be on some sort of high plateau with ups and downs, without a substantive downturn. Just sprouting stands of Aspen trees appeared among the patches of conifers. Further on down the road, an official Pike National Forest sign indicated they were passing into a federal land management area, and as such, probably with a paucity of habitation. After eight miles, according to the road markers, they began what appeared to be a long descent off the plateau. Beyond the leaving Pike National Forest sign, the group came across another log, gateway arch set back 40 yards or so from Route 9. The cut, wood, slab sign said Aspen Creek Ranch. A nice, well-kept, two-story, white siding house had a smoke plume rising from the chimney. The isolated location and the closed, metallic gate across the arch made the effort to query the owners (or occupants) less attractive. They continued southeast on Route 9. Another dry streambed paralleled the roadway. None of them had seen a title sign, and Carl was unwilling to stop and check the map. The name of the geologic feature simply did not matter beyond a potential location marker. Restraining the carts against the pull of gravity confirmed their protracted descent.

At MILE 27, a paved turnout offered a four-car-length space and a tempting respite, but the group wanted to press on. The sun was near local zenith, which meant they had plenty of daylight and great weather to move along on their journey. *Another day of better than planned movement.* The roadway continued its steady downslope grade, and eventually descended through a natural cut made by the deepening streambed just west of the road. Around a fairly tight left curve, they came upon a rather unusual sight. They first noticed what appeared to be a log-faced, in-ground shelter. They could not see a door on the clearly defined doorway, nor could they see a path to or from the doorway. It appeared to be a half-sized doorway at that. Grass grew up on top of and all around the assembled logs. Roughly 50 yards beyond the dugout, they came upon an assembled, rough-hewn, beam gateway arch. This particular arch was more notable because of the metal plate straps holding the beams in gable roof joist form cross piece between two vertical beams. The support beams were set into nicely done, five-foot high, flared, square, masonry pedestals. The wrought iron, or what appeared to be wrought iron, arched gate blocked the gateway. The red rock gravel drive looped around some trees and rejoined the road through a simple, green metal gate between two large log posts. They could not see any dwelling other than the dugout, but it was by far the most finished looking gateway arch they had seen on the entire journey so far. They did not stop to explore further. The MILE 26 marker was 70 yards beyond the fancy gateway arch. *Whatever the Guffey turn off might be should be close . . . around here somewhere.*

At the MILE 23 marker, a modest, faux log cabin home stood out as if it had just been finished. The cabin had a green, gabled roof, apparently to give the roof a copper patina appearance that looked brand new—fresh and not weathered. The grass around the structure meant that it had been there for more than one growing season. What was once a good sized recreational vehicle, a fifth-wheel trailer, and a half dozen other buildings from new to fairly old stood to the south of the nice home with other abandoned vehicles and makeshift corrals. The home sat in shadow and on a good high, tree-covered hill. They saw no signs of human habitation. The point team had to stopped to inquire whether anyone was ready to stop for the night. With another couple of hours of sunlight available, the group wanted to get another few miles behind them, so they continued walking.

A clearly man-made, rectangular pond sat on the west side of a barbed wire fence. The pond was about half full from the band of bare ground three feet or so above the water level and the straight edge of the surrounding grass. A blue road sign adjacent to the pond declared Rita's Place Café & Caldera Gallery to the left (east). *Caldera? I had no idea there were ancient volcanic calderas in this area.* Thirty yards farther on, the green road sign indicated:

◀   **GUFFEY**

CAÑON CITY   ▶

The two-lane, triangular intersection suggests Guffey may be a growing community. No one expressed any curiosity, and Carl kept his observatory thought to himself. An occupied home and garage out-building stood on the east side of the intersection. A man carrying a shotgun appeared at the door and watched. He did not wave or take any action other than to watch the group passing south down Route 9. As the modest valley opening, where the intersection lay, began narrowing down to a sharp cut, and they passed the MILE 21 marker. The valley along the dry streambed was fully in shadow and noticeably cooler. The road made a wide left curve and the valley began to widen. The roadway ahead soon transitioned to a steady rise up the shoulder of a mountain on the east side of the little valley toward a modest pass. They had to put four people in harness to haul the carts up the grade. Halfway up the hill to the pass, Carl thought, *we should have stopped at Guffey. We've had a good, long day, and this exertion is not what we need at the end of a good day. The sunlight on the mountaintops seems to be keeping everyone moving. But then, a man at his front door with a shotgun was not a welcoming sign.* The steep downgrade caution sign signaled what lay ahead, as they approached the crest of the pass. A quarter of a mile beyond the MILE 19 marker, the sun was already below the mountain ridgeline to the west. Ample trees stood on both sides of the road. The point team stood at a dirt road that broke the barbed wire fence on the east side of the road and only a simple chain blocked the road.

"This looks like it might make a good campsite," Helen announced, as the main group arrived.

"We've come nearly 20 miles today. Our best day performance so far," Carl added. "I agree with Helen. We've probably got another hour or so of daylight, but the shadows suggest it is going to darken fast. I'd recommend we set camp and get a good fire going."

"Agreed," a number of them contributed.

No one waited for further discussion. They were getting better at establishing camp as well. The fire was in full bloom in short order. They ate their evening ration with some frivolity, as the group sensed their journey was nearing an end . . . at least with respect to the primary objective.

Carl remained somber and distant. *This campsite is too close to the trees, too vulnerable.* As twilight disappeared over the tight, little valley and the vast array of stars began to pop out, they set the watch for the night. Carl tried to sleep, but found it virtually impossible. He was too uneasy about the group's location. Carl and Nick stood their watch period, but Carl kept his unease to himself. The dark of the forest all around them made the brilliance of the stars above them stand out all the more brightly.

Despite Carl's disturbed state of mine and lack of sleep, he eagerly welcomed the dawn. He felt a lot better when sunlight illuminated the western peaks, and they moved out to begin their Day 134 (T10) leg of their odyssey.

Straight away, they had a climb to complete. *Thank goodness my paranoia was not realized.* A comparatively large, asphalt-paved, turnout marked the crest of the rise. The sun had not yet broken the local eastern horizon, but sunrise was approaching, and the green road sign proclaimed their passage into Fremont County. A half-mile beyond the MILE 18 sign, they came upon an orange alert sign that read: Martin Marietta Thanks You, along with a 10-digit telephone number. *Thanks us for what? I can't imagine what a large defense contractor would be doing out in this sparsely populated part of the country—very odd.* The road traversed a long, narrow valley. A few dwellings were seen, but appeared to be devoid of human activity. Searching them was not worth the time. They kept moving. The sun finally rose above the eastern horizon and the warmth felt good. As they passed a small, man-made, pond or reservoir, no one voiced any urge to top off their water, which probably meant they would have additional opportunities ahead. The valley was widening, the grade decreasing and the hills becoming smaller as they pressed on at a good pace. The deer crossing caution sign added a positive sense to their progress. *Fresh meat would be a welcome change.* More buildings came into view, two smoke plumes rose from a modest home just south of the old, corrugated tin, covered barn and horse stalls. The point team must have piqued the attention of the occupants, since a man younger than Carl stood on the other side of a barbed wire fence, holding a shotgun in one hand.

"Where ya comin' from?" the man asked.

"We left Breckenridge a week and a half ago," Pete answered in a strong voice.

"Where ya headed?"

"Cañon City."

"Been there," the man volunteered. "More people there. We came back up here. That's quite a walk. Dedication."

"True. Why did y'all come back up here?" Pete asked.

"Nothing better there, and this is home."

"Well, we'll give it a try, but our homes are all beyond Cañon City and Pueblo."

"Good luck."

"Thanks. When did you return here?" Pete had now stopped, facing the man, as the group continued to walk.

"Two months ago. Snow still on the ground."

"Anything we should know?" Pete asked the man, from behind Carl now.

"Yes. Be really careful about three miles east beyond the US-50 junction. Bad people in that area. Travelers have had trouble."

"You made it through twice."

"Yes, we did, but others did not."

"Thank you for the warning. Have a great day. Good luck to you."

"Thank you, sir."

Pete caught up to Carl and walked alongside Carl without speaking, until they were clearly beyond earshot about a quarter of a mile down the road. "Did you hear the last part?"

"Yes. We probably should pull up to discuss our plan of action, to cross that area and to handle any bad guys."

"Good." Pete took off jogging past his formation position and reached the vanguard group, presumably to inform them of the halt guidance. As they continued their advance, Pete stood on the side of the road until he took up his assigned position.

▲ CAÑON CITY   17
◄ CRIPPLE CREEK   35

The conventional street sign at the paved T-intersection indicated the road was High Park Road and CR11 that passed over a bridge with a wider, but still dry streambed. The rising roadway seemed odd with a caution sign showing a downslope and the words "Trucks Use Lower Gear." They were still on the upslope portion of the road. The road made a 90-degree right turn and began to descend. The grade was steeper than they had seen beyond Hoosier Pass. They added a third person to aid restraint of the carts. The view of the mountains ahead of them was spectacular. The sky remained crystal clear with only a few, small, fair-weather, cumulus clouds behind them to the east. The downgrade continued for nearly three miles and eventually decreased in a picturesque mountain valley. More occupied homes dotted the valley. They passed under a tall, three-strand, high-tension power line that seemed like an artifact of the distant past. The large, log, gateway arch and sign said Lowry Ranch. The dirt road led off to a good size ranch home more than a mile away across the valley. Three smoke plumes were easily seen rising from the dwelling. *Unoccupied homes are the exception down here.* They were definitely at lower elevation. The grass was growing well and wildflowers were blooming all around them. The air smells fresh and alive with spring. The early afternoon sun told them they were now moving east-southeast. The MILE 4 marker told them they had come nearly 15 miles on Day T10 with several hours more daylight still with them. The road marker also told them they were about four miles from the US-50 junction. The MILE 1 marker instigated some joking and laughter among the group, as if they had reached the end of their journey. As they crossed a small rise and saw the US-50 T-intersection for the first time, the road sign indicated:

◀   PUEBLO

SALIDA   ▶

The point team waited at the intersection, as they had been instructed. They gathered up as they had done so many times. Everyone drank some water. Carl could see the road sign on the eastside of US-50, just beyond the intersection.

CAÑON CITY   10
PUEBLO   49

Carl turned to the group. "I do not know whether everyone heard the exchange between Pete and the man past the MILE 18 marker. Did anyone not hear it?" Helen, Holly and Alex raised their hands. "Oh yeah, sorry, y'all were out ahead of us. In summary, he indicated his family had gone to Cañon City a few months ago and returned to their home. He warned us there are potentially bad people about three miles east of here . . . on our way to Cañon City." Carl paused to allow for questions. No one spoke. "We've come 19 miles today—already a good productive journey. We have 10 miles to go," he said, pointing to his left, "according to the road sign. Also, I think Cañon City is on the other side of the second hill," Carl pointing to the southeast with the hills ahead of them illuminated by the afternoon sun behind them. "We could probably make it to Cañon City by midnight, if we kept going into the night."

"Probably not a good idea to head into a danger zone when we are tired," Hank said.

"There is that," Carl responded. "We can try to see if there is a way around that area. I don't know."

"I imagine none of us knows," Hank continued. "Several of us have driven this road, but I doubt any of us has ventured off US-50 on the back roads."

Carl nodded his head. "We have several options. One, we can press on. We will probably reach the danger area about dusk. That could give us some advantage, but as Hank indicated, we're all tired, for that action. Option two, we can encamp here . . . or at the Royal View Campground," Carl said, pointing at the large sign 20 yards to the east. "Or, we can hold up a little closer to the danger area. Anyway, there are various combinations of stopping short and dealing with any risk area tomorrow when we are fresh. Option three, from my perspective, is to make the transit during the night. We are just past the full moon, and we should have good moonlight around midnight for a few hours. So, what do y'all think?"

Everyone tried to speak at the same time. Carl tried to referee. It took about 15 minutes for a consensus to coalesce. They would camp here and head out in the morning, placing them at the risk area early to mid-morning, and potentially to Cañon City by early afternoon. Interesting enough, many voiced concerns about having time to find a place to stay at their destination. Cañon City would be the largest community they had seen in four months.

The shoulder of the road at the northeast corner of the intersection gave them the best flat ground, and there was a good stand of trees for firewood across the highway. With the decision, the whole group set to their well-rehearsed tasks. The fire was going well and they were eating their evening rations, when they spoke, again.

"We're almost there," observed Vicky.

"Yep," added Bert.

"But, that is just the end of the beginning," Pete felt compelled to add. "Most of us need to move on, to reach our homes."

"Some of us can't reach our homes," George added.

"Once we get to Cañon City, we should probably take a good rest," Pete said, "assuming we can find decent lodging, and assess whatever the situation is that we can learn, before deciding what to do."

"Each family may want something different," Hank said.

"And," Pete said with an air of authority, "we agreed that Cañon City was that decision point. But . . . ," he felt the need to add, "we have to get there first." The sun set behind the western mountains. "It's going to be dark soon. I suggest we set the watch and get as much sleep as we can. I suspect tomorrow is going to be a busy day."

Carl felt the urge to say, "I might add a little cultural note, the Arkansas River, or as we pronounce it in Kansas—the Ar-Kansas River," several people giggled, "and the famous Royal Gorge Bridge is just off to the south a short distance. The suspension bridge stands almost one thousand feet above the river."

"Are you suggesting we take a tourist excursion?" Bert asked with a humorous tone. Many laughed.

"No. We have enough to worry about. Royal Gorge is just a very impressive geological feature that is very close. I've never actually crossed the gorge on the bridge."

"It's a bridge over a deep canyon," Hank said. More laughter.

Carl let the conversation fade to memory. Folks began to move to their chosen spots for the night. They agreed to allow people to sleep without interference, except for the watchstanders, until they woke up or dawn came, whichever occurred first.

During the darkness, before moonrise, spots of light were seen or reflected to their east. It was black to the west. While there was evidence of people, they had not seen any humans, or animals, since they stopped, or during the night.

Twilight came after a quiet and uneventful night. As the sky lightened, Carl took a quick assessment of the weather and felt confident the group would enjoy yet another near perfect day on what they hoped was the last day of their joint undertaking. They tended to their personal needs to move, an hour before sunrise. Carl cautioned the point team to not get too far ahead and keep a keen eye out for human activity as well as keep track of the main group as they moved. He also reminded everyone that the risky area they had been warned about was roughly three miles ahead. They would reach the area about an hour after sunrise and the sun would be in their face.

As they moved east on US-50, Carl noticed the absence of snowplow poles on the edges of the road. *I guess snow is not as much of a problem down here as it is in the mountains.* Carl turned 360 degrees as they walked. The high mountains were clearly behind them, and the sun had begun to illuminate those distant western peaks. A half-mile down the road, a comparatively large sign on the south side of the road identified The Cactus Rose, which looked like it was a five-room motel with a gravel drive and parking area. One of the room doors was open; the others were closed. A separate residence stood just to the east. They appeared to be part of the same business, since they had identical construction appearance. The motel appeared to be a bit seedy, but it might have been better than the hard ground. That was a potential they would likely never realize.

Just beyond the motel, the green road sign said Royal Gorge ½ mile. Their first milestone marker on US-50 said, MILE 270. When they reached the Royal Gorge Road intersection, tourist shops of various sorts occupied both sides of the road. More homes appeared. This was definitely a more populated region than they were used to over the last 10 days, but still no people. The next marker they saw was MILE 272 after a protracted downhill road grade had begun.

The stench of death hit them first. As the road made a descending right turn toward the south, perhaps half dozen homes were widely scattered in the hills to the northeast. *This is probably the danger area the man in the mountains yesterday morning told us about. This is a near perfect kill zone.* Our only choices are to forge ahead under fire, try to withdraw back up the hill, or engage in a shootout. Carl noted the MILE 273 marker on the eastbound side of the road. He kept scanning everything around them on both sides of the road, looking for the slightest clue of something untoward. So far so good.

Carl moved closer to the north side guardrail. Litter hung in bushes and down the slope on the grass. He saw at least two bodies. Carl had the big M1A off his shoulder in his hands with the safety off. What looked like bloodstains could be seen on the asphalt. He scanned the houses and vegetation.

Carl luckily was looking at one of the houses and saw what appeared like a flash. Larry spun and went down. The shot report came a second later. The sniper shot came from the upper right window of the short second story of a white-sided house with a dark shingled roof.

"Take cover," commanded Carl, as loudly as he could.

"Larry's hit," screamed Pete, as he dove to protect his son.

"No!" screamed Barb and ran toward her husband and son. Another shot missed her and hit the pavement, ricocheted and kicked up a cloud of red dust from the road cut embankment behind her. The shot did not deter her, and she laid down with Larry between them.

Carl had the big M1A off his shoulder in his hands, as he hit the pavement. "White house on the hill, northeast . . . about 400 yards," Carl shouted to the long gun holders, as he laid on his back. "Should be point eight mils or 2¾ MOA elevation sight setting to get us close." He rolled over and low crawled to and under the guardrail. Grass obscured his view of the house. He slowly pushed the muzzle of the rifle through the grass. Carl set the elevation setting in the weapon's sight. He pushed a little more until his rifle sight was clear. He clearly saw the muzzle flash this time. The bullet impacted the guardrail about three yards from Carl with a very loud bang that rang for several seconds.

"Everybody, keep your eyes out all around," Carl shouted. "There may be an armed, close, contact team working with the sniper. If you see anybody—man, woman or child—anywhere around us, call out immediately."

"Which window?" shouted Hank.

"Second story, right window," Carl shouted.

Foolishly, the sniper had not moved. He was still in the same window with his rifle on a bipod. The sniper was searching for a target, when Carl squeezed off his first shot. His shot hit the siding about a foot below and to the left of the open window, kicking up a small cloud of what were probably splinters. The sniper did not twitch, so he was probably not hit. Carl noted the spot on his sight reticle, moved that spot in the rifle sight he saw to the target, and squeezed off another shot, just as two or three of the group's long guns fired as well. The sight appeared to burst and disappeared. Carl put the impact about the same distance below the first impact spot and squeezed off two quick shots, just in case the man might be wounded lying on the floor.

"Dad!" screamed Lisa behind Cart Two.

Carl instantly looked over his right shoulder first to the right, saw nothing, and then to the left. Two armed men appeared from behind trees in the wash. Under the guardrail, he could not bring his rifle to bear. He quickly tried the scurry back under the guardrail when he heard two or three shotgun blasts from the group that kicked up pine needles, dirt and probably blood. The two men dropped out of sight. Carl assumed Hank was one of the long guns on the house and was not sure if Pete was with his wounded son. "Hank, cover the house. I'm going to clear our two intruders." Carl kept low with the rifle aimed at the wash. "Nick, come with me and cover the wash." Middle son did exactly as he was ordered. As they reached the south side guardrail, Carl saw two bodies lying motionless with signs of blood. The heavy Sharps 1874 muzzle report echoed across the valley. He stepped over the guardrail, shouldered his rifle, and removed the M1911 from his jacket pocket. Carl thumb'ed off the safety and kept the pistol aimed at the two men, while he continued to rapidly scan the trees and rocks for other accomplices. He signaled for Nick to keep the shotgun on the bodies and look for others. Carl saw no reason and felt no urge to check for a pulse. He fired one round into each skull to make sure they would never bother another person. Carl quickly frisked both bodies, cleared and disabled two pistols each, and tossed the weapons in different directions as far as he could throw them. He also emptied the shotguns and tossed them in different bushes. Another loud muzzle report from the Sharps 1874 returned Carl to the scene across the road.

"Do we still have shooters out there?" Carl asked loudly from the depression of the wash.

"No," Hank answered, "just being cautious and making a statement."

"Anyone else see anything threatening?"

'No' came from several other members of the group.

"OK. When we move, everyone rise together, stay as low as you can, move steadily and as swiftly as you can sustain. If there is anymore shooting, keep moving . . . motion is your friend. The long guns will attempt to engage any additional shooters, but keep moving. Stay focused. If anyone sees any human being, please alert us. Does everyone understand?" An essential 'yes' came from most if not the whole group. "Does anyone have any questions or concerns?" Silence was his answer. Carl and Nick moved out of the wash and crouched behind the south side guardrail. "OK. Is anyone not ready to move?" Again, silence was his answer. "On three, we move. One, two, three, move!" Carl shouted.

Impressively, all 22 of the self-sufficient members stood at once, as if choreographed to precision.   Barb had Larry jump on Cart One, the boy's left shoulder now heavily bandaged and still bleeding. Lisa with Breckyn in her harness on Mom's chest climbed onto Cart Two. They did indeed move swiftly, almost too swiftly, since they were still on a slight decline in roadway grade. Several of the women had to briefly jog to keep up.

"Keep your eyes out," commanded Carl.

The shooter house still held a commanding view of the US-50 roadway and the adjacent terrain. Carl and others kept checking on that house. There was no second story window facing south. There was only one window on the south-facing side and that may have been the garage.

"Two men in the field on the right," Hank announced.

Carl and others looked over in the direction. The two men were armed and made no effort to mask their movement in parallel to the group. They were comparatively close, about 200 yards. Carl kept going back and forth from the house to the two men. With Carl's eyes at that moment on the house, the Sharps muzzle report startled him. *Damn, that thing is loud.* Carl stepped away from the group and spun, raising his rifle in the direction of the two men. Hank was kneeling on one knee with his rifle aimed in the direction of the two men. Carl saw one of the men rise from his knee, and both men ran for cover.

Hank rose and ran toward Carl, who was covering his movement. Hank stopped alongside Carl and raised his rifle, again. "One of them knelt and aimed," Hank said. "I did not want to give him the first shot."

"Did you hit either of them?"

"I don't think so. I did not have time to adjust my sight or even aim carefully. I just wanted them to hear the Sharps and feel the whizz of that heavy bullet."

Carl chuckled. "I think you accomplished that. Looks like they got the message. Let's go."

Both men rose and started jogging toward the group, now over 100 yards ahead. They caught up to the group, both winded from the high altitude and paucity of any running exercise in the last four months, just as they passed the MILE 274 marker. *Six more miles.*

"OK. We can slow down to our normal pace," Carl said somewhat breathlessly. "I think the danger has passed.

They were moving south now along a long continuous ridgeline. As Carl recalled the map, Cañon City sat on the east side of that ridgeline.

"Can we stop and rest for a moment?" George asked, gasping for air.

"Good idea," Pete seconded.

"OK. Let's hold up and take a short break," commanded Carl.

They stopped. Most of the group sat down on the warm pavement. Everyone drank water. Carl remained standing and kept searching the terrain around them. He checked the sun—not yet to local zenith. Carl joined Pete and Barb checking on Larry.

"How's he doing?" Carl asked.

"I need to stitch it up," answered Barb. "Fortunately, the bullet tore through just muscle on his shoulder. It could have been much worse for him . . . and for all of us."

Carl looked at Larry. "Are you OK to ride the cart?" Carl asked Larry.

"Yes sir, Mister Parks."

"You're such a trooper." Carl looked back to Barb and Pete. "We have another couple of hours to our destination. Let's do what is best for Larry." All three of the Higgins family nodded their heads.

Several women and men stood, as if to signal their readiness to move on down the road. They all sensed the end of their journey. Soon everyone was standing and ready. They began moving down the road at a normal sustainable pace.

The road widened to two lanes each direction as well as a center turn lane. They passed several rather nice homes at the base of the ridgeline, each with an exceptional view of the western mountains. The road sign said Skyline Drive at the intersection with a narrow road through a nicely done stone arch gateway. They could see the road ascend the side of the ridgeline to the end in what they guessed was a scenic overlook. None of them indicated any desire to see what they might be able to discover, even if it was an overlook of Cañon City. They eventually walked along the very base of the ridgeline with a gorgeous view of a large valley ahead. The MILE 276 marker established their progress. The roadway continued its steady, gradual descent. With a right curve just ahead, Carl turned and walked backward to see for himself whether they might have trailers.

Hank raised his right thumb and said loudly, "Nobody following us."

Carl raised his right thumb and answered, "Excellent."

Members of the group began to cheer when they saw the road sign on the southbound side of the wide road.

CAÑON CITY
CITY LIMIT
ELEV 5332 FT

They had not yet reached the 90-degree left turn to the east around the shoulder at the end of the ridgeline, but the sign of their achievement felt good to all of them.

The thought came to Carl, *I sure hope we find some stability down here. I sure don't want to have to walk back up into the mountains—still no people, no cars, no movement. What do they know that we don't?*

The pace remained good. The road flattened out, and they reached the big left turn. The first substantial building they reached was the Colorado Territorial Correctional Facility. It appeared to be functional, but still not seeing any people, and there were only a handful of cars in the large parking lot. At the corner of US-50, now called Royal Gorge Boulevard, and South 1st Street, the nicely done sign said, Colorado Territorial Prison Museum, Park and Gift Shop. *In normal times, that might be an interesting museum tour.*

Carl halted the group in front of the museum sign. He looked around. No people, no movement, nothing. Carl looked to the group. "We are finally here." The group silently gestured clapping and softly saying hear, hear. "It seems to me that our most immediate priority is finding lodging. We need shelter. We need to get Larry's wound properly tended to as soon as possible. We have another couple of weeks of rations, which buys us a little time, but ultimately, we must find stable sustenance. So, my suggestion, the sign back away said the business district is up this street and to the right. The main, traveled road seems to be this one—US-50. It seems to me our best chance is on US-50, so let's start there," Carl said, pointing to the east on Royal Gorge Boulevard. "What say you?"

"You've led us safely and effectively to this point," Bert said. "Your recommendation sounds reasonable. We do not know what lays ahead, so best to take one step at a time to find some form of stability."

"Those of us who need to move on," added Hank, "need to rest and recharge for a few days. So, I endorse Carl's suggestion."

Consensus came quickly. As they had done for the last nearly two weeks, they formed up for movement. The process did not take long. Less than one block later, the town hall building and empty parking lot occupied the eastern half of the small block. On the very next block, the Parkview Inn Motel stood on the far side of a small, flowing creek and directly across Royal Gorge Boulevard from Veterans Park.

"What do you say, let's start there," Carl said, gesturing toward the Parkview Motel. No one objected. They stopped at the intersection with South 3rd Street.

Carl and Pete went around to find an office. Others tried the room doors along the road. The office was around the corner at the opening of a U-shaped set of rooms around a parking area. Several abandoned cars remained in the parking lot probably disabled that night four months ago. The office door was not locked and the interior was dark. They entered and called out, "Hello?" No answer came.

"Looks like the place has been abandoned," Pete observed, "and, they only had a couple of lodgers the night of the event."

"Looks like it to me as well."

"We probably need . . . ," Pete paused, extending his fingers one at a time, clearly counting, "six or so rooms. You've got the biggest family, so up to you whether you want one, two or three rooms."

"Hopefully, these rooms use conventional, mechanical keys rather than electronic key locks."

Pete went behind the counter. He searched several drawers and found the key rack in a small cabinet below the counter desk. "Conventional keys. Do you think we should check a room to see what shape they are in?"

"A bed, any bed, will probably be better than the ground we've used for the last two weeks."

Pete laughed. "Oh so true, my friend."

"For at least one night, we can enjoy a bed. We can find another place later."

"Agreed. Let's go inform the team and get settled for tonight. As you said earlier, we need to get Larry patched up and allow everyone to get a good night's rest."

Carl nodded his head toward the group still at the intersection. The two men returned to the group.

Pete spoke, "Looks like the motel was abandoned that night or shortly thereafter. We found the keys. We," Pete said nodding to Carl, "suggest we get a good night's bed rest tonight. We can discuss the plan for the next day or so, plus it will give each family time to discuss their choices."

"Hopefully, tomorrow, we can find someone and begin to learn what happened, which should guide us in our respective decisions."

"Sounds good," Hank said. The others endorsed the recommendation.

They pulled the carts up the slight rise and into the center of the parking lot. Everyone was cautioned not to damage and be respectful of the property. They distributed keys based on the configuration chart in the office. The rooms used the night the crisis began were unkempt, but all the other rooms were as they had been left and ready for occupancy. They also agreed that it was prudent for them to post a security watch during the night. None of the rooms had a fireplace, so they agreed to set a fire on the asphalt by the carts. They would tap or consume their firewood reserve. The boys went across the street to the park and managed to find additional wood for the fire. Carl, Janet, Lisa and Breckyn took one room. The boys took another adjacent room. It was still fairly warm temperature-wise, so they waited until dusk to initiate the fire. Carl and Janet checked on Pete, Barb and Larry. Vicky and Barb had stitched up Larry's shoulder. The bullet that hit him had taken a large slice of his left deltoid muscle and fortunately had missed the humerus bone. They ate their evening rations together, as they had done for months. They also reduced the watch cycle to two males and one hour each, which would give them the most sleep. Once in bed, Janet and Carl snuggled and kissed, with the night routine set and operating. The relief felt good.

—

29

Even though their situation had not changed substantially, they all felt more positive, hopeful, and perhaps just a little euphoric. They were no longer encased in snow and ice, or isolated in the high Rocky Mountains. Despite forcing the gauntlet on the highway yesterday, the sense of foreboding or threat had diminished markedly. The relaxed morning added to an unsubstantiated feeling of safer conditions. They were close to civilization despite the paucity of people.

Around mid-morning on Monday, the 4th of May, and the 136th day of the electrical crisis, those who wanted to see what they could turn up at City Hall—Pete, Oscar, Hank, Carl, and Alex—walked to the backside entrance, the lower of two floors. The doors were unlocked. The interior was dark and unoccupied. They checked the offices on the first floor. Only the police substation and registrar's offices were locked. They found no occupants and did not find any evidence of recent activity. The second floor, which was the ground floor for Main Street, was much the same. As they turned to the west wing of the floor and building, light on the floor of the northwest corner office made them all smile. The light by itself gave them a jolt of hope. They checked the office doors on the way to the light. All were open with no occupants. As they turned to the last set of doors across from each other, an elderly man appeared in the doorway with his shadow in the light on the floor.

"May I help you?" the man asked.

"You are the first human being we've seen since we arrived in town yesterday afternoon," Pete said.

"Guilty on both counts," the man said. "Where have you come from?"

"Breckenridge," answered Hank succinctly.

"Well, I'll be damned. That is quite a way. You walked all the way down here from the mountains?"

"Yes sir," Oscar responded. "It took us nearly two weeks . . . not without problems, we must say."

"How many of you are there?"

"Twenty-three, counting a baby born a couple of months ago," Pete said. "You asked how you can help us." The man nodded his head. "We have more questions than we can count."

"Well, the best I can say is, I will do my best to answer your questions. Why don't you come in?" he said, leading them back into the office. An elegant, verging upon classical, kerosene lamp burned brightly on the desk. He gestured to various chairs and couches in the modest but well-appointed office.

The man remained standing for the moment. "Please allow me to introduce myself. My name is Angus Reed. I am the mayor of what is left of this city."

Each of the visitors introduced themselves by name only, except Alex, who added to his name, "I'm his," pointing to Carl, "youngest son."

"Where have all the people gone?" asked Pete.

"Left is the simple answer. Canyon City," he pronounced the Spanish name, "had a population of nearly 20,000 before the darkness. Only a 100 or so remain, although we have not done a head count."

"Where did they go?" Pete asked, again.

"Don't know . . . just not here."

"Do you know what happened that caused the darkness, as you say?" asked Carl.

"I've only heard rumors from people passing through headed west. No one I've talked to or listened to knows for sure. The best I can say to that question is it was some kind of attack."

"By whom?" asked Pete.

"Don't know."

"If we were attacked, what is the government doing?"

"Don't know."

"Have any of you seen any help, any government assistance?" Oscar asked.

Reed laughed a deep and hearty laugh, as if Oscar had just delivered the punchline to an exceptional joke. None of the visitors joined him. They all waited for the frivolity to subside. "Sorry. This situation is not funny, but you clearly have been so isolated, to experience this," he said, waving around the unseen scenery.

"If everyone has left, why are you still here?" asked Oscar. "There is no one else in the whole building."

"I'm too old to go anywhere. I'm still mayor of this city, and I'm here to help, as I am able . . . as we are doing now. You folks are the first I've seen in quite a few weeks now."

"Is your situation stable?" Hank asked. The puzzled expression and lack of response from the mayor prompted Hank to clarify his query. "Do you have food, water . . . the essentials of life?"

"Yes. The river," he pointed to the south, out his open office door, "is clean . . . at least the last time we tested it, and the fresh snowmelt pretty much assures that. We have to carry water once a week or so, but it's workable. Most of us up here have canned and preserved foods. We're OK for now. How about you folks?"

"We prepared a bunch of jerky the old way before we left Breckenridge," Pete said. "We still have two to four weeks of jerky left. We need to find a stable and sustainable source of food, with the supplies we have remaining."

"We can probably find some around here, but a stable, sustainable supply is unlikely."

"So, you've seen no trucks, or trains, or any other transportation of supplies?" Pete asked.

"Not a one . . . only horse-drawn wagons from farms around us, but this is not yet the growing season for crops or gardens, so we have much more work to do for stability, as you say."

"You suggest we cannot stay here. We have women and children," Hank said. "We even have an infant who was born in medieval conditions, but she survived and remains healthy. Where should we go?"

Mayor Angus Reed smiled and stared at Hank, and then glanced at the other visitors. "I have no information sufficient enough to make such a recommendation. The best I can say is, I have been told . . . with no ability to assess veracity . . . the government is beginning at the interstate network and will eventually work out from those highways and cities. I may not see the day the government arrives out here to help us."

"Interstate," said Carl. "Interstate 25 passes through Pueblo. Does that mean they might have more information and perhaps a more stable food supply than Canyon City?"

Reed shook his head. "I don't know. I've decided to stay here and care for the city I was charged to protect two years ago. If I was to guess, I would say yes . . . probably. Pueblo straddles I-25, and Colorado Springs is just up the interstate. If the rumors are true, then Pueblo should be much closer to government services than we are here."

Pete volunteered, "So we don't get crosswise with you. We arrived yesterday afternoon. We needed shelter for the night, so we commandeered the Parkview Inn Motel. It appeared to be abandoned."

"It was. It is. Please just respect the property. None of us knows when this crisis will pass, or whether the Alexanders will return. They own the Parkview."

"I would also like to report," Carl said and paused. Everyone looked at him. "Yesterday, we were attacked by a sniper in a home on a hilltop and two, maybe four, armed men at the MILE 273 marker on US-50. We killed two, probably three, in defending ourselves. One of our boys was wounded in the attack." No one spoke or moved. "As a government official, I just wanted you to be aware."

"I . . . we have no jurisdiction in that area. I will make a note," he said, jotting the information on a large, yellow pad, "for law enforcement. The county seat is four blocks over. Last time I checked, no one was there. The Sheriff has jurisdiction of that area, if we ever see him, again. MILE 273, you say?"

"Yes sir."

"I heard rumors of trouble in that area, but your report is the first actual statement. I will need your name, address and telephone number."

"I'm not sure if there is an address or phone, but my name is Carl Parks."

"My name is Pete Higgins, and I am with Carl."

"Hank Mossman . . . the same. We used to live in Golden."

"I'm so sorry," Mayor Reed interjected. "Denver and surroundings are gone." An instant cloud of gloom stifled any sound in the room. They sat there lost in their thoughts for several minutes.

"Oscar Manson . . . Santa Monica, California."

Carl picked up the thread. "Gone implies a nuclear weapon. Did you see, hear, feel anything that night?"

"I felt what I thought might have been a minor or distant earthquake, but it was not enough to get me out of bed. Other people say they saw a bright fireball high up in the sky followed shortly thereafter by a very bright light lower down. By dawn, I went outside to see what I could see, and it was just an ordinary, sunny, cold, winter day in Canyon City, Colorado." He paused, finished with his thought, but no one spoke. "I thought nothing of it, other than virtually everything stopped. We had perhaps a dozen cars and trucks that operated for a week or so, but we depleted all of our gas and diesel supplies. We have had no resupply since that night."

"What was different about those vehicles?" Carl asked.

"We wondered about that. The best we could determine was those vehicles were in metal sheds of one form or another."

"That makes sense."

"Do you know what happened?" Reed asked.

Carl smiled. "Now, it's my turn to say I don't know."

"Carl has a theory, though," Pete added.

Angus Reed looked back to Carl. "Which is?"

"The only thing that would explain all things electrical failing simultaneously is an EMP event, in this instance, a very powerful, unheard of device, since the damage appears to be far more severe and widespread than any weapon I am aware of in my military experience. The high fireball you say some witnesses reported would be consistent with that kind of event."

"What is EMP?" asked Angus Reed.

"The initials stand for Electro-Magnetic Pulse. It is a specifically designed nuclear device that emits massive, high energy, electron flux that causes induced currents in microcircuits—computers, switches, all things that have electronic circuits."

"Wow!" Again, silence occupied the room. Reed eventually noted, "That means recovery will be long."

"Yes," Carl said with solemnity, "it does." After a minute or so, Carl added, "The metal sheds would probably have been sufficient to protect the circuits of vehicles inside. Most military vehicles have shielding to protect them from EMP events."

"We've not seen any military vehicles up here of any kind since the event," Reed offered. "And, I've not tried to travel to Pueblo. I'm just too old for that kind of a journey."

"Understood," Carl said. He looked to each of his group. "Does anyone have any more questions?"

"Yeah, one question, if you don't mind," Hank said.

Reed nodded to Hank.

Hank continues, "As I recall, there were an inordinately large number of prisoners near your city. What happened to those prisoners? Have they been released? Are we going to encounter them, or have to deal with them, if they are on the loose?"

"Good question," Mayor Reed answered. "The truthful answer is, I don't know. I do know we released our prisoners from the city and county jails. They have caused no problems and have moved one. As for the state and federal prisons, I simply do not know. We have had no communications with those authorities, and we've seen no signs of them around here. If the Feds are set up in Pueblo, they may have handled all that. I just have no information for you."

Carl looked at the others, who shook their heads in the negative. "Thank you for your time and information." Carl thought for a moment. "We need to discuss what we have learned from you with our group, and then decide what we are going to do. If you have no objection, we will stay at the Parkview tonight and perhaps another day to rest up, and then I suspect we may well head to Pueblo. Like Pete said earlier, we need to find stable shelter, food and water."

"Sounds like a reasonable plan," Reed said and stood. The mayor shook hands with each of his visitors, including Alex. They said good-bye and headed back to the Parkview.

The five men returned to the group at the motel. The mid-spring day remained delightful and warm. The entire group gathered outside, some in the shade, some in the sunlight. The morning's conversation was quickly and efficiently recounted to the whole group. Very few questions were asked and answered.

"So, we're headed to Pueblo," Vicky suggested.

"That appears to be our best choice," Hank responded.

"I agree. Conditions here are not likely to be stable for us. We would burden the current population of this city by 25 percent, and the food supply would be hard-pressed to handle that burden. This is not to say that Pueblo will be in that stable of a state either. There will be other problems in Pueblo. Our first priority is food, water, shelter and safety,"

"I think we are all in agreement with that objective," Pete added.

"Based on what we heard this morning," Hank said, "we will probably find more and better information to help us make the best decision for each of our families."

"It is afternoon, now," Carl began. "I'd recommend we spend the night, maybe another day to rest, wash since the river is clean, and plan our next move." He paused to allow for questions. Hearing none, he retrieved his map and planning documents, and then continued, "My rough planning, back before we started, indicates that Pueblo is about 38 miles east on US-50. Based on our most recent days, that will take us another couple of days walking. If we start early on our departure, we might make it to Pueblo the next afternoon. It might not be so easy to find shelter as it was here."

The group unanimously agreed to the next phase of their odyssey. They drifted off into casual, low-key activities, like napping, reading, talking and whatnot. Janet pulled Carl and walked back to 1st Street, turned south, and crossed the railroad tracks, all covered with old rust indicating disuse for a long time. The river passed under a low bridge, and was running swiftly and deep. It took them a few minutes to find an acceptable area at a set of rock steps to the east of the bridge. Janet stripped naked, commanded her husband to do the same, and produced a bar of soap and room towel. The water was very cold. They washed quickly and as thoroughly as they could, and jumped out. They embraced and held each other shivering in the sunlight. They dried each other. Janet wanted to wash their clothes, but they had no spares. At least their bodies were clean for the moment.

They spent another peaceful, quiet night. Quite a few of them ruminated about the elk they passed in the mountains and how good that grilled fresh meat would taste, but they had to content themselves with their tasty jerky. By early afternoon, cumulus clouds began building very fast. The unstable air and warmer than usual air fueled the clouds. By late afternoon, they began to see lightning and hear distant thunder. Spring thunderstorms were headed in their direction. A short, covered, breezeway would protect the carts from direct rain, although the wind would likely blow rain through the breezeway. They covered and tied down the carts as best they could. Once they were satisfied with their preparations for the storms, perhaps a couple of hours away, they found the key to the ground floor restaurant off Royal Gorge Boulevard and the creek. It appeared to have been closed since the event night. The meat and other foodstuffs in the defunct freezer were all spoiled and stinking; they immediately closed the door. They found canned vegetables, beans, soups and some canned fruits. The comparatively sumptuous meal left them all full . . . in a few cases too full. They left and secured the unused supplies, cleaned up and re-locked the restaurant.

A series of strong thunderstorms rolled through and disturbed their third night in Cañon City. At least, they had roofs over their heads and walls to keep the weather out. They mutually agreed to suspend the nightly security watch during the storms. The decision to stay another night proved to be a good one. The thought of being on the open road during such storms was not particularly pleasant to imagine. The sky cleared in the early morning. The group felt it was worth the time to eat one last good meal, so they availed themselves of the restaurant, again. Even with that time taken, they struck out east on US-50 toward Pueblo just after eight in the morning.

As they moved through the rest of Cañon City, they caught glimpses of people blocks away, up cross streets. A few even waved, and their gestures were returned. Several miles later, the group found themselves in predominantly flat, slightly rolling, open country, with the mountains fading into the distance behind them—a very welcome change. They entered Penrose at MILE 289, followed by a brown road sign—Cheyenne Mountain State Park-Next Right, which seemed odd since the Cheyenne Mountain complex was north of them. Then, over a slight rise, they saw the overpass; the sign indicated exit right, and then turn left passing over US-50 to the north. Penrose seemed to be a very spread out, loosely configured community. None of them were curious enough to explore the town. As Carl took in a 360-degree scan of the terrain around them, the mountains behind them were very dim, blue-grey shapes on the distant western horizon.

The group pressed on into twilight and passed the MILE 302 marker. The terrain they had passed through was flat, reminiscent of the Great Plains of Kansas. The point group stood in a slight ravine depression in the otherwise flat ground. Widely dispersed small trees dotted the high ground on both sides of the road around them. Their choice and recommendation for this spot as this night's encampment were excellent. The boys split the task—one on the north side, the other on the south side—for an attempt to find firewood. Helen and Holly used some of their remaining reserve firewood to at least get the fire going before the end of twilight. They stuck to their routine encampment process. There were no buildings or human structures other than the asphalt roadway as far as they could see, not even power lines out there. As twilight vanished into the darkness of night, they had as much firewood as the boys could collect in an hour. They would likely have to tap their firewood reserve. Carl checked the map and estimated they had a half-day or so to go.

The night passed uneventfully and they were walking again before dawn. At the MILE 303 marker, a fairly good size residential development sat back from the highway a half-mile or so, on the south side. The horizon across the roadway remained flat and nondescript. As they walked along at a steady pace, the residential homes were closer and closer to the roadway. They crested a slight rise and homes on the south side were now about 100 yards from the road and the shapes of buildings could be seen on the horizon. As they approached, the green road sign indicated the development Pueblo West. Beyond McCullough Boulevard, businesses of various types occupied both sides of the highway. People could actually be seen moving around in what appeared to be a normal manner from days gone by, but they still had not seen a moving vehicle. They did see a few more vehicles—cars and small trucks—stranded and abandoned on the roadway. They remained the only people walking on the highway. Some of the people they saw waved, as if the group passing before them was on parade. Members of the group who expressed an opinion felt they were now in the outskirts of Pueblo. As they discussed things while they walked, the consensus wanted to press on to the I-25 junction and decide from there what to do next.

One sign made them feel better:

PUEBLO
CITY LIMIT
ELEV 4695 FT

The lower elevation offered warmer air that felt good and was quite welcomed. MILE 313 came 100 yards beyond the city limit sign. They saw the road sign for I-25 at the same time they saw the overpass that had to be the interstate highway. Shortly thereafter, they saw their first moving vehicles—an Army HMMWV ahead of two, large, M1083 5-ton Medium Tactical Vehicles heavily loaded with some kind of cargo. The sight could have been a beautiful sunset or a magnificent, powerful, rocket launch for the reaction the vehicles induced.

Carl noticed a 12-pump, 7-Eleven, gas station and convenience store on the southeast corner of the last intersection before the interstate, southbound on-ramp. The trees around the rather wide grass margin were all leafing out well—nearly full. No vehicles occupied any of the pumping stations. Only one car could be seen outside and to the side of the store—probably abandoned. Several men stood outside and a third man came out the clearly unlocked and functional, manual double doors.

"Hold up here," Carl commanded. Several members gathered around Carl. "I'm going to go," Carl said, pointing across the street to the 7-Eleven, "see what I can find out about authority." They nodded heads. "I'll take Mike with me. Better we don't overwhelm them." Again, they nodded their heads. They sat on the ground, leaning against the carts, and drank some water.

Mike and Carl approached the men, who looked suspiciously at the two, rag-tag men walking toward them. "Good afternoon, gentlemen." None of them answered and they maintained their suspicious expressions. "We just arrived from the mountains. Is there an authority in the city?"

The oldest of the three men, who were all younger than Carl, answered, "Yes. You probably need to register with the refugee center."

Carl waited, hoping for a little more information. When it did not come, Carl asked, "Where might we find the refugee center?"

"The feds have commandeered the Courtyard Marriott. That is the refugee center, now," the man responded.

"We are not familiar with the city. Where might we find the Courtyard Marriott?"

"Take Elizabeth Street," the older man said, pointing at the adjacent cross-street, "which turns into City Center Drive heading east. The Marriott will be five blocks ahead on the right."

"Thank you, gentlemen. Good day."

Carl and Mike returned to the group and informed them of what he had learned. As they walked down the city street, some stores actually appeared to be operating. People, a lot more people, walked as though this was just another normal day. The locals took note of the odd, road-worn, couple of dozen, rough-looking people, but no one bothered them or even tried to interact with them. Trees lined the street in all their glorious green foliage. The scene felt normal, even though they were walking on a city street with not one moving vehicle, well other than an occasional bicyclist. The air was warm, and smelled fresh and full of life. A few people waved from their porches, but most ignored the passing group. The seven-floor Courtyard Marriott stood exactly where the men at the 7-Eleven had said it was.

The group stopped on the street in front of the Marriott main entrance. A large, professionally done, red-lettered sign stated National Refugee Center. Numerous military vehicles stood in the parking lot. The disabled cars from the event night had actually been lifted by crane and stacked four deep along the western boundary of the hotel parking lot.

They gathered up. Carl turned to the group. "We probably would overwhelm them, if we all tried to go inside. I'd recommend one representative from each family go inside together to at least get this process started."

Janet nodded to Carl for him to represent the Parks family. Pete, Bert, Oscar, George and Hank stepped forward.

Carl continued, "I doubt they would appreciate our weapons inside. I'd recommend we leave all of our weapons out here on the carts." Everyone agreed and placed their firearms and knives on the carts. Carl laid down his rifle, removed his jacket with the M1911 in it, and removed his shoulder holster. Once the family leaders were ready, Carl gestured to the entrance.

In the lobby, a half-dozen armed military guards manned gated barriers. The lights were on in full glory. Three men in casual civilian attire sat behind the hotel registration counter and stared at the six rough looking men.

"We just arrived, having hiked out of the mountains from Breckenridge," Carl opened.

"Oh my," the man in the middle responded. "That is quite a distance."

"Over a hundred miles," Pete added. "Took us more than two weeks."

"Well," the man said, "you have arrived at the correct place. How many of you are there?"

"Twenty-three including an infant born a couple of months ago," Carl said and paused, "in six families. Each of us represents our six families," he added, gesturing to his companions.

"You are not the first and certainly will not be the last refugees to make it . . ."

"What the hell happened?" Carl interrupted.

The man held up his right hand. "Please, sir, we will answer as many of your questions as we can, to the best of our ability, but we have a process, a very necessary process, that we must follow. Please allow us to intake your families properly. You are not alone. We are taking care of refugees of all sorts in this crisis and the process works well."

"What do we need to do?" asked Hank.

"We have several steps that we must get through. But, first and foremost, do you have any individuals who need medical attention?"

"Yes, we have one young boy who was wounded in an ambush a few days ago. We tried our best to treat him, but proper medical treatment is warranted. We also have an infant who was born three months ago. She should probably be checked by a doctor as well and her birth formally documented."

"OK. We will take care of that right away. Do you need to eat?" the man asked.

"We've survived on jerky and water. We are OK . . . for now."

"But, a proper meal would be greatly appreciated," Bert said. Everyone chuckled a little, and nodded their heads, even the counterman.

"Yes, well, we'll take care of that, too. Now, the first step is to get everyone registered. We have a large conference room on the ground floor here that we will use to inform you of what has happened and what the government is doing. You will be assigned temporary rooms on the upper floors of this hotel, while you are debriefed on your experience of the last four and a half months. Depending upon your specific needs and situation, you will be helped along your way, or housed in more prolonged facilities. But, we don't need to worry about that just yet. First things first, why don't you get your whole group in here, so we can begin the process."

"We have our remaining supplies and weapons on carts," Carl said. "I do not want to leave them unattended."

"Oh my," the man said, "you cannot bring the weapons inside. However, to facilitate your registration, I can have a military guard placed on your carts to ensure they are safe."

Carl looked to the others. They all nodded their consent. "Very well."

The men returned to the group and informed everyone what they had just been told. Several of them pushed the carts into two, open parking spaces away from the vehicles. The rest of the group disarmed and stacked their weapons. A sergeant arrived and posted an Army private to guard the two carts. They were screened with hand-wand metal detectors, which they all marveled at as functional electrical tools.

Once they were through the security screening and registration process, the next activity was a medical evaluation. A dozen Army medics and nurses, with supplemental civilian nurses, examined and recorded the vital statistics of each member of the group. As they were informed, the medical screening looked for infections, diseases, parasites and other abnormalities of their ordeal. Most of the group was pronounced healthy, although slightly malnourished, but generally disease, infection and infestation free. Breckyn received special attention and a thorough examination by the duty doctor, along with an appointment with a pediatrician specialist tomorrow, after which a proper birth certificate based on Carl's notes would be recorded and issued. The wounded among the group—Nick, Vicky, Carl, Lisa and Larry—were given detail examinations by the doctor and pronounced in good shape considering their injuries, with no remedial action required.

Everything the government people have done, so far, was done with pen and paper—not a single computer or electronic device. That speaks volumes. Well, at least the lights and air conditioning work.

With the medical assessment complete, they were directed to one of the hotel's large conference rooms. More than a hundred chairs had been arranged in the large multi-purpose room, facing a podium and a couple of tables. The man in the middle at the reception counter appeared at the podium.

"Good afternoon. Welcome to Pueblo. My name is Felix Pearson. I am one of the receiving agents for the Federal Emergency Management Agency. A lot has happened since you were stranded in the mountains last winter. The purpose of this briefing is to inform you of events that night and the ensuing four months, as well as lay out a set of options to support everyone in need. Any questions, so far?" Carl was certain they all had tons of questions, but like him, they were willing to wait for the briefing. "OK, then, I would like to introduce Captain Steve Monday from our military district office. Captain . . ."

Carl recognized the shoulder patch of the 4th Infantry Division on Captain Monday's combat, forest green, camouflage uniform along with his twin, black, captain bars at the center of his chest. The last time he knew such things, the 4th ID was stationed at Fort Carson, outside Colorado Springs. "Thank you, Mister Pearson. On behalf of the Military District Commander Colonel Jason Billings, welcome to Pueblo. As Mister Pearson stated, I am Captain Monday. I am the Assistant Intelligence Officer of the 47th Regiment and currently serving as the information officer for the refugee center. You have reached safety, and in case you might be curious, today is Thursday, the 7th of May."

Carl made a quick check of his notes. *Damn, I did a pretty good job tracking the calendar. For us, it was D139 and T15, but my calendar stops now.*

"Y'all must have been through quite an ordeal through last winter and your march out of the mountains this spring. We would like to debrief you on your experience to gain information on how best to support the people of this district, but that will come later. First, it is my duty to inform you that during the night of December 19th last, the United States was attacked by disguised forces of Russia and China." Audible gasps and disbelief punctuated the captain's statement. "They used highly modified commercial aircraft on scheduled flight plans to hit major infrastructure hubs—12 in all, ranging from coast to coast, New York to Los Angeles, Seattle to Atlanta, including Denver.

Not to delve too deeply into the technical, they used small, nuclear penetrators to break up the ground, coordinated with a high yield, airburst, thermonuclear weapon and a high altitude Electro-Magnetic Pulse device."

Pete leaned toward Carl. "You were right." Carl looked at Pete and nodded his head slightly.

"The same process hit all 12 hubs at virtually the same time . . . separated by just minutes. One of their primary objectives was to render our national electricity grid inoperative for years. As you well know, I am sorry to say, they succeeded."

"Have they invaded?" asked Hank.

"No. They didn't need to. In an instant, they paralyzed our commercial and industrial capacity. Nothing works without electricity these days. They also knew that the country would have to turn its military strength inward to support the people, maintain law and order, and repair the damage. This was a well-calculated, highly coordinated attack, carefully planned over many years."

"Why?" asked Vicky in a loud, painful voice.

"They knew they could not defeat us outright, but they also believed they could render us immobile, impotent and unable to assist our allies, or to defend our interests in maintaining peace and free trade. To that end, they appear to have achieved that short-term purpose. Numerous countries have capitulated. Some are fighting, but they are overwhelmed without us in the field. My presence here is testament to that conclusion. I am here as the representative of the Commanding Officer of the 47th Infantry Regiment, 7th Infantry Brigade of the 4th Infantry Division, who currently serves as the Commander of Military District of Southern Colorado. We are a frontline combat infantry unit. However, our duty for the last few months and for the foreseeable future is to maintain law and order, and to coordinate the recovery in our assigned district. The day of reckoning for our enemies will come, but first, we must regain our strength at home and specifically our industrial capacity. Any questions, so far?"

Again, no one spoke. Carl had a bunch of questions, but he wanted to hear what the military wanted to tell them.

Captain Monday continued, "The government's recovery plan calls for us to restore the infrastructure and services along the interstate highway network, and then work our way out from there. Concomitantly, we are required to support displaced citizens, facilitate their return home," he paused, and then said with solemnity, "where homes still exist, and to be direct, put the nation back to work in facilitating our recovery as well as making preparations to take the fight to our enemies." Captain Monday paused, again, and stared at the podium before him, although Carl had not noticed any notes or papers.

"The Congress declared war on Russia, China and their allies. The United States is at war, again, and World War III has begun. As such, all citizens with military service below the age of 55 years have been recalled to active duty. It is my duty to inform you," he paused for emphasis, "all citizens, male and female, between the ages of 18 and 36, for now, are required to register for potential service in the armed forces of the United States."

"Wait, Captain," Carl interrupted. "We have families, who have no homes . . . at least none that we are sure about. Our daughter, who is in the conscription age group you stated, just gave birth to our granddaughter. Our obligation is to protect them."

"No, sir, with all due respect, it is now the countries obligation to protect your families, as you protect the Republic."

"But . . ."

"No buts I'm afraid. I presume you are prior military," Monday said.

"Yes sir. Lieutenant colonel, U.S. Marine Corps, retired."

"Staff sergeant, U.S. Marine Corps, separated," Pete contributed.

"Thank you for your service, gentlemen, but circumstances have led our country to call upon you, again."

"What about our weapons?"

"Weapons?"

"Yes, we needed them to defend ourselves in and on the way out of the mountains," Carl said. "Surely, you are not going to confiscate them, and we certainly cannot leave them outside in the weather."

"Weapons," Monday said, "you mean like rifles and pistols."

"Yes."

"We will record and inventory them and secure them until you depart this facility. Now, before everyone gets stirred up, don't get your panties in a bunch, the registration process Mister Pearson alluded to is designed to sort all that out, take care of the necessary paperwork to ensure that your families are properly taken care of and supported for the duration of your service. The process will take approximately a week. I know you have thousands of relevant questions, but I ask you to allow the process to function without resistance, and I think all of your questions will be addressed or answered. Now, one last question from me, before we get started, if you lived within a 25-mile radius of New York City; Washington, DC; Atlanta; Dallas-Fort Worth; Kansas City; Chicago; Denver; Salt Lake City; Phoenix; Los Angeles; San Francisco; or Seattle, please raise your hands." Everyone did except the Parks and Armstrongs. "Y'all are now in a special category, since you likely have no homes to return to, I'm afraid."

"Sir?" George said and raised his right hand. Captain Monday nodded his head toward George. "With respect, sir, my wife Anne and I are from England on a ski holiday in Summit County when all this transpired. What about us?"

"Yes, I'm sorry that y'all have been caught up in all this, and to be direct, you are in a subset of the previously mentioned group. London, Birmingham and Manchester were subjected to similar attacks. The process will send a message to the British Refugee Center to notify them of your identity and status. They will notify your family on your behalf. You will be handled as a displaced family, until civilian transportation to Europe can be restored."

George and Anne nodded their heads, apparently satisfied with the answer so far.

Carl raised his hand. Captain Monday nodded to him. "We also have the son of another family with us when the crisis occurred. We need to inform his family that he is safe and arrange for him to return to his family."

"Yes. Understood. Please inform the intake team of those facts. We will handle that notification immediately, and his reunion as soon as possible."

Carl nodded his head and looked to Dave, who also nodded his head.

"The hotel will serve," Monday continued, "as your temporary quarters until the registration and debriefing process can be completed. Then, depending upon your status, you will be transported to the proper facility. You will eat your meals in the hotel restaurant by floors beginning at 17:00 hours—5 PM. Your room assignments are posted in the lobby. Now, let's get your belongings inventoried and checked in. There are just a few hours remaining until evening meal is served, and I am fairly certain you will enjoy a warm shower or bath, and fresh clothes. I'm afraid our clothing supply is rather ordinary, but it is functional. Once we get your information recorded, the supply room is on the ground floor of the opposite wing of the hotel. The debriefing segment of the process will begin in the morning. Thank you very much. You are safe, now. God bless America." Captain Monday departed.

Carl wanted to intercept him, to ask more specific questions, but he chose not to do so. If he was being recalled to active duty, he would undoubtedly learn much more precise information about what caused all this damage and how it happened. There was no point in holding the whole group hostage to his curiosity.

Felix Pearson returned to the podium. "Thank you, Captain Monday," he said to the Army officer's retiring figure. "We will now complete the administrative portion of the intake process," he paused and gestured to a half dozen men and women, who came forward to the tables and set up their books. "Before we jump into all that, I wanted to add a few words of explanation to Captain Monday's briefing. As he noted, the attack on our country concentrated on our industrial and economic infrastructure. Without knowing your specific situations, I think it is safe to say that your employment has been disrupted . . . to put it delicately. Thus, your income has likely evaporated. The government has instituted a series of employment actions. First, where power has been restored, industrial capacity is being mobilized for national defense. Where employment is not yet available, the government is issuing a monthly emergency refugee stipend to ensure people can live without income. The banking system has reverted to a paper system until electronic systems can be restored. Part of the intake process is identifying your location, so that appropriate support can be provided. Once you are relocated, you will have a local contact person in case you encounter any problems with your living conditions. Now, if each family will sit down with one of our agents here," Pearson said, gesturing to his support staff, "we will get this done as quickly as possible."

Each person provided additional personal details, like last address, birth date and location, social security number (where available), relations, fingerprints and a DNA sample. As indicated, they were assigned rooms and given magnetic card keys. They were all on the second floor. The Parks were assigned adjoining rooms with a connecting doors. Lisa and Breckyn had their own room. The boys were assigned to the room on the other side of Lisa from their parents. Down the ground floor hallway in a different conference room, they picked up two sets of underwear, gray sweat pants and tops with hoods, and slip-on rubber sandals, as well as a bag of sundries for basic hygiene. Carl gave his supplies to Janet, who went up the elevator to their room. The men went outside, collected their firearms and completed the registration process, as they watched their weapons chained and locked in a windowless room; theirs were not the only weapons.

Janet sat in the room staring out the window at the city. She wanted to take a shower with her husband. They rejoiced in their simple way in the warm, verging upon hot, water, as steam filled the bathroom. The fresh simple clothes were welcome refreshment.

"What are we going to do?" Janet asked.

"We cannot worry about what we don't control."

"I understand that," she responded with distinct frustration. "I don't want to deal with all this without you, Carl. I'm afraid they are going to take you away, and I will be left here to fend for the children and myself."

"I did not hear any of that from the captain. The best we can do for now is to listen and absorb what we learn during their intake process. Let's see what the next few days turn up."

"All well and good for you, Carl. You're going off to war. I think I'm more afraid of this," Janet said, waving her arms around the room, "than I was about the blackout five months ago." She actually smiled. "As much grief as I gave you, at least we were together, and I trusted you."

"I don't know what else to tell you, Janet. We are in a safer, far more stable condition than we were just two weeks ago. So far, I think the government is handling a very difficult situation rather well."

"Yes, I agree, but I . . . ," Janet stopped with a knock on the adjoining door.

Carl unlocked their side of the door. All the children and Dave appeared at the door, and came into the room. They had all showered, cleaned up well, and dressed in new clothes. Even Breckyn had new infant attire that fit well for her. Carl took Breckyn from Lisa.

"Ah, the sweet smell of youth," Carl said, as he inhaled the scent of his granddaughter's scalp.

Everyone laughed, as though Carl's pronouncement was their best sign of normalcy they had seen in five months.

"We thought we'd stop by before dinner," announced Nick. "We've been talking."

Carl smiled, as he rocked Breckyn. "Do tell, Son."

"Nick, Dave and I want to enlist," Alex stated.

"No!" exclaimed Janet. "You cannot go. You are not of age."

"We want to ask for your consent."

"No! No way!"

Carl kept Breckyn cradled safely in the crook of his left arm and raised his right hand to stop. "Let's stop here. We just arrived. We just enjoyed our first shower in five months and will soon enjoy our first real meal in five months. I understand your sentiment," he said, looking at each of his children and Dave. "But, we do not know enough, yet. For instance, we do not know how the government intends to manage the industrial recovery and mobilization in relation to military service. We cannot have everyone in the military . . . unless we nationalize war support industries and use the military to operate the plants. There are far too many questions."

"But, Dad . . . ," Nick said, and then stopped when Carl raised his hand, again.

"Let's table this discussion for now. Captain Monday said the intake process would take about a week, so we have a few days to learn more, and see what makes sense for each of us. We do not have the authority to give consent for Dave. That said, please let Mom and I talk about this for a day or so." The boys nodded their heads in agreement. "Also, as I mentioned in the briefing, we still have to sort out Lisa's situation with the government's order. Now, I see on the digital table clock that actually works that it is nearly dinnertime. Let's make our way to the dining hall and enjoy our first real meal."

The Parks family plus Dave Baker reunited with the other members of the Building 3 Group, along with double their number of other refugees and support staff at long tables. The evening meal was simple, but hot and delicious—roast beef, corn, mashed potatoes, with delicious orange juice, and even cherry pie for dessert, served in cafeteria buffet style. They were invited to eat as much as they wished. Carl cautioned his family to avoid over-eating and to consume slowly, so they could recognize the stopping point before their consumption became problematic.

For the first time in longer than they cared to remember, they slept without interruption or apprehension. They were safe.

—

30

The debriefing process would take three full days of morning and afternoon sessions, as individuals and as families. The government wanted to know primarily where other survivors were located. It became clear to the FEMA agents that a special mission to Breckenridge by helicopter was warranted. They never did hear what was actually done, but at least they had done their part to inform the government people. Each of them recounted their experience of the last five months. Carl tried to define the location and circumstances of each life he, or any of them, had taken or likely taken. He also recounted the signs on the sheriff and police station, as well as the vacancy of the city and county offices. The 4th Infantry Division Judge Advocate General met with Carl on the third day to inform him that the homicides had been preliminarily classified self-defense in extremis conditions, and thanked him for his frankness and candor.

After supper on the third day, Pete stopped by Janet and Carl's room. "The group would like to gather up to compare notes, if that is OK with you," he said.

"Sure. No problem. That sounds like a great idea. What about tomorrow night after dinner?"

"It sounds like things are going to start moving quickly, so no later than tomorrow evening," answered Pete.

Carl lifted the phone, got the front desk, and asked for a small meeting room. One was available—Conference Room 104. It was sized for 20 people, so a little crowded for the Building 3 Group, but a few extra chairs around the periphery for the children were doable. They agreed to meet at 19:00 the following evening.

"What do you think that was all about?" asked Janet, after Pete departed.

Lisa came in with Breckyn. "That sounded ominous," Lisa said. "What does he want?"

Carl chuckled and answered, "I don't know. I imagine it may well be a final farewell before we start to disperse."

"But, we don't know, yet," observed Lisa.

"No, we don't, but others might well know what their course is. We'll find out tomorrow night."

Just then, Nick appeared, having passed through Lisa's room. "Did you and Mom decide on our enlistment approval?" he asked directly. All four boys looked quite serious. Carl hesitated and Nick continued, "Mike says he was told he will sign his conscription papers tomorrow. We would like to enlist with him."

Carl offered a somewhat surprised and shocked expression. "Well now, that is quite a lot to absorb. First, since we have all of us here and before we jump into that sensitive topic, Mister Higgins stopped by to request a group meeting. We will meet with the other families tomorrow evening after supper. I suspect we will get a more thorough exchange of status." He paused for consent. Only Mike nodded his head slightly—another sign of the seriousness of Nick's query. "OK. Yes, Mom and I have talked."

"Yes, we have," Janet interjected with some vehemence. "Your father sees things differently, so I will speak for myself." She looked directly to Nick, standing just to her left. "You are going to be 18 years old later this year. At that point, the law considers you an adult, and we," she nodded with her head toward Carl, "no longer have any authority. Alex will turn 18, next year. I will lose all of you soon enough. Mike is already of age, and we still have the grievous uncertainty of your sister's status regarding conscription. We were informally told she must register for conscription, but she would likely be suspended from eligibility until Breckyn is six, or maybe 12 months old and weaned." Janet paused to look into the eyes of everyone, including Dave and Carl. The sternness of her expression punctuated her words. "Which, I must say, is a reason to keep Breckyn at breast for years." No one laughed or even giggled. "I recognize, and in fact acknowledge, the government needs good citizens in military service. As we have learned, we are at war and will likely remain at war for years, so I cannot stop your service." Tears descended Janet's cheeks. She made no attempt to wipe her tears away or to hide her sobs.

Lisa sat next to Janet with Breckyn in her left arm, and she placed her right arm around her mother's shoulders.

Carl took Breckyn from his daughter, so she could comfort her mother.

"I do not want you," Janet spoke through her sobs, "any of you, to leave me before it is time." Janet's sobs became more pronounced.

Lisa rubbed Janet's back and patted her left thigh.

Janet sniffed to clear her nose and stifled her sobs to regain control. "I have said my peace. I want each of you to remember how I feel, to not forget my words, but I will not stand in your way." She looked again at each set of eyes on her. "Your father and I have agreed to sign your age waiver for enlistment."

Alex smiled and danced a little jig. Nick smiled and said, "Thanks, Mom."

"Please don't thank me. I am not helping you. As a mother, I only want to protect you. But . . . I endured your father's service. I shall have to endure service once again."

"We shall do our best to not get hurt," Nick said.

"I'm sure you will," Janet responded, "but, such things are not in your control. War is war. I shall proudly display my blue stars. Just do not make me a Gold Star Mother."

"There you have it," Carl inserted. "Let's take a break and avail ourselves of the 24-hour, self-serve machine in the cafeteria." The mood changed, as they enjoyed a cone or cup of soft-serve vanilla or chocolate ice cream. Laughter returned to the family, as the chatted about other less serious topics.

The following day focused on making arrangements for the next steps. As they had been briefed, Lisa and Mike completed their registration for conscription. The government agents also took down Breckyn's supplemental information to be included with Lisa's registration, including photographs of the infant. Her eligibility for conscription was provisionally suspended until Breckyn was one year old, next January. Mike opted for his preemptive choice and enlisted in the Marine Corps. In good news for the Parks family and David Baker, the Parks home in Andover, east of Wichita, was confirmed to be untouched and secure. Electrical power had been restored for Wichita and the surrounding communities, including Andover. Local law enforcement had been fully restored. Dave's family had been successfully notified of his safety, although limited communication prevailed, Dave learned that his family was safe and in good health. Carl was informed by an Army captain from the 4th IDs G-1 Administrative Division that he was tentatively assigned to the newly re-commissioned 6th Marine Air Wing, forming at Marine Corps Air Station Yuma, and potentially slated for promotion to colonel along with assignment to become the G-2 Intelligence Chief for the yet to be formed VI Marine Expeditionary Force. A government-chartered bus that somehow made it through the attack had been scheduled to transport Janet, Lisa, Breckyn, Nick, Dave and Alex back to Wichita and Andover departing in two days—Wednesday, the 13th of May. Mike would depart by rail tomorrow for Boot Camp at Marine Corps Recruit Depot, San Diego, California. They all felt events were moving far faster than any of them felt comfortable. They were repeatedly told that the Pueblo Refugee Center was only a temporary transit station.

The Higgins family joined the Parks to fill their table at supper. The evening fare this day was hamburgers and hot dogs with all the usual fixin's, French fries, iced tea or orange juice, and apple pie for dessert.

"Where are y'all going?" Pete asked, after they were all sitting and had taken a bite or two of their meals.

"Well, it's been a tumultuous few days for us," Carl responded. "Janet, Lisa, Breckyn and Dave are leaving by bus, day after tomorrow for home in Andover. Mike ships out tomorrow to MCRD San Diego. We are still debating whether to sign age-waivers for Nick and Alex. They want to join their older brother." Pete nodded his head and glanced to each of the boys, as if he approved. "I have orders to report to MCAS Yuma to join the staff of 6th MAW. I will leave shortly after Janet and the kids. They will pick me up in a Navy C-40A, at Peterson Air Force Base in Colorado Springs."

"C-40?" asked Pete.

"Yeah," Carl answered. "As I was informed, the Navy and Marine Corps replaced their old C-9s ten years ago with new C-40s that are the military version of the Boeing 737-700C airliner."

Pete nodded his acknowledgment.

Barbara Higgins looked directly to Janet Parks. "So, you're not happy letting your younger boys go off to war?"

"Nope. Fortunately, Larry is not yet close enough to even ask for an age waiver."

"Yes. Thankfully." Barb paused, and then continued, "The government people confirmed our home is gone . . . evaporated. Blessedly, we were not at home." The table remained quiet and pensive, as they all considered what might have happened. "They asked me to remain here as a serving nurse. Vicky has already agreed. However, Pete is going off to war," she paused, and said with some solemnity, "Larry and I would like to join you in Wichita, if you will have us."

"I would love to have you join us. We have done well. You delivered our granddaughter."

"Excellent. Thank you so much, Janet."

"Where are you going?" Carl asked Pete.

"Apparently, the same place as you . . . MCAS Yuma. They are trying to figure out what to do with me. At least for now, I will be assigned to 6th MEF JAG. To the Marine Corps, I'm still a non-degreed staff sergeant. They want to use my law license. They need lawyers, but no decision, as yet. I have orders to Yuma, but nothing definitive beyond that. I will join you on that transport flight. We will have to coordinate Barb's travel tomorrow."

"Excellent," Carl said. "Hopefully, y'all can get everything squared away tomorrow. Now, I noted the time. We agreed to meet with the group at 19 hundred. We'd better finish up here and get down to the meeting room."

"Before we go, what about our weapons cache?" Pete asked Carl.

"Good question. I've not really thought about them."

"Why don't we divide them up among those who want them? The ownership of personal weapons like your M1911 and Hank's Sharps 1874 are already defined. Perhaps we can ask the army to box them up to go with each family that wants them."

"That sounds reasonable to me. Let's talk to the Group."

"Agreed."

As they completed their meal, the conversation focused solely on the contrast between their physical circumstances from just a few weeks ago to this moment. They actually laughed about what they had endured. When they finished their meal, several of the children grabbed a soft-serve ice cream cone. They sauntered across the central courtyard with the refreshing sound of water splashing in the center fountain.

As they entered the room, they exchanged greetings with their comrades, some of whom they had only seen in passing over the last few days. The Mansons and the Mossmans were the last to arrive. With salutations completed, the group began to sit. Hank Mossman closed the door and joined the others at the table.

Pete began, "Each of us has expressed a desire to gather up the Building 3 Group before we began to disperse, in part to inform the group of what is going to happen next for each of us, and also to pay our respects to Carl Parks for leading us through the serious trial of the last five months. On behalf of the entire Building 3 Group, we would like to sincerely and deeply thank you for keeping us safe."

"Hear, hear," several said. They all applauded.

"Thank you all. I am humbled by your gesture. I simply did what had to be done. Nonetheless, again, thank you all very much."

"We cannot possibly repay our debt to you, Carl." Again, more cheers and clapping. "I believe we recounted in detail to the interviewers what you have done for the whole Building 3 Group. You will be remembered, and our stories will be passed down to future generations." Carl nodded several times and waved his hand. From that, Pete informed the Group of what was going to happen with the Higgins family, including Barbara's choice to join with Janet Parks in Andover, Kansas.

Carl did the same for the Parks family, including David Baker.

Hank Mossman picked up the thread. "We were not so fortunate," he began. "Our home was not vaporized like the Higgins' home, but we were informed by the government that our property was destroyed by the shockwave and subsequent fires. Betsy and I will move tomorrow to the government's resettlement camp on the outskirts of Pueblo. We are informed that they have employment services available to help us figure out how we might be able to assist the war effort. My job is gone with our community, so I'll have to find something else to do. Helen departs tomorrow for Navy Officer Candidate School in Newport, Rhode Island, while Holly has enlisted in the Air Force and heads off tomorrow for Basic Military Training at Joint Base San Antonio, in Texas. That's about it for us. We still have uncertainty, but I would like to take my moment to also thank you Carl, and convey our gratitude for taking us into the Group and getting us out of the mountains."

Oscar Manson was the next to share. "Like the Mossmans, the government informed us that our home disappeared in the attack on Los Angeles. We will join the Mossmans in moving tomorrow to the Pueblo resettlement camp . . . at least until we can figure out what is available and next for us. Emily and I are grateful our children are not old enough for enlistment or conscription, but we recognize that their time will come all too soon. Like Hank said, Carl, thank you oh so very much for everything you did to keep us safe." Carl raised his right hand and nodded to acknowledge Oscar's words.

"We were informed by your government officials," George Armstrong said, "that our home remains intact and secure, but any hope of returning to England is indefinitely postponed . . . likely years away. We are scheduled to move to the resettlement camp as well," he paused, and looked to Carl and Janet. "Anne and I discussed at dinner that if you would have us, Janet, we would like to go with you and Barbara. You made us feel so welcome and actually safe with everything going on around us. We think our best prospects are with you, if you will have us."

"We would be honored to host you both, George and Anne," Janet said to each of them. "As Carl noted earlier, our bus transport leaves on Wednesday, so we will need to make the appropriate arrangements with the government people, so that you can travel with us."

"We will do our part," Anne said.

"Perhaps we should talk to the government officials tomorrow and together."

"Good point. Agreed," Janet responded.

Everyone looked at Bert. Vicky lowered her head, not wanting to make eye contact with anyone. She also apparently wiped away unseen tears. "Well," Bert began with definite tremor to his voice. "I guess we get the trophy for the most unlucky." He stopped and swallowed hard several times, as he struggled to maintain control of his emotions. "Our home is gone, but the worst of it is, our children and grandchildren have been declared missing and presumed deceased in the attack on Denver." Again, he paused to maintain control. No one spoke. Again, he swallowed hard. "Life goes on, right? Vicky has been drafted into the nursing corps here. They are trying to find us a place to live close to here, or we will be based at the resettlement camp, and work out of there. I will stay with her and see what I can find to contribute, like Hank and Oscar."

"We mourn your loss," Carl offered, looking directly to Vicky and Bert. "If there is anything we can do to help, please let us know."

"I think the best thing for us," Vicky jumped in, now with more control in her voice, "is to maintain contact with all of you. Each of you is now our extended family, our bonds born in the crucible of trial. We did not ask for or induce this trauma, but the challenge has landed upon us. I truly and genuinely hope we can remain close for the rest of our days."

Janet stood and went around the table without taking her eyes off Vicky. She wrapped her arms around Vicky, who stood and turned into Janet's embrace. The two women held each other tightly and cried together. The other women joined Vicky and Janet, all of them in a large group hug to reassure Vicky. The rest of the Group waited patiently, silently and motionless, for the moment to pass.

Bert Johnson broke the spell. "Thank you all for your support. We truly appreciate your condolences. I propose we adjourn to the cafeteria to enjoy an ice cream in celebration of life . . . and the memory of those we have lost."

Vicky was the first to offer affirmation from inside the huddle. "Yes, ice cream!"

A number of members actually chuckled with the break in solemnity. The huddle disentangled. They made their way back across the courtyard. This time, even Janet and Carl partook of the soft-serve machine. Most of the group remained in the cafeteria as if they were going to take seconds.

Hank came over to Pete and Carl. "Did I hear correctly, you met with an Army JAG officer?" Hank asked.

"True."

"They asked me about the killings."

"They asked all of us," Pete interjected.

"What did the JAG guy say, if I may ask?"

"I told them about each and every life I took—when, where, how, and circumstances. The phrase he used was 'preliminarily classified self-defense in extremis conditions.' I'm not sure if that is a legal term, but I think it means the deaths were determined to be necessary for self-protection."

"It's not a legal term," Pete added. "But, I do believe Carl's interpretation is appropriate."

"So, we are all absolved of culpability in the deaths?"

"I would not go that far, Hank. There is no statute of limitations for homicide, and prosecutors can always change their minds. Plus, the JAG Corps officers are military lawyers, not civil law enforcement. None of us has the ability to predict how a district attorney, years from now, will respond when he is presented with dead bodies in his jurisdiction. That said, I believe we have done the correct and proper thing here . . . to be forthright and thorough in our disclosure. Even if it ever came to a trial, I cannot imagine any jury would vote to convict given the reality of the circumstances. They will likely see themselves in exactly the same terms. We have done the best we could. I say we put this behind us and not look back."

"That sounds reasonable, Pete, and you are the lawyer," Hank said.

"I agree," added Carl. "I hold no remorse. We did what had to be done."

"OK, then. I'm going to miss you guys. I guess tomorrow is the beginning of the end, when our illustrious group breaks up. I don't know how we're going to keep in touch with no telephone, no Internet, and I'm not even sure we have postal service, but hopefully, we'll figure out some means to communicate."

"Where there's a will, there's a way," Pete offered. The three of them laughed.

"Agreed," Carl contributed.

"Thanks guys. Now, I'd better get the clan off to bed. We're probably going to have a tumultuous day for us tomorrow."

"What time do y'all depart?" asked Pete.

"We're scheduled to leave by bus at nine tomorrow morning . . . at least the Manson, and Betsy and me. We'll put Helen and Holly on the bus at eight. They go to Fort Carson as their transit station. And, if Anne and George are successful with their change of status, they will now go with us."

"We'll be there to see you off," Carl said. "Mike will be on the same bus as your daughters."

"What about Nick, Alex and Dave?" queried Hank.

"Dave goes back to Wichita with Janet. His parents would not agree to sign the necessary age waiver until they saw him eye-to-eye. After y'all leave, Janet and I will sign the waivers for Nick and Alex. We think they will leave later tomorrow afternoon, but we're not sure. We've got a lot to get sorted out in the morning, so we'd better get everyone in bed as well."

The three men split and went to shepherd their respective families. It took a little longer for Carl to corral his clan. In due course, everyone headed toward sleep. Janet and Carl chose to renew their union of bodies before they drifted off to sleep still entwined.

After breakfast of scrambled eggs, sausage, hashed brown potatoes and orange juice, the entire group, all 23 of them including Breckyn, gathered in the lobby. Hugs and kisses helped Helen and Holly say goodbye to the Group and especially to their weepy parents and boarded the bus along with other people heading up to Colorado Springs and Fort Carson. From there, they would be assigned to other transport for their destination. The first members of the Building 3 Group were on their way to the next stage of their lives.

Many of the Group remained outside with Hank and Betsy until the bus disappeared heading north on I-25. Carl and Janet hugged Hank and Betsy. They would soon share the same sense of loss and uncertainty for their children.

By the time Carl and Janet left the Mossmans still outside in the warm morning air and entered the lobby, George and Anne turned the corner on the far side of the lobby, apparently intending to talk to Carl and Janet.

George began, "We took the liberty of meeting with the location manager and requested a change to our destination. Everything is arranged. Thank you so much for accepting us, Janet."

"Excellent," Mrs. Parks responded. "So, you will leave with us tomorrow?"

"That is what he said. They also indicated they would use your address for the refugee stipend."

"OK. That task is complete. Now, regrettably dear," Carl said, looking deeply into Janet's eyes, "we need to settle the paperwork for Nick and Alex."

"I really don't want to do this," she stopped to hold up her hand when Carl started to respond, "but, I know we have to do this. So, let's rip off the bandage."

Anne and George patted Janet on her shoulders, and then went outside.

Carl and Janet found Nick and Alex, and then went together to the military service room. A Marine staff sergeant asked a number of questions to ensure they were freely deciding and consenting to the enlistments. Satisfied, the sergeant presented the appropriate papers. Each of them signed their consent. With professional courtesy, Carl was allowed to deliver the oath of office to both of their youngest sons. The necessary approvals could not be received in time to make Mike's transport bus. Both boys would board another bus for Fort Carson, probably to join their older brother bound for MCRD San Diego.

With that task done, Carl and Janet found the Higgins. They changed the destination of Barbara and Larry, and had seats on the same bus as Janet, Lisa, Breckyn, Dave, Anne and George, tomorrow at midday. All of the adjustments were agreed and set.

They ate a quiet lunch of grilled chicken, scalloped potatoes, mixed vegetables, and a drink of choice. After lunch, the remaining group again gathered outside the hotel's front entrance to say goodbye to Mike. All too soon, the Parks' oldest son was away to serve his country. Next to depart were Hank and Betsy along with the Manson family, heading to the large resettlement camp just to the northeast of Pueblo. The last to leave that Tuesday afternoon were Nick and Alex. The Marine staff sergeant who processed their enlistments confirmed to the boys, and to Carl and Janet that they would join Mike at Fort Carson to their transportation to San Diego by Army railroad assets.

Dinner that evening was a rather solemn affair—very little discussion. Bert and Vicky joined the Parks' and Armstrong's late.

"We want to tell what's left of the Group," Vicky said, as they sat down, "they found, refurbished and furnished a decent apartment about two blocks away, so we will stay here. The government is going to give us a few days to get settled before putting me to work with the medical staff here in town."

"They are looking into how best to utilize my experience and skills," Bert offered, "but, they felt certain they would put me to work as well. I don't know what, yet . . . but something."

"Since y'all are staying, I guess you will be the last folks standing. The rest of us leave tomorrow. Janet and the Wichita contingent leave tomorrow after breakfast. Pete and I leave just after lunch. From that point, our illustrious Building 3 Group will be scattered to the winds."

"We will send you off properly, as we have done for everyone else," Bert added.

"Thanks, Bud," said Carl.

They said goodnight. Janet and Carl decided to take a slow, casual walk, more like a saunter than a purposeful walk, on the empty city streets around the hotel. The sky remained nearly cloudless with a light breeze. The air was warm, dry and pleasantly fragrant with new growth. They headed east to have the sun at their backs until twilight came. They looped back on a different parallel street. Just the automatic illumination of the streetlights brought an unusual joy. It was nearly dark when they returned to the hotel. The lobby was quiet.

The parents stopped to visit with Lisa. Breckyn was already soundly asleep, and Mom was reading another new book. They wished their daughter a restful night's sleep and retired to their room.

Janet suggested they take a shower together and re-consummate their union, since it would probably be their last night together for a while. Once again, they drifted into sleep still wrapped around each other.

The last day together began as another beautiful spring day. Carl did not have any baggage to load for the remainder of his family—Janet, Lisa and Breckyn. Two army privates loaded two, well packed, boxes of selected weapons for Pete Higgins and Carl Parks. Carl hugged George and Anne, Barbara and Larry, and then hugged and kissed Lisa. He also hugged Dave and wished him well. He held Breckyn for several minutes, looking into her pristine blue eyes, and smelling her scalp. *I love that unique smell.* Carl and Janet held each other for several minutes and kissed passionately several times. Carl whispered to her ear, "I love you very much."

At the urging of the bus driver, who was determined to maintain his scheduled timetable, the Wichita contingent boarded the bus, sat and looked out the window. They waved as the bus pulled away. Carl walked down the road, following the rapidly retreating bus, until he could not see the vehicle.

Pete was waiting for Carl, when he returned to the hotel. "I guess we're next."

"Yep. We have a few hours. I think I'm going to go take a nap before lunch."

"Good idea. We didn't get much sleep last night."

The two, once and future Marines did just that. They met up again at lunch with Bert and Vicky. An Army corporal driver with 4th ID shoulder patch waited for them under the entrance awning beside an Army hardtop M998 High Mobility Multipurpose Wheeled Vehicle (HMMWV), commonly referred to as a Humvee. More hugs marked their departure.

As Pueblo disappeared behind them, Pete asked, "Why do you think they attacked us?"

"My guess, we were inflicting too much pain with economic and political sanctions. We were interfering with their hegemonic designs."

"Must have," Pete mused. "They chose a preemptive attack far worse than Pearl Harbor or 9/11."

"Yeah, much worse. They needed to paralyze our military. Frankly, from a purely academic perspective, they did a masterful job of it. By taking out our infrastructure and specifically the electrical grid, they immobilized and nullified our industrial capacity in a virtual instant. Our military stocks might last several months, but certainly not for years, which is the time it would likely take to recover our industrial capacity. They learned well from history. Germany and Japan learned the hard way."

"What do you think we will do until we regain our strength," Pete asked.

"If it was up to me, I would conduct limited hit & run operations to stymie their territorial objectives, until we can mobilize our country and our allies. I think we have no choice to take the fight to both Russia and the PRC. Our fight is with the leadership of both countries—not the people. We did a masterful job of rehabilitating Germany and Japan after the Second World War. We can do it again with Russia and the PRC, after this Third World War."

"I wonder how many died in the attacks?"

"My guess . . . probably millions."

"Then, we should just nuke the bastards. The area bombing of Japan and Germany certainly killed that number, and they recovered."

"Who knows? They may have already done it . . . although I suspect not," Carl answered with solemnity.

"Hummpf."

The two men rode the rest of the way lost in their silent thoughts. The drive north on I-25 took an hour. The driver took them directly to Peterson AFB and the flight line terminal. Carl and Pete were informed the Navy C-40—the military version of a Boeing 737-700C airliner—was on approach. The driver departed.

Carl and Pete watched the aircraft land and taxi up. Surprisingly, the pilot did not shutdown. A Navy PO1 loadmaster/crew chief came quickly down the extendable ladderway, and directly to Carl and Pete. He asked for orders and IDs, ticked the names off of his clipboard list, and asked them both to board and take any seat they wished. Carl and Pete did as instructed. The aircraft was only about half full. They found two seats together, sat and buckled in. With no fanfare or ceremony, they received a quick, but thorough safety briefing from the crew chief, and then they were off to the next phase of their lives.

The end of the beginning had come.

—

Cap Parlier

Author

—

Cap and his wife, Jeanne, moved from the Great Plains of Kansas to the warmth and diversity of Arizona. Their four children have established their families and are raising their grandchildren. Their first grandchild and granddaughter became an adult herself and graduated from university. Cap is a graduate of the U.S. Naval Academy, a retired Marine aviator, Vietnam veteran and experimental test pilot, and has finally retired from the corporate world to devote his time to his passion for writing a good story. He has numerous other projects completed and in the works including screenplays, historical novels as well as atypical novels at various stages of the creation process.

—

Interested readers may wish to visit his website at <http://www.parlier. com> for his essays and other items, or subscribe to his weekly Blog: "*Update from the Sunland.*" Cap can be reached at: cap@SaintGaudensPress.com.

—

Copyright © 2019 Cap Parlier
All rights reserved.
ISBN: 978-0-943039-51-0
Printed in the United States of America

www.ingramcontent.com/pod-product-compliance
Lightning Source LLC
Chambersburg PA
CBHW020655110726
47901CB00001B/196